RUNNING WITH THE PRESIDENT

A Conspiracy of Love, Lies, and Political Mayhem

AUGUST MARTIN

Co-written by AUGUST MARTIN JR.

Redwood Publishing, LLC

Published by Redwood Publishing, LLC
Orange County, California
www.redwooddigitalpublishing.com

ISBN: 978-1-956470-88-8 (hardcover)
ISBN: 978-1-956470-89-5 (paperback)
ISBN: 978-1-956470-90-1 (e-book)

Library of Congress Control Number: 2023910621

This book is a work of fiction. Names, characters, business, events, and incidents are the products of the author's imagination. Any resemblance to actual persons, living or dead, or actual events is purely coincidental.

ACKNOWLEDGMENTS

This book is dedicated to Elsie Martin, who is not just an amazing mother and wife, but also a woman who would be running a Forbes 500 company right now if she had been born in another era. Elsie is a brilliant leader—strong and resilient. When my father had the idea to open a shelter for at-risk children, it was my mother who brought it to fruition with her tireless efforts. Elsie raised hundreds of thousands of dollars to purchase the home and coordinated volunteers to donate their services to open the doors in 2002. Since then, the Children's Guardian Home has helped over 15,000 children, and my mother has raised over six million dollars to keep the home open by hosting twenty-one fundraisers at her and my family's ranch in Farmington, California. *Running with the President* owes its existence to Elsie's unwavering support. Whether she was encouraging my father to work on it or motivating me to complete it, she remains the inspiration behind this novel. Thank you, and I love you, Mom.

Thank you to my father, August Martin Sr., for having the vision to write this story, with its colorful cast of characters with which we can sympathize, characters that often operate in the gray zone. August was a true renaissance man. After having worked as a dairy farmer for fifty years, at the age of fifty-six, he began composing poetry, took up the violin, and wrote this novel. August's inspiring life is a testament to the fact that it's never too late to pursue one's passions!

A special thank you to my sister, Lisa Martin, who lovingly worked on this novel with our father over thirty years ago!

In 1996, Peggy Marie brought this book to APA talent/literary agency where she worked, and was given notes on how to shape the book to make it work better. Now all these years later, those notes were put to use with her help in story plot ideas, edits, diligence and creativity.

Thank you to Latoya and Lisa for the countless hours they spent editing the initial drafts of this novel. Their input, changes, and ideas helped create a compelling story.

And finally, thank you to Sara and Avery for their final edits on the book and for their efforts in bringing this novel to publication. Their attention to detail, advice, and honesty helped fine-tune this story and bring it to life.

CONTENTS

PROLOGUE

The neighbor can hear the noise from a block away, and over his lawn mower. He doesn't even bother looking up this time. He already knows all too well the sound of the oversized red four-by-four pickup truck that will soon drive by, always just a little faster than necessary. He curses, knowing no one can hear him over the sound of the mower. When he turns the mower in the other direction, he sees two men get out of the truck and make their way to the front door of the one-story pale-green house with gray trim that sits in the middle of the cul-de-sac. He notices one of the guys grabbing two bulky army-green bags from the cargo area and heading to the front door with its *No Soliciting* sign prominently displayed.

The door looks similar to the others in the neighborhood; however, it's actually reinforced with steel, should anyone get any ideas. The men nod at the small camera in the upper right corner of the door. Then the shorter guy, who's wearing a blue flannel shirt, takes a key from his pocket. While it may look like a regular key, it's far from normal. The moment it's inserted into the lock, there is a series of noises from inside the house, faint enough that they can't be heard from the street. It sends a signal to the people inside, telling them more members of their group have arrived.

The neighbor sees the guys disappear inside the house, and he shakes his head in disbelief. People have been coming to and going from this house over the past few weeks, ever since these new neighbors moved in. He hates their big, loud trucks and is annoyed that they park wherever they want, sometimes ending up on curbs. It's like nails on a chalkboard. This was a quiet family neighborhood, but now these new neighbors are wearing thin everyone's patience. On top of all this, two huge satellite dishes clutter up the roof. The neighbors even removed some of the beautiful old trees, only to put up ugly high fencing, giving the once-lovely home the look of a compound. It now stands out in this otherwise small suburban neighborhood. He can't wait for the neighborhood association meeting next week. There will be much discussion about these new neighbors. He wonders how much more of this they can take.

Just as he goes back to tending the lawn, a dark-blue four-door sedan speeds by and pulls up behind the red truck. He notices a tall, nicely dressed middle-aged man in a blazer getting out of the sedan. The new visitor looks less like the guys who usually show up and more like someone who actually could be part of the neighborhood. As the man begins walking toward the front door, the two men who arrived earlier step outside to meet him. Even from a couple of houses away, the neighbor can see they are having a heated conversation, so he turns off his lawn mower and pretends to futz with its controls. He overhears bits and pieces of their conversation, including the name "Rockefeller" more than once. When he lifts his head to look at them, they finally notice his presence. He gives the guys a casual wave, but they do not return the gesture and quickly head back toward the house. They pause by the door while the guy in the flannel walks over to lock the gate behind the sedan and then returns to the house.

The three men enter the single-story home. To their right is the kitchen area, with a group of guys sitting at the table, shooting the shit. The new arrivals nod to the guys, then head to the left, where six men and two women sit at desks that line the living room wall. They wear headsets as they type on their keyboards and stare at the oversized monitors in front of them. Along the other wall is a huge screen with a map of the United States, featuring colored dots spanning coast to coast. Some of them are blinking.

A door flies open as an older man exits the basement to greet the tall gentleman from the sedan.

"Hello, Gruff," says the man from the sedan.

"Good to see you, Rockefeller," Gruff replies as he runs his hand nervously over his unkept graying beard.

Rockefeller follows Gruff back to the basement door, where he enters not just a code, but also a palm print. He then undergoes an eye scan, and the door, constructed from three-inch-thick reinforced titanium steel, finally opens with a buzz. At the bottom of the stairs, the basement, which has been sound-proofed, contains a cell phone jammer so that no one can make outgoing or take incoming calls unless they're using a satellite phone. There's no chance of this place ever getting hacked. The team has nicknamed the basement the War Room. Two men are monitoring a large map of the world, similar to the one upstairs. A red triangle frames the area surrounding the capital city of a Midwestern state. Gruff calls over one of the men and tells him to update Rockefeller.

"Yes, sir," says the skinny young man wearing jeans. He then turns to Rockefeller. "So far, we are on schedule. The team up-stairs has infiltrated the top ten social media sites with thousands of fake profiles that have continuously spread our messages over the last two weeks. Additionally, we are getting a lot of traffic with the videos we created. They seem to work especially well, as it's hard to tell the real footage from the footage we created. We have over five hundred new members joining each day and paying their membership fees, and we have thousands of members, all over the country, reposting our messages on a daily basis. The country seems to enjoy getting worked up; it's easier than one would imagine."

Rockefeller nods and asks, "What about the weaponry? How well are we stocked?"

A short, stocky man in his early fifties stands up from his chair in the corner of the room and walks over to them. He clears his throat and, with a voice rough from years of smoking, replies, "Sir, most of the weaponry is located off-site in a large warehouse about ten minutes from here. It has around-the-clock security. Together with what we have here, we are armed to the hilt. Weapon donations have exceeded our expectations, and we are about three weeks ahead of schedule. There is also enough manpower signed up to cause a ruckus no one will ever forget."

The men spend another five minutes answering their leader's questions until he seems satisfied. Rockefeller then spends another ten minutes in private with each of these senior members. Each of them is in charge of a specific part of the plan. All information is on a "need to know" basis, just in case any of them are captured and questioned by the authorities. No one but Rockefeller knows the entire plan. Everyone else only knows the part he or she has been given to play. As their mantra goes, "It's all for the greater good."

As Rockefeller gets up to leave, he takes a last look around. He's feeling especially proud today, having accomplished so much in just ten months. Rockefeller and Gruff make their way upstairs.

At the front door, Rockefeller says, "I will be in touch, Gruff. And thank you for the new satellite phone." He tucks the phone into the breast pocket of his new Tom Ford blazer. On the way back to his sedan, he smiles to himself with pleasure at what he will soon be accomplishing: stopping Dumont's plan to dismantle the America he loves.

CHAPTER 1

BUTTERFLIES

▷ **Lance – Greenville, South Carolina**

The presidential candidate groans as he climbs out of his uncomfortable hotel bed and attempts to determine which part of his body hurts the most. Years of wear and tear have finally caught up with him. Hard work, sports, and a politician's lack of sleep have each claimed their effect on his body. He stretches out his bad shoulder and massages his knees, which always make a clicking sound when he first stands up in the morning. He heads to the bathroom to rejuvenate his body with a hot shower.

As he washes himself, his mind walks through the events of the day ahead. He looks forward to his final speeches and loves the idea of rallying these American voters, convincing them his ideas will get them back on track.

By the time he's dressed, it's almost 7:00 a.m., time to meet and greet the voters here, in Greenville, South Carolina. He knows that time is passing quickly, and he wants to get the most he can from this campaign stop. Due to his packed schedule, he needs to get this over with as fast as possible. Lance Dumont wants to win, and he knows he's the best man for the job.

An aide walks with him down the long, sleek hall, at the end of which they take the glass elevator down to the hotel lobby.

The sun shines through the dozens of glass panels positioned high above them as they exit the elevator. A group of journalists are waiting to barrage him with photos and questions, as are his supporters and, as always, a handful of agitators.

"Nationalist!" yells one heckler. Lance isn't sure where the shout originated from; he just smiles.

"Socialist!" rings out from another area, to his left.

But Lance just keeps smiling and waving, wondering how these people think he can be both a nationalist *and* a socialist. He just laughs it off, as usual.

But then comes an actual question from a real journalist: "So have you changed your mind yet about downsizing our military?"

For this question, the candidate stops in his tracks and turns around to answer. "No, I haven't changed my mind. Shifting some of our budget from the Pentagon, FBI, Homeland Security, and CIA to local initiatives, like beefing up police salaries, battling homelessness, and dramatically decreasing your taxes, is my promise. And it's a good one. The doubters in this lobby will be thanking me in a year when the streets are safer and the middle and lower classes have more money in their pockets. In fact, you will *all* thank me later." At a lanky six foot three, Lance towers above most of them. Beneath his nicely cut Brooks Brothers suit exists the frame of a former college football linebacker. He would be an intimidating force if it weren't for his dazzling white smile and hearty laugh, which accompany most of his remarks. His vision is controversial, and although it has created a lot of enemies for him, it has also pushed him to the top. He is different from his opponents, and *people want different.*

"We'll believe it when we see it!" shouts a journalist in her twenties to cheers from the crowd.

"Well then, you can vote for me, and you *will* believe it! We need to enact real change here, in America, not just be talking mouthpieces who don't keep their promises or stick to their ideas. I know there are many individuals in the high ranks of government agencies who are scared to lose their status quo. And they are correct; they should be scared. I'm ready to put this country on a budget and make sure that people like you and everyone else in this room get better jobs and more money in their pockets and grow their small businesses. The fat cats in government and at large corporations are going to have to start paying their fair share of taxes; we can't keep supporting them. That's social welfare." He winks as cheers rise up from the crowd. He then smiles and waves as he walks out of the bright lobby and into his waiting black Lincoln SUV.

His aides join him, and they head to a rally for the homeless—or rather, the "unsheltered," as Lance so often corrects people. He's a firm believer that the first step in getting people off the streets is to find them a place to sleep and keep their possessions safe. He knows something must be done for them, and he has a lot of specific ideas that were shaped during his undergrad years, bolstered both by his social sciences major and a personal experience in his younger years. This rally will be good for his campaign and will satisfy his personal goal to help the people who need it the most in cities all over the country.

After the unsheltered rally, he has a speech at another rally: the unions. Then, at the end of the day, he has a town hall meeting to attend. All in all, it's a busy day, but no one—not even Lance—is expecting what will soon transpire.

☙❧

At 9:00 p.m. that evening, Lance arrives back at his hotel, but he's not alone. Nearly a dozen scruffy-looking unsheltered men and women who've been awaiting his arrival are now following him toward the door to the lobby, trailed by campaign aides muttering restlessly among themselves. Lance glances over his shoulder at his surprise entourage. He knows his aides don't appreciate his desire to connect so personally to this group, but there's not much they can do about it. It could open the door to unpredictable situations that may or may not backfire on his good intentions. But Lance never thinks about that. He just does what he feels is right in the moment, and inviting these people into the hotel for a shower and dinner on him is the first time all day he feels like himself.

Lance's aides follow his direction, taking the men and women to Lance's floor, where they all take showers and get cleaned up in the empty rooms reserved for security briefs and meetings. Lance enjoys watching their expressions as they take it all in; he knows how much they appreciate the gesture. He can overhear them talking about little things, like the extra-large fluffy white towels and the contrast between their newly showered selves and their appearance upon arrival—not unlike the disparity between the rich and the poor in this country. Lance outfits the men with clean clothing brought in from the closet in his room, his personal wardrobe. He has also had clothes specially delivered for the women. While his aides take pictures of all of them together, he asks them to refrain from releasing the pictures to the press. This is a very personal moment for him, and he doesn't want public credit for it, just his own satisfaction that he's able to give these special people something nice.

Lance then asks his guests to stay for a while so they can have the opportunity to eat dinner together in the dining area of his large suite. Within twenty minutes, security opens the oversized double doors so that the hotel staff can wheel in the ordered carts of food. All of this will be charged to Lance's personal credit card, not to his campaign. He makes a note of this on his phone to ensure this will occur.

As they begin eating, Lance switches into candidate mode and decides to ask his guests for their thoughts on current events in the country. He truly wants to hear their advice, as who else would have better insight into what *they* need to get out of their current situation and how to prevent it from happening again.

Lance looks at those gathered around the table and says, "Listen, I need your help. I want to know what each of you would do if you were the next president. I truly want to know how I can help, should I be elected."

An older man named Oscar is the first to speak up. Staggering slightly as he rises, he explains that he is disabled from his time serving in the US military. He describes himself as a proud veteran who has fallen on hard times because he has not been able to work full time. "If I were president, I'd ask the people of this country to love their work, to be proud of what they do, to work hard and deliberately. Making one's living isn't a class thing. Blue collar, white collar—hell, no collar! We just need opportunities."

Another guest, a tall man with long hair and a boyish face, cuts in: "Maybe we, the people of this great country, should be able to talk more to our president, the way we're doing here. Make him available to us, the American public, to hear firsthand what we are dealing with on a daily basis. Make him listen to what we have to say, good and bad."

"So do you believe you know more than the people I surround myself with?" Lance asks with a hint of sarcasm. "After all, each of them is not only college educated, but has been doing what they do for quite some time."

The group falls silent except for one woman, who says, "That could all be true, but sir, who put you and the others through college? And who elected you to your positions? Isn't it the working-class people out here, those who pay taxes by working everyday jobs, who make all of this happen? And how about all those companies who employ people like us at all levels, from the janitor to the CEO? The products and services they sell to people around the world are taxed and help many people go to college. The whole economy begins with and relies on the working class and the local businesses that make each community thrive. In contrast, in a socialist society, the money would be cut up like a pie, with all pieces being the same size to be shared equally. In a capitalist society like ours, there must be profit, or the system does not evolve and flourish. And in our case, as homeless people, our system has fallen short. That is what needs to change."

Lance—the man, not the candidate—looks at her with surprise. The others nod their heads in agreement, as if listening to a preacher and recognizing she has included them in her sermon.

The man with the long hair clears his throat and speaks again. "I *do* believe our judgment is keener. We put value on all the small things in our everyday lives, especially the freedoms we enjoy to go out and do random things, like go to the store or a ball game. On the other hand, *you* can't just go out and eat a hot dog or hang out with anyone you want in public. Your life is not private. We are, in a matter of speaking, free to do as we like, while your life is not so free. There's always someone who knows your exact whereabouts at all times."

"That's true, so very true." Lance puts a finger to his chin. "I've never thought of it that way. I guess, in some ways, you guys are richer than me. I don't mind my position of status, but to be so free . . . I'll tell you what," he adds, grinning, "one day, say, if I'm elected, I'll sneak off and we can maybe play some cards, drink some beer, and shoot some hoops or go to a ball game."

"You don't mean that, sir, do you?" Oscar asks eagerly.

Lance's smile melts into a tired frown. "As much as I would love it, you are all probably right: it can never be that way, though I wish it were possible. But sometimes I wonder if maybe you and

I—and the rest of the world—can just coexist peacefully, forget all of this government stuff, and live for the moment. Wouldn't that be nice?"

James Edwards, Lance's campaign director, looks at the presidential candidate and says quietly, "I hope we don't get any backlash for this, sir. I know it's going to be hard for you to be unable to do things like this in the future—connect with people you treasure the most. I admire your desire to help the unsheltered. I don't know what drives you, but I *do* think you can make a difference in their lives."

Lance looks at James. "Thank you, James. How much time do we have left here with these ladies and gentlemen?"

"Oh, about ten more minutes," James answers promptly. His soothing voice is comforting to Lance. He sounds as though he would do an excellent job of narrating books. "It's getting late, sir, and I've got to whisk you off now, as Rose requested—well, *ordered* is more like it," James says with a smile. "You've got to get to sleep at a decent hour. She said to bring you to your room early, and now it's nearly 10:00."

Lance turns back to his new friends. "Well, everyone, I really enjoyed being with you tonight. But we've got just enough time left for you to tell me some of the jokes that are going around about me out there on the street."

The guests look at one another, clearly unsure if this candidate really wants to hear the things being said about him. Lance looks at James and then the rest of the group, shakes his head, and breaks into laughter. By the time Lance begins his goodbye to his guests, another five minutes have elapsed. James gives his boss the eye. Lance knows what this means, but he doesn't care. He's enjoyed his time with them. He admires how they hold their heads up, no matter their status in life, and the fact that they, too, can help shed light on what the American dream truly encompasses. Lance lingers by the table before finally exiting into the long hallway, James trailing after him.

"James, have you ever met my wife, Rose?"

"Of course, sir," James replies, having been asked this rhetorical question dozens of times over the past year. "You have introduced me to her about a hundred times, and I'm sure it's going to happen again. You miss her on these trips, don't you?"

"I do. I've always enjoyed beseeching her for everything—in a teasing manner, of course—whether I'm asking for a squeeze, a cuddle, a hug, or a kiss. This, in some way, has become our foreplay. Sometimes it's in the manner of a boy begging for her attention; others, a man feeling a little jealous. It all depends on my mood or the situation." Lance pauses to look at James, "Don't all my roads lead to her?"

James just smiles in reply.

Before they retire to bed, Lance asks to be kept updated on his five children and how they're coping. He knows they, too, are tired of being on the campaign trail. Soon, they'll be returning from all parts of the country on his behalf, which means they'll be a step nearer to completing their campaign duties. Lance sighs. He's more than ready for this campaign to end.

In the morning, Lance's group checks out of their hotel in Greenville to head back to their headquarters in Columbus, Ohio. Lance stretches out in his airplane seat, trying to find a comfortable position in which to sleep, but his rest is interrupted when James sits down next to him with an update on his family.

"Sir, your daughter Edwina has made her school aware of a very surprising interest, one that has raised eyebrows."

Lance gestures for him to continue.

"Sir, she has informed them that she wants to become a nun."

Lance almost spits out the water he just sipped. "*What?* What did you just say? Is this for real?"

The look on James's face lets Lance know that, yes, it is. Softly, James says, "Rose has made some inquiries into this development and will update you after some more conversation on the matter."

"Wow! I'm surprised to hear that. Everyone knows Edwina is quite religious in her own way, but this is a big leap." A long, awkward silence passes before Lance continues, "I just don't understand. Edwina, while being a devout Catholic, was such a tomboy when she was younger. And now she wants to be a *nun*? I didn't see this one coming. Did Rose have any more to say about why Edwina chose such a path?"

"Not really, sir; I think she was just as flabbergasted by the announcement as you are. I felt it wasn't really my place to ask questions."

Lance nods pensively before switching to work mode. "James, I'm thinking about the big agencies that I'm looking to downsize—specifically, the heads of these agencies: Schultz, Noakes, Johnson, and Cummings, as well as his sidekick, Ackman. What do you think of this cast of characters? To be honest, I've only dealt with the CIA director, Schultz. Let me just say that I don't like him. I haven't met the others, but I'm hoping they aren't as difficult as Schultz."

"Well, I haven't met them all either, just the FBI director, Anita Johnson. I'm a big fan of hers. The first female director of the FBI, she's a badass and a very nice person, an absolute keeper. The head of the Secret Service, Alexander Cummings, has my respect. Worked his way from the bottom up. He's the first Black director of the Secret Service, but he's a little hard to figure out. Talks a good talk, but I don't know enough about him yet. His chief of the Uniformed Division, David Ackman, is known to be a go-getter, but he's not to be trusted. It's said that he would do anything to get his boss's job. *Anything.* But that's just the rumor mill. And then there's Keith Noakes, head honcho at Homeland Security, which oversees the Secret Service. He's a newbie to the arena, but people like him. Guess he's a no-nonsense, level-headed guy. Haven't heard a bad word about him," James replies. "*Yet,*" he adds slyly, raising his eyebrows for emphasis.

Lance nods in acknowledgment and looks out the window. The rest of the one-hour plane ride is spent in silence, which gives Lance some extra time to sleep, and James, the time he needs to catch up on work.

They make it back to the Ohio campaign headquarters before noon. The Dumont campaign headquarters is in a tall office building overlooking all the other buildings near the Toledo and Ohio Central Railroad Station. As a kid, Lance loved the station because he enjoyed "riding the rails," as he and his friends liked to call it. It represents the American spirit of travel and shipping. He's pleased this way of life is seeing a revival now, thanks to the building of more and more public transportation and railway infrastructure. One can create his or her own destiny on the train while observing the beauty of the country.

CHAPTER 2

THE PRICE OF YOUR CANDIDACY

▷ **Lance – Columbus, Ohio**

O nce inside the expansive lobby of his campaign headquarters, Lance can only think about finding his Rose upstairs, as he heads toward the elevator with his Secret Service special agents in tow. But he soon realizes he should've known better, as once he is spotted, he's accosted by a burly man who wants a few words with "his candidate." Lance tells his special agents it's OK and allows the man to approach him. He'll have to hear him out; it's just part of campaigning. Afterward, he can go find his Rose.

The impromptu discussion with the man, who turns out to be a local blogger, takes much more time than it should. While Lance wants to have this type of interaction with members of the public, he also has a schedule to follow.

Twenty minutes later, exhausted and more than a little irritated, Lance follows James to the conference room upstairs. Sitting alone on the other side of the room, head bent while staring at her laptop, is Rose, his wife of a lifetime. Lance's steps quicken into an energized stride as he crosses the room. Rose stands to greet him, and he kisses her on each cheek—a tradition they've maintained since they first met. Lance wishes he could show her much more affection right now, but alas, there are people around.

"I've missed you so much," he whispers into her shiny black hair, taking in the familiar smell of her cream-colored skin. "I'm so glad to be back, at least for a little bit. We're almost at the finish line, my love."

Rose squeezes his hands. "I know, I know. I've missed you too." As she sits back down, her determined deep-brown eyes return to the screen of her laptop.

Lance is baffled by her subtle reaction to his return. He'd been expecting a much warmer reception. Maybe the news about Edwina has Rose's mind elsewhere. "Do you know Edwina wants to become a nun?" he asks. When Rose doesn't respond, more questions tumble out of him: "Has she asked for your input? Maybe some advice? Do you know anything about this? Don't you think this is out of the blue?" Exasperated, he adds, "What's happening to our family?"

Rose looks at him with a somewhat vacant gaze. "Just take it slowly. I'm sure she's got her reasons. But who knows—maybe we'll never understand her motivations, and it may never matter. I, for one, am excited for her and support the idea of it wholeheartedly."

"Really? Well, I'm just surprised by the news. There's just so much out there to be experienced. And she wants to become a *nun?*" Lance feels disappointed that he didn't receive the news directly from Edwina. He will never say it out loud, but she is his favorite child. He bites his tongue for a moment but then realizes he can't stop himself: "Why was I the last to know? I really thought I'd be the first person she'd talk to about her vocation." Lance can't look at Rose. He doesn't want her to see the tears in his eyes.

"I'm sorry, Lance. You are gone most of the time. Don't be hurt. I'm sure she will confide in you if you two ever get a chance to be alone—but given your schedule, I don't see that happening anytime soon. It's the price of your candidacy."

Lance walks over to the large window and looks out at the darkening stormy sky. He can almost feel the clouds wrapping around his mind. It's as if they want to get a closer look at the man he has become, and he's terrified of that. He's not yet ready to acknowledge that man. Rose's words hit hard: the price of his candidacy. If losing his connection to his family members is the price he has to pay now, what will the price be if he becomes president? He shudders at the thought.

Frustrated, he returns to Rose's side to review the giant stack of paperwork that has accumulated over the last two days. Most of the staff is on lunch break, with only James remaining.

"Why don't I give you guys some alone time," James offers softly as he grabs his bags and leaves the room, shutting the door behind him ever so gently.

Lance looks at his wife, who places her finger to his lips, as if she knows what he's about to say. She always knows. Before he can speak, Rose takes a deep breath and then confesses, "I was going to surprise you with the news about Edwina. Guess James beat me to it."

"*Surprise* me!" Lance exclaims. "First of all, we aren't even practicing Catholics; we only go to church on holidays and occasions like weddings, baptisms, etcetera. And honestly, isn't she too damn smart and pretty to become a nun?" When he sees Rose's eyes narrow, he hastily adds, "Maybe I shouldn't have said that. It's not quite what I meant."

Ignoring her husband's gaffe, Rose continues, "You know that she has a big, charitable heart, and maybe she feels this is her way to give back. She's got to do this in her own way. You know she's been thinking about a life of service for a while now. It's in her blood. In that way, she's just like you."

Lance lets out a big sigh and hugs her tightly for nearly a minute, not wanting to let go of this momentary reprieve. But Rose gently eases herself from his arms and sits back down, nodding at the stacks of their personal mail, which has been neatly stacked in a box in the corner of the conference room. Together they review their bills and investments, but Lance finds it difficult to concentrate.

"What happened to the kids supporting us more on this campaign?" he asks as he peruses a bill. "Feels like they're just showing up on the campaign trail now, in the last two weeks. Where the heck have they been?"

He peers at Rose, but she doesn't look up from the paper she's holding or give any indication she even heard his question. She just carries on with her paperwork, so Lance lets it go.

☺☺

Hours later, they head to the hotel, which is conveniently located just a couple of blocks away. The Hilton on North High Street in downtown Columbus is just enough distance from his campaign headquarters to afford Lance a few blocks to walk off the stress from each day. Lance and Rose walk hand in hand, their security detail about ten feet behind them, enjoying a quiet moment, as the street is surprisingly empty for this time of day.

When they reach their suite, they get situated for the evening. After changing, Lance crosses the room to open the curtains. The room feels instantly freer to him.

Rose looks up from where she's sitting at the dining table. "What's the matter, Lance?"

Lance is a poet at heart, so it's no surprise to Rose that his answer comes in the form of a question: "Do we put our lives on display for the world to see as we try to find a comforting tune on the jukebox? And if so, for how long will that comfort last? Will I someday forget who I used to be as a child? I never want to forget playing with butterflies and all the other sweet, innocent things I used to do. I don't want the presidency to change who I am, Rose."

"You never told me you played with butterflies, dear," Rose replies distractedly. She walks to the bathroom and grabs her hairbrush as Lance follows. "I do want to know about these butterflies," she says as she combs her hair, which falls just past her delicate shoulders, making sure to keep the curl at the ends. Lance delights as he watches her ritual. Like her namesake, Rose is petite and beautiful. Above all, she exudes class, is ever loyal, and is the rock of their family.

"I had four glass cases I hung about four feet from the ground. I filled them with my butterfly collection," Lance says. "The cases were suspended above these beautiful purple hydrangea bushes; the bottom and sides were glass, and I installed a removable screen on the top of each case. After some time, I had collected almost ten butterflies from the farm, all different types. And, of course, all the butterflies had funny names, like Wiggles, Boeing, and Dimples. I would take them out sometimes and walk around with three or four on my shoulder, right through the house, and not one would fly off me. This amazed my mother. They loved water with a little bit of sugar mixed in."

Rose sighs and changes the subject: "How do you want me to wear my hair tomorrow? Up in a bun or like this?" She allows her hair to fall past her shoulders again and then shakes her head. "Never mind. I'll wear it down. I hate seeing all this gray coming in." As Lance looks at her in the mirror, she adds, "I'm sorry, Lance. Continue your story. How did you find time for that? I thought that when you were a kid, all you did was work on the farm nonstop and that your dad didn't allow time for such lighthearted play."

"That's true to a degree. We did have to get up early every morning to feed all the animals on the farm, plus I had baseball and homework. My father believed in developing good work habits early, *really* early, like when I was four or five years old, from what I can remember. When I was about eleven, I thought I could carry enough wood on my back to warm everyone on earth. I felt invincible." Lance is surprised by how easily he can bring himself back in time to his home outside of Dayton, Ohio. He yearns for those years when life's pleasures were so simple. He wonders to himself how this young farm boy who loved butterflies wound up running for president of the United States. Being president wasn't a childhood dream of his; he just wanted a job that would help people.

With a glass of water in hand, Lance follows Rose to the bedroom area of the large open suite and leans against the dresser, scanning the room for a chair in which to make himself comfortable. He misses his favorite chair at home, the one into which he nestles each night to watch TV. This thought makes him realize he has spent too much time on the road campaigning and misses all the little things that make a house a home. He decides to hop up and seat himself on the dresser, exposing his mismatched socks. When Rose looks at him and rolls her eyes, Lance knows what she's thinking.

"What are you going to do about your inability to match your socks? Do you want to give the press something else to ridicule? I can hear them now: 'If he can't match his socks, how can he run a country?'" They both laugh.

As Lance looks down at his socks, their laughter intensifies, as it often does in their lighthearted moments together. He runs his hand through his hair, which is still as thick and wavy and the same sandy-brown shade as it was in his youth. He has no patience whatsoever in managing it, but he appreciates that it's still thick and full. When the sun hits it just right, its streaks of gold make him appear younger than his forty-nine years. His complexion appears fair in the winter, but come summer, the sun effortlessly tans his skin, imparting a golden hue that reflects his Italian heritage.

He moves to sit in a chair by the couch in the living room, just beyond the bedroom, turns on the TV, and puts his feet on the corner of the coffee table as he watches some of his speeches from earlier today on the news. "I look tired, don't I?"

"Yes, I've noticed that, and so has most the world. Even the children have commented." Rose's voice softens. "Why don't you go to bed early tonight, like right now, please?"

"I can't even remember how many days are left until Election Day; it's such a blur at this point."

Rose turns around to look at him, a small smile on her lips. "Three days from today, Matches."

"Matches!" Lance bounces back. "Rose, you haven't called me that for a very long time!" The nickname brings back old memories from college. When he played poker with his friends, matchsticks were used as chips for betting, and as he was good at the game, he always had plenty of matchsticks to give away to his friends. It was around that time when people began calling him Matches. The moniker stuck with him through the rest of his term as an undergrad at Georgetown University and well into his graduate years, when he first met Rose and she learned the story behind it.

Leaning back in his chair and fanning himself with a folded newspaper, Lance looks out at the full moon against the dark of night. He thinks to himself that the nights are getting longer, and having been raised on a farm, he knows that the migration of the birds will end soon. It's a sign that another year will soon pass, this one marking his twenty-sixth year since he met Rose. He turns to her and admires everything about her, noting how beautifully she has aged. She's even more lovely today than she was the day they met.

Lance thinks back to their first meeting. It was at a friend's party in Washington, DC, months before he graduated from grad school at Virginia Tech. Rose had overheard someone call him Matches and teased him about his nickname. Right then, he knew she was something special. He felt so completely alive when his gaze met her deep, dark eyes for the very first time. To this day, her eyes still make the night race with the heat of their passion.

As midnight approaches, Lance leads Rose to their bed and turns off the lights one at a time. He gently slips off her nightgown with one hand while removing his clothes with the other. Within seconds, they are pressing their bodies together on top of the oversized bed. Hungry for the taste of her sweet skin, he kisses her neck, then uses his tongue to trace a path to her nipples until he finds his way to the warmth below her belly button. He eagerly consumes her until she convulses in pleasure. She grabs his head and pulls it back up from below her hips to kiss his lips. Their tongues find their way to spots both familiar and new. She pleasures him with her mouth until he can't stand it any longer and climbs on top of her. After coming to climax with all the energy they have left, they lock eyes and push their hips as close together as they can until they both release. And like so many nights before, their wet bodies collapse onto the bed next to each other, too tired to stand.

Lying there in the dark, Lance notices the glow coming from his watch, which makes him shudder. He moves closer to Rose and whispers in her ear, his lips pressing against her lobe, "I hate these damn things."

"What's that, dear?" Rose replies sleepily.

Lance isn't ready for bed, as his mind is still racing. "Watches!" he says loudly, startling her as she presses against him. "They bug the hell out of me! But on the other hand, they also give me a lot of beautiful moments, especially when I'm with you." He grabs her hand tightly.

"Listen, Lance, I get it. You feel like the clock is ticking and running your life right now, but it's what you signed up for, just like when you were governor," Rose says wearily. "Don't worry so much; it'll be fine when the campaigning is over. You'll have a large team managing that time for you, making sure it flows correctly. But for now, let's just be quiet and get some sleep. I'll make the room really dark, just like you like it, OK? Then you can relax some . . . for me?" And with that, she kisses him on the cheek and walks over to the window to pull the curtains tight so that light cannot find its way through.

Five minutes pass before Lance breaks the silence: "Being president is going to feel like living in a beehive. I'll be like the queen bee, with everyone pushing me here and there. Then they'll all look at their damn watches, and I mean *all* of them, and then off they'll go again, to another point, from A to B, and so on." He waits for a response from Rose, but there's only a long silence.

Suddenly, Rose throws her side of the covers off of her and climbs out of bed. She balances her tired body on her feet, which are pained from having worn heels all day, and pads unsteadily across the room to turn the lights back on.

"Rose?" Lance raises his head, blinking in surprise. "What made you do that?"

"You're not going to sleep, and you need to! But it is what it is."

Before he can respond, Rose walks around to his side of the bed and tears the covers from him, startling him into a sitting position. Without a word, she begins to rub his tense shoulders.

The knots begin to melt beneath her grasp. Leaning over him from behind, she embraces him and pulls him toward her chest. Lance holds her clasped hands to his chest and bends his head to kiss her fingers.

"I'm scared, Rose. I'm really scared," he says in a small voice that's hardly recognizable.

Rose's voice is full of affectionate determination: "There's something in the wind, the water, and everything that surrounds you that makes you special. Not just to me, but to the entire country, and we all need that kind of person leading us. Someone different, someone people can relate to. Don't take my word for it; read the papers. The stories are all out there." Leaning further over his shoulder, she kisses him ever so softly on the mouth.

But Lance's work is never finished. His eyes begin to blink impatiently as he grabs some papers from the bedside table and embarks on a review of tomorrow's speech. It's after 2:00 in the morning when he finishes making corrections and memorizing the more poignant parts. He puts down the papers and realizes he needs sleep in order to be ready for the day ahead. Rose went to sleep over an hour ago, so Lance decides to call it a night and turns off the bedside lamp.

After some time, Lance finds he just can't get to sleep. He lies there in the dark, staring at the ceiling, the windows, the door. The sour aftertaste of dinner lingers in his mouth, making him wonder if he forgot to brush his teeth. Or perhaps it's the strain of the campaign and its effect on him. Most likely, it's what tomorrow and the following grueling days will bring after he takes off from John Glenn Columbus International Airport. He's tired of campaigning and wants to skip straight to the real job of being president. *No*, he thinks tiredly, *the campaign isn't over yet.*

CHAPTER 3

THE CANDIDATE

▷ **Lance – Atlanta, Georgia**

Just two days before the election, Lance and James rush through the doors of the Hilton and into a waiting car that's headed toward yet another flight. Their first stop will be Atlanta. They are an hour behind this morning, and tensions are running high.

On the way to the airport, James tries to engage his distracted boss. "We're going to have to put on a big public media blitz here, as the polls show the incumbent is not far behind us."

Lance doesn't take the bait; he's too busy staring out the window and wondering what he's gotten himself and his family into. When the car screeches to a halt, he jumps out and follows James through the airport's automatic glass doors, taking in the familiar sounds and smells. He hurries through the airport while drinking from a travel mug the size of a coffee pot; he needs the jolt of caffeine to pick him up. They board the plane for their final swing in the two biggest battleground states, Georgia and South Carolina.

Once settled in the back of the plane, Lance yells, "Hey, James!"

"Yes, sir? How can I help?" James replies while making his way from the front, sitting down next to Lance, and fastening his seat belt.

"Just thinking—if I win this election, how do you think it will affect my way of life?"

Lance watches James as he adjusts his shirt and straightens his cuff links. He wonders if James will finally give in and tell him what he *wants* to hear. Lance has always wanted his and his family's lives to be similar to the way they were when he was the governor of Ohio. It is something he has said from the beginning of his campaign: the presidential office should be more accessible and relaxed than its historically out-of-reach reputation. He doesn't take his eyes off James while he waits for his answer and remembers how James showed up in his life like a gift from the powers that be. He knows James is his rock and he wouldn't have gotten this far without him. It seemed as though he showed up out of nowhere, but thank God he's here.

The plane begins to level itself out, so James unbuckles his seat belt while trying to avoid his boss's question. Lance notices that he's making James anxious and watches him run his hands over his salt-and-pepper hair, adjust his gold-framed glasses, and make sure his tie is straight. He is always dressed impeccably; it's the first thing people notice about James when they meet him.

Somewhat reluctantly, James turns to face the presidential candidate. He smiles from one side of his mouth and fixes his bright-green eyes on his boss. He looks him straight in the eye and asks, "What do you mean by 'affect your way of life,' sir? In what regard?"

"What I mean is, can I use the drive-through to get a burger? Can I do the things I did before all of this started? Will I be able to do whatever this heart of mine so desires without a bunch of fanfare? Hell, in Ohio, people weren't surprised to see me at a McDonald's!"

James smirks. "Just between you and me, what do *you* think? Just to get a burger will take a caravan of limousines, special agents, and possibly local police escorts. We've gone through all this before. How many cars will have to pass through that damn drive-through window so you can get a McDonald's shake and burger? But if you really want it, I think it will be possible. Of course, it might be a ten-thousand-dollar burger at the end of the day and a whole lotta effort for a cheeseburger, but it'll be possible. If that's what you want and it will make you be a happy president, sir, then that's what will happen. But Washington, DC, is not Ohio. If you really want to be free, you are going to have to run away! But good luck doing that with a couple dozen special agents knowing your every move."

Lance leans back into his seat, covering his eyes with his hands and laughs at himself. "I can see the headline now: PRESIDENT DUMONT ESCAPES WHITE HOUSE FOR CHEESEBURGER!"

He rises from his seat to stretch out his lanky six-foot-three frame and pulls up his pant legs to make sure his socks match. He's relieved to discover they do. Tugging on his wedding ring, he turns his head and looks back at James, wondering if he can trust him with his most secret thoughts. But he knows James is right: DC *isn't* Ohio, and most likely, he won't be able to genuinely trust anyone except Rose and his children.

"I think you're going to be one hell of a funny president," James says with a laugh. "Voters are starting to like you for the funny, quirky things you do. The things you pull with all those elderly ladies—they just love it when you say silly things to get them all riled up. My father was also a flirt with women of a certain age; it's that Moroccan blood we have in us. My father was really good at it, like a stand-up comedian. Everyone leaves laughing and more in love with you and life itself. You're the same as my father, and they love you for those qualities. Maybe it's because you're a funny guy with a passion for honesty. Those are the things that move people toward you; it makes you one of *them*. It could just be the way you say hello, Lance. For a lot of people out there, it's like coming inside from a cold rain."

"James, you haven't called me Lance since we met." Lance's mind wanders back in time to when he met James just over a year ago at his second major public event. James walked up to him and introduced himself as his new campaign director. It was not a request, but a statement. Lance shakes his head, remembering how taken aback he'd been, but he'd loved James's confidence. Impressive from the very moment they met—and with a background in marketing communications from two of the most prominent schools—James was just the upgrade he'd been looking for, and neither man has looked back since.

"Sorry, sir," James says softly.

"Oh no, that's all right. If you like, you can call me Lance whenever you want."

James laughs as he says, "I think you're endearing yourself to women on the campaign trail, but you *do* flirt with them all."

They laugh along with the onboard team members as well as a number of the reporters.

James glances down at Lance's finger, which is resting on a silver button. He then bolts upright in his seat. "Wait! You've had the intercom on all this time, sir?!"

"Maybe!" admits Lance with a laugh.

Suddenly, everyone on the plane grows quiet and looks down at their phones. The company that is handling the polling just sent a text message to all on board with the latest numbers. The polls now show their opponent is just one point behind them. Statistically, it's a tie. Lance is down three points since the last poll, thirty-six hours earlier.

Lance takes one look at the message and swears through his teeth. "Are you shitting me?"

"I'm afraid not, sir," James says.

"I mean it, James. Can I carry enough votes here?"

James doesn't answer. Lance makes sure the intercom is off, then leans in. "James, *can I?* You know what I mean. Do I have the juice to get enough votes to pass the electoral line?"

"Of course you do. People just need to see the truth in all you've been saying. Just promising them something doesn't make it all come true. The voters must know that their government is by the people and for the people. But still, that's often not enough. You want to show them you are strong enough to carry this load for them."

"Well, how do I prove to them I can do this, James? I know I can do it."

"Let me put it this way, sir: You're a man with a well-used ruler. You are constantly measuring the size of every detail, measuring the width to see if you can fit it all on your shoulders, as there is so much to carry. So, yes, I believe you have enough juice to pull off a victory for the people of this country. People like you because they believe you are a man of character and someone they can trust. At this point, it's up to the voters. We've done all we can do. Ultimately, they will vote with their conscience, and that's how you will win."

☼

They land in Atlanta, the stop before South Carolina, to try to steal the hearts of more voters in another state that's too close to call. After campaigning for most of the day, Lance begins to tire and the streets start to blur together. They arrive at a part of town called Buckhead, the uptown residential and commercial section of Atlanta. There is an area within Buckhead called "The Hill," a tiny city within a city that houses dozens of homeless men and women. They even have their own barber.

25

Today, many more people have shown up, both sheltered and unsheltered. Lance stands in the bed of a large truck, which has elevated him several feet above the crowd. The cold wind cuts right through his overcoat, and he shivers. He delivers a moving speech about the disparities in America and reiterates his plan to shift funds to domestic initiatives, including housing for the unsheltered. That part of the speech always brings cheers from the audience. As with every speech he gives, Lance ends with a call to action.

"How many of you are registered to vote? Lemme see those hands high in the air!" Lance's voice is jubilant. Key to his campaign has been his plan to get everyone, including the homeless, registered to vote. Nearly every person in the crowd raises a hand. After the speech, Lance makes his way down from the truck bed. James ushers him inside the waiting Lincoln.

"James, that was motivating! Thank you for making this special stop happen. I know we have a tight schedule these last couple of days." Lance pauses to find his next words, then says, "I can imagine their daily struggles. The unsheltered could be our neighbors, our brothers, or our mothers. They always know who's telling the truth and can't be fooled for a minute. You know how much I empathize with the unsheltered, James."

"Yes, sir, I do know."

Lance pauses for a moment and stares out the window at the crowd that is now dispersing. He begins to tear up. "I'm sorry, James; it's just that this is a lot sometimes—to keep seeing it and take it all in."

"It's OK, sir."

"Actually, it's *not* OK. I have been meaning to confess something to you. It's something I've only told Rose, and it has to do with my past. I've confided in you about so much, and you know I trust you, but there's something you should know." Lance gathers himself together and turns to look at James's worried face. "James! Don't look so scared; everyone has skeletons in their closet! And don't worry; this information won't take down the campaign. Well, at least, I don't think it will. Anyway, my obsession, a word you used a few months ago, with the homeless pandemic, has a backstory, and it's a doozy that I'm sure will surprise you." Lance's voice cracks as he says softly, "I was once homeless myself." He then takes a long drink of water as the SUV heads back through the streets of Atlanta, in the direction of their tour bus.

"Wow," replies a visibly surprised James. "I didn't expect that. Please tell me about it; I really want to know."

"Well, it was during my undergrad years. As you know, my parents didn't come from money. It was hard to make a profit from the farm, and they barely got by. It was my second year at Georgetown, and my scholarship was in limbo because I had missed the reapplication deadline. It was summer, and I was working an unpaid internship at the National Archives in Washington, DC. My university counselor convinced me to take the position, and I was too embarrassed to say I had no money, even though she knew I was on a full-ride scholarship. The scholarship didn't pay for summer housing, so I had to move out of my apartment. On the weekends, I worked at a run-down fast-food joint. During the week, I worked nights, delivering pizza so I could have enough money to pay for gas, car insurance, food, and a local YMCA membership, so I had a place to shower. I lived in my old, beat-up car for the entire summer."

"That must have been quite an experience," James replies humbly.

"To say the very least. I did meet some of the kindest and most interesting people I've ever met. But I also saw a lot of terrible things happen to the people who society had left behind. The spiral of the streets can be unpredictable. I was fortunate, as I knew I had options. It was that experience that shaped my future. It's why I ran for city council once I left grad school and went back to Ohio."

"Thank you for sharing this, sir. It means a lot to me on a personal level, and it does explain a lot. Can I ask you a question?"

"Of course."

"I know your journey from city council to mayor of Dayton to governor of Ohio, but what made you build a campaign for the presidency centered around downsizing our military and intelligence? I've done my research and combed your old speeches. Nothing gives. What happened?"

Lance isn't quite sure he trusts James enough to tell him the truth, so he decides to tell him half of the truth: "It's simple. A lot of the homeless men and women I met were vets who not only served our country in wars created by our own government overseas, but also were neglected upon their return by those same organizations that sent them there. On top of that, as governor, I experienced firsthand the power of small local government initiatives, like incentivizing infrastructure and small businesses, increasing salaries for the police force and teachers, and cutting taxes for the middle and lower classes. Now, if I reach the top, I can make nationwide changes that will transform the fabric of our nation. Power will be returned to the masses, away from large government, foreign military operations, and corporate welfare. My agenda is focused on domestic issues."

"Your strategy has definitely won you fans and enemies on both sides of the fence. I have to say, one of the reasons I joined your campaign is that you are a different type of thinker. You look at both sides and the bigger picture. I respect that." James hesitates and then adds, "Excuse me, sir, but I have to tell you what's on my mind. You must know that this information is valuable, about your having been homeless, and, if leaked to the media, could be dangerous to the campaign. On the other hand, if it's spun correctly, it could be a huge benefit to the campaign. It would give you 'man of the people' credibility like nothing else could."

Lance pats him on the leg. "That's why only three people know about this, James. Now let's get out of here." Lance lets out a small sigh as they board the bus for the airport. The pair sits in silence during the ride. He hopes that his entourage won't lose its enthusiasm during these last stops of the campaign and that he can finish this trip without offending anyone with his choice of words. It is yet another reminder for him: politicians are only as good as their last misspoken word.

◎◎

The bus nears the Signature Executive Terminal and Hangar, which is located at the north end of Atlanta's Hartsfield-Jackson airport. From here, they will head to South Carolina, their final campaign stop. Lance gets out of the bus with his security team behind him, then sneaks away to a more private area of the terminal to make his "feeling so lonely" phone call to Rose. She's in the Sun Belt area of the country, actively dodging some of the protestors who are letting out their frustrations about their financial struggles. Their fear of the unknown is real. Most of them are worried and wondering if they can make it through another year without losing everything they own. Their last hope is help from Dumont if he is elected. They want some of those big agency and military budgets funneled back into their midsize towns and businesses.

"These protestors have *you* in their minds, Lance. You!" Rose reassures him over the phone. "I'm reminding myself that they only want good for this country, just like you keep saying, and although they are here to protest us, my heart goes out to them because we are all in this together. Somehow, honey, you've managed to upset both parties. Some of the protesters are calling you one thing, like a 'crazy liberal,' while others are chanting 'conservative fascist.' Darling, you are going to have to pick a side at some point," she teases before changing the subject. "When do you land in South Carolina?"

"We are supposed to be departing in about thirty to forty minutes, which will have me arriving about two hours from now," Lance replies while looking at his watch and finding that it's already 8:45 in the evening. "That should put us there pretty close to 10:30. I'm going to try to sleep on the plane. I'm so damned tired, Rose. My throat is raw from speaking nonstop. I feel like my lungs can't take in enough air to catch my breath, and my stomach is telling me "No more coffee." He subconsciously rubs his stomach as though it may help. "James has been especially good to me during this last part of the campaign tour. He is on top of everyone, going over schedules for tomorrow's new set of stops and speeches. Sometimes I feel like he's got my days planned for me all the way to my second term's campaign start date, less than four years from now!" Lance says jokingly.

Rose coughs and pauses for a moment before replying, "I've told you before: James does not run your life, nor should he make your decisions. You can't put so much trust in one person. It's late, so don't get me started; I want to sleep well tonight. We can talk about this reelection thing another time. It's a family decision. And may I add that you aren't president yet, so get some sleep on the plane."

Lance knows Rose's feelings about James. He wonders how many times she's told him that he shouldn't trust anyone, not even James. But now is not the time to bring it up, so instead, he says, "OK my love . . ." But these words are drowned out by the sound of a loud boom, which is quickly followed by another, even louder *BOOM*. There's a pause followed by a half dozen or so smaller booms. The sound is deafening. Everyone in the small private terminal starts screaming and running as they see the explosions light up the terminal next to theirs. Lance can see flames shooting at least fifty feet in the air. Members of his security detail grab him so hard that his phone falls from his hand and slides a few feet away.

He can hear Rose's voice screaming, "Lance! Lance! Lance!? What was that? What's happening? Lance!?" as he's thrown to the ground and covered by members of his security team.

The rest of them draw their weapons and yell, "Everyone *GET DOWN* . . . down on the ground—*now!*"

CHAPTER 4

BOOM, BOOM, BOOM!

▷ **Lance – Atlanta, Georgia**

Some people have started running toward the windows. Lance wants to warn them that the glass could explode on them and cause serious harm, but he's prevented from doing so by the special agents who are covering him with their bodies. It's complete mayhem. Lance is shouting at the agents, telling them to get off of him, but they are busy yelling to panicking people to take cover. The twenty-five or so people in the private terminal are diving under tables and chairs, while some are running from the terminal. Lance has lost his phone in the melee, which just seems to worsen as the explosions continue: *Boom! Boom! Boom!* Though now, they're less loud and frequent as the first ones.

Lance attempts to grapple with what's happening around him as he tries to move in the direction of where he last saw his phone. All he can think of is what Rose is hearing. Clearly this is an attack. Some type of assassination attempt? Maybe it's an attack on the airport itself and has nothing to do with him. But he knows that's unlikely. He's heard too many Secret Service briefings about the organized groups that vow to stop at nothing to make sure he's not the next president. Right now, no one seems to know what's happening.

He finally spots his phone just a couple yards away. As he moves closer to it, another agent grabs his ankle and pulls him back. "Sir, we've got you covered. We will be getting you out of here as quickly as possible."

They stand Lance up and move fast, shielding him with their bodies, weapons drawn, pushing people away as they walk him to a more protected area. Once they have Lance in a secured conference room within the terminal, they check him over and ask him if he has been hurt in any manner whatsoever. Lance is visibly shaken by all this. He knows he is OK; he's just concerned about what's happening and wonders where the attackers are and if they are closing in. He also wonders if anyone has been hurt or killed.

Lance turns to the closest agent and asks, "Do we know what's happening? Has there been any gunfire? Anyone hurt?" But, of course, no one has answers yet.

His security personnel are on high alert as they bark coded commands to one another over their radios. They are also in touch with the air traffic control tower, which reports that the explosions came from the end of the terminal used by UPS Airport Hub. They tell Dumont's team to stay put until they find out what has happened. Lance looks around and realizes he feels so very helpless. He's humbled by these men and women who are putting their lives on the line for him and is amazed by what they do for their country.

The explosions have ended, and now the sounds of sirens fill the air. Lance and his team can see smoke just outside the terminal, on the east side, which is used for UPS shipments. After what seems to be an eternity, Lance asks if anyone can provide more information about what the hell is going on. Everyone is jumpy and still unsure of the threat level. His mind goes back to his phone that must still be lying on the ground. He hopes Rose didn't hear everything. He just wants to speak with her and tell her he is OK.

◎◎

After all that occurred last night, the campaign team is on edge today. Lance went to bed at 3:00 in the morning. After waiting for two hours at the Signature Terminal, they finally learned that the explosions came from a shipment of fireworks that were inadvertently ignited. This information led to a two-hour discussion once they landed in South Carolina at 1:00 a.m., and the discussion turned into an argument via conference call between Lance, Secret Service Director Alexander Cummings, Homeland Security Director Keith Noakes, and James Edwards. Lance's security team took the opportunity to try to convince their boss to request more security precautions. Homeland Security had already received a record number of threats on Dumont—greater than any four-year period for a sitting president, let alone a candidate. Despite his countless conversations with the Secret Service and Homeland Security, Lance has been blasé about the threats and has continued to refuse to add any more security agents to his team. He feels his entourage is big enough and doesn't want to tarnish his reputation as a candidate who is always accessible. Lance pointed to the fireworks explosion as another example of Homeland Security blowing things out of proportion. "No pun intended," he added, but no one laughed. In the end, they came to no resolution and just agreed to disagree. Yesterday was a long and awful day, and the team is unsure of how the press will cover the incident.

Despite the scare and long conversations, Lance feels positive and grateful today. He's in more hopeful spirits than he has been in for a while. South Carolina is his last campaign stop, and for the first time in two weeks, he and Rose will be meeting up to campaign together. They have been splitting up their visits to cover more ground on this final stretch. Rose arrives at the hotel at 10:00 a.m., and they steal thirty-minutes together in the suite to catch up and share a few moments of intimacy before their campaign day begins.

☼☼

Seven hours later, at the end of the long day filled with stops in three counties, Lance and Rose board their private plane to Columbus, Ohio—this time, thankfully, with no fireworks. Lance leaves South Carolina while looking forward to reuniting with his children back home. This will be the first time in a while he has been with the whole family: his wife, Rose; his two sons, Thomas and George; and the twins, June and Edwina. He knows they are all looking forward to being together again, as the last year has been hectic. This brutal period he has spent on the campaign trail will finally be over. The election is tomorrow.

After Lance and Rose land in Columbus, Lance says good night to his team and heads up to the family's private quarters in the Hilton hotel across the street from the Greater Columbus Convention Center. The top floor has been reserved for the Dumont family members and their team. A bonus is the private elevator access. As Lance enters the suite, he glances around. His kids look exhausted, draped all over the room like zombies, limbs spread out over sofas, legs and arms dangling from chairs. Even though they are completely wiped out, they jump up to greet their dad, particularly happy to see him after the airport scare. Edwina is especially emotional and gives him a long hug, her tears soaking into her father's shirt. She has taken a lot of personal shots from the media, and her quick temper hasn't always been portrayed in the best light.

The family's conversation flows easily for some time, and then the fireworks incident comes up. They all express their relief at finding out it was simply bad timing. The Dumont kids are especially eager to share with their parents their experiences on the campaign trail.

After a brief pause following their wrap-up, George sits up and pushes his wavy sandy-brown hair behind his ear. He then turns to one of the twins and asks, "Edwina, is it really true you want to become a nun?"

For support, Edwina glances at Thomas, her older brother in whom she confides, then turns her gaze back to George. "Yes, it's true. I think I can help this world in some small way. I'm not going to be a shut-in, nonspeaking, habit-wearing type of nun or anything like that. But . . . well . . . I'm still thinking about it, what it will look like for me. I think it might be a good way for me to give back to society and help others. You know, sort of like Dad's reasons for going into politics."

George gives his sister a big hug. Thomas walks over and joins in the embrace. Lance, with tears in his eyes, then joins the trio. He tells Edwina, "I promise to be supportive. No matter what you decide to do, know that I will always be on your side. I'm sure you will help a lot of people, Edwina." He kisses her on the forehead.

It's nearly 1:00 in the morning, and considering everything that has happened over the past day and a half, and the fact that no one has really gotten any sleep, they are ready for bed. They say their good nights. No one is thinking of him- or herself, only of the others, especially their father. Now is the time to get serious, as things are about to change, no matter which way the election goes.

ELECTION DAY

▷ **Lance – Columbus, Ohio**

The morning begins with the entire family seated around the table, enjoying a large breakfast. Today is the big day. Reporters, pundits, supporters, and campaign organizers have been arriving since early this morning from all parts of the country. There are TV news stations with cameras and crews setting up at the Greater Columbus Convention Center across the street. At the end of their meal, Lance and Rose enjoy a moment alone at the table while everyone else goes to their rooms to relax a bit before the hectic day gets underway.

"I hope you ate something substantial instead of just having coffee, Lance. It's going to be a very long day," Rose says as she moves from across the table and sits down in the chair next to him.

"I feel like a fish out of water, like I can hardly breathe." Lance pushes away his plate full of food, stands up, and starts pacing the room.

"Come back to the table and eat, right this minute," Rose commands.

Lance notes her authoritative tone and returns to his seat.

"You will be the most amazing president, Lance. I don't even know if I've ever taken the time to tell you that. You're honest, smart, and have good intentions. And you have common sense ideas for turning this country around. You will be the best president we've ever had. Forget the naysayers, the haters, and the media—right now, Lance. It's just you and me. Today will be your day. I just know it." Rose gives him a quick, reassuring peck on the lips, then rises from the table to get ready for the day ahead.

☯

A couple of hours later, Lance, Rose, and the children head downstairs to a small conference room in the hotel and join the group gathered. There is a palpable buzz of eagerness in the air, and Lance can't help but acknowledge it as he addresses his team.

"Today is the day!" he shouts to cheers from members of his team. "Our jobs are done, and all we can do is remember that we did our best. I'm grateful for your hard work and commitment to the change we hope to make in this country. Now, let's just pray for a win!"

His team claps and hollers, but Lance feels a sense of loss as he exits the room. This is the last time he'll be in the company of all the members of his campaign team. Tomorrow they will go their own separate ways. If he loses, they will be moving on to other jobs. But even if he wins, most of his wonderful team members won't be joining him in the White House.

James leads Lance to a small meeting room for a briefing with four officials from the very agencies he's looking to downsize, including the CIA, the FBI, the Secret Service, and Homeland Security. This room down the hall was set up just for this reason. What was to be a thirty-minute security briefing turns into an hour-and-a-half heated discussion about the scale of these agencies. The clear disdain for Lance's plan to cut their budgets is etched on their faces and in their tones.

"Please, everyone, let's settle down," interrupts Lance as one of the briefing agents rants about the value of his work and its importance to the country. "Look, everyone, I'm not going to diminish the importance of the CIA or any other federal organization, or the value of these briefings, or any of the important work done by your organizations; I promise you that. And I will extend an olive branch to you right now: all four of you can be on my security advisory team. I need your blunt and honest feedback. We will comb through the budget line item by line item. And if you don't think something can be cut, then it won't be. But trust me, I will challenge you. If you can defend your position, I will be your biggest champion." The CIA representative looks unconvinced and rolls her eyes, but Lance ignores her reaction. He knows her boss, Director Donald Schultz, has been one of his biggest opponents. He doubts he can win Schultz over, but he will cross that bridge when he comes to it. He thanks the agents and sends them on their way, knowing that if he's elected, it's going to be a battle every day.

Lance returns to his team down the hall to get caught up on the numbers. After many hours of being glued to the TV, the team members are relieved that the long day is coming to an end. It's early evening on the East Coast, and Lance has gathered together those closest to him: his family members, friends, and campaign staff. The large-screen monitors cast an ominous light on their faces. Lance grabs Rose's hand for a moment. It seems as though every person in the room is holding their breath, their hearts skipping a beat as they watch and wait for the election results. In half an hour, voting will come to an end on the East Coast. Some positive numbers have already come in from the Midwest, along with encouraging early results from the West Coast, where they still have a few more hours before the polls close.

Lance anxiously glances from monitor to monitor, each displaying a different news channel. He's trying to gauge what's happening in hot spots around the country, and to understand and digest some of the intelligence information he received earlier from Homeland Security regarding extremist groups. He wonders if he missed anything during their heated discussion.

Lance walks over to sit next to his vice-presidential nominee, Jennifer Alvarez, and Jennifer's husband, Nick. They chat for a bit, then turn back to the monitors. Within seconds, out of sheer exhaustion, Lance doses off in his chair for about twenty minutes.

☺☺

It has just turned 9:00 p.m. on the East Coast, and all the polls are now closed. The results are coming in fast. At one point, the votes begin to avalanche for Lance, but then, just as quickly, they shift in the opposite direction. The numbers are rolling in from not just the presidential election, but also from the state and city elections and the ballots' propositions.

Lance thinks back to the hard days he spent planning his campaign, struggling with the Midwestern humidity, lack of sleep, bad food, cold coffee, and the constant smell of exhaust from the campaign's tour buses. While he knows he will miss those days, he's glad they are over. He rests his weary head in the palms of his hands, now wishing for this night, too, to be over.

Rose sits silently beside him, and as usual, he turns to her plaintively. "Rose," he begins, "I don't know how this is going to end. It's up to the people of this country to step up and speak out. I know I can't keep my promises without reaching across the aisle and having support on both sides of the political spectrum. I'm willing to compromise; that's for sure! How will I help these farmers, retailers, manufacturers, and janitors if we don't work together? I'm 100 percent human and can only be successful if everyone comes together and works with me, not against me."

"You need to get out of your head and just enjoy this for the moment that it is," Rose replies gently. "For better or worse, this will be the biggest day of our lives. Let's just be present for it, OK?"

With that, the pair head up to their hotel suite to get ready for the evening. Lance showers, and they both get dressed to meet the staff, reporters, politicians, and friends they have invited to watch the results filter in from across the country in the large ballroom of the Hilton. When they enter the crowded room, everyone cheers, and Lance is overwhelmed by all the people as well as the noise coming from the numerous televisions scattered throughout the room. Lance first notices his children, then turns to see nearly every person who helped in the Ohio campaign office, close family friends, and tons of media—cameramen and reporters who all want time with the family. He and his family members are being bombarded with questions, and Lance's anxiety is through the roof.

As he looks around the room at the people gathered here to support him, he is suddenly overcome with emotion and gratitude for all they've done to make this moment happen. He also realizes that tonight isn't just about him. Nearly every person in this room has risked so much and worked so hard; they are all stakeholders in the outcome of this election. He breathes deeply and takes comfort in knowing they are in this together. Win or lose, they will stand tall in the end.

Lance gracefully moves about the room and spends his time shaking hands with those who extend theirs. He attempts to thank each person individually while also taking time to answer questions from the media. As Lance glances at the large clock on the wall, the TV announces that it's been an hour since the polls closed in the Midwest. The reporter goes silent for a moment while the onscreen numbers show that Jeffrey Thomlinson, the incumbent, is moving ahead in not just the popular vote, but also the electoral vote. He's been in office for just four years and has been plagued by low polling numbers and numerous unfulfilled promises. Lance is hoping to make Thomlinson a one-term president. The anxiety level in the room begins to rise considerably, with the loud hum of voices growing more desperate by the minute.

CHAPTER 6

THE DUMONTERS

▷ **Lance – Columbus, Ohio**

t's been two hours since the polls closed on the East Coast. The entire group that had filled the Hilton's Aminah Robinson Grand Ballroom has now moved down the street to the Greater Columbus Convention Center. The enormous Battelle Grand Ballroom is packed with thousands of attendees from all walks of life. These are the passionate voters and supporters who have backed Lance for the last decade—not just from Ohio, but from all across the country. Backstage, the Dumont family and close staffers stand by while watching four small TV monitors. Lance wipes the sweat from his forehead with his handkerchief. The headlines change almost simultaneously: "Arizona, New Mexico for Dumont." Suddenly, the numbers are beginning to shift in Lance's favor. Arizona, with their eleven electoral votes, and New Mexico with their five, both go to Dumont. The convention center explodes with thunderous shouting, stomping, and clapping. Immediately afterward, Ohio is called in Lance's favor. This big jump of eighteen electoral votes puts Lance in the lead for the first time all evening. "Whoop!" and "Dumont!" along with other cheers fill the room. Can he, the underdog just one year ago, actually pull this off?

The crowd begins to gather in front of the podium on the small stage. The electricity in the air is palpable. Lance's campaign staff, including all the people who have been there for him since the beginning, are starting to feel it too. It's looking more and more like he might actually pull off this incredible feat, and he, Lance Dumont, will be the next occupant of the office of president of the United States.

Standing in anticipation, they all watch the screens, waiting to hear if the pundits will call the election in his favor. Just then, the screens flash to the words "Lance Dumont — Surprise Win," followed by "Dumont Elected President of the United States."

The images on the screens once again change, bringing viewers inside President Thomlinson's election night party. The whole world watches the incumbent come to realize he has lost the election. Clearly surprised by the results, President Thomlinson forces a smile and begrudgingly announces his concession to Lance Dumont.

Back at the Dumont party, the crowd is screaming, crying, and cheering. Balloons and confetti drop from the ceiling and cover the Dumontier's, a term the Dumont kids use to describe their father's most enthusiastic fans. Rose bursts into tears as she hugs her husband. The kids join in one by one until they've gathered together in one big group hug, tears of joy streaming down their faces. Behind Lance, James and the campaign heads begin getting everything into place for Lance's victory speech, which will take place in about twenty minutes. They nudge the family members to take their places on the stage. It all seems to happen so quickly that Lance feels dizzy with joy, excitement, and the realization that he has just been named the president-elect of the United States. *He actually won!* He secretly wonders to himself if a mistake has occurred.

As he's being moved toward the podium, Lance mumbles to himself, "This can't be real," but it is.

Rose senses his emotions, takes his hand, and says, "Lance, I can't believe what's happening. This was just a pipe dream, but here we are." She wipes away his tears and gives him a crowd-pleasing ten-second kiss.

Lance gathers close his beaming family members. It feels to him as if the stage lights have become brighter and harsher, but he's no longer overwhelmed and suddenly feels energized by this incredible win. The worry and pressure from the past two weeks seem to melt away in the heat of the lights. Onstage, along with the Dumont family, stands the vice president-elect, Jennifer Alvarez, and her family. Lance and Jennifer join hands and then raise them in unison while simultaneously waving at the massive crowd. They've rehearsed this part, but without the tears and glory of this victory. Together they share in a genuine moment of sheer bliss. Lance knows nothing in his life will ever compare to this moment.

James walks up to the podium, shaking hands along the way, until he reaches Lance. He then gives him a bear hug that takes his boss by surprise. But it's all so very good, as this is a moment to be cherished. As James takes hold of the microphone, he uses his other hand to attempt to quiet the ecstatic crowd. He then announces, "Ladies and Gentlemen, I am proud to announce that the results are in, and it's official: we have won the presidential election! Everyone please welcome our president-elect, Lance Dumont, and Rose Dumont, our incoming first lady!"

Cheers boom from the enormous crowd as Lance and Rose step forward for the cameras, smiling and waving as they savor the moment.

Once the cheers finally die down, James takes Lance backstage and says, "There are a few close states that are being verified, and then it will be all over with. You will be well ahead of Thomlinson. You will have won by a landslide, sir. After the official results are announced, you can return to the stage and make your acceptance speech. But let me just say how proud I am to have been on your team, no matter what happens."

Lance's radiant expression suddenly changes as he begins, "What's going to—"

As if on cue, a tall, intimidating figure approaches them and extends his hand. "Congratulations, Mr. President-elect. Alexander Cummings, director of the Secret Service. It's a pleasure to finally meet you face-to-face under such wonderful circumstances. Zoom doesn't foster personal relationships like the real thing. I look forward to getting to know you. My job is to familiarize you with your new security detail teams, and I will vet each person with you over the next few days." With a wry smile, Cummings adds, "You will be seeing a lot of me and my team over the next four years . . . more than you'd probably like."

As they shake hands, Lance isn't sure what to make of this sudden and unexpected appearance by his predecessor's appointee. He knows Cummings is a valued and tenured member of the Secret Service who climbed his way to the top with a reputation of being fair and honest. He remembers that the director is also the first African American to lead the organization. Lance wonders why Cummings chose *this* moment, in front of the cameras, to introduce himself. But now isn't the time to start analyzing the internal politics of this new office. It is time to celebrate.

He thanks Cummings and then turns back to James, unable to stop a wide grin from spreading across his face. "This is it! I am no longer just the nominee; I'm the president-elect, and come January 20, the president of these United States of America! It feels right, James, and I couldn't have done it without you."

"Thank you, sir." James gives him a brief smile and pat on the back. "It's been my pleasure to be a part of all this."

Lance has so many mixed emotions going through his mind. He feels like he is on top of the world, yet he also feels as if a judge were pounding her gavel on his body. The lines he'd planned to say tonight are rushing through his head, but he's not sure if he'll be able to remember them all. He's going to be the next president of the United States. This is it. His long fight has finished, and now he realizes what lies ahead of him is not going to be an easy feat to accomplish. But as long as he has the right people in his corner, he will make it happen and keep all of his campaign promises. As he stands here, thinking through all of this, a surge of people are reaching out to him. Some are trying to grab his hands; others are clapping him on the back. All are offering their congratulations to him, his family, and his campaign team.

Moments after the official announcement is made on television, the Dumont family heads back onstage along with Vice President-elect Jennifer Alvarez and her family. A raucous crowd roars at their approach, waving American flags, posters, and lighted cell phones in the air. Lance delivers his victory speech. He's nervous, tired, and emotional, and it is apparent in his voice. It's shaky in the beginning, but then it smooths out by the time he thanks Jennifer Alvarez for all her help and touts her breaking the proverbial glass ceiling by becoming the first vice president of Hispanic descent in American history. Lance is proud to have such a diverse administration planned for his tenure. He thanks all those who have helped him achieve his goal and vows to work hard and make good on his campaign promises.

By the time Lance has conversed with what feels like everyone in the convention center, he is exhausted. Still, he finds a bit of energy left to play a little game with the Secret Service, inspired by something he once read Teddy Roosevelt did. He makes his way through the crowd, looking over his shoulder to see if the agents follow him, which, of course, they do. Then he makes the same circle again, but quicker this time. Once again, they stay close to him, not missing a beat. Then the president-elect backs up in a quick succession of steps, and, without warning, darts to the side, never looking back to see if they are keeping up. The special agents follow in his steps while shooting confused but mildly amused looks at one another. Lance gives them a big smile and a wink. This is his way of trying to get them to warm up to him. If they are going to spend a lot of time together, they might as well find some enjoyment in the job.

By 3:00 in the morning, all the fanfare and big celebrations have officially ended. It's just the family and James gathered together once again in their hotel suite. They are situated around the coffee table and still reveling in what has taken place over the last seven hours.

Lance stands. "I want to thank you guys—my core team: Rose, James, Thomas, George, Edwina, and June. I am the next president because of the six of you in this room. Especially you, Rose." He bends over to take her hand and kisses it. "I know it hasn't been an easy road for any of you."

George stands. "The Monsters!" he yells as they all stand and raise their hands for high fives to celebrate their moment of triumph.

Lance just shakes his head, but he can't help grinning.

June asks, "Come take a picture with me, Daddy, for my Insta, please?"

Lance, of course, gives into his social media guru daughter. He knows this means that pictures of him and this private family celebration will be posted to her various sites, but he owes his sweet June this and so much more. After all, she was key in helping, along with his media team, to navigate a complicated social media landscape throughout the campaign. They stand together while June sweeps her long brown hair from behind her back so that it falls over her chest, her standard selfie pose. But before she can even raise her phone to take the picture, Edwina snatches it from her grasp.

"That's all you ever think about: *yourself!*" Edwina snaps, her hazel eyes on fire. "You can't be posting pictures of our lives now! Don't you understand how much danger you're putting Dad in? This is a private moment, and all you care about is getting more attention. Dad's already getting daily death threats, and now here you are, exploiting him."

An awkward silence falls over the family. June begins to cry, and Rose gets up to comfort her. Lance looks shell-shocked by Edwina's cruel outburst.

Thomas turns to his father. "Edwina is kind of right, Dad. There are many people who would like to see you dead . . . but at the same time, there are others who would like to see all Americans dead. We all have to be careful. *You*, most of all, have to be very careful. No more goofing around with security. Please? Do it for us."

"Sure, Edwina has a point," George adds, "but she didn't need to go so overboard on June. We've got to stick together." He puts his arm around June as Edwina glares at him.

Lance, realizing Edwina and Thomas are right, says, "Guys, this is just the beginning for all of us. Of course we are more at risk now than we were when I was governor. And it's all because of me, because of my decision to run for president. I know we discussed it long ago, but here we are now. This is a whole new level of scary; I get it. I am sorry that we may all be in a somewhat constant state of worry over the next four years." He looks down at his hands, unsure of what to say next.

With a knock at the door, room service saves everyone from the moment. An early breakfast has arrived, and along with it, the bad air in the room is quickly replaced by the sweet aroma of pancakes and bacon. The kids joke about being "hangry" and exhausted, and begin devouring their food. Once they've had their fill, June and Edwina apologize to each other.

"Dad," Edwina asks softly, "are you *really* aware of the dangers you face? I assume you have been briefed by the Secret Service and all, but have you been properly briefed by, say, the CIA, FBI, and/or Homeland Security on *all* the possible threats? I've been studying the topic and just finished a great book that sheds light on one of the possible truths behind the assassination of JFK. You should know you can't trust *anyone*, Dad. I'm being serious." Edwina's face is full of emotion as she says this.

June, who usually keeps her opinions to herself, chimes in, supporting Edwina's argument. "You especially need to listen to the Secret Service. No more games, Dad, like the one you played tonight! We know it's not going to be easy for you. I can appreciate that you hate losing any ounce of privacy you have left, but that's the decision you made. We are all in it together now, whether we like it or not."

Thankfully, Rose is there to stop them from diving deeper into this discussion. Before the children can say anything more, she commands, "Let's all go to bed. I'm still your mother, so you have to do what I say. Good night. I love you guys." The kids obey without complaint, sheepishly heading off to their bedrooms.

Lance smiles gratefully at Rose, takes her hand, and leads her to their bedroom without turning on the lights. As they slip into bed, he feels the presence of the special agents outside their hotel room door, protecting him from whatever and whomever is out there.

"I hope you listened to the kids tonight," Rose says gently. "They aren't wrong. We've had this discussion: you need to take the briefings more seriously, especially when there are threats against you. Now go to bed, Mr. President-elect." She laughs softly, then kisses him on the lips for a long, delicious moment before laying her head on the pillow.

Lance can hear the concern in Rose's voice, even as she pretends there is none. Butterflies begin to fill his stomach. His mind is far too muddled by thoughts of what took place tonight: *he,* Lance Dumont, has really been elected president of the country he loves so deeply. It's now 4:45 in the morning. They have been up for almost twenty-four hours straight, and he's so tired. He takes a few deep breaths to revive his weary mind, but it's of no avail, and he drifts off to sleep.

☺☺

The next morning, the president-elect calls James to discuss the next steps. As with past administrations, the process of briefing the new administration will begin within weeks.

After ten minutes, just as Lance is preparing to end the call, James says, "Sir, nothing needs to happen right away. I'm in meetings all day, preparing what comes next for you. In fact, I think that starting tomorrow, you should take a few days off to do whatever you please. After today, there is nothing scheduled for you over the next week, though there are things related to the campaign that will need to be wrapped up soon."

"Thank you, James. I do want to join the security briefings taking place today with the leads of the security branches. Are the guys from Homeland Security, the CIA, and the FBI still scheduled?"

"All lined up. And I emailed you the list of calls scheduled today with eleven world leaders who want to congratulate you personally. I've prioritized the members of G-7, just in case you don't get to the rest." James clears his throat before adding, "By the way, sir, there is one thing that is going to be required of you after the holidays, and that is a code you need to create."

Confused, Lance asks, "A code? What type of code? I haven't heard anything about this."

James continues, "It's a new protocol Homeland Security wants to implement. It's more precautionary than anything and is to be used in case of a kidnapping, an assassination attempt, a terrorist attack, or anything of that nature. If such a situation should occur, this code will identify you as being the actual president if you're ever in the hands of an enemy. Given today's level and range of threats, there are a lot of crazy, dangerous scenarios that can take place, even here on our own turf."

"What about my fingerprints? Aren't they enough? Why not just add a retinal scan as well?"

"Safety is a number one priority, and this is just part of that process."

The annoyance is clear in Lance's voice as he says under his breath, "What are these people going to think of next?"

In a calming but authoritative voice, James says, "The new protocols are something you must, and I stress, *must* follow. If anything should happen, and you are not able to provide the code, you will *not* be identified as the president of the United States, and that just isn't a scenario we want to think about. Anyway, aside from this and the calls I mentioned, you are mostly on your own over the coming week, with nothing really pressing on your agenda. Therefore, it might be a good time to take your family on a little trip, as you never know when your schedule might be this open again."

Lance thinks about this for a moment and replies, "Thanks, James. You're right; that's a good idea. The family could use a little break. If possible, I think I'd like to take my family to a tropical island, as that's something we've talked about doing for years."

"Of course, Mr. President-elect. I was hoping you'd agree. This might be one of the last opportunities for you all to squeeze in some peace and fun before you take office. After that happens, the presidency will fully consume the lives of all of you."

Lance asks James to arrange a trip to Saint Croix, instructing him not to tell anyone who isn't on the "need to know" list, in order to preserve the family's privacy and prevent the destination from being leaked to the press.

James responds, "You do realize we will never be able to sneak you out of here without the media's notice, right? They are waiting not only to see their new president, but also to hear from and speak to you. I don't know how you plan to avoid the public eye on vacation!" James laughs in surprise.

Lance realizes this is one of the first of many battles he will lose and begins to concede that his life now belongs to the citizens of the United States, whom he cannot fail.

CHAPTER 7

THE DUMONT CODE

The family trip to Saint Croix was just what the Dumont's needed. Plenty of sun and family time. But most of all, it was a chance to be away from the media. And now the holiday season is in full swing as the family members come together again in Ohio. Christmas is starting to feel like a warm blanket enveloping them on a cold night. Rose asks the children to start making lists of their belongings that need to be moved into the White House.

Christmas in Ohio wraps up quickly for Lance, and he soon finds himself back in DC. On his agenda for today, which James and his staff prepared for him, is his meeting with Homeland Security at their headquarters, located across the Potomac River from Ronald Reagan Washington National Airport, where they will create the code. Lance's SUV pulls into the parking lot of the massive headquarters, an impressive building. Lance and his security team make their way into the underground garage after having the vehicle checked by the parking security team, and step into the elevator, which in and of itself, is something to see: cameras in all four corners, voice recognition to open and close the doors, and palm print scans to access specific floors. It's lit up as brightly as an operating room. Lance notices the harsh florescent lights reflected in everyone's pupils.

Homeland Security Director Keith Noakes and Secret Service Director Alexander Cummings are waiting in the generously sized room to greet Lance. Noakes's dark complexion stands in contrast to his light-gray suit, and his quiet demeanor belies his fierce reputation. Lance looks away from Noakes and notices that there are no windows; the room is stark and modern with nothing on the walls. Voices echo in here, which forces everyone to keep their voices low. Lance shakes hands with each director and they exchange pleasantries. As he's about to sit down, the door opens, and in strides the director of the CIA, Donald Schultz. Lance is a bit taken aback, as James didn't mention that Director Schultz would be attending. Fortunately, Lance's face doesn't betray his thoughts, and before he can think twice about it, he's shaking Schultz's hand. It's just the three of them in the room.

Director Noakes doesn't acknowledge Schultz, who kicks off the meeting without hesitation. "Mr. President-elect, does anyone in your family know where you are today?"

All eyes turn to Lance with a strange intensity, as if this is the first of many tests he has to pass.

Lance clears his throat and replies, "If you're asking if I've told my family about the code, the short answer is no. As you already know, the only person who knows about this meeting is James Edwards . . . oh, and my special agents, I suppose."

A long, uncomfortable silence fills the room.

"That's good, sir," Director Schultz responds as he unbuttons his suit jacket. "However, it's time for you to be made aware of something." He appears to pause for effect, then continues, "And that is that James Edwards is one of us."

"One of us?" Lance asks. His eyes widen in surprise, and he works hard to stifle a gasp.

Schultz continues, "Yes, let me clarify: He works for us. He's an agent of the CIA and reports directly to me."

Lance can no longer hide his reaction but maintains his composure. He doesn't look away from Schultz, and their eyes remain locked. Lance won't back down, not this early in the game—if that's what this is, some sort of game that everyone in the room has been playing and he's only just now been invited to the table. But it is very clear from the note of victory in Schultz's tone that he thinks he has already won.

"I take it you're surprised, sir?" Director Schultz asks, letting the question hang in the air. With a hint of a smile, he continues, "Agent Edwards has worked for the CIA on and off for nearly six years now. He left the agency to get into politics and, as you know, built a solid reputation as a political strategist in a short span of time. The agency took notice of this, and I asked for him to be reactivated about a year before he joined your campaign team. Mr. President-elect, with all due respect, sir, in the world of politics, there are no coincidences. Once we knew you were putting your hat into the ring for president, we knew there was a chance that you could be our next commander in chief, and we made sure that Agent Edwards was at the top of the list to run your campaign. Selecting him would be the wise choice, and you did just that. We wanted Edwards to be at your side from the beginning. It was a way for us to learn who you are. We wanted to get to know your personality, your habits, any proverbial skeletons in the closet, and most of all, the identity of those with whom you surround yourself behind the scenes."

Lance noticeably stiffens, unsure of how to reply. Schultz must've seen this coming. He nods to the other two directors and says, "Can you guys give us the room for a few minutes?"

Once they are alone, Schultz stands and walks over to a table on which food and beverages are laid out. "Well, sir, I'm sure you have some questions. Anything specific you want to know regarding this new information?"

Lance is angry, but he's trying hard not to show it. He clenches his jaw and makes a mental note to nominate a new CIA director as one of his first actions as president. Right now, he doesn't care if this dinosaur has been working for the CIA for thirty years. After enjoying that thought, he says, "What the hell is going on here? I've had the wool pulled over my eyes this entire time? Is this some sort of revenge for our fallouts when I was governor, Schultz?"

"I'm sorry for this surprise revelation. This probably wasn't the right moment to tell you, but I felt you needed to know about James as soon as possible, especially since I've heard you are planning to make him your chief of staff."

"This doesn't make sense; cut the crap!" Lance blusters. "How the hell did I, as a candidate running for president, have a CIA agent operating—*heading*—my campaign for the presidency? This can't be legal, dammit! This isn't some small country with a dictatorship. This is the United States of America, and last time I checked, we were still a democracy! This is a perfect example of an overfunded, out-of-control, unhinged agency."

Lance can see the rage in Schultz's dark eyes. *Good*, he thinks.

"Listen, I understand your frustration, but if it makes you feel any better, President Thomlinson also had no clue about this. He was not involved in any way. He was never 'in on this,' so to speak, and it wasn't sabotage. In fact, I was never given any inside information about your campaign or strategies. All intel was purely about *you*."

Just as Lance is about to threaten Schultz, a man and a woman enter the room through a disguised door in the middle of a nearby wall, along with a Homeland Security agent. Lance is dumbfounded. He hadn't even noticed the door before their entrance.

Director Schultz says, "Well then, looks like it's time for you to create your code. This is the combined direction of the Secret

Service and Homeland Security, so I will be stepping out now. Thank you for your time, and I will see you at the next briefing, Mr. President-elect." With that, Schultz exits the room without answering any of the questions Lance wasn't even given an opportunity to ask.

What the hell just happened? Lance wonders.

As soon as Schultz leaves, Directors Cummings and Noakes reenter the room. At the same time, a large screen descends from the ceiling, and a small computer center is revealed when part of the wall opens. The woman walks over to the chair in front of a computer, sits down, and begins typing on the keyboard. At the same time, the Homeland Security agent hands Lance a page of typed instructions. Once he has finished reading them, Lance nods his head in acknowledgement, and the agent leaves the room. The lights dim, and the proceedings begin.

Director Cummings turns to Lance. "As you know, the reason you are here is to enact our new coding system specifically set up for security purposes in relation to the office of the president. To be more precise, sir, you are here to create this code—a cipher, if you will. If someone or some organization, whether it be domestic or international, should happen to gain access to you, we will be able to verify your identity when you are located. For instance, in the case of a kidnapping, by using this code, we would be able to unmistakably authenticate your identity. Your ability to decipher the code would let us know that we are negotiating for the right person. There is no way we can use fingerprinting, retinal scans, or voice recognition. They just aren't secure enough in this day and age. They can all be easily hacked and faked. Simply put, this new code is set to be foolproof. This is all new for us too, as you are the first president for which this code will be created. One thing you might be happy to learn is that the code was given an official name just this morning." Noakes appears to pause for effect. He smiles at Lance before adding, "We've named it the Dumont Code."

"Thank you, Cummings, for the explanation," says Homeland Security Director Keith Noakes. Lance notes a slight irritation in his tone. "The code process was developed by my team here at Homeland Security. I've been a proponent of the code from the very beginning. We can't be too careful given the current global political climate, as well as our own here at home." With that, he looks at Cummings, then turns back to Lance. "We are taking extra precautions wherever we can. The war on terrorism is always an uphill battle for a man in your position. With the way things are now, we knew we had to up our game, so to speak. If there is anything you want to say or any questions you might have as we continue, please feel free to interrupt at any time during this process."

"I'm good, Director Noakes. Thank you," Lance responds before adding with a smile, "I must say, I especially like the name."

Both directors return the smile, and Noakes turns to Cummings. "Thank you for coming today. If you'll excuse us, Director Cummings, we will begin the process."

As Cummings says his goodbyes, Lance notes the tension between the two directors and wonders what's really happening behind the scenes. He's almost positive this has been a turf war, as protection of the president has always been the sole responsibility of the Secret Service. But since that agency has been overseen by Homeland Security since the latter was established after 9/11, the lines have become a bit blurred.

Noakes produces an electronic tablet and says, "Mr. President-elect, we will provide you with sets of numbers, symbols, and words on the electronic pad in front of you to begin the process. No one will be able to see what you're typing in response to them. The good thing about this particular new protocol of code creation is that *you* are the most integral part of the code itself. It will make the code authentic to you, and you will be able to decipher it at any time."

Lance shoots him a puzzled look. "Decipher? I thought I would be creating a code I would then memorize."

"This is not based on basic code or password memorization. Technology has come a long way. It would be easy to crack a simple code composed of some letters and numbers. Some portions of the code will use memories from *your* life, so that only you will be able to decipher the code. In essence, *you are the code*."

"That's a lot to unpack, Noakes, but I like the concept. I'm ready to move on."

They spend the rest of the morning working to ensure the new Dumont Code is to Lance's liking and impossible to hack. The matching up of numbers and letters, coupled with the symbols provided to Lance and others that Lance, himself, has selected takes hours. Each of the two Homeland Security programmers works on a separate laptop. In the end, only the president-elect and the actual program itself will know the entire code. They first focus on the numbers. Lance reacts quickly and types as fast as he can. The letters make things a bit more complicated. They want the code to be strong, but not so complicated that Lance can't decipher it under stress. Lance selects special memories from his past for added security. He then requests the use of images, and Noakes embraces the idea. After four hours, they are ready to test the first portion of the code. A virtual reality headset is used to simulate stress scenarios. Lance is blown away by the technology. In one moment, the VR experience places him in a prison cell; then, just as quickly, he's blindfolded while being hauled away in a helicopter. The realism of the VR is impressive. He's slowly beginning to understand the need for all this security.

After the test, they break for lunch, and Lance gives Rose a call to see how her day is going.

"Any luck in choosing your new staff members?" Lance asks as he bites into his roast beef sandwich. "I'd focus on selecting your deputy director of events first so you can get your scheduling in order. Equally as important is your designated special assistant, and, of course, your press secretary. These three individuals will be integral to you, dear; then they can hire the rest of your team."

"No, I'm sorry," Rose replies. "I've not started any of that. I know it's crazy, but I keep procrastinating because I'm not ready to give up being able to do some of these things on my own. It's getting a bit overwhelming. Also, I just learned that there's a man who will always sit outside our door, even when we sleep. Is that really necessary? Isn't the White House itself secure enough? It feels like such an invasion of our privacy, Lance."

"Yes, dear, it has been part of the Secret Service's protocol for decades. He is there for security reasons. My security team members are supposed to stick close to me at all times. You must remember this from when I was governor, but please, let's not worry about all that right now. They say those people don't hear very well, anyhow," he adds jokingly. "Also, I'll be home a bit late, but I still want to have dinner with the family, so wait for me, please."

They spend another ten minutes on the phone as Lance finishes his sandwich and Diet Coke. He has loved this combination ever since his college days. They say goodbye, and Lance checks his voicemail. He'd planned to call James after lunch, but after what he has learned today, he decides the call can wait.

◎◎

Twenty-five minutes later, Lance finds himself back in the room with Noakes and his staff. He turns to Noakes and asks,

"How many people know about the Dumont Code?" He smiles inwardly while saying the name aloud.

"Ultimately, there will be only eight of us who know about the existence of this code," Noakes reassures him. "The two of us, the two Homeland Security programmers we've been working with, Vice President Alvarez, Agent Edwards, Director Schultz, and Director Cummings. As I stated before, only the highly secured computer application itself knows the entire code, but even then, just in pieces. It can't be hacked to reveal the entire code. No one can access the code via the program, not even you. But you, of course, will be the only actual *person* who knows *how* to decipher the code. It's completely unique to you, Mr. President-elect." Noakes pauses, then adds, "I must say, you have come around quite quickly to understanding the code development. I especially like your suggestion to pair prime numbers with their corresponding letters in the alphabet. That definitely does create a great base. What you do with the images will be interesting. Additionally, your unique symbol submissions and personal photos can help, especially in high-stress situations. We will test this with VR again after it all comes together."

After an additional four hours and too many variations to count, Lance finally finishes creating his code—the Dumont Code. Before they leave the room, they speak to the two Homeland Security programmers who've been working in tandem with Lance. He thanks them for their patience and acknowledges their brilliance in creating the structure for the code.

On their way to the elevator, Director Noakes stops and asks Lance, "May I confide in you, sir?"

"Yes, Director, of course you can."

"Well, I've been in DC for nearly twenty years, and I've seen a lot."

"I'm sure you have, Director. That's probably how you got this role."

"Yes, yes. But what I'm about to tell you needs to remain between us only."

Lance's casual tone stiffens. "It will. I promise."

"Don't ever trust Cummings *or* Schultz."

CHAPTER 8

INAUGURATION DAY

▷ **Lance – Washington, DC**

nauguration day has finally arrived. The previous twelve days have been packed with preparation for the family's move to the White House, the finalization of Cabinet picks, and other staffing priorities. Lance has been working fourteen-hour days, mostly apart from his family. The First Family arrives at Pennsylvania Avenue early in the morning to get ready for the swearing in and the passing of the torch, so to speak.

Hours later, they arrive at the Capitol and take their places in front of the crowd of spectators. Lance looks over at President Thomlinson and his family. He no longer harbors any bad feelings about the man despite all his awful name-calling and attacks on Lance and his family. He realizes that Jeffrey is just another political pawn, much like he, himself, will be. Maybe insiders such as Schultz played *him* too. *Perhaps,* Lance thinks, *I'm not so different from Jeffrey. Everyone is just trying to do something good for this country, and over time, some people lose their way.* Lance makes a silent vow to avoid losing *his* way, no matter the temptations. He brings his mind back to the moment.

Time passes quickly, and the chief justice of the United States, Scott Landry, prepares to administer the thirty-nine-word presidential oath. Lance places his right hand on the Bible, and the aging justice begins to speak. Maybe it's because this is all too much to take in, but Lance's mind momentarily slips back to when he was a small child. *Where have all my days at the farm gone?* he wonders. *It feels like it was just yesterday I was there, and now, as if by magic, the entire country is now my responsibility. And Chief Justice Landry, he reminds me of my father; he even kind of looks like him. They both have hands that are big and strong.* A tear finds its way to the corner of Lance's eye as he wishes his father could be here to see this moment.

Lance looks well beyond the ceremony that is being played out around him. It's as if he's floating above the inauguration, watching himself. At first, as Rose said, this was a pipe dream, and yet now here they are, standing in front of the world as the national anthem is played. He's jolted back into the moment and discovers he's already smiling and waving. For the first time since he won the presidential election, Lance feels at ease with his victory. Maybe it's having his family by his side that's giving him this feeling. His younger brother, Joe, and his family; his mother, Lucinda; his wife, Rose; and his kids—they give him the strength and courage to claim his spot in history.

��

The next day comes too quickly, and Lance finds himself in the Oval Office, as if he just woke up here. The morning is a whirlwind of new faces and rooms he has never visited. Unexpectedly, everything Lance thought would go wrong actually goes smoothly and better than he anticipated. The Senate and House members on both sides of the aisle are very cordial, offering him their congratulations throughout the day. Lance can't help but wonder just how soon this will all come to an end, especially once he proceeds with his agenda and tries to get bills passed. He's sure to see a whole different side of these people.

Lance has made time in his schedule for the one-on-one meeting with James. He's put it off too long and wants to clear the air. He's still hurt by James's double-agent stint; the man needs to decide who's side he's on. Lance can't allow his chief of staff to work for the CIA. Part of him regrets giving James the job. This meeting will either make or break their relationship. They haven't been alone together since Lance learned that James was leading a double life, acting as his campaign director by day and a CIA agent by night.

Lance is sitting behind his desk as James enters the room. It's immediately apparent that James is nervous. Lance doesn't bother standing to shake his hand; he simply points to the chair in front of his desk. James obeys the command, silently walking over and taking a seat. They both begin to speak at the same time; clearly, they've spent some time rehearsing their speeches. Lance puts up his hand to stop James. After a short, uncomfortable pause, Lance changes his mind and waves his hand, allowing James to speak first.

Surprisingly, James stammers a bit as he begins: "Mr. President, I-I cannot even begin to explain how s-sorry I am for betraying your trust. I can only imagine how you must feel. I take full accountability for my actions." James exhales deeply and continues, "To work for you was a dream come true. If it meant working for the CIA to realize that dream, well, I was willing to pay that price. I didn't know you at the time; I just knew I wanted to be a part of your vision."

Lance puts his hands together, as if preparing for a prayer. He rests his chin on his thumbs, readying himself.

"Thank you for the apology, but I want to be direct. I have to ask you something, and I need an honest answer. I'll give you one crack at this." Lance looks James directly in the eyes, watching him as he sits up straighter in his chair. He then asks,

"Why should I trust you as my chief of staff?" The gravity of the question is clearly evident in his voice.

James clears his throat before replying, "Because, Mr. President, I never divulged anything that Schultz couldn't get through his regular channels. He has people everywhere. There's very little any of us can hide from him. But your secrets were my secrets; I promise you that, sir. And I will continue to protect those secrets. That's something I know how to do well. My allegiance then and now has always been to *you*. I managed Schultz and fed him false pieces of information to satisfy his demands—to keep my job and keep him at bay—and it worked. What he knew about you and your campaign contained fragments of truth but was often based on falsehoods. The CIA taught me how to do that. In fact, it's part of the reason I believe I can be a strong chief of staff. I can't make it any clearer in words, but I can show you with my actions. I can also assure you that nothing truly private was ever passed along to Schultz; I swear to God."

"I see," Lance replies. "Well, I, too, will have eyes and ears everywhere. This job is still yours. But you will have to prove yourself every day, James." He pauses, then adds, "You owe me *big-time.* I don't know how you will make this right, but I'm sure the time will come, and you'd *better* step up when it does." Lance knows their friendship and working relationship have both been bruised, but deep down, he hopes they're not broken.

"I know I owe you, sir, and I look forward to earning your trust and paying you back."

"Good," Lance says. "Also, I don't want you to have any further contact with Schultz or anyone else in the CIA without my clearance. Anyway, I plan on nominating a new CIA director soon. Now let's get back to business. Do you remember when I promised to thank the people of this country for their support? I told them I would do so fifteen days after my having taken the oath of office. I also said I would thank them on the same special spot where I declared my candidacy for president: on the steps of the New York State Supreme Court Building. You know that building, the beautiful, old one that has so much history behind it, with those beautiful steps leading up to it."

"Yes, I know it, sir—all too well, as it was bitterly cold and icy on those steps when you announced your campaign, much like it probably is now. It was a unique announcement, the first one made outside a candidate's home state. You made it seem—I don't know—spontaneous."

"Maybe it was," Lance says slyly, remembering how angered James was by his last-minute decision to make the announcement on that day instead of waiting for their return to Columbus.

"Can't you postpone the trip until the spring months, when the weather is a bit, well, more favorable?" James challenges.

"No. I made a promise. And I keep my promises, just as I expect you to do." Maybe this was an unnecessary crack at James, but Lance couldn't help himself; he's still angry about the betrayal. "And this has to be done as promised: on those steps within fifteen days—not earlier, not later, no matter the weather. I'm just giving you a heads-up on this, James; I'm not asking your opinion. It's going to happen. So I need you to support me and help me convince everyone else that this is a good thing and to start working on the trip *now*."

"Yes, Mr. President. If this is what you want, I will support your decision and will immediately tell the Secret Service Advance Team to get started."

Lance turns around to look out the window at the pouring rain. "It looks cold out there. I worry about the unsheltered and all other people who are cold and hungry at times like this."

"I know how you feel, Mr. President, and I agree. Something has to be done, and we will take action," James replies without looking up from his schedule. "Regarding the trip, the exact date would be the fourth of February. You can keep the promise you made to the voters. I understand your desire to keep your promise, but it doesn't change the fact that the weather doesn't care about it. Let's just hope for the best with Mother Nature."

"I know, I know. Thank you for understanding my wish to do this. A promise is a promise, and I don't want to start off my term by breaking a simple one like this." Lance's voice takes on a pleading tone as he adds, "Also, please help me convince Rose to come with me. You know she hates traveling in the cold."

"Yes, Mr. President. I will do my best to convince her. This can be her first official outing as First Lady. It's important that she's there with you. Remember, per protocol, Secret Service will notify the other two agencies automatically, so Director Schultz and Director Noakes will soon know about this trip."

"Is that protocol really necessary? This doesn't involve them in any way."

James looks at Lance, mildly surprised. "Allow me to impress upon you again, Mr. President, the importance of this new reality—*your* reality. It's all about security. Every move you make is monitored by Homeland Security, and sometimes the CIA and the FBI, per protocol."

"Damn it! It's just a small trip to make a small speech—one that I will write and you'll review, changing it ten times." Lance cracks his first smile of the day. "It's not really something to be made into a big deal. It's not enough for the other agencies to even be involved in. Isn't Secret Service's involvement enough? By the time we're back, they won't even have known we were gone!"

"Mr. President, have you forgotten what really goes on in this world? These agencies are just doing their job. You, of all people, should know that procedures can't be changed. There's a lot of planning that goes into even the smallest trip—like getting a hamburger." James stifles a laugh, then continues, "And since we are on the topic of people just doing their job, I do want to go on record right now and say that the weather is supposed to be extremely nasty for a couple more weeks, and I think you should consider moving your speech to a better date, weatherwise. *And there's still an inordinate amount of death threats coming in every day.*"

"Very well, let's be sure to make a record of that!" Lance says sarcastically. "But we are still going. When it comes to keeping promises, I won't budge, not now, not even an inch." Lance looks up at James. "And you can wipe that smug look off your face."

"Well, ten days ago, I remembered the promise you made to the voters on those courthouse steps. I knew you would want to go back there in just a few weeks, so I had a talk with Cummings."

"What did he have to say about it?" Lance asks, pleased that James had remembered the promise and anticipated Lance's request.

"Cummings said his team isn't ready. And given the weather, it makes the area harder to secure and control. He asked me to dissuade you if you brought it up. Expect him to fight you on this one."

"Well then, I'm looking forward to that argument with Cummings." Lance turns to look out the window again at the rain, trying to ignore James's concerns. He then looks back at James. "Is that it?"

"That's it. Do you want anything else at the moment, Mr. President?" James asks as he removes his glasses and pulls a cloth from his jacket to clean them, something he does at least ten times a day. It's more of a habit now than a necessity.

Lance gestures for James to stand next to him. "Look out there. Can you imagine how many people are walking around out there at any given time? Some have no home to go to and no one to help them. They are lost souls who want to do better and make their lives better."

"Yes, sir," James answers.

"Well, I work for them now. I promised to help, and that job started today. They may not have much, but they have me in their corner. There's now someone out there in this world who loves them very much. Now let's go keep some promises!"

⊚⊘

It's two weeks later, and the weather in New York has remained rainy and cold. The night before they are set to leave, it finally quits raining and snowing, but the wind turns cruel, and ice remains a factor on the highways. In the residence section of the White House, Rose stands looking out into the night as Lance stretches out on a recliner.

"You know, I'm beginning to get used to all of this," Rose murmurs.

Lance looks up and smiles at her. "That's good, honey. I'm glad. Although I'm still not quite sure that anyone can completely get used to living in the White House. I was worried about you for a while, but I wanted to stay out of your way so you could do what you needed to in your own way. I know people were all over you at the beginning, demanding more time from you each day, but that's to be expected the first couple of weeks, and I just didn't want to add to all that."

"I know." Rose turns away from the window and comes to stand next to him, one warm hand on his shoulder. "You remember that Thomas and George are leaving us soon to get back to their own lives now that the campaign is over and you're settled in the office. They'll go back about their careers and schooling. But they agreed to wait until you get back from your trip so we can spend one last day together."

"What about their safety when they go back to their regular lives?" Lance asks. "I just haven't had the time to look at the report put together by the Secret Service on what will be provided for each of them. Were you able to take a look at it?" He knows he's treading on thin ice because Rose had wanted to let the three of them leave earlier but he'd insisted that they stay a little longer to make sure their security detail was covered.

"I've already spoken to Director Cummings," replies Rose with no trace of animosity. "They're all set up. I've met with each of their special agents personally. Honestly, the kids are more anxious about you and this silly trip to New York. On top of that, they are constantly watching the news and are worried that your enemies are already plotting against you."

"Wait a minute. Why do you think this trip is silly? I made a promise, and I want to start my term off right. That's definitely not silly."

Rose grabs his face with her hands and says in a stern tone of voice, "Look at me, Lance. They say it's going to be one of the coldest days in decades. There's a major cold front coming down from Canada, and you want people to show up and risk their lives? And then you want them to deal with those freezing winds slapping them in their faces as they stand on those icy sidewalks and steps for hours? All this so that you can keep a promise that I'm sure no one even remembers! You should cancel the trip . . . or at least postpone it. I'm sure people will understand, honey. Please."

"If I cancel now, what message does that send?" Lance pulls his face from her hands, the volume of his voice rising. "Then everyone will say, 'Look! He's starting it already, breaking promises, even one as simple as this!' Listen, as much as I appreciate your trying to protect me, I'm still going. I really don't want to talk about it anymore. It's settled and done. Honestly, Rose, I can't afford *not* to go. I need people to know that I am as good as my word."

"All right!" Rose snaps. "Just deliver your speech quickly, and then get out of there. Can you keep that promise?"

"I promise. Just a quick hello, a few words, a lot of thank-yous, a couple of talking points, and then we're out of there. Thirty minutes max!" He grabs her hands. "And thank you for agreeing to come with me. I know it's the last thing you want to do right now."

CHAPTER 9

HIT THE GROUND

▷ **Lance – New York City, New York, February 4**

As the president's motorcade approaches the New York State Supreme Court Building on Centre Street, over two thousand people, mostly supporters of the new president, have already gathered on the sidewalks. They wave as the president's vehicle passes. Lance looks at Rose, unable to hide his loopy, half-triumphant smile.

"Look at everyone, Rose. Imagine, they came out in this weather for me, for us! Thank you for giving in and letting me have this day. It means the world to me."

"I'm so proud of you, and I'm happy that you're happy," Rose replies. Then her smile disappears as she adds, "But please be careful standing out there in this crazy weather and walking on those icy steps. Remember, Lance, you agreed this is just going to be a quick speech. And please follow whatever your Secret Service detail tells you to do. They've already been complaining that you haven't been following their directions. These guys did a lot of prep in advance of this trip, and they truly have your back."

The motorcade finally comes to a halt at the bottom of the forty-four steps leading up to the courthouse. Lance can see a light snow falling outside. At least the rain has stopped, but unfortunately, it left behind the ingredient needed to make ice. The wind, however, has not given up and continues to blow hard. Attendees hold their coats closed with gloved hands. Rose rolls down the window a notch, and Lance leans over her shoulder to look up toward the podium that's been set up for his speech. He then glances in each direction of the sidewalk. For a moment, the steps look like frozen rock on the side of a mountain.

Rose shivers as a gust of wind blows through the open window. She gives Lance a sideways look. "Are you sure you want to go out there? I mean, just look at it all. It's got to be at least minus twelve degrees out there with the windchill."

Lance kisses her cheek. "These people are waiting for me. I have to do this speech now. If I leave, how would that look? I'll be done before you know it. Thirty minutes tops, I promise." He holds up two fingers, like an obedient Boy Scout.

They wait for the other VIPs to show up, including the mayor of New York City and two local senators. After they park, a Secret Service agent jumps out of the SUV to open the door for Lance and Rose. Another huge gust of cold wind rushes into the vehicle. Rose raises her arm up over her face, as if to protect herself from the wind's attack, and they exit the SUV together.

Huddled against Lance, Rose shivers. The wind is relentless as they begin to walk down the snowy sidewalk leading to the steps. Lance looks at Rose's high-heeled shoes. They're clearly not appropriate for this weather. She starts to slip on the icy sidewalk after just a few steps. Lance grabs her arm tightly to keep her from falling to the ground and realizes she will never make it up the steps. He wonders if she planned it this way, but it doesn't matter to him. More than anything, he wants Rose to be safe. The Secret Service stops to confer with Lance regarding the situation, and they agree that Rose should remain by the SUV with her detail, as it will be impossible for her to make it up the slippery steps.

Lance turns to her while she holds her coat together with gloved hands in the blustery, practically blizzardlike conditions. "Rose, we think it's best you stay here by the vehicle, as it will be too difficult for you to get up those steps in this weather." He hugs her and adds, "It will make me feel better knowing you are safe down here. Lloyd, Karen, and Ryan will stay down here with you."

Rose doesn't argue and gives him a quick kiss. "Don't worry, honey; I will be listening to every word. Remember that I'm down here supporting you. Just be quick!"

They part ways, and soon Lance is shaking hands with some of the local officials. He decides to embrace the cold air while trying not to show its effect on him. When everyone is ready, they begin to proceed slowly up the icy steps as the crowd around them cheers. The higher they climb, the stronger the wind seems to grow, which forces them to walk a little slower. As they pause momentarily, Lance can hear the grumblings of his staff and some of the officials, but they press on, ignoring the sting of the wind that's biting at every uncovered part of their bodies. Finally, after what feels like forever, Lance reaches the podium, where the microphones are patiently waiting. Silently, his staff assembles behind him, tucking their faces into the collars of their coats. After his Secret Service agents situate themselves around him, Lance turns to the crowd, eagerly awaiting his speech, probably so they can return to the comfort of their homes.

As Lance looks deep into the crowd, he feels overwhelmed by the support of the people who've shown up to hear him speak, especially in this brutal weather. It hits his heart in all the right spots. This is his first public speech since he took the oath of office fifteen days ago. As he looks out at the two thousand or so constituents before him, he notices how similar they look to one another, all bundled up against the cold. From his vantage point, they all seem to be wearing the same dark-gray overcoats, scarves, and hats. He notices that many have their hands in their pockets and some have wrapped their scarves around the bottom half of their faces for warmth. This reminds him to be quick, as he promised Rose.

Members of his Secret Service detail are in their respective positions and are communicating through their earpieces, some speaking into their wrist microphones. They signal that they have secured the area, and Lance is given the nod to go ahead. All the while, Lance has been noticing that some of the people are slipping a bit as they stand along the sidewalk and on the lower steps. Many are holding on to one another for support.

Since this speech is taking place outdoors in this weather and on the stairs, Lance cannot rely on the teleprompters he's grown accustomed to. So he begins the speech he's only partially memorized, knowing that he will probably be winging some of it.

"Thank you all for your support! I'm humbled that you came out for this, despite the weather."

The crowd cheers and then quiets down.

Lance quickly thanks the elected officials who are present, before continuing, "It was on this very spot exactly one year ago, on these very steps, that I announced I was running for president of this great country. That day launched my campaign for the highest office in the land, the presidency of the United States."

The crowd cheers louder this time, though the applause is muffled by their gloves.

Lance smiles. "Even though I was not remotely close to being projected to win when I entered this race, I know I am here because I spoke from my heart throughout the entire campaign. Many of the policies I spoke about I truly believe in from the bottom of my heart, and it seems they are the ones you want as well."

More cheers rise from the crowd. Despite the terrible weather, they are excited to hear this man, who offers them hope, finally speak as their president. The movements in the crowd are making Lance's detail a little nervous; they stand alert and stay in constant communication.

Lance continues his speech, even though his fingers are numb. "We can do this! But we have to do it together. Change will come, though I'll be the first to admit that the wheels of government can turn slowly. However, I hope to speed up the process by reaching across the aisle to work with everyone. And I will compromise; I've always made that clear." Lance pauses, then adds, "Maybe today was not the best day for this, weatherwise, but I wanted to start my presidency off the right way, by sticking to the first promise I made, which was to return to this very spot and thank you in person fifteen days after my inauguration. So here we are!"

Everyone claps in acknowledgment—not just of the fact that he is humble enough to admit he might have picked the wrong day, but also of his apparent willingness to fight the weather in order to start off his presidency on the right foot.

As he looks out at the crowd, Lance wonders, *Why was I so stubborn in insisting this happen today, making all these good people brave this weather just to hear me speak?*

Just as Lance begins the final section of his speech, covering his top three initiatives, a quick flash of gray to the right catches his eye. As he turns to look, a hand suddenly grabs his arm and someone near him shouts, "Hit the ground!"

CHAPTER 10

THE BOTTOM STEP

▷ **Lance – New York City, New York, February 4**

L ance looks to see who grabbed him and realizes it's one of his agents. Instinctively, he shakes the man loose and turns to his right again to see what the flash of gray was all about. Just then, in the same spot where he saw the flash, he sees a small object rolling from the left side of the courthouse. He squints to make out what it is that's coming toward him. His security detail also notices the cylinder and the trail of smoke coming from it.

Shouts come from every direction, as the same Secret Service agent grabs Lance's arm again. Another agent steps up to cover him but suddenly falls to the ground, blood quickly spreading across the back of his coat. Lance nearly trips over him as he tries to shake the other agent off his arm. He just wants to move forward faster and on his own, but this agent is preventing him from getting out of harm's way. Lance begins to take the steps two at a time to escape whatever is going to happen next. Just then, the agent who previously attached himself to Lance also falls to the ground. More blood. Lance looks back and sees that two more of his agents are also on the ground. He wonders if he's on his own now and suddenly feels hot. He attempts to wipe what feels like sweat off his face but sees that it's actually blood. He wonders if he's been hit and doesn't know it; he's too numb to feel anything.

He decides to keep walking as quickly as possible, removing his overcoat so he can move faster. His front foot lands awkwardly on the next step. Just as he catches his balance, a loud boom cuts through the air. A hot white wall of light fills his vision until all he can see is smoke and fire. He slips again and falls to the ground, then tumbles down several steps.

◎◎

Lance isn't sure if he blacked out. What felt like minutes had only been seconds, and whatever was happening is real and hasn't stopped. Then Lance hears the most horrible noise he has ever heard: automatic gunfire coming from all angles, accompanied by screams from the rapidly dispersing crowd. Bullets ricochet off the steps and into the crowd. From the ground, Lance can see bodies falling and wonders if it's because of the icy sidewalk or because they've actually been hit by the bullets; it's almost impossible to tell. Lance remains sprawled halfway down the steps, shifting ever so slightly, wanting to get to the bottom so he can run to Rose. He lets the slippery ice slide him slowly downward, step by step.

When he opens his eyes again, he can't see any Secret Service agents around him. He remembers they were the first ones hit by the gunfire, *but all of them? That can't be.* Now he can't hear anything at all, as the last explosion blew out his ears. As Lance glances over his shoulder to try to comprehend what is happening, his gut wrenches at the sight of unmoving bodies surrounding him, some in pools of blood. He decides to crawl to get back to where he last saw Rose, standing by the SUV with three Secret Service agents. He prays that they managed to get her into the bulletproof vehicle in time. But as he tries to move from the danger and get to his knees, a sharp pain strikes him in the face and sends him spiraling backward headfirst. He slams into the concrete. Complete blackness.

When Lance wakes for the second time, what he sees can only be described as a full-scale attack. It's most definitely an assassination attempt. It's hard for him to tell what exactly is going on, as it's all happening so fast. His hearing has returned, and the sound of gunfire and screams combined makes him feel as though he's in a war zone. For the first time, he notices a man wearing a red bandana, his gun blasting at the dispersing crowd.

Lance turns his head in the other direction and sees three uniformed police officers and Secret Service agents trying to outgun the attackers, but they aren't succeeding, as they're clearly outnumbered. It appears clear to Lance that members of his primary security detail were the initial targets and were most likely the first to go down. Those who are left are attempting to dodge bullets while desperately trying to locate the president.

"Can anyone see him?" yells one agent into his body microphone.

"No eyes on the president yet," returns a voice.

Just then, more bullets spray from surrounding buildings, targeting these agents. Lance wants to stand up, wave his arms, and tell them he's not far away, but the sounds of the melee taking place around him drag him into a semiconscious state. His body isn't responding to his brain's commands. His face and head throb with escalating, excruciating pain. The metallic taste of iron fills his mouth. He attempts to speak while trying to blink away the spots that blur his vision. Then a bolt of pain shoots through him like a hot iron, searing through his body as if every nerve were on fire.

While trying to figure out a way to stand up, Lance hears another yell that cuts through the air around him: "Mr. President! Mr. President! Goddammit, where is the president? Where the hell is everyone?"

Thank God, thinks Lance as he jerks his head up to see where it came from. Blood spills from his mouth and pours down the back of his throat, nearly choking him. His head falls back onto the cement step. He peers through the haze of smoke around him and dimly registers that the amount of rapid fire is beginning to decrease. Now he can clearly hear the horrific screams of those who were caught in the cross fire. So many innocent civilians who just moments ago were cheering for him are now either injured or dead. *This is all because of me,* he thinks.

Lance manages to roll his body onto its side. Pain surges through him, but he can now see the SUV next to which he last saw his Rose. It isn't far, just a few dozen steps away. The thought of seeing Rose gives him the energy he needs to attempt to stand, but he simply can't. So he decides to half drag, half crawl his way toward the vehicle. His hands immediately begin to slip on puddles of blood. He's not sure if it belonged to him or another poor soul. He looks up again to see Secret Service agents returning fire from behind the SUV. Realizing Rose must be inside, he is thankful it's bulletproof. He wonders what she's thinking. *"Rose,"* his mind pleads.

Lance attempts to scream for help, but something is clearly wrong: no sound comes from his mouth, just a strangled mess of guttural noises and a gush of blood. Indescribable pain accompanies this, like none he has ever felt. Then dizziness overtakes him as his body gives out. Lying motionless on the step, he forces himself to keep his eyes open and not give up. Using his hands to feel the ground, he realizes he has finally reached the bottom step. He's too tired to do anything other than wait here on the cold step, on top of the blood and ice, and stare up at the gloomy gray sky above. He's sure they will soon find him; after all, he's the president. It's only a matter of time, and Rose is just yards away.

Groaning, Lance lifts his head one last time, and for a second, the pain feels like it's leaving his body. He feels peaceful as he gazes up at the heavens and notices a beautiful silhouette of sharp angles and gray corners against the darkening sky. The loud gunfire exchange above him slowly fades. He stares in awe at the clouds, and even with all the chaos surrounding him, the impressive beauty of the sky is not lost on him.

As thoughts stream through his injured head, a massive weight suddenly barrels into him, knocking him off the last step and onto the icy sidewalk. Disoriented and still losing blood, Lance struggles to rise, only to fall facedown against the frozen ground. Just as he catches his breath, there is a sudden indescribable pressure on his body, as if the Running of the Bulls festival is taking place on his backside. The stomping sends throngs of pain through his legs, back, arms, and head. He covers his head with his arms as he realizes it's the remaining members of the crowd trying to escape, now that the gunfire has subsided. Just moments ago, they were braving the weather to listen to his speech, and now they are running for their lives. They scream as they try to hold on to one another, grabbing at the nearest person for help. With the human spirit comes panic, and panic turns to fear. Fear of death equates to a melee of screaming people scrambling for safety.

Breathless again, Lance tries to force oxygen through the blood in his mouth. He breathes in and out, as slowly as he can, trying to time his exhalation to the intermittent stomps on his back. Stabbing pains overwhelm him. He welcomes the numbness afforded by the icy pavement below his chest. His right knee has been twisted so severely, he feels it may snap under the next stomp. His fingers curl in on themselves as a burning sensation seizes his head. His eyelids flutter and close. The last memory that goes through his mind is of the beautiful cloud formations above. He hopes they're still watching over him.

CHAPTER 11

HE HAS A PULSE!

▷ **CIA Director Schultz –**
New York State Supreme Court Building

I t has been over forty minutes since the attack began. CIA Director Donald Schultz arrives at the New York State Supreme Court Building with his team. They are there to fight off any remaining attackers and find the president. Most of the NYPD officers and Secret Service agents in attendance were either injured or killed. James Edwards was aware that Director Schultz was in New York City for work at a CIA field office, and Schultz is thankful for the coincidence and that James contacted him immediately. When the attack began, it was clear the situation was more than the Secret Service could handle. James contacted Schultz immediately and told him to bring a hell of a lot of backup.

There are now well over four hundred bodies lying on the ground, either injured or dead. The scene is quickly overrun by ambulances, medics, firefighters, NYPD officers, CIA and FBI agents, and, of course, Homeland Security agents. The courthouse building and surrounding area are not yet secure, so the process of helping those on the ground begins precariously.

Schultz quickly takes over, although no one is sure if he has jurisdiction over the situation at hand. "Half of you focus on locating the suspects. I want the other half of you to find President Dumont. Notify me the moment you find him. Locating him is our number one priority." He gestures with his right hand to split in half his team of thirty-four agents, and they go their separate ways within seconds.

He turns to James and says, "What the hell happened here? Clearly, the Secret Service wasn't prepared. They are going to have Cummings's head." He then speaks into his radio: "I want you guys to remember that this scene is still active."

Yards away, an agent, with his gun drawn, is moving from person to person. He radios in excitedly that he's found the president.

"Tell your team to cover him immediately!" yells Schultz to the NYPD chief.

The nearest NYPD officers make their way toward the president with their bunker shields in hand. Within seconds of reaching him, they use their shields to create a protective circle around him—nine officers facing outward with guns drawn. Each is willing to take a bullet for the president, aware that a remaining attacker could open fire at any moment.

Schultz makes his way over and breaks through the circle. He crouches next to the president. He can see that Dumont has been shot, possibly more than once, and is now lying face down in a pool of blood. He leans in closer and gently takes the president's wrist.

"He has a pulse!" exclaims Schultz softly. Dumont's sandy-brown hair and tailored blue suit stand in stark contrast to the crimson puddle surrounding him. He sees the president's overcoat a few steps up from the sidewalk, with its American flag lapel pin.

"Thank God it's him," says Schultz with a sigh of relief. "Now, agents, step back, keep cover, and let's get the medics in here!"

At this point, the head of the Secret Service Uniformed Division arrives on-site. David Ackman is ambitious and reports directly to Director Cummings, but everyone knows he'd throw his boss under the bus to get his job. The guy is ruthless, but good. He joins the group surrounding the president and asks Schultz, "What are you even doing here? This is *our* jurisdiction. Cummings told me to take over."

Schultz is sure Ackman's lying. "The question is," Schultz snaps, "why the hell weren't you *already* here? Edwards called *me* the moment the attack started, and thankfully, I was already in town for business, so I rounded up my team and came here immediately. You should be thanking me, Ackman. Clearly, you and your team are understaffed and were unprepared for this attack. It happened on *your* watch, not mine. We are just here to help clean up your mess. And *we* found the president. You're welcome."

By this time, the scene has been secured, and the officers and medics can move about more freely in helping the victims, some of whom are moaning as they come to in a state of dazed confusion. Others aren't moving at all or making any sounds. Medics shout instructions to one another as they assess the fallen and tag them as needed.

"Gentlemen, this is no time for this bullshit. My friend and boss," James wipes a tear from the corner of his eye, "could be dying, and the two of you are having a pissing match." He shakes his head and kneels down next to one of the medics tending to the president. "What do you guys need?"

The medic doesn't look at him as he replies, "We are keeping him still and monitoring his vitals until we get a stabilizing board over here. We want to be as careful as possible in case he has injured his back or neck. He's lost a lot of blood."

"Can you confirm he's been shot?" James asks the medic, panic in his voice. From James's point of view, Lance Dumont looks dead. But the medics are too busy to answer as they prep the president to be taken away safely to one of the two best-rated hospitals in New York City: New York-Presbyterian/Weill Cornell Medical Center on 68th Street on the Upper East Side of Manhattan.

Within seconds, a couple of paramedics exit an ambulance to prep the president for transport. They place him onto a gurney with a stabilizing board beneath him, careful not to worsen any neck or back injuries he may have. Though they have done this hundreds of times before, they've never done it for someone so important, so critical to the country. It's clear they're aware of the responsibility bestowed upon them. Once the president is safely on board the ambulance, James begins to step up into the back to escort the president to the hospital, but he's stopped by Chief Ackman. Schultz can't help but smile as he stands by, watching the scene play out in front of him.

"Excuse me, Edwards; we've got this. This is *our* job," Ackman says, softening the blow with a cocky smile and a hand on James's shoulder. "Maybe you should check on the president's family. I can't imagine what they are going through right now."

CHAPTER 12

CATATONIC

▷ **Rose – New York State Supreme Court Building, Day 1**

Rose is catatonic. She can't move, not even an inch. As soon as the attack began, her security personnel put her inside the bulletproof SUV and told her not to budge. They let her know that even an inch of movement could mean the difference between life and death. So she has been lying down for over an hour, her cheek pressed against the leather seat. She is scared to even breathe and has been waiting for what feels like an eternity. She has spent the time alternating between praying and thinking about simple, happy memories, such as taking the kids to school and celebrating their birthdays—anything to take her mind far away from this awful moment in time.

Rose can faintly hear the victims' screams as the ear-splitting sounds manage to penetrate the soundproofed vehicle. And she *wants* to hear them. She wants to be with these people. For the majority of the past hour, her body has felt frozen from fear and cold, but the numbness is now beginning to subside. Now she just feels listless.

"Rose?" asks a voice.

She jumps at the sound of her name and quickly recognizes the voice, though it doesn't belong to Lance. She turns her head and opens her eyes to look up at the now-open door near her feet.

She is relieved to meet James's reassuring gaze. He opens the door wider and offers her his hand. She gladly takes it, letting him pull her up into a sitting position. Slowly, she exits the vehicle and shakes her body to loosen her stiff joints. As her eyes begin to adjust to the light, she is struck by terror and panic. Her body starts to give out, and she collapses against the side of the SUV. James grabs her just before she slides to the ground. The scene that is unfolding before her is like no other she has seen, either in person or on TV. She begins to tremble, and James holds her closer.

"James—*oh, James!* This can't be real!" Rose shrieks, her voice cracking. "What happened here, James? Where is Lance? Is he all right?"

"He's . . . he's alive," James says slowly. "We found him. He was unconscious, but he had a pulse. That's the good news. It looks like he was hit by one bullet, maybe more. They are on their way to New York City Presbyterian Hospital, where they've got a Level I trauma center prepared for his arrival and specialists on the way as we speak. We'll meet them there. I had my assistant notify your children and make arrangements to get them to New York as quickly as possible. I'm sure they are already on their way."

"The children! My God, they aren't going to forgive me for letting Lance come here today. They called this his 'whimsical speech' because of this weather. Little did we know that it wasn't the weather that we should've feared. I never would have imagined *this* . . ." She trails off as she begins to cry. She knows Edwina will be especially upset, and then there will be Thomas, reproachful in his silent judgment. She can hear it now: "He would've listened to you," he'll say. "If you'd asked him one more time to stay home, he would have." The guilt gnaws at her as James guides her back into the SUV and tells her that they'll soon be leaving for the hospital. And just like that, he's walking down the sidewalk, talking on his phone. And Rose is alone again.

The sounds of screeching sirens pull Rose out of her horrified daze. Dozens of police cars and ambulances are surrounding the courthouse, and people are flooding the streets, as they've just heard the news. She hopes the arriving civilians are here to help, not to take photos for social media. EMTs and paramedics spread out among the injured, dropping down on their knees to help those who can be treated immediately, and loading others onto stretchers in preparation for a trip to the hospital. Rose watches, amazed by the sight of so many fearless people stepping in to help, comforting the victims in any way possible, even if it's by using their own jackets to protect the injured from the icy cold. As her gaze pans upward to the people collapsed on the icy steps, her breath catches in her throat. The paramedics and those assisting them are struggling to keep their footing, often slipping and falling as they try to help. Not far down the sidewalk, a young man takes off his bright-yellow jacket and covers a woman in an effort to help her stay warm until help arrives. Rose swallows heavily. She's not sure if she's actually tasting blood or if it's simply her imagination, but it's terrifying just the same. "I need to help these people," she says to herself, but she can't move.

James climbs into the front passenger seat of the SUV, and the driver begins to steer the vehicle away from the horrific scene. Rose presses her cheek against the cold glass of the window next to her. Drops of blood have dried on the outside of it. Whoever they are, she hopes they're alive. But from the looks of it all, it's clear that there will be many casualties and that some of them will not make it to a hospital in time. She closes her eyes and says a prayer for the victims.

The SUV makes its way through the chaos and winds through the haphazard blockades created by all the police cars, ambulances, and government vehicles. The sirens and red-and-blue flashing lights from multiple police cars and firetrucks warn incoming traffic to stay away. The sight of all this help brings Rose some comfort as she turns away from the window while the driver navigates through the busy streets of New York City.

"James," she says finally, her tears again flowing freely, "do you think he's going to survive this?"

"Of course he will, Rose," James says, dropping all formality, but she can see he's avoiding her gaze. "We will be at New York Presbyterian Hospital in just a few minutes. And don't you worry; we will get to the bottom of who did this and why. It's going to be OK."

She shoots him a knowing smile, gently acknowledging his half-hearted attempt to make her feel better. They both know nothing is going to be OK. Things have been forever changed.

CHAPTER 13

I CAN TELL YOU EVERYTHING

▷ **CIA Director Schultz –**
New York State Supreme Court Building, Day 1

irector Schultz takes a look around at the aftermath of what happened at the courthouse today. Standing at the bottom of the steps, he can see medics attending to victims as best they can, trying to diagnose the extent of each person's injuries before using the triage tag system of being able to distinguish the direst of cases from the less dire. Medical doctors and nurses have also made it to the site, and there are teams on hand setting up medical tents to cover those waiting to be transported to the largest local hospitals. Those with less severe injuries are being treated on-site. On the other end of the steps there is an even more somber area, which is dedicated to collecting those declared dead at the scene. There is pandemonium all around him, as the press has also arrived and is now milling about, trying to get information from anyone who will speak to them. But barricades have been set up and cameras have been prohibited in order to protect individual privacy. Schultz covers his eyes as if not to see the pain, but he can still hear some victims crying for help. However, he isn't there to help the victims, at least not in that way. He is there for a much more important reason.

Schultz makes his way around the scene, searching for any surviving perpetrators of this heinous act. He imagines it may be hard to distinguish the victims from the attackers, so he starts looking for small, distinct things, for instance, a scarf or patch that could identify a group with which they're affiliated. But it would be easiest to tell who's who by the weaponry they're carrying or the flak vests they're wearing under their black overcoats. He can only hope he finds an attacker who's still alive; the Almighty could at least give him that on a day like today.

As his eyes scan the scene, he removes his overcoat, acting as though he is looking to cover one of the bodies. Without anyone's noticing, he pulls out his weapon and hides it under the coat, which he quickly hangs over his arm. He continues his search for any attacker who might still be showing signs of life. He finds his guy about twenty yards away, an assault weapon lying by his bleeding shoulder. It seems his vest partially protected him from the hail of gunfire that was aimed at him. He's moving slightly, and that's what caught Schultz's eye.

"Thank you," Schultz whispers as he looks skyward.

When he reaches the man, he stoops down and confirms what he'd assumed: the man is still alive. Schultz takes his overcoat and covers the wounded attacker. From a distance, it looks as though the CIA director is leaning over to help this man. He leans in very close to the attacker's ear, then slips his Glock 19 closer, twisting the silencer onto it while sliding it toward the attacker's head. All of this is hidden beneath the overcoat. Schultz can see that the man is severely injured and bleeding profusely.

"The president is still alive," Schultz says calmly, a glimmer of menace spreading across his face. "You did not succeed, and soon you will die."

The man's eyes widen when the gun makes contact with his temple. He raises his head a bit to speak. "I'm sorry. I'm sorry," he pleads.

"I know you are," Schultz replies without emotion.

"Wait—don't do this! I can tell you everything!" the man begs. "Please!"

Schultz laughs at him and says with a snarl, "It's too late for you."

Suddenly, the attacker goes for his weapon. Schultz is expecting this and uses a knee to lock the man's arm down before he can grab his assault rifle. He shoves the barrel of his Glock, with its suppressor attached, against the attacker's skull and pulls the trigger. Schultz rises quickly and checks to see if anyone is looking in his direction. No one seems to notice him in the pandemonium, nor hear the sound of the shot amid the sirens and whirring of the helicopters above. He walks away from the man without looking back.

◉◉

Schultz makes his way back to one of the tents where the agencies have set up shop. Soon, evidence collection and the investigations will begin. The CIA and FBI will be partnering with Homeland Security to create a command center here so that they can coordinate and share information regarding the attack, something they don't usually do, and heads are already butting. This development is per the request of the acting president, Jennifer Alvarez. Their first priority is making sure the victims are taken care of without destroying any of the evidence. The Secret Service has well over two dozen casualties, brave men and women who defended the president with their own lives. The next priority is to begin an investigation into the attack.

The entire area, consisting of six square blocks, is now locked down. There were reports of snipers shooting from nearby buildings, so the perimeter of the crime scene is sizeable. An attack of this scale will take the entirety of all three agencies to find out who is responsible and bring justice to the victims and their families. Director Schultz sets up a ground control communication center with a line directly to the White House in order to provide briefings in real time. He easily takes command and makes sure one of his trusted assistants acts as his eyes and ears on the ground in his absence.

He turns to his assistant and says, "I want to know what they know as soon as they know it. Got it?"

"Yes, sir," Agent Parker replies. "As always, you can count on me."

THAT'S NOT HIM

▷ **Rose – New York Presbyterian Hospital, Day 1**

Rose paces up and down the white-tiled corridor of the ICU, staring daggers at the three men who, in her opinion, allowed this to happen: Director Schultz, Director Cummings, and James Edwards. All four children have already arrived by helicopter from DC, a short ninety-minute trip. They sit in chairs alongside the wall, ashen-faced and solemn. They've asked to go into the room to see their father, but it's every hand on deck to make sure the president survives.

Rose turns on her heel toward Director Schultz, who has just arrived and is standing next to James and Director Cummings. "What in the *hell* happened today?" she asks in a voice so low and filled with such aggression and accusation that everyone takes a step backward. In that same calm, angry tone, she continues, "Wait, no, no—how could *you* let this happen?"

The men just stare at her, their faces devoid of expression.

Rose raises her voice while maintaining her calm. "Do we not have more than enough agencies in this country, filled with supposedly competent people, making sure things like this don't happen on American soil? Really, I don't understand any of this!"

None of these guys is willing to be the first to respond.

Rose feels her hands twitch. She really wants to reach out and slap each of them. Her eyes narrow and begin to burn with an indescribable pain. Part of her is looking for comfort while the other is looking for blame.

Thomas walks over to his mother's side. "Mom," he begins softly, but Rose pushes him away. She is not done speaking.

"Damn it to hell! Each of you! You've let me down. You've let my children down. Not to mention the entire country! Who knows how many people are injured, wounded, or—worse—*dead*, all because of your negligence and blatant incompetence. The three of you are to blame for this fiasco, this . . . this . . ." She doesn't finish the sentence because there are no words to describe what happened this afternoon. The word *attack* certainly doesn't begin to sum up the horrific scene at the courthouse.

James steps forward. "Mrs. Dumont, you know I didn't want this trip to happen. Neither did Cummings. I tried talking him out of it and told him I didn't support it. And I know you begged him not to come to New York. But you know how insistent he was on keeping his first campaign promise. We just couldn't convince him otherwise."

"Don't you *dare* blame my husband for this!" Rose sputters, clearly disgusted by his feeble attempts to shift the blame. James puts his head down and steps away from her.

Cummings steps forward and clears his throat. Rose's eyes follow him; she's irked by his overconfident, nonchalant manner. "The truth is," he says, "we shouldn't be arguing over who is to blame right now. We'll find that out soon enough. But we all knew the weather forecast, and that it really wasn't wise to do this today. The truth is that we didn't have enough time to prepare. I told your husband this, but, as Edwards said, he wanted to make good on his word."

"I don't give a damn about Lance's promises; none of you can blame *him* for this!" Rose turns to Cummings. "Take some accountability and admit it: you could've stopped this from happening!" Rose turns to James and Schultz. "And God help me—if and when I get my husband back, we will see to it that there won't be another opportunity for you to do this again. I will personally make sure of that."

Just as James and Schultz simultaneously begin to speak, Rose raises her hand, stopping them in their tracks. "I don't want to hear your excuses or whatever it is you are going to tell me. Honestly, I could have done a better job of protecting him than all of you put together! Might I remind you all that I delivered my husband safely to you fifteen days ago, and you nearly returned him to me in a coffin."

At that exact moment, a tall, dark-haired man with a somber face enters the hallway. He is dressed in a shirt and tie with a doctor's white coat on top and a stethoscope around his neck. He approaches the group and asks Rose if she is Mrs. Dumont. When Rose nods, he extends his hand to shake hers. Rose does not return the courtesy.

"I'm Dr. Kellerman, and I'm in charge of your husband's care," he says.

Schultz steps up to Dr. Kellerman. "I'm the director of the CIA, Donald Schultz. Is there somewhere private where we can speak?"

Rose turns to the doctor to protest, but before she can, Dr. Kellerman speaks, ignoring Schultz. "Mrs. Dumont, your husband is stable right now. He's going to survive, but it may be a long road to recovery. It appears he took a bullet through his mouth, which entered under his jawline. It traveled upward and exited through his left cheek. It took out some of his teeth and gum tissue and fractured his jaw. We'll wire his jaw shut for the next week or two while things heal. His teeth can be replaced later, but he won't be able to speak for some time—for just how long, we don't know yet. It could be anywhere from ten days to a couple of months. It's just too early to tell right now. Along with his oral injuries, he's sustained a concussion, which we are monitoring closely. He has several broken bones in his hands, ribs, and left ankle. We are still reviewing scans to determine if anything, such as shrapnel or bone fragments, needs to be removed."

Director Cummings speaks up. "As you can imagine, Dr. Kellerman, we are going to need a lot of staff on this floor. I head up the Secret Service, so we will have staff stationed throughout the hospital and at all entry and exit points. We are in discussions already with the hospital CEO."

The doctor nods.

"No!" yells a voice. It's Edwina. Her mouth is trembling, and there's a mixture of angst and rage in her eyes that Rose has never before seen. "I don't believe you, any of you! T-t-that man in there isn't my father! That's not him; it *can't* be! You need to be looking for him, not protecting a stranger!"

Everyone stares at her in shock, but no one moves, except Rose. She steps forward and with a swift hand, slaps her youngest daughter across the face. Edwina stumbles backward, her hand flying up to her cheek as she glares at her mother with a mixture of shock, surprise, and fear. Then she takes a few steps backward and lowers herself slowly into the chair where she'd been sitting, next to her sister, June. A red streak spreads across her cheek, and her eyes promptly fill with tears.

"If that's not your father in there, then who is it, Edwina?" Rose snaps at her daughter angrily. "How could it possibly be someone else? How dare you even say such a horrible thing! Why *would* you even say that?"

"I d-d-don't know, b-but I know that it's not Dad! He wouldn't have let this happen to him!"

Rose swears under her breath and turns on her heel, flinging the following command over her shoulder to June: "Take her out of here before I lose my mind. Now!"

James steps in and puts his hand on Rose's shoulder in an attempt to calm her, but Rose isn't having any of it. She brushes him off with a glare and steps away.

Obliging her clearly distraught mother, June wraps her arms around Edwina's shoulders and leads her down the corridor, speaking to her softly as they walk.

Rose waits until the twins are out of sight before turning back to the doctor and directors, who are now talking among themselves.

"I'm sorry to interrupt your little powwow here with the guys," Rose says sarcastically to Dr. Kellerman, "but again, how long do you think it will be before my husband will be able to speak?"

The doctor looks at her cautiously. He is a bit flummoxed, given what he just witnessed. "It could be anywhere from ten days to a couple of months, Mrs. Dumont, if everything goes as planned. But again, at this point, it's just too early to tell. The next forty-eight hours will be critical. But I won't lie to you, it could be double that amount of time if there are complications. We will continue to conduct MRIs, CT scans, and other tests to understand the full extent of his injuries, but this is what we know at the moment."

"If anything else comes up, please let me know first. My family and I will be by his side night and day. From now on, all medical updates will go through me. He may be the president, but he's first and foremost *my* husband."

"Of course, Mrs. Dumont. Rest assured, he's in the best place in the world for head trauma. As long as there's no permanent brain damage, he'll be OK. He might not look or sound the same at first, and he may not be able to move like he used to for a while, but with time and treatment, that can change. Most importantly, he is alive, and he will live."

"Thank you, Doctor." Rose lets him leave and then turns to Schultz, her voice hardening, which aligns with her body posture. "Director," Rose says snippily, "as soon as you are able, let me know how many victims, Secret Service agents, and police officers lost their lives today, as well as how many were injured."

"Yes, ma'am," Schultz replies calmly.

Rose turns to James. "Find out what's happening with these people, as I want to make sure they are getting the best care possible, both mentally and physically. And their families too. I want details on everything."

She turns to walk away but stops herself and looks at the Secret Service director. "Mr. Cummings," she says coldly. "Find out what happened there today, how it happened, and—most important of all—who is responsible for this reprehensible attack against the president, the country, and our democracy. Now, if you will all please leave us alone, we need to be together as a family, and you've done enough, or should I say, *not* enough. I can't stand the sight of any of you right now."

CHAPTER 15

HIDDEN POCKET

▷ **Doris – New York State Supreme Court Building, Day 1**

An eerie silence envelops the courthouse grounds as Doris Machado hurries back to the man she saw earlier, lying on the sidewalk. She arrived at the scene an hour ago and has already helped seven victims into five separate ambulances. The paramedics want her to come back to the hospital with the next victim she helps. They said more nurses are on their way and will continue to assist the injured.

Earlier, when she first noticed this man, she passed him, assuming he was dead. Now she wants to double-check to make sure. He's lying quite still, so she crouches down next to him and gently wipes his face with her coat sleeve. She can now see that he's breathing, but just barely. A lock of blond hair falls over her face as she leans in closer and removes one of her gloves in order to check his pulse. When she confirms he's alive, she lifts her arm in the air, signaling to an ambulance to get ready to load. Minutes later, two paramedics come over to lift the man onto a gurney. The tiniest whimper escapes his lips. Doris lightly touches the victim's shoulder and then stands up, lifting her gaze into the crowd until it meets the eyes of a man standing some thirty feet away. The moment she catches his gaze, he turns, walks away, and disappears into a sedan.

Doris fidgets while the ambulance loads the man into the back, alongside another patient and then gives her a sign to scramble in before the doors shut. She shifts her body in the cramped space until she's sitting directly beside the man, who is beginning to regain consciousness. He is twisting his head back and forth, writhing in pain from the bullet that must have grazed his jaw or his cheek. Or both. There's just so much blood.

"Shh, shh," she whispers, cradling his ice-cold fingers in her warm hand as she leans over him. "Just try to relax."

She gingerly wipes a wet towel across the side of his head, where another bullet must have grazed him. His eyes briefly flickering open, the man moans, and his free hand reaches for the shiny red ribbon attached to her lapel. Doris glances downward. Her first instinct is to move away, out of his reach, but the man's helplessness and intensity change her mind. Perhaps this is all he needs to take his mind off the pain. She bends down, allowing his fingers to touch the ribbon. A calmness washes over his otherwise pained expression, and he closes his eyes as the paramedic tends to him.

Ten minutes later, the ambulance doors swing open. The other patient, a woman, is pronounced dead on arrival. She'd lost too much blood over the course of the day. Her nurse takes her death in stride, leading her gurney straight to another room farther down the hall. Victims, whether dead or alive, can't remain on the gurneys; they all need to be returned immediately to the courthouse for more victims. Doris absentmindedly wonders where they are stacking the dead bodies.

As the man's gurney is rushed through Lenox Hill Hospital, Doris sticks by his side, anxiously stealing glances at him while they twist and turn through the hallways. He doesn't move or make a sound.

In a curtained space within the emergency department, Doris reaffirms to herself that she won't let this man be the next to die—not on her watch. With expert precision, she snips off what's left of his suit to allow her assistant to start dressing his wounds. Doris checks the pockets of his suit jacket and pants. She finds neither a wallet nor identification. No matter. That can be dealt with later. Doris tags him as a John Doe, scoops up the rest of his clothes, and puts them into a plastic "belongings" bag before hurrying back to her patient. She tries not to imagine the hundreds of belongings left behind on those icy steps back at the courthouse.

Due to the massive influx of patients, Doris's John Doe has waited for two hours before he's finally visited by the attending doctor, Dr. Brian Dansby. Doris begins telling Dr. Dansby that she has already started the double IVs with saline drip has done her best to stop the bleeding with compressed bandages.

Dr. Dansby takes a preliminary look at the patient and practically screams at Doris, "This man has clearly lost a lot of blood! Call upstairs, and get me six units—no, make that eight units—of O neg blood now!"

Dr. Dansby carries on with his examination of the patient as Doris scrambles to schedule the blood transfusion. Even though he has been sedated, Doris's patient keeps jerking about, so she fastens him to the hospital bed to prevent him from flailing and accidentally pulling out the needles.

After stabilizing the patient, Dr. Dansby looks at Doris and says, "Looks like you have him listed as a John Doe. Do you want to double-check his clothing for some identification before we continue? That way, the front desk can begin the process of locating and notifying his family while we work on him."

She nods in agreement, but before she retreats back to the nurses station, where she left the patient's bag, she notices that her patient's eyes are glued to where the ribbon had been on the lapel of her overcoat, even though she has since changed into her light-blue nurse's uniform. She smiles at him and heads out of the room to retrieve his bag of personal items.

After returning to his room with the bag, she removes the patient's clothes and lays them ever so carefully on a metal table. She again searches every pocket, but she still can't find any ID. She begins to put his suit jacket back into the bag but stops short when she feels something inside the lining. A hidden pocket? She finds the discreet opening, places her hand inside, and pulls out an official government-issued identification card. She wonders if he is one of the many Secret Service agents who was gunned down at the courthouse. When her eyes travel to the name listed on the card, her mouth opens, but no sound comes out.

Doris knows this must be a mistake. Even so, her legs wobble at the thought, so she grabs the back of a nearby chair to keep herself from falling down. She quickly searches for more hidden pockets, triple-checking his pants and the lining of his jacket to see what else she can find. She wants proof. This just can't be right. Maybe this guy is some kind of fanatic who's obsessed with the president? Maybe this ID belongs to one of the president's assistants or someone who's supposed to throw his body in front of his boss to protect the country? She looks at the ID again and starts to sweat. Abandoning the clothes, she sits on a folding chair and crosses her arms over her chest, holding herself tightly. The man in the hospital bed does not look like the man on the ID card; that's for sure.

Doris hears a booming voice calling her name from down the hall. It's Dr. Dansby. Before she can rise from her chair, the doctor appears in the doorway, the bright hallway lights pouring in from behind his stocky frame.

"It's just me," he says, noting her startled expression.

Doris tries not to tremble as she hastily pockets the identification card. At just five foot nine, Dr. Dansby is not an intimidating figure. But Doris is not one to keep secrets, especially from a doctor she deeply respects.

"You scared me!" she says.

"I'm sorry; I'm just looking for the patient's details, at least his name, so that I can finish my paperwork before the next shift takes over. The day's been insane, and it's getting late. I just want to get this done and go home at some point tonight, Doris."

Doris suddenly feels sick. She wonders what she should do.

"Doris! We are all exhausted," Dr. Dansby says impatiently. When Doris doesn't respond with the patient's name, he persists. "There's already enough to do; I can't chase the details here!"

"I-I didn't find any form of identification," Doris stammers. "What should we do?"

Dr. Dansby squints at her, ignoring her question. "You look pale, Doris. Maybe you need a bite to eat. You were out there in the cold for how long?"

Doris lowers her head and silently prays to God for strength. She just wants to be alone with her thoughts, and she wishes Dr. Dansby would leave.

"Well then, he's a John Doe for now. We will circle back later and figure it out then. I'm sure someone will come looking for him soon," Dr. Dansby says. "Oh, and since he's a John Doe, please fill out the form, noting any distinguishing moles, tattoos, scars, or birthmarks. You can just put his personal belongings back in the cabinet and go home after you've completed the form. We've all had an awful day, and you've witnessed more than any human should ever have to see. I'm sorry you had to go to the courthouse today. Why don't you finish up, and I'll join you in a few minutes so we can stitch him up."

Doris bites her tongue as Dr. Dansby leaves the room, fighting with herself over the mystery man lying in the hospital bed. She stares at her John Doe. She examines his arms and legs so she can fill out her Unidentified Persons Form. He moves slightly as she's searching his body, but so far, she has found no distinguishing marks. She pulls back the sheet that covers his upper body and carefully searches his chest. No unique markings. She gently lifts his left shoulder, then his right, and does the same with each of his hips. Just then, something catches her eye. She turns up the lights in the room and pulls out her phone to use the flashlight function. She sees a scar on the lower right side of his back. It looks old, and she wonders if it's from a childhood accident. Regardless, she notes the scar on the form. She then stands back and studies the man. Could he really be the president of the United States? Impossible. She heard earlier they have President Dumont at New York Presbyterian Hospital. So if that's the case, who is *this* guy? She either has a devil or an angel on her hands, and she deeply hopes it's the latter.

Doris feels herself swaying, but she's not sure if it's from exhaustion or fear and shock as a result of what she witnessed on those courthouse steps. She presses her hip against the bed for support. Bending down to get a closer look at the man, she whispers, "Please don't be *him*." Suddenly, a terrible thought flashes through her mind: What if this man is one of the bad guys? And if he is, will the rest of the terrorists come looking for him? She closes her eyes and childhood memories swim through her mind: butterflies with broken wings, baby birds that fell from their nest, and crickets that can't jump. A warm glow encompasses her, and the corner of her mouth lifts as she remembers caring for these wounded souls when she was just a little girl. It was these experiences that told her she'd be a nurse someday.

Doris opens her eyes and looks at the ravaged man lying before her. The warmth disappears from her body as reality dawns upon her: This is real. Today was real. And this officially unidentified man is still here. She knows this is not a dream; it's a puzzle. Hopefully, it's not a puzzle of nightmares. She has to put it together, and fast, but right now, there's no way to know how many pieces there are.

When Dr. Dansby returns to the room, Doris helps him re-clean the patient's wounds, swallowing every urge to tell him what she found in the patient's hidden pocket. Are they helping a man who could've been part of the attack or just one of the president's assistants? The entire side of the patient's face has ballooned so much that he could be anyone. Half of his head has been shaved to treat his wound. Is this guy even going to make it? The MRIs that were taken a few hours ago indicate minimal internal bleeding. That's good news, but there's still a dangerous amount of blood putting pressure on his brain. Only time will tell. Hopefully, the patient won't die of a stroke in the meantime. The medications should help prevent that from happening.

Dr. Dansby stares at their patient and then turns to Doris. "Have you ever seen this guy before? He looks sort of familiar to me. I don't know what it is. Maybe I'm just tired, and all the patients are looking alike to me." He appears to wait for a response from Doris, but when none comes, he begins rebandaging the patient's wounds. "Today's attack was the worst we've seen since 9/11. I don't think New York City can handle this again. So many dead, and even more injured. Most of the patients' injuries resulted from the stampede of people running away from the bullets, not the bullets themselves. It must have been mayhem. All this pain and destruction of life just to get to the president. It makes me sick. I was willing to like Dumont even though I didn't vote for him. I hope they catch those monsters."

Feeling dizzy and parched, Doris reaches for her nearby water bottle and drinks from it. Someplace under her tongue, there's enough moisture to feel her lips again. She closes her eyes. All she wants is some time alone with her thoughts and to be able to erase everything she saw today. The mass of bloodied bodies suddenly appears in her mind's eye, so she opens her eyes and puts a hand on her cheek. She's momentarily relieved by the renewed warmth of her hand, so she presses her other one to her face as well before looking up at Dr. Dansby.

"Yeah, I hope they get all of them. Do you think our John Doe here will make it?" she asks hopefully.

Dr. Dansby frowns. "I can see you've taken a particular interest in this patient, haven't you? I've told you before, never get attached to a trauma patient. It will break you. And you've been through enough of these heartaches." He gives her a sympathetic look and asks, "Are you listening to me, Doris?"

"I was just wondering if he'll be gone before my next shift," Doris replies defensively. She can't help but feel attacked for her care in looking after patients. "I've loved every one of my patients. I take each and every one of their cases personally. Even when I'm at home, I worry about them. That's just me. I can't help it. It's why I'm here; you know that!" Not quite sure why she's this angry, she takes a deep breath.

"I didn't mean it that way, Doris. But from the look on your face after you searched his personal items, it seemed like you were already very worried. I figured being at the scene of the tragedy got to you." Dr. Dansby says. "I'm sorry I brought all of this up. You are an incredibly good nurse. What's more, you are an exceptional human being. Let's get this guy all fixed up so he can go back to his loved ones. I'm sorry. I didn't want to upset you; I only wanted to caution you."

After they finish bandaging John Doe, they wheel him into the operating room. Over the course of the next hour, Dr. Dansby carefully stitches up the injured areas of the patient's scalp and left cheek. Doris realizes plastic surgery might be necessary in the future, depending on the patient's ability to recover.

After they bring John Doe back to his room, Doris asks, "Do you still want the next step tomorrow to be another MRI?"

"Yes. We need to see if the blood in his brain is draining on its own. I don't want to open him up. It's too risky. Right now, I just want him to make it through the next forty-eight hours. Also, make sure he gets a full-body x-ray later tonight so we can see if there are any broken bones. The radiology department has been backed up all day."

"I'm really worried that there might be some bullet fragments moving around in there," Doris says somberly. "Like traveling landmines. Maybe the last MRI didn't catch everything? We've got to make sure before we do anything else, right?"

"You're right. The MRI might have missed something, but we won't know anything for some time." Dr. Dansby straightens his shoulders. "For now, schedule him for an x-ray as soon as possible. When the results come in, we'll learn what else we need to address tomorrow. Now please go home and get some rest."

Instead of heading home right away, Doris waits restlessly with her patient by her side. She's unable to stop her thoughts from spiraling into full-blown anxiety. Two hours later, she takes the patient down to the radiology department for his x-rays.

An hour later, the night-shift doctor, Dr. Liz Chen, emails Doris that the patient's x-rays show no broken bones. The doctor says her key concern is the swelling from the shot that grazed the side of his head. The blood needs to drain, just as Dr. Dansby said. An MRI tomorrow will tell them if the blood is dissipating.

Doris knows she should be home by now, but instead of leaving the hospital, she locks herself in a private bathroom and pulls the patient's ID from her bra. Sitting on the lid of the toilet, she considers her options. There are so many ifs—one hundred ifs for this John Doe, and another hundred if he's really the president, which she's sure he can't be. Assuming that not all the attackers were killed or captured, this guy could still be in danger, especially if he is one of the attackers. And even more so if he's the president. "He's not the president, Doris!" she says out loud. "But then . . . who *is* he?"

Restless, Doris rolls up her sleeves to wash her arms and neck, a nervous habit she adopted when she was an undergraduate nursing student at Washington State University seventeen years ago. The water is ice-cold, and her hands shake beneath the faucet, just as they did back on those courthouse steps. She looks at her reflection in the mirror, unable to stop all the questions from barreling through her mind. She wonders if she should just talk to Dr. Dansby in the morning and hand over what she found. Maybe he can handle it so that she can move on. She should make it *his* problem. This is above her pay grade.

Doris opens the door and takes a seat by her patient's side. He's quiet now, but his breathing is labored. She checks his vitals again and again. Then she examines the swelling on his head. She isn't sure if it's getting better or worse, but it looks redder than before and slightly larger. Maybe it's just the lighting. Doris clenches her fists in frustration, fighting back tears. Should she walk away without saying anything, or should she tell the media they have the wrong guy at New York Presbyterian Hospital? She closes her eyes only to once again see the mass of bodies on and beside the courthouse steps. *Don't close your eyes, Doris,* she tells herself. Then she again sees the name on the government-issued ID, and fear grips her tightly. Something feels wrong about this guy, and she can't quite pinpoint it. Her gut is usually right, and it's now telling her that this patient is trouble. She sits nearly motionless in her chair, only moving to make sure an ice pack is applied to the patient's head every hour. She shuts off the overhead light in the room and is instantly soothed by the sounds and lights emanating from the vital signs monitor. She wants to close her eyes, but can't bear to see the bodies again.

CHAPTER 16

THE SCAR

▷ **Doris – Lenox Hill Hospital, Day 2**

When the light of the sunrise leaks through the room's blinds, Doris barely acknowledges it. The sun takes forever to make up its mind, playing hide or shine for well over an hour. She eyes it groggily, wishing she could just skip town and go to the countryside, where everything is sweet and fluffy, like cotton candy, and the sun heals all. Here, in New York City, the emergency rooms are still overwhelmed, helping the rest of the victims from yesterday's massacre. Doris considers herself lucky that her ambulance got this John Doe to the hospital quickly; the line was long, and there weren't enough first responders available to help at the scene. He could easily have lost his life while waiting, as did many others.

Angela Woo, Doris's close friend and colleague, enters the room. "Oh, honey, you look a mess," she says, shocked. "Now I know you haven't been home yet. Go the hell home! What are you doing to yourself?"

Doris doesn't turn around. "I can't leave him, Angela. I don't know why, but I just can't."

"I know why; we both know why. He's not Daniel, Doris. He's not going to die on you just because you left. You have to know that. The best thing you can do for this patient is to take care of yourself so you can be in a better position to properly help him get out of here." Angela's tone is no-nonsense, just like she is, but she is happy to see her good friend. Angela is one of those people who are naturally smart, and she is more mature than her thirty-one years.

Doris nods in agreement. Angela gives her a kiss on the top of her head before leaving the room. But Doris doesn't go home. She ices John Doe's head. Then she lies down on the cot she set out earlier and goes back to sleep.

☺☺

Thirty minutes later, Doris wakes from an unnerving dream about her late husband, Daniel, the only man she has ever loved. It was so real that she jumps off the cot and rushes to John Doe's bedside. She knows it was just a dream, but secretly she's hoping that it wasn't, and Daniel will be lying there. She'll still have time to save him. But, of course, it isn't Daniel. She rushes to the bathroom and throws up in the toilet as her tears finally flow freely. She sits on the cold floor until the tears and convulsions have stopped. Then she lifts herself to her knees, still over the toilet, and says a prayer out loud: "Don't let this man die, God. Give me another chance! Help me! Tell me what to do. Give me a sign." She slowly stands, her legs still shaky, then makes her way back to the bed to put another ice pack on her patient's swollen head.

An hour later, Dr. Dansby returns to the hospital and makes his rounds to visit his patients. Doris can hear him talking to the nurses and asking about her. They tell him Doris hasn't been home yet.

His footsteps grow closer until his shadow fills the door. She turns to see him leaning against the doorframe, playing with a pencil between his fingers.

"You know, I was at home thinking of you, Doris. I was wondering how you're going to handle having been present on the scene at the courthouse. Especially since it's only been a year since Daniel passed."

Doris looks away from him, feeling like he should be thanking her for her dedication to saving the lives of their patients. Sure, she may be a bit obsessed with her job, but this job has been her saving grace.

"Please look at me, Doris." Dr. Dansby puts his pencil into his shirt pocket and continues, "What are you doing to yourself? You shouldn't have been here all night. The night-shift nurses told me you hardly slept. This John Doe has been here for one night and is already sucking the life out of you. I'm going to ask you to go home, and if you don't, I might have to pull you from caring for this patient and put you on leave. You need to get some professional help; you can't keep burying your pain in your work."

Instead of replying to Dr. Dansby, Doris hums to herself as she moves the ice pack from the patient's face to the side of his head.

"Doris, I'm serious. If you don't go home, I'll—"

"OK, OK!" she snaps, glaring up at him with her puffy, bloodshot eyes. She knows he's right, but the thought of being home alone with her thoughts scares her too much. "I promise I'll go home and sleep."

"That's all I am asking. Your personal connections to these patients aren't healthy. But do the right thing, and take care of yourself first. I'm thinking you *will* do the right thing—*now*. I'll have the nurses take over on John Doe here. He will be all right. I'll also pay more attention to him today; I promise. You know I'm on your side, so no push back here. I'll do my part if you do yours. I'm counting on you."

"Thank you. I'll see you tomorrow then," Doris says sheepishly.

"And Doris, you aren't getting off this easy. Once this mess settles down, I'm talking to human resources. They will set you up with a therapist. With the loss of Daniel, and now this courthouse disaster, we are going to get you help." After Doris turns to leave, he jokingly adds, "And don't roll your eyes!"

@@

Forty-five minutes later, Doris is back at home in her four-story brownstone on the Upper West Side. Her home is her haven and the result of the large insurance payout she received when Daniel succumbed to cancer. She remembers scolding him for paying so much money for life insurance. He would always joke that he was worth more dead than alive. She hated that policy because it was a reminder that, at some point, their relationship would end. She wishes she could still be in their small one-bedroom apartment, making dinners, watching movies, and taking two-hour walks on those balmy summer nights. But it was all out of her control; he had made her promise to buy a place on this block. She granted his dying wish and purchased her unit, which she turned into a shrine for Daniel. There are signs of him everywhere in the house, and that's the only reason she ever enjoys coming home. But today feels different, and the normal comforts don't seem to be working. Something feels wrong.

She turns on the television, hoping to soak up as much information as possible about the courthouse attack. Maybe there's something that can shed light on the mystery man back at Lenox Hill Hospital. Predictably, all of the cable news channels and even the networks are 100 percent focused on the massive attack. It has been just over twenty-four hours since it occurred, but it feels like days. Images of the president fill the screen. News reports confirm that all but five of the president's Secret Service detail were killed. She wonders if one of those agents is her patient. *That* would make sense. She hopes they'll show images of some of the agents, but of course, they don't.

Doris flips to the next channel to find the anchorwoman in midsentence. The caption below her face reads *GOVERNMENT INVOLVEMENT?* Doris turns up the volume.

"We've had multiple callers," the anchorwoman continues, "who've asked to remain anonymous, claiming that they work for the government. Each of these callers insists that a government agency is behind the attack and are urging us to investigate. Our team of reporters are doing just that. There's more to come this evening as we interview well-known government conspiracy theorist Richard Brown."

Doris mutes the TV. All the information is overwhelming. She wants to close her eyes, but she doesn't want to see the bodies on the steps again. She decides to take out her laptop and look for more information online. While searching, she comes across numerous photos of President Dumont. She finds some pictures of him taken when he was in his twenties and is surprised by how much he looks like Daniel. They are both so handsome. Doris is shocked that she didn't notice the similarities earlier. They both have hazel eyes, sandy-brown hair, and high cheek bones. They're both tall, with broad shoulders. Daniel. She shakes away the memories.

Ten minutes pass, and she's still looking at the photo of the president in his twenties. Maybe there's something that can help her answer her burning question. She scrolls through images until she stops on a group of photos taken during the president's trip to Saint Croix in December, just weeks before his inauguration. They are clearly photos taken by paparazzi. The then-president-elect and his family are enjoying some time on the beach. Doris then comes across a picture of Dumont taken from behind, wearing nothing but swim trunks. Out of sheer curiosity, she clicks on the image and zooms in. Squinting, she grabs her reading glasses so she can see more clearly. She zooms in closer on his lower back until she sees the scar.

"Oh my God! It's him!"

CHAPTER 17

ONE MINOR SITUATION

▷ **Rockefeller – Langley, Virginia, Day 2**

Rockefeller steps outside his office and looks for a quiet spot to make a phone call. He's always surprised that it's so difficult to find privacy in a building that's over two-million square feet. It's been a hard week, and he's barely slept. The president is still alive, and the press is saying there's a good chance he will survive, despite his brain injury. He's not quite sure how things went wrong at the courthouse. How the hell did his team not accomplish its goal? Everything had been going according to plan, but the weather proved more challenging than he'd expected. And sadly, there were a lot more casualties than he'd wanted. His trigger-happy soldiers did what they love best, damn them. Even sadder to him is the fact that he now has to do the hardest job: cover their footsteps. He steps into the stairway of the 1950s-style monolithic structure and places a phone call using his Alcatel A206.

Gruff answers the phone on the first ring. "Yes, sir?"

"It's cleanup time, Gruff. Don't let anyone screw this up. We have to make sure no one talks. You know what to do. Hit each of the five hospitals they've mentioned on the news. Use your top people, and have them do their damn homework before they get there. Remember, they need to know the name of the spouse or one child of each nurse or doctor on staff. It's all about leverage. I want all nine of our missing members located and eliminated in the next seventy-two hours."

"Understood and agreed. I secured all the hospital staff members' names yesterday, and the team started getting information on each of them last night. I've been quizzing them this morning, and they will be ready for the night shift. Just glad none of our guys wound up at Presbyterian; that would be difficult to access, as security there is tight. We are still working our contacts there to see what we can control. The president's doctor, Kellerman, may be accessible. He has a young wife and small children."

"Good. Keep on it. I'll call you in the morning. I will want a detailed report. I want to know everything: who your team speaks to at the hospitals and what they find out. They need to get the job done." He pauses for a moment before adding, "Are you sure these members know what to do? I don't want them backing out at the last moment."

"They are more than willing. These are our most dedicated elite Brigade members. Each will carry multiple vials and will make sure this goes unnoticed. It will be clean. I promise. No trace."

"Tell them I will personally reward them for each member they successfully handle."

"Will do."

Rockefeller hangs up the phone and puts it back in his jacket pocket as he enters the long, empty gray hallway. He straightens his suit and tie and returns to his day job, where he will have a whole new set of problems to handle today.

☙❧

The next morning, Rockefeller's Alcatel rings. "Tell me you have good news," he says as he heads to the stairwell at the end of the hallway.

"I do, sir," replies Gruff. "Three down; six to go. Hopefully, we can finish the job tonight."

"Well done. Any issues?"

"No, sir."

"I want no surprises here. Tell me everything."

Gruff goes into detail on each of the three members who were given injections. He lists each staff member encountered along the way and what was said. "Luckily for us," he says, "my guys had no bad encounters. These hospitals are still a mess from the attack. Their uniforms and credentials were nearly perfect—at least, good enough for the night shift." He pauses, then adds, "Wait a minute, sir. You should know about one minor situation."

"*What* situation? You said there were no issues!" Rockefeller barks.

"Well, it wasn't really an issue, but our guy who went to Lenox Hill had an encounter with two nurses. He was in a room where there was an unidentified patient—a John Doe, as they call them. The nurses didn't believe our guy worked for the hospital and wanted to see his identification. Guess he pulled a knife on them, but—"

Rockefeller doesn't let him finish. "What the hell? *A knife?!* This is an issue, Gruff. This is bad."

"It was handled just as we discussed. My guy was ready and knew where one of the nurse's kids goes to school. He knew both the boy's name and school. He told them what would happen if they talked. One of the nurses immediately started crying. He had them stay in the patient's room while he finished his rounds on the floor. Don't worry; I promise there will be no issues stemming from this incident."

"Well, that's why we do our homework. Always pays off."

"Yes, it does, sir."

"Make sure you take down the names of the nurses, just in case."

"Already done."

"Good. And this John Doe—did your guy get a good look at him?"

"He did, he wasn't one of us."

"OK. Thanks, Gruff. Any news on Kellerman?"

"No, sir. Give me forty-eight hours."

"All right. Make sure tonight goes just as well. Let's get those last members. We can't risk anything. Now go make it happen."

With one hand, Rockefeller folds closed the phone and slides it into his jacket pocket. He then uses his work phone to call his next pawn. He hopes there's still an opportunity to finish the job he started.

THE MAN WITH THE HOODIE

▷ **Doris – Lenox Hill Hospital, Day 3**

Doris returns to Lenox Hill Hospital for her shift, anxious to look at the scar on her patient's back. She has to be 100 percent sure. Though she still hasn't had a full night's sleep, she's wearing a bright smile today, hoping it will cover the panic she's feeling inside. Her mind has been reeling, trying to figure out just *how* the president of the United States has wound up in her care. She feels confident the hospital will take good care of him once she confides in them. The decision was an easy one to make, but telling them needs to wait until she can make sure it's really him.

Doris finally makes her way to his room and closes the door. She immediately lifts the sheet from her patient while gently pushing him onto his side and pulling open his hospital gown. The scar is the first thing she sees. She pulls up the president's vacation photo on her phone and zooms in again, holding the phone next to her patient's back so that the scars are side by side. They're identical. Starting to sweat, she opens the door to tell Dr. Dansby before she loses her nerve. She was sure he wouldn't believe it, but *now* she has proof.

The moment she puts her hand on the door, it flies open in her face, and she stumbles backward, nearly falling to the ground.

"Doris!" exclaims Angela. "We've been looking for you everywhere!"

Alice Waters closes the door behind them, her bracelets shimmering under the bright lights of the hospital room. Alice is a fifty-five-year-old, tall, slender Black woman who always sparkles—literally and figuratively. She's the type of person who speaks to anyone who will listen and is always ready to show you pictures of her three beautiful children. And most important of all to Doris, she's one of her best friends.

"Why, Angela? What's wrong?" Doris asks, worried by their urgency.

"Where have you been?" Alice demands.

"I came in late because I needed a little extra time at home. I have . . ." Doris can't seem to find the words to finish her sentence. How does she even begin to tell them that the president of the United States is lying in this room?

"You need to sit down, Doris. We have something urgent to tell you. But you need to swear it will stay between the three of us," Angela says while pulling up a chair for Doris.

"We had an encounter last night," Alice begins. Her voice is shaky, and her eyes begin to water.

"Guys, what's wrong? You're scaring me!" Doris exclaims.

"At around 2:00 this morning, Alice and I were doing our paperwork. From the corner of my eye, I saw a male nurse entering your John Doe's room. I had never seen him before and noticed that he was wearing work boots—like those yellowish-brown construction ones, you know?

Doris nods.

"He also had a hood hanging out the back of his scrub top. He looked clearly out of place, so I told Alice and asked her to come with me to check it out."

Alice takes over, adding, "He had closed the door, which was also strange, so we knocked first. There was no answer, so we opened the door and found the guy sitting in that chair." She points to the chair in which Doris is now sitting. "He was reading your patient's paperwork. He barely bothered to look up at us until we asked him what he was doing in the patient's room. He smiled and said his name and held up his ID card, but neither of us have ever seen him, so we asked who he reports to and when he started. And so he stands up, pulls out a knife, and comes toward us. It was awful!" Alice's shaking takes over her body.

"Doris, he knew who we are," says Angela. "He knew our names and where we lived. He even knew Kevin's name and where he goes to school."

"What? How is that possible?" Doris turns to Alice. "Why would he know your son's name, Alice?" Her mind starts spinning again, just when she'd thought this was almost over.

Alice shakes her head and replies, "I dunno, he said if we told anyone that we saw him here, if we reported it to the hospital or police, that he would hurt Kevin." She bursts into tears and is unable to continue.

"We don't know what he was looking for, Doris," Angela says, "but we knew we had to tell you since we found him in your patient's room. We are in danger, and so are you. Who is your John Doe? Maybe he's one of the terrorists?"

"Oh my God. I'm sorry. I'm so sorry," Doris says, now pacing the room. She's not sure if telling Alice and Angela that he is the president will help or hurt. She immediately decides she won't put either of the women or their families in any further danger. She won't tell them. At least, not right now.

"You didn't do anything, Doris. It's not your fault. We're sorry to tell you this, but we felt we had no choice. We've all got to be careful," Angela says, remarkably calmly. "The worst part is that before he left, he told us, 'I'll be back in a week to make sure you've kept your mouths shut.' What should we do?"

"It's good that you told me. I needed to know. I will figure this out, I promise. You guys have been here way too long. Go home to your families. Make sure they are OK. And make sure you stick together." Doris walks over to give each of them a long, tight hug. She truly doesn't want to let go.

⊚⊚

After Alice and Angela leave the room, she turns her attention back to her patient. She can't find it in herself to think of him as President Dumont. Doris looks at his chart and breathes a sigh of relief upon seeing that his vitals have improved. She places an ice pack on his swollen head then double-checks the chart to make sure all his meds were administered while she was away. Taking care of him is just the distraction she needs while she figures out what to do now that he's in danger. They are all in danger. Alice and Angela could've been hurt. And Kevin, he's just a twelve-year-old boy. Whoever is behind the man in the hoodie has connections and must be part of something bigger.

She's just about to lift a bandage to inspect his head wound when there's a tap on her shoulder. Doris turns around, expecting Dr. Dansby, but to her surprise, it's a police officer in full uniform.

"Excuse me, ma'am?" he says gingerly.

"You scared me!" Doris barks.

"I'm sorry; I'm just passing through the floor. I'm looking for a patient by the name of Vince Guthrie." The handsome police officer towers above her while he holds his hat in his hand, like it's a bouquet of flowers for a lover. His chocolate eyes are deep and penetrating, so she diverts her gaze. It's like riding in the back seat of a taxi: don't make eye contact with the driver in the rearview mirror. Your eyes will reveal too much.

"No, sir, I haven't come across anyone by that name. Why do you ask?"

"Vince Guthrie is my father. He was in the crowd to see the president speak, and I think he was probably injured—or worse—during the attack. He hasn't been home since." The young police officer's tone has completely shifted. He pushes back his dark-brown hair with one hand while the other still holds his hat. Doris can hear the worry and sadness in his voice. "He's just over six feet tall, forty-seven years old, and has a full head of light-brown hair. I know you see many patients come through here, but . . ." His voice trails off.

Doris can't help but feel for the young man. The description of his father is not too different from that of the president—and perhaps thousands of men in New York City, she supposes. Little does this guy know who's lying next to them. She needs to get rid of this cop right now. "I'm sorry to hear that," she says. "If there is anything I can do for you, just ask. You can also talk to any of the nurses, the office, or the front desk. I will keep my eyes and ears open. I promise."

The police officer leans over Doris's shoulder to take a closer look at the man in the hospital bed. Doris tries not to tense up, but she knows there isn't much to see due to the bandages.

"Who is this gentleman you have here?" he asks. "It looks bad. Will he survive?"

Doris tries to keep her voice from shaking as she replies, "This is a patient from the courthouse. A bullet grazed his left cheek, and another grazed the same side of his head. His family is devastated. He's stable now, so hopefully, he will make it through OK."

The police officer nods and turns to leave, but quickly turns back to face Doris. "What's his name?"

"I'm sorry; that's private patient information. You understand."

"I see."

"Is that all, Officer?"

"Actually, I was wondering if there are any unidentified patients here?" Officer Guthrie clears his throat.

"I—" Doris hesitates and then spies Dr. Dansby walking past. "I don't think so, but you can ask the doctor about your father. Dr. Dansby—he just walked past, and he can help you with that."

Officer Guthrie thanks her, and as he exits the room, Doris heads to the door and quietly closes it behind him. She's bought herself a few minutes, if that. She doesn't want the police involved, not after the threat from the man in the hoodie. She's not taking any chances. She yanks the bag of clothes from the cabinet, dumps the items onto the floor, then quickly runs her fingers across the lining and pockets, feeling for anything that the officer may find, anything *she* may have missed. Sweat drips from her upper lip as she gathers the president's clothes and puts them back in the bag, which she places back in the cabinet. As she's straightening herself up—adjusting her hair and wiping the sweat from her face—the door opens behind her.

Officer Guthrie stares at her, his eyes traveling from her matted mess of hair to her heaving chest. He smiles as he says, "Relax, ma'am. You are not on the Ten Most Wanted Fugitives list."

Doris doesn't laugh at his half-hearted joke. The officer straightens his tie as if it were out of place, but Doris knows the gesture is fake. There's nothing wrong with the position of his tie. Her mind dances with uncertainty. Should she smile or say something? The officer is waiting.

"Hello again. You startled me," she croaks.

"You're still here," he says coolly.

"Of course I'm still here; this is my job," she replies a little too defensively.

"Yes, I know," Officer Guthrie says, nodding. "Never mind. Why did you lie to me? Dr. Dansby told me this patient is a John Doe."

"Because you can see this man is *not* your father." Attempting to change the subject, Doris adds, "I still can't believe what happened yesterday. And right here, in our own backyard. *Again.* Makes me sad for us all. New York City has suffered so much."

"I know. It's been hard on all of us," he says as he tries to make eye contact with her. Doris turns away as he continues, "You know everyone thinks our government was behind this."

Doris freezes and turns, looking him directly in the eye for the first time since they met. *"Excuse me?* There's no way. That makes no sense. I, too, saw the cable news coverage of the conspiracy theories, but, as usual, they are just filling airtime until they have more information on the terrorists. That's all it is."

"That's what all you civilians think. And that's how the government wants to keep it. Trust me, ma'am, there are entire government agencies who didn't want Dumont to win. Well, *actually,* no agency was behind him. He was going to shrink those agencies and direct the money toward police departments, schools, and tax breaks for regular folks. I voted for him. We deserve better pay."

"Yes, yes you do," Doris agrees softly.

"The terrorist attack is all we've been talking about at the police station. Most of the guys are betting that the government is behind this one. *I'm* sure of it. If I was one of the Dumont kids, I wouldn't trust anyone with my dad's life. I wouldn't be surprised if someone finishes him off in his hospital bed. That's the real reason why the hospital is blocked off. It's not just to protect him from the terrorists. There are a lot of corrupt leaders, even in our own police force—officers who actually work for the FBI or the

CIA. I've even met some of those guys. I had a colleague who found out his captain was a double agent: police captain by day, FBI agent by night. Those people know everything. They listen to us via our phones—Siri, Google Assistant, you name it. The good news is that maybe we will have a female president sooner than we thought." He gives Doris an awkward wink and half smile.

Doris turns away and grabs the nearby desk for support, but she quickly recovers before he notices. Her mind is racing, and all she can think to say is, "I'm so sorry about your father. I really am. What's your name?"

"Jack Guthrie. And you are?"

"I'm Doris."

"Pleasure to meet you, Doris."

She watches his eyes fall on her bare neckline, and then he looks away rather hastily.

"Best of luck, Officer Guthrie."

"Call me Jack. And thank you. I definitely need some luck. It's now been two days since the attack, and this is my fifth hospital. After this, I will be checking the morgues."

Doris's heart breaks for this man. Without thinking, she walks closer to him and gives him a hug as she wipes a tear from her eye. "You will find your father, Jack. This won't be the end. You have to keep hope alive. Even if there's just a little left, hang on to it fiercely. That's more than many people get. Trust me; I've been there."

◎◎

Doris heads home after her shift, changes into a comfortable pair of pajamas, and pours herself a glass of red wine. Then she goes to find her bottle of Xanax. A self-medicated night of sleep is what she needs to be ready for tomorrow. Just hours ago, she was about to tell the hospital that the president was lying in that room.

But now, after listening to the news, hearing what happened to Alice and Angela, and getting an earful of government conspiracy theories from Officer Guthrie, she's not quite sure how to keep this man safe. As usual, her mind travels to Daniel and the mistakes she made with him. When Daniel was in the hospital, she assumed she could go home and get some rest. She assumed that the hospital staff would stay on top of his care, just for a few hours. But she was wrong. There aren't always people looking out for your loved ones. Only you can do that. She regrets leaving his side and trusting others. This time, she's not going to make the same mistake that could lead to another loss of life, especially one this important to the country.

"Daniel, if you are listening, please give me a sign telling me what to do." She says this aloud, mostly to hear his name but also to help her focus. "Think, Doris, think!"

After another glass of wine, she heads to the bathroom to take the Xanax and get ready for bed. Her bathroom is small, with old pink tiling. She hated that tiling when she moved in, but now she loves it. Ever since Daniel died, the bathroom has felt like her safe place—a place where no one can get to her.

"A safe place." She says this out loud. That's what *he* needs; he needs a safe place. But then what? What did that officer say? That he wouldn't trust the government to keep Dumont safe. Daniel would say, "Trust no one, Doris." He always told her she's too trusting and that the world doesn't work that way. After what's happened over the past couple of days, she can see that her late husband was right. She can't trust anyone right now. For the first time since this ordeal began, she finally has some clarity. She realizes that the only safe place for the president is with his family. But how can she possibly make that happen?

CHAPTER 19

THE BRIGADE

▷ **Doris – Lenox Hill Hospital, Day 4**

Doris wakes from her medicated sleep cautiously optimistic. Plans seem to be presenting themselves to her as if by divine intervention. She goes online and looks up some names. Thirty minutes later, she comes up with a believable combination: Elliot Greene. She will tell Dr. Dansby that the hospital received a call from his daughter, who had been calling all the hospitals, looking for her father. Dr. Dansby won't question her or think twice about it. The hospital was such a disaster right after the attack that everything fell through the cracks. Why wouldn't the same be true for his patients' files? She could doctor the file with the required documentation. The doctors would quit asking so many questions about her patient, and this would buy her enough time to figure out how to get the president safely to his family.

She makes it to Lenox Hill in time for her shift, feeling rested and ready for what the day will throw at her. After catching up on her paperwork, she emails Dr. Dansby and tells him about Elliot Greene and his daughter, Allison, who called from Europe. She elaborates maybe more than she should, but she is feeling confident. After sending the email, she returns to her "Elliot Greene."

"Elliot?" she whispers to him, but, as usual, he doesn't respond. Dr. Dansby still has Elliot sedated, which means he's not moving much, and most of the time, his eyes are closed. But the sound of his new name is perfect; he even looks like an Elliot. Doris is partially glad that he still can't talk, as it buys her more time. The doctors have presumed that this John Doe has lost his memory but expect that it could return at some point.

On her lunch break, Doris sits by Lance's bedside, watching him sleep and wishing she could sleep as soundly. She wipes her forehead and then runs a damp towel across Lance's, taking care to tread lightly around the black-and-blue marks. At least his condition isn't as dire as it looks, or so the doctors say.

While keeping a close eye on him, Doris turns on the television for an update on the Courthouse Massacre, the official name chosen to reference the day of the attack and attempted assassination of President Dumont. So much is still unknown. Doris has had a terrible time trying to sort out fact from fiction, though there are a few facts that have been confirmed. The Secret Service announced that at least twelve domestic terrorists got away that day, and that they're part of an extremist group called the Brigade. All that is known is that the Brigade is made up of many members with military backgrounds. Apart from that, no one has any idea how many members there are or how far their reach extends. The government is confident that the organization is large since the attack was executed on such a grand scale. The media, however, has numbers all over the place, some putting the group at over two hundred, noting that there had to be a large staff working behind the scenes in order to execute such an elaborate attack. They also believe that such an attack would require inside information. *There it is,* Doris thinks, *connections to the US government.* Doris isn't sure what to believe, but she knows one thing for certain: the man lying next to her is still in extreme danger.

The anchorwoman on the cable news channel Doris is watching turns to the latest coverage of yesterday's bomb scare at New York Presbyterian Hospital. Officials located a genuine bomb and managed to disable it before the hospital had to be evacuated. This was a benefit of having a bomb squad on full-time duty at the hospital since the president of the United States was in residence. Strangely enough, the Brigade did not claim responsibility for the bomb. *Then who is responsible?* Doris wonders.

Doris sinks back into her chair and looks over at Lance, who's sleeping. She ought to feel relief, but none is forthcoming. Only four Brigade members have been captured. Four out of twenty, or four out of two hundred? Neither number provides much comfort. She wonders how many died at the courthouse. The numbers have not yet been released.

Doris is aware that she still has to figure out what to do with the president. She knows he can't stay here; it's just too dangerous. She feels certain that this Brigade group is looking for him. The man in the hoodie is likely proof of that. Eventually he, or others, will return to the hospital. She wonders if anyone other than her is aware that the wrong man is lying in bed at New York Presbyterian Hospital. If so, it won't be long until someone from the government comes looking for the president. She needs help. Outside help.

The name comes to her at once: Fatima—her younger sister, who lives in Santa Fe, New Mexico, and who also happens to be her best friend and confidant. No matter how far-fetched her story is, she knows Fatima will believe her. She *has to*. Doris refuses to believe otherwise. She pulls her phone from her pocket, but just as she's about to dial her sister's number, a prick of paranoia hits her: What if she's being monitored? She stares at her phone, worried it might be compromised. Officer Guthrie's face materializes in her mind's eye. Is he watching her? Thinking quickly, Doris pockets her phone and heads to one of the pay phones in the hospital. It's like 1994 here, at Lenox.

Fatima answers on the first ring, much to Doris's relief. "Hello?"

"Hey, girl, it's me. I can't talk long. I have an urgent request. Please don't ask any questions, and more importantly, please say yes to what I'm about to ask you." Doris doesn't want to give her sister any time to say no. "I need to meet you right away, somewhere between New York and New Mexico. Really—as soon as possible."

"Hey, slow down, sis. What's going on? Why are you calling me from an unknown number? Are you in some kind of trouble?"

Fatima had not wanted Doris and Daniel to move to New York. She firmly believes big cities equal big trouble. Doris realizes this story will confirm those fears.

"No—well, *yes*—but it's not what you think. You'll have to trust me on this. You won't believe what I have to tell you, which is why I need to see you face-to-face somewhere between our cities. I need you, Fatima. Please help me, I-I'm scared. I don't know what I'm doing."

"What do you mean by 'between our cities'? And what kind of trouble are you in?"

"Well, I'm thinking St. Louis. Is that OK with you? Tomorrow?"

"But what's the hurry? And if it's so important, why not tell me over the phone right now?"

"I can't! I can't explain, Fatima! The phone—they might be— never mind. I just can't say it here. Fatima, please meet me tomorrow. I'm in danger."

"OK, OK. Tomorrow, then."

"Thank you!!" Doris replies.

"I'll have to call in sick. Should be all right though," her sister says, anxiety audible in her voice.

"Fatima, seriously, you're the best sister ever."

"Yes, I am," Fatima says with a laugh. "But you're OK for now, right, Doris? Do you know how worried I am now?"

"I know. I'm sorry. I'm OK at the moment, I just—I need to talk to you in person. Tomorrow at four at . . . at the St. Louis airport bar called Eighteen 76 in Terminal 1?"

"Sure, Doris. I'll see you there tomorrow. I love you."

"I love you too, sis."

CHAPTER 20

MEET ME IN ST. LOUIS

▷ **Doris – St. Louis, Missouri, Day 5**

When Doris arrives at the St. Louis Lambert International Airport, the first thing she notices are the beautiful arched windows, ceilings, and skylights throughout Terminal 1. For a moment, she takes in the warmth of the winter sun streaming in through the skylights. A thought flashes through her mind: she wishes she had made more time to travel with Daniel to see more of the America she loves. He had urged her to be more adventurous, take more chances in life, and explore the country with him. But Doris always found a reason to stay close to home. So many regrets.

She quickly finds Eighteen 76 in Terminal 1 and finds a quiet spot to sit down. Her stomach is in knots. With no sign of Fatima, she is consumed by fear. Maybe Fatima's phone is monitored, and a Brigade member kidnapped her. But when the clock strikes four, Doris looks up to see a familiar tall, slender brunette heading her way. Fatima's long hair is pulled into a loose ponytail, and she's dressed in athletic wear. Her smile is as big as a basket. Doris is so happy to see her sister's kind face. Grabbing her bag, she sprints to Fatima and wraps her up in a bear hug, squeezing so hard she thinks her arms might fall off. Tears stream down her cheeks and disappear into the shoulder of Fatima's dark-blue shirt. Both sisters shed tears for the time lost between them. Phone calls and texts can't replace face-to-face connection. They look at each other for a long time without speaking, smiling all the while. It's almost as if they have never really *seen* each other before.

"Doris, I'm so glad you're OK," Fatima says with a sniffle. "I can't believe what I've been seeing on the news. I have been trying to call you since the attack, but you haven't picked up. Thank you for at least answering my texts so I'd know you were safe." Her face darkens. "Can you believe what this world has come to? They nearly killed our president and murdered so many people in the process. I-I just can't believe it."

"That's actually why I'm here. Everything you just said." Doris's voice drops to a whisper. "That's it, the reason I needed to meet with you."

Fatima looks deeply into Doris's dark-blue eyes. "What do you mean? Are you connected to this somehow?"

"Yes, but by mistake. I-I'm not sure you'll understand." She takes her sister's hand and leads her to the table she'd picked out earlier in the corner of the bar.

"What do you mean? Doris, don't play games with me. I paid all of this money to fly here, called in sick to work, and now you're saying I won't understand?"

"Don't get mad at me, Fatima. I've been through hell back in New York!"

Fatima bites her lip. "Well, what's this hell all about? What happened?"

"I'll tell you, but let's get a drink first," Doris suggests, realizing she still hasn't let go of Fatima's hand.

"Jesus Christ, Doris! Can you not dig your nails into my skin?"

"I'm sorry." Doris lets go of her sister's hand and waves down a server. After they order a couple of cocktails, she leans in close to Fatima.

"I've never felt so alone. I feel like I've been chosen out of everyone else on Earth. It's as though I've been the one picked to . . . He reminds me of Jesus on the cross. I see him like that when I look at him in the hospital bed. At other times, I see Daniel. I don't know why. And I truly believe that only you and I, as sisters, can bring him back from near death and deliver him back to our country. Maybe we aren't the best people for the job, but we can *try* to help save the country."

Doris stops to breathe and notices Fatima's look of frustration and fear. The server reappears with their drinks, but Fatima doesn't touch hers.

"Doris, just say what you need to say, and cut out the garbage. What do you mean, 'Jesus on the cross'? You're worrying me!"

"The president!" Doris blurts out. "He's not at Presbyterian Hospital, as the country believes. He's in *my* hospital, on *my* floor. He's my patient and under my supervision. They brought in the wrong guy! It was some kind of awful mistake. There were literally dozens of lifeless bodies lying on top of one another. It was hell on Earth. I haven't been able to get the scene out of my head. I'm sure you've seen the images on TV."

Fatima's face is blank with shock. She opens her mouth to speak, but Doris isn't done.

"Fatima, I have the *real* President Dumont, and I'm the only one in the world who knows this. Well, now *you* know too."

"Shit!" Fatima shouts as she springs from her chair. Everyone in the bar turns to look at her.

Doris attempts to yank her back onto her seat. "Sit down! I'm in enough trouble already. Someone might be watching. I'm paranoid and scared enough as it is."

"Wait, OK, wait." Fatima holds up her hands then finally reaches for her cocktail. "How do you know he's really the president? This seems impossible."

Doris guzzles down her cocktail, and leans in. As quietly as possible, she begins her explanation: "I have his ID, government issued with his full name and details. It was in a hidden pocket in his suit jacket. Lance Dumont, male, born August 1, 1974. But that's not really how I know. When I saw the ID, I was sure my patient *wasn't* the president. As you said, that would be impossible. I was sure it was an aide or Secret Service agent who'd been holding the ID, or a fanatical fan, or maybe even a Brigade member, but *not* Lance Dumont. But when I checked him in to the hospital, I noticed a scar on his back. The next day I was looking at pictures of the president and found one taken when he was at the beach just before Christmas. I zoomed in on the image, and he has the exact same scar in the exact same spot. The patient is the same size, weight, eye color, and hair color as well. A bullet grazed his cheek, his *left* cheek, and another grazed the same side of his head, so it's hard to look at his face and see the handsome Dumont we see on the news. I'm sure he will never really look the same as he used to. You and I are the only two people in the world who know this. The most powerful person on Earth is *our* secret." Her last sentence makes her cringe. *What a thing to be proud of.* She can tell by the twisted look on Fatima's face that her sister isn't proud of what she said either.

"So that's what you wanted to tell me? You wanted to rope me into this mess too?"

"No, it's not just that. Fatima, I need your help. Please. I don't know what to do. Have you heard of the Brigade? They're the domestic terrorists responsible for the attack. The government says many members are still at large." Doris motions to the server to bring another round.

"Of course, but—"

"And then there's all these conspiracy theories about our government being involved. It makes sense. How else could they have executed such a large attack? Trust me; I've thought about this *a lot*. It's all I can think about. I was at the scene. I don't get how the Secret Service could've missed all the militia members hidden throughout the audience and in the nearby buildings. Don't they clear locations before the president's arrival? This has never happened before—not like this. This is very different than the Kennedy assassination or the attempt on Reagan's life. They had to have had inside help. I know I sound crazy, but you've got to believe me. I even talked to a cop who insists this is an inside job. Sorry—that's another long story. Anyway, I don't know who to trust. The Brigade is hunting the president, and I-I can't go to government officials, not if they're the ones who let this happen in the first place! I'd be delivering him to his grave. I'm not gonna have someone die on my watch again." Doris pauses for air, and the server approaches with their second round of drinks. "And then, of course, there was the bomb they defused at Presbyterian. The Brigade said they weren't behind it. So someone else is after Lance Dumont."

"Good Lord, honey. This is a lot to take in," Fatima says, reaching for her drink.

"I know it is. And on top of all this, at some point soon, somebody is going to find out that President Dumont is not at Presbyterian Hospital. And that somebody, whoever that may be, will come looking for him." She stops, unsure if she should tell her sister about the guy with the hoodie who came to Lenox Hill and threatened Alice and Angela. She decides to hold back that information for now, as she doesn't want to worry her sister any more than she has already. So she continues her nervous rant: "I'm already involved by having stayed silent for so many days. I didn't mean to—but now I'm in too deep."

She collapses into Fatima's arms, crying softly. She can sense Fatima's hesitation, but after a moment, she feels her sister's arms close around her firmly, rocking her back and forth. This is really what she needed the most from this short visit.

"I need proof, Doris," Fatima says after several minutes of silence.

Doris lifts her face and looks up at Fatima, who keeps talking.

"Look, what you just told me is, frankly, unbelievable. I need to know you're not crazy. I mean, this whole thing is crazy for sure, but I need to know *you're* not crazy."

Before Fatima finishes her sentence, Doris is already reaching into her bra. With a flourish, she pulls out the card and hands it over.

Fatima takes her time in reviewing the details listed on it. Doris nurses her second drink as she watches her sister's gaze slide methodically across and down the card. An audible gasp escapes her. The next moment, she's draining her glass and then reaching for Doris's. Doris hands it over without hesitation, hoping Fatima's stomach is steady enough that she doesn't just throw it all back up.

After draining Doris's drink, Fatima just sits there, slumped over the table with the ID card in her hand. She doesn't move. Her eyes are closed.

Doris waits, counting down the seconds until she loses her patience and reaches over to grab the card from Fatima's fingers.

Her sister finally opens her eyes, looking dazed.

"Do you believe me now?" Doris asks in a low whisper. "My nerves are shot from keeping this to myself. And I wish—God, I wish—I could just make this disappear. But I'm determined to do the right thing, Fatima. To do something big in my life. Something important. I need this. I'm embarrassed to say this out loud, but I *need* redemption."

She can feel the tears welling in her eyes as she talks, and when she looks at Fatima, she sees the pained resignation in her sister's face. She knows Fatima won't fight her on this, not when she gets this way. She doesn't even need to say Daniel's name. Her sister knows her situation all too well.

"OK, so what's your plan?" Fatima asks earnestly. "Have you been able to speak to the president? Is he able to talk or walk? I mean, if and when he's able to do any of these things, or if you come clean, you will be the scapegoat." She pauses, her hands grasping at the empty air. "How would our government even acknowledge that they've had the wrong president? The country is already furious with the lack of security. And—oh God—when the media gets ahold of this! When the attackers find out . . . shit! I don't want you dead, Doris. Nothing is worth that—and I don't want the president dead either, but . . . I can't imagine a good ending for either of you."

Doris motions for the server and orders a third round. "OK, so this is my plan so far. As soon as Elliot—that's the name I gave him—is well enough to leave the hospital, I'll get him the hell out of there. I don't know how yet, but I will. We won't be able to fly without proper identification, but I can rent a car, hopefully under your name, and drive to New Mexico. We can hide out at your place until we figure out how to deliver Elliot back to his family without getting someone killed. I know I can trust his family. That's my plan for a happy ending. What do you think?"

"That's . . . well, I'm not thrilled about opening up my house for terrorists to find us, but it's as good a plan as any. I mean, what else can you do? Of course, you could just take a chance and turn him in, so to speak."

Doris shakes her head, not taking her sister's bait. "I can't. I can't risk handing him over to someone who may be trying to kill him. I have to do this *my* way."

"I know—but he's a time bomb, Doris. Once they find out they have the wrong guy, all hell is going to break loose. There will be madness in DC! New York City will go crazy. There will be rioting in the streets. The Pentagon will have people looking everywhere."

Doris gives her a knowing look; then Fatima reaches forward and clasps Doris's hands in her own. "OK, OK, I'm sure you've thought of all this, but I just want you to be safe."

Doris grips her sister's hands tightly and then glances down at her watch. She has to catch her plane if she wants to get back in time for work tonight. But she needs her sister to know how much she appreciates this—all of it. A warm smile spreads across her lips as she raises her head and catches Fatima's eyes, hoping she can tell her everything with just one look. It's her 'special smile,' as Fatima calls it. A smile for a sister and a best friend, and it never fails to warm Fatima's heart.

"I've missed your smile," Fatima says. "And I especially miss *you*."

Doris's eyes well up again, and she squeezes their hands together. "Me too. I love you. Thank you for listening to me, Fatima, and for . . . for everything. I don't know how to thank you enough."

"We're sisters," Fatima says simply. "We will always be there for each other, no matter what."

CHAPTER 21

RIBBONS

▷ **Doris – Lenox Hill Hospital, Day 6**

oris arrives back at the hospital after midnight—just over an hour late for her night shift. Lance looks better than the last time she saw him, just eighteen hours earlier. The swelling on the side of his face has gone down a bit. The best news is that while she was away, he said his first few words, although none of them were intelligible. It was a miracle they'd all hoped for but didn't expect so soon. Dr. Dansby is planning to remove some of the stitches from Lance's mouth and lips over the next couple of days.

She looks at the calendar on her phone. There are just a few days left before the hoodie guy comes back. There's no way she's going to have Lance still at the hospital, putting her best friends in danger. Doris needs the next few days to plan and prepare for their departure from Lenox Hill. All the what-ifs rush through her mind. What if Lance really doesn't have amnesia? What if he freaks out when he fully comes to, and rejects Doris's help? What if he starts talking and exposes his identity, risking their safety? Part of her just wants to get the hell out of here and walk out the door without saying goodbye. The other part wants to have a chance to talk to Lance for the first time.

Doris keeps the television on the news channel and listens intently to the handsome anchorman as he says, "According to our sources, the president's recovery isn't coming along as well as was initially reported. The acting president, Jennifer Alvarez, is expected to speak at a press conference with the president's doctor, Dr. Dennis Kellerman, first thing in the morning. What we have been told is that President Dumont may not be able to speak for at least a few weeks, maybe even longer. Yesterday, they had to induce a coma in order to keep his vitals stable and allow time for healing. It's a short-term loss for a long-term gain, as his doctor put it."

Doris grabs the remote and switches channels only to see another overly made-up anchorman fill the screen. She wonders why these talking heads need so much makeup. The anchorman seems to be in the middle of his segment. "When we come back, we will continue our report on the Brigade and the new revelations about the militia group's history. Later in the hour, we will discuss other similar extremist groups and how they may have been involved in the Courthouse Massacre, and possibly with the bomb planted at New York Presbyterian Hospital just days ago."

Every media outlet is fixated on the Brigade, with each presenting its own estimate of the number of members. The official size of the organization is still unknown. Doris fears that soon, neighbors will be pitted against one another, not really sure if the extremist they know is part of a militia group. Some news outlets believe that the Brigade was just a conspiracy theory ignited by the US government to cover their own tracks and hide something much more sinister. Every news channel is chasing any militia or conspiracy story to fill their twenty-four-hour news cycle. But there is one thing almost everyone in the country wants: to have the perpetrators of the attack captured so the world will know why this happened and justice can be served.

Doris rubs her eyes wearily. She hasn't had a good, nonmedicated night's sleep since the attack. Every time she closes her eyes, she is back at the courthouse steps, covered in blood, with the sounds of the injured and dying ringing in her head. And now there's more to worry about. As soon as the guy at New York Presbyterian wakes up, they'll know he's not the president, and all hell will break loose. Then the search for the whereabouts of the real president will begin. She's sure that the security agencies will stop at nothing to find Lance Dumont once they know the truth. Before this happens, she needs to be far away from New York City with Lance. But getting in touch with his family without the authorities finding out is an entirely different challenge.

She glances over at her patient, wondering if he will remember trying to pull himself toward her, trying to reach the red ribbon on her lapel. She wonders if he can recover enough from his head injury to make it out of Lenox Hill. When, or even *will*, his memory return? Will he be able to tiptoe back to the things that made him who he was before being shot?

Doris leans over Lance and rubs his shoulders as he looks up at her. She gives him a smile, and to her delight, he attempts to return it. He reaches up to hold her shoulders with both hands, and she pulls him up into a sitting position for the first time. He begins to say something, but she gently puts her index finger to his lips to tell him not to talk. With his left hand, he takes hold of her finger and gives it a gentle squeeze.

After some time, Lance tries to speak again, but the stiches that bind part of his lips and connect to his left cheek pull, and the pain prevents him from moving his mouth. Doris realizes this and puts a finger to his lips once more. Then she moves closer.

"Lance? Lance? Lance?" she asks slowly and clearly. "Can you hear me, Lance?"

To her dismay, he pulls his head back as if to avoid the sound. He then uses a hand gesture to request a pen and paper.

She leaves his side and fetches a blank piece of paper and a pen, then slides them into his grasp. It takes him several minutes to maneuver the pen between his fingers and, his fingers begin to tremble as he moves his hand across the page. He's trying to write, but the scribbles are failing to form letters. Frustrated, he throws the pen and paper at one of the curtains, glaring at it as if it's to blame.

Doris walks around the bed and opens the curtains gently so that he can see out the window. After about ten minutes of watching the rain hit the glass, he tries to get up. Doris moves quickly to give him support. She motions for him to wait while she grabs the walker. With her help, Lance makes it out of bed for the first time, and together, they slowly make their way to the window. He brushes his head and lips against the cold glass. His tears gather on the window and race the rain down the glass. She watches, knowing that she has been the director in this movie they are making. For both their sakes, she hopes Lance turns out to be a good actor.

After a few minutes, she pulls him from the window, wrapping her arm around his waist while pulling his other arm up around her shoulders. Intertwined, they walk to the doorway, from outside of which some of the staff are watching. Lance raises his head to return their smiles, half of his mouth lifting into a sagging grin. Doris gently turns him around and helps him back into bed. Her underarms are sweating so much that she's sure there are visible pit stains on her top, and the back of her neck is damp as well, but Lance doesn't seem to notice. Instead, he points to where her lapel would be if she had one on her scrubs, and draws a heart. Doris does the same, smiling widely. He then twice repeats the gesture. She nods, gratification welling up inside her.

It's clear he remembers she was the one by his side on the day of the attack; it was her ribbon.

Wearing a big grin, Angela saunters into the room. She may have a small frame, but she always fills up the room with her big personality. "So, my dear, what's he trying to say to you? What's happening here?"

"Do you remember that red ribbon I sometimes wear on my jacket? The one I wear in memory of Daniel? Well, I was wearing it on my overcoat when I first saw Elliot at the courthouse. I remember grabbing it just before I left for the courthouse. I knew I'd need Daniel's strength with me on such a horrific day."

Angela started at Lenox Hill at the same time as Doris, nearly ten years ago, and Doris still feels grateful to her for being there during the darkest days after Daniel's death.

Lance waves his hand, tries to speak, and then turns his head and points at Angela.

Angela looks at him and nods. She then turns to Doris and says, "I love that you wear that ribbon, Doris. And what is your character of a patient wanting?" She smiles and walks over to Lance, placing her hand on his shoulder.

Lance points upward to Angela's head.

"Ah! Angela, I think he wants the ribbon in your hair!" Doris says.

Angela removes the ribbon that's tied her hair into a ponytail. Her long, dark hair falls down her back as she takes Doris's hand and ties the black ribbon around her wrist.

Lance points at the ribbon then at Doris's face repeatedly, like a toddler does when he has discovered something clever.

Angela winks at her. "I don't know what you've done to this guy, but whatever it is, it's made him remember you. You may be the only thing he *does* remember." She pauses before adding, "Girl, maybe we should call you Ribbons." She laughs heartily.

Her signature laugh can be heard halfway down the hall of their floor on any given day.

"No way, sweetheart!" Doris can't help herself and joins in the laughter.

"Listen, if any guy called me Ribbons, I would never let him go. Why don't you just let him? And don't tell me that he's not special, Doris—I mean, Ribbons!" Angela giggles like a teenager.

"If you only knew—"

"Don't change the subject. Besides, *I* love the name. And don't worry, I won't tell anyone else about it, I swear."

Doris opens her mouth to argue, but Angela quickly loops her arm through Doris's and guides her into the hallway, pulling the door half closed behind them.

"So, Ribbons." She winks again, then sobers. "Seriously, be careful. We don't know if this is the man that guy was looking for. He said he's coming back in a few days, remember?"

"Of course I remember. I promised I will take care of this. I have a plan."

"I'm not sure I want to know about it." Angela says.

"You *won't* know . . . until the end."

"That man, his knife, and his threat—that's all I've been able to think about. Alice too. We drop our kids off at school and worry that they may not be there when we arrive to pick them up."

"I'm sorry." Doris can't think of anything else to say right now.

"It's not your fault! Anyway, I looked at Elliot's file. That was some crafty thinking—his daughter in Europe. I hope you know what you are doing." Angela pauses, then turns to look at Doris, "I'm also worried about you—that you are getting too attached, like before. Remember, none of your patients are Daniel, honey. You can't redo the past."

Doris can't help but grimace. First Dr. Dansby, now Angela. Doris hates these conversations about Daniel, so she just goes along with them. "Thanks, Angela. I know, and I won't. And I—Doris—promise to be a good girl. But Ribbons—you know she can't be trusted!"

Angela laughs aloud and slaps Doris jokingly on the shoulder before heading down the hallway to attend to her patients.

Doris returns to Lance's bedside. As soon as she's close enough, he grabs her arm, plays with the ribbon around her wrist, then points to the door, gesturing for another walk.

They make it to the door one more time with the use of the walker. But before Doris can open the door, Lance signals that he's too tired to go any farther. She takes him back to his bed and readies herself for the end of her shift. As she says goodbye to Lance, she says a silent prayer that God will give her enough time to figure out a plan to help save this man.

CHAPTER 22

ANYTHING IS POSSIBLE IN DC

▷ **Rose – New York Presbyterian Hospital, Day 6**

Rose is looking out the window of the car. She sees bodies sprawled across the courthouse steps and sidewalk. She rolls down the window despite James's protests. The cries, moans, and screams of the victims overwhelm her.

She suddenly spots Lance lying on the ground. She opens the car door and runs toward him, but just as she gets close, he stands up and starts running away. He turns to smile at her, gesturing with his arm for her to follow—and she does. She runs after him through the dark streets and alleyways of New York City until she reaches a dead end. She cannot see Lance anywhere.

"Lance! Lance!" she shouts as loudly as she can.

"Mrs. Dumont?" says a voice from behind her.

She turns to see Director Cummings.

"Where did Lance go? Did you see him?"

"No, ma'am. He's dead, remember?" Cummings replies.

Rose wakes from her dream. Her heart feels like it stopped for who knows how long. Then she realizes her sheets are wet, and she suddenly feels cold. This is the third night in a row she's had the same dream—or rather, nightmare. It's the same thing over and over again. She tries to put it out of her head as she jumps out of bed to take a hot shower.

"Damn you, Lance, and that stupid speech," she murmurs on her way to the bathroom.

After a long shower, Rose dresses and returns to her *living* nightmare. She's tired of spending her days and nights at the hospital. But she's not just tired; she's also mad and looking for someone to blame. So she picks up the phone and calls Acting President Alvarez.

Jennifer Alvarez grew up in Illinois, the granddaughter of Cuban immigrants who came to the United States just before the Castro regime took over. Lance selected her as his running mate not only to secure the crucial Hispanic vote, but also to represent a demographic that is often overlooked. During his days back on the farm, Lance came to know many of the migrants who traveled to the US for harvest season, and he heard many horrible stories of the plights they faced back home. He also selected Alvarez because she is respected by her colleagues on both sides of the aisle. She's known for being tough, but she's also someone you'd want to have a drink with at the bar. She is tall and intimidatingly pretty, with long, wavy brown hair. She was the first in her family to go to college—and not just any college; she is an Ivy League graduate. She can be funny and always speaks her mind—qualities Rose loves the most about her. Jennifer has proved to be a friend and confidant over the past twelve months. Of course, Rose never expected this friendship to blossom, but it did, and right now, Rose needs a friend more than ever.

Jennifer's aide quickly connects the call, even though her boss is in a meeting.

"Hello, Rose. Everything OK?" asks Jennifer earnestly.

"I'm good. I just need to speak with you rather urgently to discuss something important. But I *am* aware you're busy running the country," Rose adds with a laugh.

"Never too busy for you, Rose," Jennifer quickly replies. "When do you want to talk?"

"I'm sorry to ask this, but as soon as possible? I need to have a private call with you. No aides or assistants. Ordinarily, I would have requested a face-to-face meeting, but both of us are basically prisoners right now."

"You can say that again. How's tomorrow morning?"

"Perfect. Thank you, Jennifer. I promise to make it worth your time."

"No promises necessary, Rose; I'm at your disposal. Talk to you in the morning."

For Rose, tomorrow morning can't come quickly enough.

☯

Rose has mapped out the entire conversation she is about to have with the acting president, knowing she will have to craft her words with care.

She makes the call to the White House and is immediately connected to Jennifer. The pair exchange pleasantries for a few minutes. Then Rose shifts to the business at hand: getting to the bottom of who really did this to her husband and why.

"Let me get to the point, Jennifer: I need your help to determine who's responsible for all of this."

"The Brigade? Every agency we have is on top of that, Rose. You know that. You get the briefings."

"I don't believe everything I read in those briefings," Rose retorts. "You don't believe it's just the Brigade, right?"

"Actually, I *do* believe that," Jennifer responds matter-of-factly.

"OK," replies Rose calmly, "then let me ask you a question: Did Lance ever tell you that James worked for the CIA while he was Lance's campaign director?"

"Excuse me? That's impossible."

Rose can hear that her friend is genuinely taken aback by the news, so she continues, "I was just as shocked, which brings me to my point: Maybe the Brigade had inside help."

"Don't feed into the conspiracy theories, talking heads, and extremists. That's what they want us to do—believe there was someone else pulling the strings. An alternate truth. There's no way. Impossible."

"As impossible as James working for the CIA?"

"Well . . . I . . ." Jennifer stammers, "I dunno. I guess anything is possible in Washington, DC, and I can tell from your tone that you have your own theory. So, let's hear it; I'm open, Rose."

"In a very short period of time, I've learned that the rules DC follows are not the same as those of the average American, or even state politicians. I am convinced that there is no way something that massive could've happened in this country without someone allowing it to happen."

"Allowing it to happen?" Jennifer asks somewhat mockingly. "Come on, Rose. Listen to yourself."

"I've thought about this long and hard. Trapped here, in the hospital, it's pretty much all I can think about. I don't know if James had anything to do with it, but I wouldn't put it past his old boss, Director Schultz. As for the other agency heads, I consider them all guilty until proved innocent. Especially Director Cummings. You have to admit, as the person responsible for protecting the president, he's the most to blame for all of this. And that's why I wanted to talk to you. I need your help. I can't do this alone."

"My help? What can I do?" Jennifer asks, clearly surprised by Rose's request.

"You are the only insider I trust. And you are the acting president of the United States. You can do a lot. I want you to be open to my plan. If not for me, do it for Lance, or just do it for our country."

Jennifer says nothing for what seems to Rose to be an entire minute. Finally she replies, "Yes, I will help you. But what exactly do you need?"

"I want you to open up a congressional investigation into the February 4 attack to find out why our system failed. And I want you to put public pressure on the agencies that failed to flag the risk the Brigade posed to our country and to Lance in particular. Specifically, pressure on Cummings and Schultz. Oh, and the head of the Secret Service Uniformed Division." She pauses to remember his name, then continues, "Ackman. I don't like him. Anyway, I want them to feel the heat. Get the media on them. Please. You know Lance would want this."

Again, Rose waits patiently for Jennifer's reply. She knows her request is not a small one.

Finally, Jennifer speaks: "He *would* want this. You're right. Cutting financing for incompetent, overstaffed agencies was at the top of his agenda. That's why many people voted for him. I will gladly take on that challenge, Rose—for you and for Lance."

Rose smiles triumphantly, thanks Jennifer, and spends the next twenty minutes detailing the intricacies of her plan.

CHAPTER 23

WHY THE RIBBON?

▷ **Doris – Lenox Hill Hospital, Day 7**

The next day, Doris enters Lance's room and opens the curtains for some morning sunshine. Lance appears lifeless, but his eyes are open; he's just staring at the wall. She walks over to his bedside, leans in close to him, and says his real name again, just as she did yesterday: "Lance? Lance? Lance? Can you hear me, Lance?" No reaction. She then says the names of his wife and children: "Rose, June, Thomas, George, Edwina." Still no reaction; he just stares at the ribbon pinned to her scrub top. Since he'd responded so well to Angela's black hair ribbon yesterday, Doris decided to start wearing the same ribbon she wore on her overcoat the day of the attack. Lance's gaze travels upward until it lands on her face. He looks sad and tired. She wonders if he wasn't able to sleep during the night shift.

She's glad she wore the ribbon to work today. For many months after Daniel's death, she'd worn it in his memory. She'd never imagined it would lead to *new* memories, perhaps even a new opportunity to get it right.

Doris decides to give Lance a pen and paper in the hope it will cheer him up. Lance is reluctant at first, but then takes the pen and begins to draw crude pictures of what could be trees and butterflies. It's hard for Doris to tell. His art is slightly better than that of a three-year-old, but at least this is progress.

She leaves the room to get more paper, bigger pieces this time. She wants Lance to grow strong, like the butterflies in his picture, so he can fly out of Lenox Hill Hospital *tomorrow*.

Today is the day to push him. When Lance's mood improves, she encourages him to walk to the end of the hallway. After he has finished his lunch, she makes him walk down the hallway again and then around the corner to the end of the next one. She proudly watches him show off for the staff. His smile stretches his mouth and cheek a bit too much, which brings tears of pain to his eyes. With his head still half bandaged, he looks like a wounded soldier as he waves to the nurses. Lance points to them and then to the ribbon on Doris's scrubs. The nurses look to Doris for an explanation. She tells them that he's just a big goofball. She knows if the nickname Ribbons gets around, it will stick to her forever.

Right now, she's looking forward to Lance's stiches being re-moved, as well as the majority of the bandaging on his head. She has been pushing for this over the last two days. She needs Lance to look less like a patient in twenty-four hours, when they'll leave the hospital. Her mind drifts to the man in the hoodie and what Angela told her he'd said, "I'll be back in a week." Those words ring in her head every day.

⊚⊚

At the end of the day, Doris slips away to meet with Dr. Dansby and two of the ward specialists in a small meeting room on the ground floor of the hospital. She's been dreading this meeting, but she won't give up. She can't. The doctors have threatened to move Elliot to a residential treatment facility to get the specialized care they believe he needs.

"Let's try two more days here," she argues. "His progress has been significant. Give me a little more time, please. I know he will continue to make big improvements. I promise." She flashes her famous smile. "You know the quality of my work. Let me try a little longer, please."

These guys know her history, so they are easily convinced that more time might just do the trick. Doris is stubborn and persistent, but usually right. She goes on to explain her plan, including the therapy schedule and the methods she will employ to ensure his recovery, both physical and mental. But in reality, this patient will be gone before they know it.

"Why have you taken such an interest in this patient?" one of the specialists asks. "I mean, you can barely see his face with all those bandages. How are you connecting to a patient who looks more like a mummy than a man?" No one laughs at his poor attempt at a joke.

"To be honest, I've had a very traumatic life experience. I can't even begin to explain what it was like at the scene of the Courthouse Massacre. That's my connection to him, my empathy for him. From the moment I found Mr. Greene on the sidewalk below those courthouse steps, I knew I could save him. That's it. Nothing more, nothing less. This is me doing my part, like everyone else here."

The two specialists turn to leave. Doris smiles again with the satisfaction that she has won this round. She pushes her chair back from the old oak table and leaves the room to head back to her station. But Dr. Dansby stops her along the way.

He looks at her, then at the ribbon. "Why the ribbon?"

His question takes Doris back to when she found it in a boutique many years ago. She first noticed the lapel ornament when she was paying for a dress she'd fallen in love with. At its crest, a vibrant red silk ribbon was elegantly wrapped around a ring, forming a circle. Its delicate tails then cascaded gracefully downward.

When she arrived home that evening, Daniel noticed it immediately. She remembers this moment as clearly as she would if it took place last week. Daniel told her it was beautiful and that it complemented her blue eyes. He then said he loved it when she wrapped her long blond hair into a bun, explaining how it looked to him like a bouquet of sunny marigolds. He was poetic, romantic, and always by her side. She loved him more than life itself, and over the past year, she has felt her loneliness grow deeper every day.

The sound of Dr. Dansby clearing his throat brings Doris back to the present. Her cheeks feel hot. "When Daniel told me how much he loved it, I began to wear it every time I left the house. He went wherever I went. After he was gone, I continued wearing it. It was my way to keep him with me. I stopped wearing it on a daily basis a few months ago, and I haven't worn it to work until recently." She hesitates briefly before continuing, "Now I wear it because Elliot seems to respond so well to me when I do. The ribbon seems to be all he remembers from the day I found him."

The doctor smiles, a rare occurrence. "I've worked with you for a long time, Doris. And I know we've had this conversation already, but still, I'm worried about you. I did talk to human resources, and they are looking for a therapist. As you can imagine, they are in high demand right now. I just want to make sure you get through all this. You've been through a lot over the last year."

Doris changes the subject: "Thank you for agreeing to remove Elliot's stitches and bandages."

"You were right; it's time. He's healing perfectly."

As planned, Doris sows some seeds of deceit: "I've heard his daughter—I think her name is Allison—is already on a plane back to New York. Guess she was in Europe. She should be here tomorrow. That will make Elliot happy. Hopefully, seeing her will trigger his memory."

"That's good news, Doris. I'm sure it will help him."

With that accomplished, Doris takes the elevator to the second floor and heads to Lance's room. She sits at the foot of his hospital bed and watches him sleep. She thinks about his safety, and her mind starts racing again.

With just hours to go, Doris's plan is coming together. Yesterday, she called the hospital's administration department, saying her name was Allison Greene. She said she would be back in the States within twenty-four hours and she would be coming straight to the hospital to see her father. Now all Doris needs to figure out is how exactly to forge the discharge paperwork, which requires a doctor's signature.

She tries to picture herself on the run with Lance and wonders how to hide a man whose image has been seen millions of times. She tries to guess just how many pictures must have been taken of the president during his campaign. But President Lance Dumont and Elliot Greene do not look much alike now. After losing nearly ten pounds, having his wavy hair shaved, and gaining some significant facial scarring, he looks more like a war veteran, albeit a handsome one.

"Doris?" A dark, curly head of hair pops around the corner.

"What's up, Alice?"

"I have it on good authority that you're pushing poor Elliot to the brink. If you keep this up, you can both enter the next marathon!" Alice shakes her head with a chuckle, and her shiny rhinestone necklace swings loosely around her neck. No matter what, she always finds a way to wear a little sparkle in her outfit. "At least he's recovering quickly; it'll make your job a little easier."

Doris smiles with pride. "Yes, he is doing well. Thank you. I've been worried about his ankle. It was so swollen from the fall down those slippery steps, but he's walking so much better now."

"Yes, but . . ." Alice pauses, her voice uneasy. "I'm scared for the two of you, and for the two of us left behind."

"Leaving is the right choice," Doris says quickly. She told Alice and Angela about her plan to leave the hospital with "Elliot" yesterday when they had their morning break. "That man is coming back in a couple of days. You two have kept your mouth shut, just as he demanded, and you can tell him that Elliot's gone home with his daughter. This is the best we can do."

Alice tears up. "Maybe *we* should have left with our families."

Doris puts her arm around her for comfort. "You know you can't uproot your families. You have jobs, school, and support here. This was our best option. The three of us agreed to this plan."

"I know. You're right, but—"

"But nothing. We have a plan; let's stick to it. It's a good one. I just need you two to cover for me, and soon this will all be over. Once that man sees you haven't gone to the police and that Elliot is no longer here, there will be no reason for him to return."

"But where will you go, and what will you do? The burden's fallen on your shoulders. That's not fair to you."

"It is fair; this is something I *want* to do. You just have to trust me on that."

Alice gives her a hug and then leaves Doris with her thoughts. Doris putters around Lance's room, tidying things up and stealing glances at him every now and then. *Tomorrow feels too soon,* she thinks to herself.

Moving silently across the room, she bends over Lance.

"Lance, wake up. Lance?" His eyes open slowly. "I want to help you, so you're going to have to hear me out and trust me. I need to know you can understand me. Smile if you do."

Lance gives Doris a puzzled look, points at the ribbon on her scrub top, and smiles.

Doris softens her expression and lowers her voice. "Lance, you can call me Ribbons. It can be our secret code." She pauses to make sure he's really listening. "But what I really want, more than anything, is for you to start speaking, saying anything, just a word or two. You need to show me you can do it. I know you can. Do it for Ribbons."

He looks at her in his boyish way and stretches out his arms. Doris grins and hugs him tightly. Then Lance takes her hands and gives her the smile she's been waiting for since the day they met. That smile of encouragement is all she has really needed.

As she goes back to straightening up his room, a sudden exhaustion hits her down to her bones and casts doubt into her mind. *Where am I going to get the strength I need to leave with him?* she wonders. Overcome by the flood of emotion and fatigue, Doris sinks her face into one of Lance's extra pillows and cries a symphony of tears.

☺☺

Doris leaves work early to purchase all the things she needs to take with her to her sister's home in New Mexico. She started the list three days ago, and as of now, it includes, among many other items, new clothing for Lance, healthy snacks, and enough bandages and antibiotic ointments to make sure Lance's wounds remain clean and sterile. The biggest challenge so far was getting Lance's prescriptions, drugs that will prevent infections and keep him on the road to recovery while keeping him calm. But thanks to Angela's help yesterday, Doris was able to secure all that she needed—no questions asked.

Without thinking, Doris pours herself a large glass of wine and switches on the TV. Almost immediately, she regrets her decision to turn on the television. ABC is debuting its new show,

American Extremists, a six-part series that explores the radicaliza-
tion of American citizens, cult aspects of extremist organizations,
and the brainwashing of their members. The Brigade is just one
US-based antigovernment militia group. It happens to be the largest, but the series focuses on five additional groups as well. These
groups have three things in common. First and foremost, they
have a common objective: to overthrow US officials who are not to
their liking and replace them with their own leaders. Second, they
are fear-based groups. Fear is their religion, a god they worship
more than the Christian God whose word they claim to follow.
Third, they're angry. As with the gangs that have been around
for decades, members join these militia groups to channel their
anger and frustration about life not going their way.

Doris sinks into her couch, sipping absentmindedly from her
wineglass. A deep sense of purpose replaces her anxiety and
fear. She's now certain that running with the president is the
right thing to do, no matter how crazy it seems. The threats are
real and increasing every day. With a trembling hand, she grabs
her list and looks it over. She adds to it several types of soft fruit,
knowing Lance's ability to chew will be limited to soft foods.
She's bought protein bars and nuts for herself and applesauce
and bottled protein shakes for Lance. These staples should suffice
between stops at the fast-food chains along the highways.

Closing her eyes, she leans back and allows herself to dream
of wide-open spaces and the wind in her hair, getting away from
the hustle and bustle and the danger of the city. Last night, Doris
came across a website on which people can create identity cards.
She created an Illinois driver's license in the name of Allison
Greene, age twenty-four, and already filled out the official discharge form. All the hospital needs is the proper documentation.
Angela and Alice promised to handle the doctor's signature.

Doris and Lance are ready to run.

CHAPTER 24

NEW RECRUITS

▷ **Edwina – New York Presbyterian Hospital, Day 8**

I t was crowded at the hospital, particularly in the ICU. But five days ago, a makeshift suite, right next to their dad's room on the fifth floor, was created for the First Family, one of Rose's many demands. They now have the entire floor, which previously housed staff members' offices. Acting President Alvarez readily agreed to provide financial support to the hospital to make sure that it could continue to accommodate victims of the Courthouse Massacre and cover the cost of their care.

This morning, Thomas and Edwina are alone in the mini kitchen after a night shift at their father's bedside. Thanks to their mother's twenty-four-hour schedule, ensuring their father is never left alone, as well as her paranoia following the massacre, the responsibility became that of her children, as they're the only ones she trusts. She especially doesn't trust the Secret Service, whose agents are permanently stationed outside their doors, a situation Edwina finds irksome. Her mother requested that some other division's people replace the Secret Service agents, such as National Guard soldiers, but her request was denied.

Tipping her chair onto just its rear legs, she leans backward to see if anyone is around. The hallway is mostly empty, so she gets up to shut the door, catching a glimpse of the straight-backed agents posted right outside. She knows this won't provide total privacy, but she likes the feeling of having something solid between her and *them*. At least then, she can pretend no one else is there. There are always people around—so many doctors and nurses in and out of their dad's room at all times of the day and night. And of course, there are the Secret Service agents. Edwina doesn't hold anything against the agents themselves; it's what they represent that doesn't sit well with the Dumont family: a government they don't trust. Her whole family has been watching the news, and she's sure her mother and siblings have their own conspiracy theories about the attack, but they've kept those thoughts to themselves. At least, they have until now.

Edwina settles herself back in her chair and grabs an apple from the fruit bowl on the table. She pulls out her phone and scrolls absentmindedly through her texts, munching noisily.

"Edwina," says Thomas.

She can hear him, but she pretends she can't.

"Edwina!" When she still doesn't look up, a small, squishy object hits her squarely in the chest. Edwina yelps and brushes it off before realizing it's just a grape.

"Geez, Thomas. What's up?"

"What you said the other day—I mean, the more I think about it, the more I think you were right." Noticing that Edwina looks lost, Thomas taps his fingers impatiently on the table. "I believe they *did* bring in the wrong man. Maybe this guy is *not* our father."

Edwina stops munching and looks at him, her face frozen.

"I'm serious." Thomas leans forward, clasping his hands in front of him. "There have been many attempts to murder US presidents over the centuries. And you remember all the death threats Dad was getting. Anyway, for the past few days, I've been noticing small things about whoever that is in the hospital bed. Things that just don't look or feel like Dad. I know his face is mostly covered in bandages and tubes, but I remember his hands and arms looking different. And it's not just that. I don't know what or who to believe. Maybe that's because of the news; I dunno. What I *do* know is that I don't want to piss Mom off or have her freak out again. But that attack—it was way too big to have gone unnoticed by the CIA, FBI, *and* Secret Service. How could they *all* miss it? There had to be someone or some organization within our government on the Brigade's side to help them go unnoticed. It would've been impossible otherwise. So, if that's the case, who helped them? How deep is this, and who can we trust?"

Edwina smiles at Thomas with confidence, realizing that perhaps she *does* have an audience. "I think anything is possible. Look at Kennedy; they never found a motive, and they never found out who was *really* responsible for his assassination. That was decades ago! I'm sure it was our government. Most people agree. Like Dad, Kennedy wanted to change things too fast." She pauses before adding, "So what can we do?"

"If we start snooping and Mom gets ahold of it, she'll lose her mind. Maybe we can start asking questions casually and see if stories match up? And if this isn't Dad, then where is he? Is he even alive? I mean, where do we begin to look? Maybe this is all crazy, and we've just been cooped up in this hospital for too long. If only Dad, or whoever he is, could talk."

Edwina straightens up, dropping her apple core to the floor. She retrieves it and continues: "What if the doctors are also involved? That would change everything! Maybe they're keeping him in a coma on purpose—preventing him from waking and talking! Is there anyone here we can trust? Maybe we need to start thinking about bringing in our own team of doctors, ones who know Dad and who we know and trust."

Thomas stares at her. "Wait, remember what they told us?" he asks. "Dad was found with his overcoat off; it was lying near him on the steps. Who removed it? Was it him? And why? It was freezing. Also, did the Secret Service or any of us check his clothes to confirm they're his? And now that I think of it, I remember how frightened James, Schultz, and Cummings looked when you told them they brought in the wrong guy."

"Exactly what I've been thinking! Do we know where his clothes are from that day? They must be here, in the hospital."

"I think Mom asked, and the Secret Service said they'd follow up and not to worry about it. I thought nothing of it at the time." Thomas grips the edge of the table. "What the hell is happening here?"

Edwina hoped she was wrong when she shared her fears about their father, but her gut told her she was onto something. "If only we could tell Mom—she'd know what to do."

"Oh yeah—*you* tell her," Thomas says rolling his eyes. "The best thing to do is to tell George so he can help us. Let's not tell Mom anything until we have proof. *Anything.*"

Later that afternoon, while their mother is meeting with Dr. Kellerman, Thomas and Edwina lead George to one of the empty meeting rooms. Upon entering the room, George, the tech geek that he is, checks the room for bugs and locks the doors before they sit down. Normally, Edwina and Thomas would be teasing him about his paranoia, but things are different now.

"What's going on? Why are you guys so serious?" George asks when he's done securing the room. "Before you ask, I haven't said a damn thing to the press or even left this building!"

"Calm down, George. For once, it's not about you." Edwina looks at Thomas and then blurts out, "We think that isn't Dad in the bed next door."

George rolls his eyes and shakes his head. "Not this again. Come on! Really? I thought Mom set you straight. And now you too, Thomas? You don't think that's our dad in there?"

"Just listen to us for a second," Thomas proposes. "Sit down. I thought this sounded crazy when Edwina said it on the day of the attack, and I know it still sounds a bit crazy. We hope we're wrong, but if there's just a 10 percent chance that we're right, we owe it to Dad to look into this. If that isn't him, and he's still out there, we've got to find him before anyone in the Secret Service, CIA, FBI, and especially the Brigade does." He bites his lip. "Unless the Brigade already has him."

George slowly sits down, his voice low and verging on anger. "Why on earth would you want to find Dad before the Secret Service and CIA do? They're *our* people, for Christ's sake! Shit— please don't give me any of that crazy media brainwashing stuff! What's with all the suspicion? Our Dad may actually die here, and we're wasting time dreaming up conspiracy theories for shits and giggles?"

"Think back to the presidential assassination of John F. Kennedy, or the assassination of Bobby Kennedy," Thomas urges. "No one knows who really killed them or why. What we do know is our government holds many secrets about both and was most likely involved in some way. And it could've just happened again—with our dad. Think about it, George. The massacre proved that they can't be trusted. I don't understand how you can defend a government that let this attack happen. Aren't you angry with them? Aren't you angry that so many people died, many of them civilians?"

George sighs. "OK, OK, I'll listen. But it better make sense, because if your crazy accusations get beyond these four walls, it'll be one of the worst things that could happen to our family. But if any of this is true, then we're all in real danger."

"We know." Edwina's expression hardens; she's glad her new recruit is open to coming on board. "If these agencies were working for me, I would fire all these sons of bitches and start fresh. And I would do it before they could even reach for the door."

"I don't believe my ears! Such language! And from a soon-to-be nun, no less." Grinning, George wags his finger at her.

"Well, I never!" Thomas adds with a laugh.

Edwina ignores them. "The more I think about Dad, the more my conviction feels right. If we can find his clothes, we'll at least have some proof that it's him, right? We'll also need to secretly test his DNA to see if it matches ours. I'm more than happy to give blood."

Thomas looks thoughtful. "Now that I think about it, no one has provided us with any proof that it *is* Dad. Sure, he looks kinda like Dad, but that's about it. It's impossible to tell with all the tubes and bandages. Has Mom even looked closely at his body for any distinguishing marks? She knows his body best. Do you guys know of any scars he has that we should be looking for?"

George shakes his head. "I don't know of any, but you know . . . now that I think about it . . . Dad would be recovering a lot quicker. Dad is, or was, in great shape, strong and unshakable. The doctors keep saying recovery has been much slower than expected. Dad is a lot of things, but slow isn't one of them."

None of them speaks for a while. They're thinking about all the possible scenarios—as well as some *impossible* scenarios.

Thomas is first to break the silence. "Guys, maybe it really is Dad down the hall. Maybe it's just that we don't want it to be him. Like you said, George, we want to believe our dad would never allow this to happen. And if it did, he'd be walking and talking by now." He lets out a heavy sigh. "But of course, we think our dad is Superman. He became the president of the United States, for Christ's sake. But he isn't infallible. I don't know. This all feels overwhelming. We're all alone in this—no one to talk to and no one to trust. And the world is watching."

Edwina wants to refute his reasoning, but she knows she can't. He has a valid point. There are too many questions without answers and no one who can help them. They can't even leave the hospital by themselves to grab some takeout, let alone go searching for their father. But that only means they have to get creative in the face of danger, and Edwina knows that's something she's good at.

CHAPTER 25

SAVING ALL OUR LIVES

▷ **Doris – Lenox Hill Hospital, Day 8**

Tonight's the night. Doris pulls the gray rental car, which she rented under Fatima's name, around the corner of the hospital, away from the parking lot's cameras. Psyching herself up, she exits the vehicle and walks through the sliding doors for what will probably be the last time in her life. This final trip to her floor will be either the best choice or the biggest mistake she has ever made. Only time will tell.

Her walk to Lance's room is quick. Since it's the night shift, there are fewer workers on the floor, so she slips into his room without anyone seeing her. Lance is sleeping peacefully, so she grabs the thermos of coffee she prepared and gently shakes him awake.

"Good morning, Lance. I hope you slept well." She offers him the thermos of coffee with extra cream and sugar, just the way he likes it. He eagerly accepts it. Suddenly she's overtaken by a memory of Daniel, who also liked extra cream and sugar in his coffee. How did she not recognize that similarity until now? She shakes her head to get Daniel out of her mind. Now's not the time.

"I'm looking forward to our adventure," she says as she helps Lance into a fresh pair of underwear and a T-shirt covered by a clean hospital gown. By now, it's nearly 5:30 a.m., so Doris heads over to the nurses desk and tells them that the hospital's discharge planner called to advise her that "Elliot's" daughter has finally arrived to take him home. None of them even bother to look up—except Alice, that is. Doris chose this timing on purpose; she needed Alice and Angela to be there.

"Elliot is so excited to see his daughter. She's downstairs waiting. I hope he recognizes her." There's still no response from anyone at the desk.

Alice walks over to Doris and whispers in her ear, "I hope you know what you are doing."

"Hopefully, I'm saving all our lives, including his."

"I know you are. But just the same, be careful. I love you." Alice wipes away a tear.

Doris squeezes Alice's hand but avoids looking directly at her. She knows Alice has a million questions to which she doesn't want to know the answers, and Doris wouldn't answer them anyway. It would put Alice and Angela in even greater danger.

"Before I forget, I left some of Elliot's paperwork on his bed. His daughter filled it out, and it includes a copy of her driver's license," Doris says loudly enough for all to hear. "Do you mind grabbing the paperwork and finishing it, dear?"

As Alice walks away, Doris steers Lance down the hallway in a wheelchair, standard practice when discharging patients. They get into the elevator and head to the ground floor. When the doors open on the first floor, she ushers him into a janitorial supply room down the hall and around the corner without anyone seeing. They slip inside, and she locks the door behind them, keeping the lights off. The green exit sign above the back door provides enough light for them to see. Doris pushes aside a supply box to reveal her hidden stash: a plastic bag filled with clothes.

Doris dresses Lance first: black socks, a black sweater, khakis, and black sneakers. His clothes hang on him a bit, but other than that, he looks like just another man in his forties. Now that he is dressed, she examines his wounds and finds no bleeding. "Thank God," she says under her breath. The fresh skin on his face still looks raw, but she hopes the fake reading glasses and cap she purchased are enough to hide the wounds that will surely scar him for life. She's planning to bandage them later so they don't get infected.

Switching focus, Doris pulls from the bag her own change of clothes: black pants, a white blouse, and comfortable but fashionable shoes for the long trip ahead. She takes her hair out of the ponytail it's in and brushes it out. The red ribbon on her blouse matches her red earrings. Glancing at herself in her pocket mirror, she's satisfied no one will recognize her. After all, they've never seen her with her hair down or dressed this way. Plus, she hasn't interacted much with anyone on the ground floor. Working in a hospital with thousands of employees means it's easy to go unrecognized. She grabs the remaining wardrobe items from the bag: two black overcoats to keep them warm.

"OK, Lance," she says as she turns around to help him up. "Let's get the heck out of here!" She then leans in close and whispers, "And from now on, you have to be Elliot when we're out there, so just play along."

Lance grins, and she directs them out of the room via the exit where trucks usually pull up to unload janitorial supplies. The best part of her plan is that the door's alarm hasn't worked for over a month. She knows a lot of the staff members have been using this convenient exit to steal a smoke, but thankfully, no one is there as they hobble out into the dark. Doris navigates Lance to the small ramp, avoiding the stairs as she embraces the early-morning air. It won't get light outside for at least another forty minutes.

As she walks Lance to her car, Doris feels grateful for human habits, in this case, those of Travis, the night shift security guard. She's known him for years and picked up on the fact that he is truly a creature of habit, never failing to take his breaks at exactly the same time every shift—like clockwork. He also never fails to extend those breaks by an extra ten minutes, allowing her to pad her timing. Lance follows her guidance and stays close to the hedges of the parking lot. She can feel him shivering.

"I know. I'm sorry it's so cold, Elliot," she whispers, puffs of warm breath escaping from her mouth.

She quickens their pace. Once they reach the car, she opens the door and carefully guides him into the passenger seat, which she has already placed in the reclined position, with a big pillow strapped to the headrest. Doris tucks him in and adjusts his seat belt. Then she gets into the driver's seat and pauses. Staring at herself in the rearview mirror, she thinks, *What am I doing?*

"Snap out of it!" she hisses aloud, but she sees only fear in her eyes. Tilting the mirror, she angles it downward to reflect her ribbon, which she previously pinned to her new black overcoat. "OK, Ribbons, this is *your* moment. Please take it from here. Doris can't do this."

She places her hand on Lance's leg and pats it gently, then shoots him a nervous smile. While pulling a bag from under her seat, she asks him to remove his cap and glasses. There's already a bit of dried blood from one of the healing wounds on the side of his face, so she carefully applies a small bandage and then reaches into the back seat for an ice pack. She suddenly freezes.

"Damn it!" she exclaims. "I forgot ice packs! I knew I'd forget *something*, Elliot." It was inevitable. There were too many things on her list.

Lance fidgets beside her, whimpering as sweat starts to bead on his forehead and above his upper lip. She wipes it off with a tissue and looks in her purse to see if she mistakenly put the ice packs in there. Nothing. Maybe she put them with the rest of the medical supplies, but that bag is buried deep in the trunk. She can't be unloading suitcases from her trunk so close to the hospital. Frustrated and unsure, she hovers her hand over the key to the ignition. She knows she needs to get the hell out of here now.

A sudden bang on the window nearly makes Doris jump out of her skin. A yelp escapes her throat. The silhouette of a dark figure taps on the glass, motioning for her to roll down the window. Doris gulps. It has to be Travis, the security guard, here to bust her. If only she hadn't forgotten the ice packs, she'd be gone by now.

Sighing, she rolls down the window, but instead of seeing Travis's stern, grizzled face staring down at her, all she sees are two hands holding a stack of ice packs. After a moment, a familiar face comes into view.

"Angela?"

"Hey, honey." Angela drops the ice packs into Doris's lap and grins.

"What the hell are you doing out here?"

"I thought I would be your angel of mercy tonight. I knew you'd need one, you crazy girl. I don't know who this guy is, and I don't know why there are people after him, but I know you are trying to help us all remain safe, so thank you for that. You also know we will cover for you. Alice and I have your back. I found the papers on Elliot's bed. It's all good. We know what to do; we will get the signatures for his release. I don't know how, but I *will* make it happen. I don't know how long it's going to take the hospital to figure this all out. We are lucky this place is such a mess right now. I hope you know what you're doing. But I don't know *what* we will do when that guy comes back. It'll be any day now."

"Just tell him the patient's daughter checked him out of the hospital. Give him the full file if you need to; it will lead to a dead end. Just keep your family safe."

She grips the steering wheel tightly as Angela leans in and pushes a lock of Doris's hair behind her shoulder. Her face is soft; her voice, sad. "You're going to get far away from here, right?"

"Yeah, that's the plan. I know you deserve more of an explanation, and I promise to give you one, to tell you the truth, but I can't right now. You just have to trust me." Doris squeezes Angela's hand.

"I do. But you bet your ass I'll be holding you to that promise," Angela says with a chortle.

Doris smiles. "Thanks again, Angela. And thank Alice for me. I can't tell you where we're going; you already know too much for your own safety. Play dumb for me, will you? Just this once, please play dumb."

"I'll stick to the story," Angela promises, her voice wobbling ever so slightly. "Just be careful."

Doris starts the engine. "Stay safe! I love you, and I hope I'll see you soon."

As Doris rolls up the window, Angela calls out softly, "Goodbye, Ribbons!"

Doris considers saying something in return but decides it's best to keep her mouth shut. *Ribbons.* The name sounds good on her. She tightens her grip on the wheel. *Well, Ribbons, it's up to you now.*

CHAPTER 26

WELCOME TO NEW MEXICO

▷ **Doris – Highway 70, Indiana, Day 8**

The trip from New York City to Santa Fe takes around thirty-one hours if one drives straight through with no breaks. Doris has divided the trip into five six-hour segments. Each segment will end at a rest stop along the way for a two-hour nap, and they'll take one restroom-and-food break at the halfway point. The whole trip will take almost two full days—an exhausting experience, but one she's well prepared for, thanks to her job. She's grateful that long shifts and lack of sleep were part of her training.

Doris is viewing the road trip as an opportunity to talk to Lance so that he can get to know her a little better. This is partly to keep her awake while driving for so long and partly to share with him her life story during the times he is awake. She isn't sure what he overheard about her story during the first segment of their drive, but she feels it is important to say it aloud to him— even if he doesn't understand all of it.

After a long nap, they get back on the road for their third segment of the trip somewhere in Indiana. Doris picks up where she left off before the rest stop. "I know I've mentioned Daniel's name a hundred times. But he really *was* my everything. I feel like my life didn't really begin until I met him, when I was thirty-one years old. Sounds sad when I say it out loud, but it's the truth. We left Washington because we wanted to start our life together somewhere new—where neither of us had ever lived. We were both obsessed with New York City, so it was an easy decision. We agreed we'd give it six months. If we didn't like it, we would move. But, of course, we loved it—all the nuances, the beauty of feeling like we were a part of so much one moment, and all alone, the next. We absolutely *loved* the museums, in particular, the 9/11 Memorial & Museum. I'm sure you've been there. The visit can be draining, but it leaves you believing in people again. All those heroes from that day and beyond. I was always envious that I never got to be there during that period. I would have loved working the hospitals during that time and helping those people."

She wipes a tear from her cheek.

"Just thinking about it makes me cry. I wanted to be there. I almost flew across the country to see how I could help. But of course, I couldn't. No one could fly, and I wasn't even a nurse yet. But I knew that's what I wanted to do with my life: help people during a crisis. In fact, that sad day in American history validated my desire to become a nurse. It all clicked after that, and that's when my path became clear to me." She turns to look at Lance, and his eyes are heavy.

Six hours pass, and it's now time for a quick bathroom break. Doris is craving salty snacks. As they sit in the car, enjoying their convenience store treats, she feels some relief that they have reached the halfway point without any issues. Lance is holding up well and is in good spirits. She's glad that he's been eating solid foods without issue.

Lance falls asleep by the time they are back on the freeway. five hours later, he is still sleeping when they pull into the parking lot of McDonalds. Doris takes the opportunity to get out of the car, stretch a bit, and get some fresh air. She watches him from a distance and can't help but smile. She is finally doing something important in her life—even if it fell into her lap. Maybe she's changing the course of history. This is *her* chance to make a difference, and for that she is thankful. It's her job to protect Lance from the US government, the Brigade, and all the other extremist groups now taking up arms.

When Doris goes back to the car to wake up Lance, she finds he's still sleeping soundly, so she decides to get back in the driver's seat and try to steal some sleep as well. Upon waking three hours later, she is startled to see a police car parked next to them. She looks around. The parking lot is nearly empty, and it's dark. What time is it, and how long have they been here? Worried she's about to get an unwanted visitor, she pretends not to notice the police officer and hopes he will drive away. But no luck.

The officer rolls down his window and motions for her to do the same. "Everything OK in there?" he asks.

Doris reluctantly rolls down her own window, but just a few inches, "Hello, officer. How can I help you?"

"I was asking if you two are OK, ma'am," he replies sternly.

"Yes, sir. We're fine. I was just resting my eyes while my husband was sleeping. We stopped for water and some snacks." Doris flashes her winning smile, hoping that a little charm might make this problem go away. But her smile fails her this time, and the police officer gets out of his car with his flashlight in hand. He turns it on and shines it through her open window. The beam of light moves from her face to Lance's and then finally down to her cleavage, where it lingers just long enough to make the officer soften his tone.

"I didn't mean to startle you," he says, turning off his flashlight. "Just trying to do my job. The way you just looked at your husband reminds me of how I look at my wife."

"That's OK, officer; I understand. I'm glad you checked up on us. He was in a terrible car accident recently. It nearly left me widowed." In order to display her old wedding ring, she presses her left hand to her chest, as if the memory of even speaking about it pains her.

The officer's eyes soften further, and Doris tries to ignore the guilt of using a relic from her past as part of her plan. But she didn't have much choice; the ring is her best way to legitimize their relationship during their trip. She had struggled with the decision. After all, it was the ribbon on her lapel that represented her late husband, and now the ribbon is her link to Lance. On top of that, she is using her wedding ring to protect him—or rather, the both of them. For a fleeting moment, she feels guilty and second-guesses her intuition. But it doesn't feel wrong in her heart. Daniel always said her intuition was her gift. It proved to be correct dozens of times over the course of their marriage.

"We're on our way to St. Louis, to my brother's home," she continues. "He's away on vacation for a month and said we could use his house to recuperate. There's a wonderful rehabilitation center a mile away."

"I'm so sorry, ma'am." The officer straightens and gestures around the dark lot. "But you've gotta be careful about being in an empty parking lot in the middle of the night. I see a lot of bad things happen on the road. There are a lot of predators looking for vulnerable people, which the two of you definitely are." His expression changes. "Why don't you just get a motel? That would be a lot safer than sleeping in your car."

"Thank you, sir. Perhaps we will."

Doris turns to Lance and grabs his hand; it's as cold as ice. The window has been down too long. She has to get rid of the police officer.

"Can I offer you any assistance?" the officer asks.

"Actually, I don't want to leave him in the car alone. Would it be a bother to get us some water and snacks if you're going into the store? Anything will do just fine."

"Of course, ma'am."

Doris smiles and hands him a twenty-dollar bill, then watches him walk away. Once his back disappears into the store, she turns to Lance, shaking him gently by the shoulder.

"Elliot? Elliot! Honey, pay attention. I need your help. Can you do something for me, Elliot? Just wake up, please."

Lance comes to quickly, rubbing the sleep from his eyes and trying to adjust his vision. His eyes fall upon her ribbon as she pulls a bottle of smelling salts from her purse. She holds it beneath his nose, watching his eyes open wider as he inhales. She hopes this works, that the police officer will see he's OK, leave, and forget he ever saw them. As Lance shakes his head, snorting, she puts her purse in the back seat and rolls the window down again just as the door to the convenience store opens and the cop strides toward them, plastic bag in hand.

"Here you go, ma'am." He offers her the bag and some change through the window.

"Thank you so much," she says earnestly, reaching through to shake his hand. "Really. Thank you, sir. You should be proud of the work you do."

He lets his hand linger on hers for a moment, then opens his mouth to speak, but she can see him change his mind. He appears happy to have helped. All of a sudden, he takes out his phone and starts typing.

Doris has to know, so she asks, "Are you texting your wife?"

"No, ma'am. Just logging my work. We have to record each interaction—and license plate, if there's a car involved."

"Oh. Well, is that really required? That seems like a lot of unnecessary work."

"It's my job. I have no choice. Is there a problem with that?" he asks in a slightly concerned tone of voice.

She regrets her choice of words. She's irritated but needs him to move on. "Of course not. Thanks again, officer, and be safe out there!"

Doris smiles as she rolls up the window. The cop waves good-bye and she returns the gesture. She opens the bag to find some orange juice, chips, cheese sticks, and a Snickers bar. She smiles to herself, knowing that the junk food will help calm her nerves. Lance drinks the orange juice in a couple of long gulps and devours the chips by the time they've hit the freeway.

Another three hours crawl by, and her mind is racing faster than her rental car. She has so much to tell her sister. As of right now, this part of her plan, getting to Fatima's, is almost complete. The rest she still has to figure out, like how to rehabilitate the president and contact his family. She speeds up as she tries to put it all out of her mind for now.

Suddenly Doris sees a "Welcome to New Mexico" sign. As she passes it, she makes the sign of the cross and thanks God for a safe trip. Over the past two long days, her old-school paper map hasn't failed her. Thankfully, Lance has been sleeping for much of the trip. The rest will do him good since their next adventure is just beginning.

Three hours later Doris taps Lance on the leg and says, "Elliot, wake up. We're almost there! Elliot, honey, we're safe."

WHAT MAKES HISTORY

▷ **Doris – Santa Fe, New Mexico, Day 10**

Doris pulls onto Fatima's street and sees her sister standing in the middle of the road, waving excitedly. Fatima has never been one for discretion. Doris steps out of her rented Nissan sedan and rushes to her sister with open arms. The two sisters hug in front of the 1950s white stucco house, then look at each other as tears fill their eyes.

Doris asks Fatima to open the garage door so she can help Lance out of the car without the notice of Fatima's neighbors. Once that's been accomplished, Lance extends his hand to Fatima. As Doris introduces them, Fatima's eyes open wide and her hand rushes to her mouth. She turns, runs to the nearby trash can, and throws up. After a moment, she stands up straight, wipes her mouth with her sleeve, and returns to the two of them, apologizing along the way.

"I'm so sorry; I don't know what happened!" Fatima stares at Lance, searching for President Dumont's face, hidden somewhere under the bruises, healing wounds, and scruff. "He looks like he got beaten up by a group of guys at a bar. He looks bad, Doris. Poor guy."

"Honey," Doris says, putting a hand on her arm, "He can understand you. And yes, it looks bad, but he's healing quickly and did well on the trip. He's going to be all right. Why don't we go inside?"

Fatima takes her sister by the hand and leads her inside the house. Together, they take Lance to the bedroom so he can lie down. The sisters then head down the darkened picture-lined hallway to the living room, where Fatima pours two glasses of rosé. Doris looks around, admiring the bright, open space; whitewashed walls; and colorful Southwestern decor. Interior decoration has always been Fatima's forte, while Doris has consistently shown a keen eye for fashion.

Once they're seated on the couch, Doris grabs her sister's hands tightly. "It's so good to see you, my love!"

"You too, sis. Now that we have more time than we did at the airport, give me all the details. I want to know everything," Fatima says as she cradles the bowl of her wineglass with both hands, as if readying herself for a long story.

Doris spends the next forty-five minutes recounting her tale from the beginning. First, she details the horrific scene at the courthouse, when she first came upon the president on the sidewalk beneath the icy steps. Then she tells Fatima about the cop who was looking for his father at the hospital, news about the Brigade, media reports about government involvement, the bomb at Presbyterian, Lance's health status, her exit strategy at the hospital, and the falsified documents—all of it.

Fatima finishes her second glass of rosé then says, "That's a lot to take in. I'm sure it's even more to experience. So what's your plan?"

"Like I said before, I will find a way to get him back to his family safely," Doris says defensively. "Fatima, after seeing him today, tell me from the bottom of your heart: What would you have done?"

"Honestly, I don't know what I would've done in your position. It's just that this is hard for me to wrap my head around. I don't know how we can handle all of it by ourselves."

As soon as the words leave Fatima's mouth, Doris can see that she regrets them.

"I'm sorry, honey," Fatima adds quickly. "You've done a great job of taking care of him. Really. I mean, given what he's been through, he could look a lot worse, and you even dressed him up for a two-day car ride! Only you would think of doing that. You've always loved dressing the part."

"Thank you. I also need to tell you about an incident at the hospital."

"Yes, tell me," Fatima says eagerly.

"Well, about a week ago, there was a man in scrubs who was wandering around our floor at the hospital, but he was wearing work boots and had a hood hanging out of the back of his scrub top. Angela and Alice noticed him go into Lance's room, so they went in to ask who he was." Doris wipes a tear on her sleeve and says quietly, "He pulled a knife on them and told them to never report his being there. Then he threatened them and their families. He even knew the name of Alice's son and where he goes to school."

"Lord! Are you serious?" Fatima asks as she reaches over to hug her sister. "You are brave, so brave."

After a couple minutes of silence, Doris says, "I need a small, silly favor. Please don't call me Doris in front of him. He doesn't know me by that name, only by the name Ribbons."

Fatima tilts her head and squints her eyes. "Ribbons?"

"You know the red ribbon I started wearing when I was with Daniel? Well, that's how he recognizes me. It seems to be the one thing that soothes him. I was wearing the ribbon when I arrived at the courthouse. Since then, he has clung to the ribbon like it's the last thing left of his memory."

"Yes, of course I remember it. I was wondering why you were still wearing it when you arrived today."

After a sudden flashback, Doris says, "This reminds me of the secrets we used to exchange in the haystacks when we were kids." The sisters were raised on a dairy farm in California's Central Valley.

"All we had was each other back then," Fatima replies. "We used to complain about not having any neighbors within miles and having to spend our time playing with only each other. Now I'm thankful for that. I wouldn't have had it any other way."

"Me too. But I don't miss working with Dad—waking up every morning at 6:00 to help with the cows."

"Really? I miss the dairy. I miss it all," says Fatima wistfully.

Their father was of Portuguese descent, which is how Fatima got her name. He was also Catholic and wanted to honor Our Lady of Fátima, the Portuguese name for the Blessed Virgin Mary. Doris has always been thankful that she was named after their grandmother on their mom's side. It's a good old Irish name, albeit a little boring, but she's always been OK with boring.

They finish the bottle of rosé and head to the bedroom to see if Lance is still asleep. It's almost 1:00 p.m. He is sitting up when they open the door, his eyes open and blank.

"Elliot, honey, we're home." Doris sits on the bedside, rubs his arm, and turns to Fatima. "He looks more tired than I expected."

"The dark circles underneath his eyes, Dor—oh!" Fatima giggles. "I mean *Ribbons!* You have your work cut out for you. And you know what? I like the way that sounds. Ribbons. Riiiiibonnns." She stretches the word out, rolling it off her tongue like she's trying to taste it. "It's going to take some time getting used to it and remembering it, but Ribbons it is." They both laugh.

"To be honest, I like the way it sounds too. Elliot, why don't you lie down and relax; you need to get some rest." Doris pauses, her expression now solemn. To Fatima, she says, "He hasn't lifted his head straight up since we left the hospital, and sometimes he seems disoriented. But I've got to start to rehabilitate him, or I'll lose him mentally. I've got to keep him connected and stimulated."

"Doris—oops, I mean Ribbons—can I help?" Fatima asks while watching them—the patient and his nurse.

Doris turns away, uncomfortable with the way Fatima is looking at them. Her sister is watching them closely—the way they're sitting, touching, and speaking—and Doris can tell from the slight frown on her lips, she doesn't approve. She knows what Fatima wants to say, that this isn't a normal relationship between a patient and his nurse. She leaves the room with Fatima, closes the door, and then speaks before Fatima does.

"I've got this, thank you. At the hospital, he wouldn't respond to anybody but me. And Lord knows, you've done enough already by housing us."

Fatima dismisses this with a shrug, but her tone turns serious. "You'd better get this right, Doris . If you don't, I don't even want to think of what could happen. You know they'll charge you with everything they can think of—kidnapping, attempted murder, and treason, for sure. Just whatever you do, don't let him die. Oh God, I didn't even think of that. Did you?"

"Yes, I've thought of it many times. I'm not naïve." Doris replies. "But I've got this. I saved his life—not just there beneath those steps and in the hospital, but also by removing him from harm's way." Doris shakes her head. "You don't know what went through this head of mine; my brain must look like Swiss cheese! And right now, I feel like it's covered in mold. I'm exhausted, and I can barely think. And I still have to figure out how to contact his family. But in the meantime, I have to find a way to get his memory back. I have a lot on my plate." She realizes she sounds defensive, but she feels attacked.

She's not sure anymore how this will end—or even *if* it will end. She thinks back to the day they met, with the cries of all those victims surrounding them and the pain on their faces. The sounds and images have filled her dreams every night since. But that is for the historians to write about, because that's what makes history. Her story has all the elements, and she just wants a happy ending to it—not Daniel's ending. This time it will be different. She can save this man; she's sure of it.

Fatima puts her hand on her sister's shoulder, as if to remind Doris that she's still in the hallway with her. "Get some sleep, Doris. You must be exhausted. I love you very much. Whatever happens to us, I'll be proud of you for being so brave."

Doris heads to the kitchen as Fatima walks down the hallway to her bedroom. She fills a glass with tap water and holds it up to the light, watching the water swirl. Fatima's words echo in her brain, the thought of Lance dying at the house. Her body stiffens and her mind races: *Will I have to run and hide for the rest of my life? I'll have to cut and dye my hair, throw away all my clothes, change my name, and maybe even leave the country.* After a minute, she comes to her senses, shaking the glass of water as if to help clear her mind. She then heads back to the guest bedroom to get some sleep.

When she returns, Lance is still sitting in the same position on the bed. She sits beside him, and he turns to face her. For a moment, she doesn't recognize him. He looks less like her hospital patient and more like a stranger. His eyes are suddenly clear and focused. His posture is straight—and his head, held high.

In a soft, sweet voice, Doris asks, "Elliot, how do you feel? Do you need some water?" Lance doesn't respond, so she gingerly guides him into a position in which his head is on her lap. Leaning over him, she pulls the covers up to his chest, then rubs his forehead and the back of his neck.

After some time, she begins to sing a song she loved as a child—a tune her mother made up: "I wish I was your button / For your dresses and blouses of cotton / I will be there when you're lonely and cold / We will always be together, I am told."

Lance turns his head to look up at her. He then tries to pull the ribbon from her blouse.

Doris continues singing while holding back tears. She's had so much loss in her life—her parents, then Daniel, so many patients, and then all the lives at the courthouse.

When Doris reaches the end of the song, Lance gives her a sweet smile. She smiles back, and in an attempt to get comfortable, she opens the top two buttons of her blouse. Her ponytail relaxes on the side of her exposed shoulder as they lie down together. Suddenly, Lance attempts to sit up, turning his head to look at her. She wonders if he wants to get a look at her bra or just the ribbon again.

"Before we nap, let's get cleaned up," she suggests, standing up. She holds out her hand and waits for him to take it. He does.

Carefully, she leads him to the bathroom and turns on the bathtub faucet. Lance doesn't move as she takes off his clothes and then guides him into the tub. After soaking a sponge in the bathwater and rubbing soap into it, she gives him a sponge bath, like she did so many times back at the hospital. But this time, it feels different. Dangerous.

CHAPTER 28

PLEASE BE THERE

▷ **Edwina – New York Presbyterian Hospital, Day 13**

After an afternoon of looking at family pictures, Edwina suddenly jumps up from the couch, leaves the makeshift Dumont suite at the hospital, and walks quickly down the long white hallway. She ignores the staff members she passes along the way, as well as the Secret Service agents guarding the ICU room in which her father *may* be lying. She doesn't want to be right. Being right would suck. She opens the door and stops in the doorway.

"Hello, Dr. Kellerman. Where's George?" Edwina didn't expect to find her father unattended by one of her siblings, especially with the doctor in the room.

"I'm sorry to startle you, Edwina. I'm just checking your father's oxygen levels. The reports are coming in inconsistent, and I thought I should try to figure out what's going on."

Edwina watches as the doctor places the device that was on her dad's finger into his coat pocket.

"Right, and my brother?" she asks, not bothering to hide her irritation.

"He just went to the bathroom. I was—"

"Hi, Edwina!" George passes by her, entering the room with a spring in his step. His expression changes the second he notices Dr. Kellerman. "Oh, hello, Doctor."

"Hello, George. If you both will excuse me," Dr. Kellerman says awkwardly as he heads for the door. Everyone in the room is well aware that the First Lady demanded that no hospital or government personnel ever be alone with her husband without a Dumont family member present.

"I really had to go to the bathroom!" George says defensively after the doctor is out of earshot.

"It's OK. It's not your fault. Kellerman knows the rules. Mom's not going to be happy."

"Do we have to tell her?"

Edwina ponders the question. "I guess not if it was just for a couple of minutes. Let's not add to her worry. She's up to something. She's been holed up in her room for the last two days, and I've hardly seen her. It's not like her."

"She hasn't said a word to me. As always, I've just been avoiding her so I can stay out of trouble. Does seem like she's looking for blood, and I don't want to get in the way."

"Well, I'm early for my shift, so go get some rest, George."

The siblings hug before George leaves the room. Edwina waits a couple of minutes, then pokes her head out the door to make sure no one is headed her way. It's a long hallway, and she knows she has a guaranteed forty-five seconds of alone time with her dad.

Edwina immediately takes out her phone and sets it down on the bed. Then, with one hand, she pushes her father's hip upward. With the other hand, she pulls open his gown, happy to find it isn't tied in the back. It is hard to see clearly, so, as planned, she grabs her phone and snaps three flash photos. She quickly moves to the other side and repeats the motions.

"Please be there, *please*," she pleads aloud while opening her photos app. She squints at the first image. Nothing. She zooms in on the image of his backside. Still nothing. Quickly, she scrolls through the next five pictures, zooming in on each one. Nothing. Nothing at all. No scar.

Tears well in her eyes as she begins to feel the weight of the entire country on her shoulders. She lowers herself to the floor and closes her eyes.

CHAPTER 29

THE WOUNDS WE CANNOT SEE

▷ **Doris – Santa Fe, New Mexico, Day 14**

On the fifth day at Fatima's house, the sun pokes its light through the venetian blinds, causing Doris to stir. An involuntary gasp of surprise escapes her mouth when she sees Lance just inches away. Her face breaks into a sleepy smile.

"Elliot, good morning. You're up early."

Lance looks at her with confusion, which makes her laugh.

"You look like an orangutan with that beard and messy hair. I don't think we can let it grow any longer. You need to look like an Elliot again. Let's get you cleaned up. I'll borrow a hair and beard trimmer from Fatima. In the meantime, let's eat! Ribbons is hungry."

They head to the kitchen for a breakfast of poached eggs with bits of bread mixed in, just like her father used to make. She watches Lance take a cup of orange juice and drink it unaided and without spilling. Just a couple of days ago, she had to help him with the smallest of tasks.

"Elliot, do you know what we're going to do now?" She knows from experience that patient engagement is the best thing for mental rehabilitation. "We're going to get you cleaned up! You're going to take a hot shower, and then we'll clip your beard and hair. No more baths! Won't that be nice?" He looks at her like he doesn't understand a thing she's saying, then frowns. She ignores this, and they head back to the bedroom.

"I hope you are ready for this, my Lone Ranger!" She wants him to take a shower; the exhausting and awkward sponge baths need to end. "We're going to take off your clothes; then in you go, OK, Elliot? I know you're going to love it. It's like rain. You remember, don't you?"

She tries to reassure him while removing his clothes, which is made easier this time thanks to his help. He pulls an arm out of one sleeve of his pajama top and then pushes his pajama bottoms down. Once naked, he just stares at the shower spray as though he's not sure what to do next. As steam begins to rise in the room, he reaches out to touch the water. Then, just as quickly, he pulls his hand back.

"OK, Elliot. Even if I have to tie you up, we're going in." Doris strips down to her bra and panties and steps into the shower.

"Look, Elliot! Look at the water hitting my face." Doris turns her back to the showerhead, lifts her hair, and piles it on top of her head with a hairband that was on her wrist. She looks over at him with a smile.

Lance reaches in again and touches the hot water with his hand.

"See, Elliot, it doesn't hurt. In fact, it's going to make you feel so much better! Come on in!"

He looks at her, then at her bra.

"What's up, Elliot? Oh right, the ribbon! No problem, I'll get it." Doris sticks one leg out of the shower and leans forward, unclasping the ribbon from her nightshirt. She then pins it to her bra. As she gets back in the shower, Lance follows without hesitation, his eyes on the ribbon.

She turns him around and aims the spray onto his neck and back. Lance stiffens as the force of the water hits him, so she places her right arm around his waist to help him relax. He does so, and Doris begins to gently wash his back, shoulders, and neck with a washcloth while humming softly. She flashes back to memories of Daniel. He used to love super-hot showers. She realizes how similar Lance's shoulders and body are to Daniel's. She shakes her head and opens her eyes wider. *This is not Daniel,* she reminds herself and speeds up the process. Steam rises around them as she adjusts the water temperature, hoping the hot water will strike a positive note deep inside his memory and help heal the many wounds she cannot see.

"When we get out of the shower, we're going to trim your hair and beard. Remember? I'm also going to let you brush your teeth on your own. You're going to have to start helping so I can figure out what the hell we're going to do next."

It takes them some time to finish showering. Doris hands him the washcloth and guides his hand with hers.

After stepping out of the shower, Lance tries to dry himself off, but halfway through the process, he stumbles and nearly falls. Doris leans him against the bathroom sink, rushes into the bedroom, grabs a small chair, and brings it back to the bathroom. Despite the weight he's lost, Lance is still too heavy for her to fully support.

After they're dry, she decides to keep the momentum going by having Lance brush his own teeth. She applies toothpaste to his toothbrush, then guides his hand over his teeth, minding the healing wound that starts at the corner of his mouth and continues upward along the side of his face.

The next step is too dangerous to let Lance do, even with guidance. Doris holds Fatima's electric trimmer in one hand and carefully trims his head and beard, wondering if he's ever had a beard or even stubble in his entire life. President Dumont is perceived as the all-American, clean-cut boy next door. She's pretty sure he's never shaved his head. Who would ever shave off that gorgeous head of hair? With the five-o'clock shadow of a beard that's left on his face, a buzz cut, and extensive facial wounds, Lance looks very little like his former self. In a way, Doris likes this version better. He's more approachable.

They move to the bedroom, where Doris takes out a sweat suit she purchased back in New York. Again, she lets Lance take the reins, turning what's typically a one-minute process into one that takes nearly half an hour. Doris constantly reminds herself that this will be worth it, that every minute invested in Lance's eventual independence will have a domino effect on his development. She hopes the Dumont family will be grateful for all she's done.

She takes him to the full-length mirror in the hallway and playfully spins him around, careful not to let him trip over his own feet. For a finishing touch, she spritzes him with some cologne she found in Fatima's bathroom, leaving him smelling like a cedar forest in spring.

"You clean up well, Elliot," she says. "Let's rest a bit before lunch. I think we both deserve it after that experience!"

⊚⊚

An hour later, Fatima calls out to let them know that lunch is ready, so Doris walks to the kitchen with Lance. She tries to help him eat, but he pushes her hand away and slowly feeds himself. She smiles, remembering her plea to him in the shower. She's very impressed with his progress thus far. It takes him nearly forty-five minutes to finish his meal, but Lance's determination is heartwarming to witness. After lunch, he takes his plate to the sink and washes it, giving Doris some much-needed sister time with Fatima.

A bit later in the day, Doris leads Lance back to the bedroom. She puts him back in bed, turns off the lights, closes the blinds, and then hangs blankets over the blinds to prevent any sunlight from sneaking in. Doris knows this much: Lance needs a lot of sleep right now. The sleep he got in the hospital was far less than ideal due to medical interruptions every few hours and the constant noise of an overcrowded hospital.

Doris knows the window for Lance's mental recovery is quickly closing. If his memory doesn't return soon, he might be lost in a fog forever. There is no high-tech equipment here, and she has no medications to help him get better, only some to help him feel better. She has to try something different, something aggressive.

After Lance falls asleep, she borrows Fatima's laptop and spends the evening researching post-traumatic amnesia. It turns out that in most cases, recovery is simply a waiting game. But in their particular situation, time is of the essence, so Doris takes a look into a possible solution she comes across. It's called stimulation therapy. There are a limited number of case studies on it, but it's better than nothing. And it's all she has right now.

There are several different types of memory triggers. The link between them is that they are all highly emotional situations. Doris looks at the options—pain, anger, sex, and cold-water immersion. "Stimulation," she says aloud. She immediately dismisses the sex option; she hasn't had sex since Daniel and certainly can't have sex with the married president of the United States.

She then considers the other types of triggers. Pain and anger would be easy to administer. After another hour of searching, she stumbles upon a case study from Brazil in which a patient's memory was triggered via the element of surprise. This option for home rehabilitation treatment should begin after the patient wakes from a deep sleep. She decides to combine two of the triggers, surprise and anger. Perhaps coupling stimulation therapies will speed up his progress. Time is running out.

CHAPTER 30

THE ELEMENT OF SURPRISE

▷ **Doris – Santa Fe, New Mexico, Day 15**

One of the few things Doris is sure about is that Lance cannot live his life this way; it isn't right. He didn't ask for what happened to him at the courthouse. Lord knows, he didn't deserve it. She is determined to save him, and she has succeeded at that so far. The stimulation therapy she read about last night may be her only hope, but part of her wonders what she will do if it actually works. That thought makes her panic. *Stop it, Ribbons!* she thinks. She has no choice. If his memory returns, she will figure out what to say to him. She can manage this; losing Daniel was a hundred times harder. So, deciding to go ahead with the stimulation therapy, with a focus on the element of surprise, she puts together a plan.

She decides to give Lance an hour and a half of deep sleep. In the meantime, she changes her clothes for the experiment and puts her hair in a bun so it's out of the way and not easy to grab. The article advises caution because most patients react violently, and Doris imagines Lance's reaction will be no different. When she hears his gentle snoring, she switches out his nightstand for a hard chair—nothing too comfortable, so she can stay alert. Next, she partially opens the bedroom door so that the hallway light is funneled onto the lower part of his body. The article explains that if the patient wakes up swinging, the bright light will momentarily blind them, protecting the instigator. Doris isn't sure he's strong enough yet to really hurt her, but she's not willing to take the risk. She is facing enough challenges as it is.

"OK, you've got this," she whispers to herself.

Doris takes a deep breath and sits down in the chair, nervously twisting in her hand a feather she found earlier. The plan is to arouse him from deep sleep. The concept relies on one's ability to find the right balance between waking the patient and triggering their deeper emotions. Doris tries not to think about what the doctors would say about this therapy—Dr. Dansby in particular. He consistently relies on medication and would be adamant that this therapy is unacceptable. But Doris has no choice. She gently starts brushing Lance's face with the feather, trying to irritate him just enough to induce the intended reaction. Lance awakens unagitated and limply swats at the air with one hand.

"Go back to sleep, Elliot," she says softly. "It's OK. Go back to sleep. I'm here."

She lets him fall back asleep and restarts the stimulation process again an hour later. Each time he wakes, his reaction intensifies.

Second round.

Third round.

Stifling a yawn, Doris opens the door for the fourth time. She gets back on the chair, this time, just behind his line of sight. She passes the feather over his face, wiggling it back and forth with increasing speed. Lance jolts up from his pillow, agitated and emotional. His arms flail in the half-lit room, desperately reaching for something to grab. Doris bolts from her chair and squats on the floor just in case he turns around and hits her. Her lips curve into a grin when Lance picks up his pillow and swings it around, trying to hit anything. Doris only steps out into the light once he has tired himself out and fallen back on the bed.

"Elliot, what's the matter, honey? What's wrong?"

He just shakes his head and closes his eyes. Within minutes, he's asleep once again. After another round, Doris feels like real progress has been made. Lance's awareness seems to have improved, and his reactions to each stimulus have become stronger. Deciding to give him a break, she leaves the room. It's nearly 11:00 p.m.

She finds Fatima sitting in the living room, reading a book. Her sister looks up as she takes a seat next to her.

"Well, how's the patient, Doctor? You two skipped dinner," Fatima says.

"I think he's doing well. I could've sworn he tried to speak. Maybe it was just loud grunts. Either way, progress has been made." She can't help but let her voice drag; as satisfied as she is, she's drained and scared. Everything has taken a toll on her—the escape from the hospital, the ongoing nightmares from the courthouse, and now the fear that the president will die at her sister's house. She needs a distraction. "How's work?" she asks.

"You know, same as always," Fatima replies. "I'm still living paycheck to paycheck, but I love my job at the law office. Sure, sometimes it's stressful, but it's good enough. I'm not living beyond my means. I have everything I want. You know me; I like a simple life. With no children and no boyfriend, my life is uncomplicated. So, to answer your question, I guess I'm saying that work is good. I am good." Fatima fiddles with the corner of her book. "So what's with the ruckus in the bedroom? What the hell are you two doing in there?"

Doris laughs. "Well, to be honest, I've been kind of winging it. I have no meds for him, so I found an online therapy and stayed up very late researching it. It's a type of stimulation therapy to trigger his memory; it's like jolting your patient back to life. From what I've read, the statistics aren't great. It rarely works. The practitioners themselves have to go through a lot. The idea is to get the patients worked up, then calm them down, and repeat. It's supposed to activate hormones as well—something to do with the angry reactions it causes. I dunno. It's all I have to go on right now." She speaks softly, trying to convince herself as much as Fatima. "And it's better than doing nothing."

"Doris, I . . ." Fatima bites her lip, eyes shadowed with concern. "I'm not sure that's the right approach. I don't want you to put yourself in danger. I mean, *look* at you. You look as if *you're* the one who needs help."

"I'm fine," Doris replies, but in the back of her mind, she *knows* she needs help. Daniel pops into her head but just as quickly vanishes.

"No, you're not!" Fatima exclaims. "Don't do this, please. If something really bad were to happen to you, then it's me who has to figure out this whole damn thing, and then what the hell am I going to do with the president? It's too much for me. Maybe you should focus your energy on contacting his family."

Ignoring her sister's plea, Doris smiles weakly and tries to put the thought of Lance's family out of her head. *One thing at a time.*

"Nothing is going to happen to me, Fatima. I'm as strong as a horse and as fast as a rabbit." She winks and changes the subject back to something she can control: his therapy. "I've made the room as dark as possible. After Lance is asleep, I open the door to let in just enough light to blind him after I wake him up with a feather. He hates it, which is perfect. Something's clicking. And really, that's all I need—to fire up his brain, to trigger his thoughts.

And I'll tell you what: he's a great swinger! He almost got me a couple times, but he isn't quite quick enough yet. I guarantee you, though, that soon enough, he'll find me, and when he does, I'll know he's coming around. Next, I'm going to immerse him in an ice bath. I'll need you to run to the store to buy ten bags of ice."

"All right, I can do that. Has he been eating enough?" Fatima asks. "I think he needs more protein. I know it's good for the brain. And you could use some calories too, some comfort food. I can make some hamburgers tonight. Doris, please, I want to help. Let your sister take care of you. Please?"

Doris nods wearily and stares out the window. "Maybe you are right. It is becoming too much. To be honest, sometimes I don't know if I really *can* help him, and I wonder if I was fooling myself when I left the hospital. I was just so scared. Every time I hear a noise, I think it's the FBI or the CIA. Last night, I dreamed that I slipped him back into the hospital, left a note for the staff, and fled the country. What the hell have I done?"

Fatima says nothing.

"Do you want us to leave?" Doris asks, her voice wobbling. "I know this is a lot for you too. You're putting your life on the line for us. We can find a hotel and—"

"Of course I don't want you to go!" Fatima interrupts. "Back in St. Louis, I said I'd help you, and that hasn't changed. But I have to ask you something personal. Promise you won't get mad, OK?"

Doris nods.

"Do you love him? Like, *really* love him? I mean, you've done so much for this man and risked even more. And if you don't love him, then what is this really about? Lance isn't Daniel."

Doris doesn't try to stop the tears from rolling down her cheeks. She knew it was just a matter of time before Fatima mentioned Daniel's name in all this. She gives in, just a little. "Maybe, yes, in my little fairytale, I do." Her body shudders with relief at the admission, but she avoids looking at Fatima for fear of seeing judgment and disapproval on her face. But deep in her soul, it feels good to have said it aloud.

They sit in silence for a few minutes, then Doris continues after some thought. "It's been five days since we got here, and it's given me time to think. At my core, I'm a mother hen who never got to have children." She ekes out a pained smile. "So, part of why I feel so strongly about Lance is because I want to take care of him, but more than that, it's because I know I can save him. I can save this one, Fatima. I screwed up with Daniel, but it won't happen again. I also want to protect him, and in the process, do something for my country." She pauses and her face reddens. "And I do love him, but it's a different kind of love. I can't explain it. I also understand that my days with him are numbered. It's often easier to fall in love with someone when you know it's *not* going to be forever. It's like when we'd go on vacation when we were young and single. We could meet a guy and fall in love because we knew it was just for the moment. There was nothing to risk because we knew when it would end. And right now, I'm living in the moment."

Fatima sighs. "I'm sorry, Doris—really, I am—for questioning you. I know you didn't ask for this to happen. And you don't have to keep on explaining yourself for my sake. I realize he just landed in your lap, and you have made the best decisions you could have with such little information. I also know you have done so with the best of intentions. And you definitely did the right thing in protecting your friends while also saving Lance. I'm all in—100 percent. I'm just really scared."

"Me too, Fatima. Me too."

CHAPTER 31

THIS CAN'T BE POSSIBLE

▷ **Rockefeller – Langley, Virginia, Day 16**

Rockefeller stares out the window of his large office and smiles. He's happier than he has been in two weeks. Even though his day job has been a nightmare, his side job—really, his passion—has been a success. None of the Brigade members have talked, and anyone who was a risk has been eliminated. He loves that word. *Eliminated.* So effective. Efficient. His special phone vibrates in his jacket pocket. A smile spreads across his face as he answers.

"Update me. How's our patient?" Rockefeller says confidently.

"The patient will not be coming out of his coma anytime soon. Our new friend Dr. Kellerman assures me he won't awaken him until you give the command, as you requested." Gruff then adds, "But there's more news about this patient . . ."

"Yes? What is it?" Rockefeller asks impatiently, not liking Gruff's tone.

"Well, we have a problem."

"I need to know *everything*, Gruff! Just tell me."

"Dr. Kellerman has been with Dumont for just over two weeks, as you know. And he's been consulting with the president's doctors, of course. It's per protocol—couldn't get around that. He asked for all the president's medical records, and in going through them, he noticed a discrepancy in Dumont's blood type."

"What exactly are you trying to say?"

"Well, I'm getting there. The reports that were sent over indicate his blood type is A-negative. However, Kellerman's test showed that it's O-positive. So Kellerman tested it again and confirmed the O-positive result."

"So Dumont's doctor has it wrong. Who cares?"

"That's what I thought too, but I had Kellerman fingerprint Dumont, just in case. That wasn't easy. As you know, a Dumont kid is always on guard duty. So we just adapted one of those pulse oximeters to take a fingerprint. You know, those small devices doctors use to measure heart rate and oxygen saturation."

"Don't say what I think you are going to say, Gruff!"

"Exactly. I had the fingerprint run through the system via one of our Brigade insiders. It didn't match Dumont's. Not even close."

"They pulled in the wrong frickin' guy? This can't be possible! *Damn it!!*" Rockefeller shouts into the phone.

"I know. It's definitely not Dumont lying in that bed at Presbyterian."

"Just when I thought we had him! Where the hell *is* he?!"

"I don't know."

"Damn it!!" Rockefeller thunders. "Do you think the Secret Service has the real Dumont somewhere else?"

"I doubt it. Dumont's whole family is there, and Director Cummings shows up at Presbyterian all the time. It would be too good of a show; I don't think they're that competent. You know that."

"True. That bunch of idiots couldn't pull that off. But that doesn't answer the question—where the hell could he be?"

"My best guess is that he's dead. Maybe in some morgue, tagged as a John Doe."

"That would be ideal," Rockefeller says under his breath.

"But don't worry—I have a plan. My team will go back and check all the John Does in the hospitals and morgues. I will connect with the data team to supply a list of all those hospitalized as well as those sent to the morgue. We will find him. Got to finish this right, sir," Gruff says confidently.

"Gruff, then who *is* lying in that hospital bed?"

"Vince Guthrie, a retired NYPD policeman. And get this, his twenty-six-year-old son is an active NYPD officer, just like Daddy was. His name is Jack."

"I don't like that at all. Let's make sure this young cop doesn't come snooping around for his father."

"Will do, sir."

"I'm surprised Rose Dumont hasn't noticed that the guy isn't her husband. Very strange. Something's not at all right here. Anyway, in the meantime, go ahead with your plan. Send as many Brigade members as you need to, move fast as hell, and make sure no one gets caught."

"What if we find Dumont?"

"Eliminate." The word makes Rockefeller smile. "Even if your guys aren't 100 percent sure, eliminate. Take fingerprints, and we can confirm after the fact. We aren't going to have another screwup."

"Got it," Gruff says, then hangs up.

Rockefeller picks up his work phone and dials.

The call is answered on the first ring.

"James Edwards speaking."

CHAPTER 32

SOMETHING HAS CHANGED

> **Doris – Santa Fe, New Mexico, Day 18**

For the past three days, Doris has been repeating the different stimulation therapies: cold immersion in the bathtub, followed by sleep sessions and surprise triggering with the feather. With each session, Lance's reactions have improved, but he's exhausted from having been on an emotional roller coaster.

During today's trigger session, his fingers get caught on Doris's tank top and accidentally rip it open. With her breasts partially exposed, she freezes like a cobra ready to strike back. Lance looks frightened. He reaches for her torn top to look for the ribbon, but it fell off and is now lying on the floor. He doesn't see it there and clumsily tries to put the torn pieces of her top back together. Doris waits for the moment when he will touch her breasts. But he stops within an inch of her nipple, lets the torn piece drop from his hand, and turns away.

For a split second, she feels rejected—then ashamed for those same feelings. She gets off the bed and puts on a shirt. For a moment, she hates that damn ribbon. She knows she's being ridiculous, but it's been over two weeks, and Lance can't see *her*—just the ribbon. It's been over a year since she's really been *seen*. She pauses for a moment and wonders how many other women in their late thirties feel unseen on a daily basis. Maybe she's asking for a lot, but she needs some recognition from him in return for all that she has risked, all she has done, even if he isn't aware of any of it.

Doris returns to the bed and sits with her back to him. Suddenly, she feels his hands on her shoulders. He begins to massage them gently. She closes her eyes. Finally, she gets something in return and releases a deep, satisfied sigh. She looks at the lonely ribbon on the floor and brushes it under the bed with her foot. She then turns around to face Lance. His hands move from her shoulders to her breasts. Instinctively, she slaps him across the face, forcing him backward on the bed.

The slap unlocks a scream followed by a fully formed word: "Mom!"

His first word is "mom"? she thinks. *My God, does he think I'm his mother?* Feeling guilty, she uses all her strength to pull him up into a sitting position, but he immediately falls backward again.

Lance puts his hand to the left side of his face, removes it, and looks down at the fresh blood. The slap has torn the scab on his cheek. A stream of blood mixed with fresh tears runs down his neck. He sits up and wipes his face with his hands while staring hard at her. He looks different to Doris. *Totally awake,* she thinks. *No . . . aware.* He's present in a way she hasn't yet seen him. He looks into her eyes and then down at her chest.

"You know I'm not your mother, right, Elliot?" She speaks slowly and softly. "What is your mother's name?" Doris feels hot all of a sudden and notices that they are both sweating. Lance tries to speak but is clearly pained by the effort.

"I'll get a towel. Don't move. Just stay right there," Doris says before hurrying off to the bathroom.

She grabs a blouse on the way back and quickly puts it on before she sits down. Then, using the damp towel, she dabs the blood from his cheek and uses the other side to wipe the sweat from their faces. She turns her back to him to finish buttoning her blouse, but she can feel his eyes watching her.

Doris coughs to get his attention. "Well, what's your mother's name, Elliot?" She wishes she didn't sound angry.

When she turns to look at him, he looks up at her, even more present than before, but the sound he makes doesn't form a word. She retrieves a pencil and paper from the desk across the room. He eagerly grabs the pencil in his right hand and tries to write. The letters don't make sense. It looks as though he's trying to spell a word—Lckia?

"Is it Vicki?" Doris asks, desperate for a breakthrough.

He shakes his head and moves his hands from side to side in a "no" gesture. A burst of excitement floods her chest. This is the first time he's communicated with both his hands and his head. Something has changed. *Thank God*, she thinks.

"That's good, Elliot! You're starting to think for yourself." She isn't sure if this will be a good or bad thing for her. She has been both waiting for and fearing this very moment. "OK, honey, just focus. I'm going to try and guess your mother's name, and you tell me when I get it right. Is it Lucy?" His reaction brightens. "Lucia?"

Lance studies her mouth as she repeats the name Lucia.

"Lucinda?" Doris asks.

Still sitting up in bed, he begins to rub his stomach with joy, as if he's just tasted something he likes. He nods vigorously.

"Lucinda! Lucinda is your mother's name?"

He smiles.

"Thank you, Elliot! Thank you!"

Doris hugs him tightly, her heart bursting with both fear and joy. Then she leans back, patting the space next to her for him to lie down. He does, but he's trembling from the trauma of the moment, so she grabs his cold hands and rubs them gently. After a moment, she pulls a soft-spun gray blanket over the two of them and adjusts the pillow underneath his head. As he closes his eyes, she tells him a story about a girl and a glass slipper, pausing frequently to make sure he's listening. Toward the end, she hums a tune before realizing he's asleep. Shortly afterward, she, too, drifts off.

After a few hours of sleep, they wake to the smell of Fatima's cooking and head to the kitchen for an early dinner. Lance's appetite is in full swing. He finishes two helpings of pork chops without looking up from his plate.

Doris gives her sister the full update on Lance's progress. As they talk, Doris can sense him paying full attention to their conversation. She wonders if he's understanding their every word. She decides to start watching her words more carefully from now on.

After dinner, Doris leads Lance to their bathroom to get him into a hot shower. This time, he gets in without any coaxing. Lance navigates the shower easily—taking time to wash his arms, back, and neck. She puts a fresh towel over the shower door and leaves the bathroom to give him some time alone to finish showering and, following that, dry himself off.

Afterward, they brush their teeth and climb into bed. She waits for him to fall asleep, listening to his breaths fall into a deep, slow rhythm before tiptoeing out of the room to say good night to her sister. She finds Fatima having a glass of wine on the couch and sits down next to her. She positions herself far back on the cushion to keep her bare feet from touching the cold floor, just like she did when she was little.

"Well, how's Lance doing?" Fatima asks.

"He's doing so much better every day. It seems my home-spun therapy is working. His mind is slowly returning home to his body. It's as if they were disconnected by the trauma." Doris pauses to take a sip from her sister's wineglass. "Oh! And he spoke! Well, just two words. His first word was *mom*. And then I asked him what her name is, and he tried to tell me. After some time, I figured out that it was Lucinda. I wasn't sure if that was true, so I did a quick search on the internet, and it's correct. Either way, I think he's coming around. Maybe it's the therapy, or maybe it was just a matter of time and rest. I'm just thankful that he's improving."

"Honey, speaking of moms, don't you think it's time you figure out how to reach out to his family? It's been a week since you got here."

Doris can tell her sister is worried. She wishes they could just celebrate this progress, but her sister keeps speaking.

"I'm concerned that you are getting in over your head, emotionally speaking. Let me help you figure out how to contact the Dumonts. Please."

Doris doesn't want to have this conversation, but she does want to appease her sister. "OK, OK. I hear you. And yes, of course you can help me find his family. I have no idea how the hell we can do that without involving the authorities, but I welcome your assistance. You've always been the clever one in the family." She's hoping the compliment will get her sister off her back.

Fatima takes the bait. "All right then, I will start researching tomorrow and report back to you. You can trust me on this."

"I know. I love you. Sleep tight, sis."

Suddenly, a loud scream comes from the bedroom. They rush to the room and hurl open the door. Doris runs over to grab the ribbon from under the bed. She attaches it to her bathrobe before turning on the light. The sisters find Lance shaking with cold and mumbling to himself. Neither of them can understand a word of it. It's like he's speaking another language. Doris takes off her bathrobe and wraps it around him. Now in just her pajamas, she snuggles up close to him from behind and embraces him tightly.

"Can I get anything for you guys?" asks Fatima.

"No, I think he's OK now."

"All right, just holler if you need anything," Fatima says as she closes the bedroom door behind her.

Doris begins to talk to Lance softly, trying to focus his attention on the sound of her voice. After a few minutes, he stops shaking. Using the sleeve of her bathrobe, she wipes the sweat from his forehead.

When she changes her position on the bed in order to face him, she notices the clarity in his eyes and an alertness that wasn't there just an hour before. She wonders if this is what progress looks like.

Holding him tightly, she whispers, "Did you have a bad dream? What do you want me to do, Elliot? Do you want me here, or do you need to be alone?" He doesn't react, so she decides to keep quiet. But just then, he bolts out of bed and heads toward the closed door. She rushes forward and grabs him tightly around his waist until he's no longer moving.

"Elliot, it's OK."

She wonders what would happen if he were to wake up in the middle of the night, realize who he is, and escape. She can just imagine him in his pajamas, running down the street, claiming he's the president of the United States. She can't risk that. He needs to be watched constantly from now on. There's too much at risk. So after she gets him settled in bed, she grabs the chair she used during therapy and wedges the back of it securely under the knob of the bedroom door.

CHAPTER 33

WHERE'S YOUR RING?

▷ **Rose – New York Presbyterian Hospital, Day 24**

Rose Dumont wakes up in a sweat. The first thing that pops into her mind is Edwina. One of the most awful mistakes she has ever made is slapping her daughter when she said the man in the hospital bed is not her father. Rose believed the Secret Service and CIA completely. Sure, she questioned their competence after the Courthouse Massacre, but aside from that, she trusted them to do their jobs. But that was in the beginning, and since then, so much has changed.

Rose has become so engrossed in following the latest news reports that she has removed herself from her husband's twenty-four-hour bedside schedule. She has left that responsibility to her children, who have been fulfilling it without complaint. Sure, she has visited her husband's ICU room, but never without one of her children present, and often, a nurse or doctor.

She has been obsessed with researching the Brigade and has spent the last two weeks interrogating the CIA, the Secret Service, and the FBI. The news networks have consistently pointed fingers at the government, with their round-the-clock coverage pointing out every detail that was missed on February 4 and every error that was made. This media frenzy has been fueled by Acting President Alvarez's off-the-cuff comments. The focus is mostly on the Secret Service and, subsequently, Director Cummings. Rose has met with the director a handful of times to ask every question she can think of. She's done the same with CIA Director Schultz and FBI Director Johnson. So far, their explanations are consistent. These institutions have traditionally only focused on international terrorism, not homegrown militants. They didn't take the threats seriously. To Rose, the ignorance and arrogance of these organizations and their leaders is beyond comprehension. They haven't changed in decades. That much is clear, but nothing Rose has learned has led her to believe that any of them were behind her husband's attempted assassination. What frustrates her the most, however, is a gut feeling that's telling her that the opposite of this may be true.

The only other person Rose is aware of who shares these feelings is Edwina. From the start, Edwina has been going against the grain. She doubts the trustworthiness of the agencies and of the hospital staff. Rose suspects her daughter shares her gut instinct that something is wrong.

After combing the internet for hours, as she has been doing for far too many nights, Rose takes a walk down the stark white hallway to Lance's room, the click-clack of her shoes echoing against the walls.

"Hello?" she announces softly as she opens the door.

"Mom?" asks June, clearly surprised by her mother's sudden appearance. "What are you doing here? Is everything OK?"

"Everything is fine, honey." Rose kisses her daughter on the cheek. "Listen, I can't sleep, and I decided I need to be with your father. It's about time I start helping out. I'm ready. I want to be here."

"You have enough on your plate, and we all agreed to handle this for you so that you can manage the rest, Mom."

"There's nothing to manage right now. Really, I need to be here. Please."

June smiles and takes her mom's hand. "I'm sure Dad would love that."

"Go to bed, and get a good night's sleep, OK? I love you."

"I love you too, Mom. Good night," June says as she quietly leaves her mom alone in the room.

Rose stares at her husband, wondering how many days it has been since she's seen him. Guilt gnaws at her, but she distracts herself by rubbing Lance's forehead. She then grabs a chair and pulls it closer to his side so she can sit while holding his hand. It feels so different—thinner. She pulls his hand closer to get a good look at it, then wonders if she's ever really paid attention to all the physical details of the man she's lived with for the past three decades. She has taken so much for granted.

Edwina pops into her mind, and Rose wonders why she thinks this isn't Lance. She looks at his hand again, then at his finger, where his wedding ring should be.

"Where's your ring, honey?" she asks him, as if he could hear her and respond. She's surprised that there's no pale, untanned line where his ring would be. Has he already lost his deep tan in just a few weeks? She finds this strange but suspects she's being paranoid.

After a moment, Rose walks over to the room's entrance and turns up the dimmer switch as far as it will go. She looks closely at her husband's face, then focuses on his lips. She kisses him softly but feels nothing. Then she takes off his blanket and tugs down the top of his hospital gown, exposing his chest. It feels like it's the first time she has ever really looked at her husband. And the strange thing is that it doesn't *feel* like her husband. Feeling a surge of panic, Rose pushes him onto his left side and opens the back of his gown, exposing his right buttock and right lower back.

"Where is it?!" she practically shouts. Even though her husband played sports throughout high school and college, he has only one scar on his entire body. He got it as a boy, climbing through a barbed wire fence on his family's ranch.

But now, it appears, that scar is gone.

"Holy Mother of God."

CHAPTER 34

WALK BEFORE YOU RUN

▷ **Doris – Santa Fe, New Mexico, Day 24**

Lance's progress has been swift. Six days have passed since he uttered his first word, and now he is finally able to talk, read, and write. He is by no means back to normal, but Doris feels that his recovery to this point has been nothing short of a miracle. Things have come back to him—basic abilities, but not his memory. Doris is somewhat grateful for that under the circumstances. She needs more time before she can handle a fully functional President Dumont. She fears the pace of his progress, as the balance of control is changing—something for which she isn't prepared. She didn't expect Lance's physical strength and capacity for conversation to improve so rapidly. Knowledge of his identity and memories of his family will surely return to him soon, so she knows her time is running out. It's a matter of days, not weeks.

At first, they ventured out of the house for short walks. Within four days, they were walking six to ten blocks in a day. Lance enjoys walking by the small stores and restaurants in town, people-watching along the way. Doris has kept him in sunglasses, a buzz cut, and a tightly trimmed beard. The wounds on his face are healing well but still draw attention from those they pass. While still handsome, he definitely doesn't look like his former self anymore.

Doris feels pride when they are together. Her feelings have deepened, especially now that his personality is emerging. She didn't know what to expect, but she didn't think her spending time in his company would feel so comfortable.

Perhaps the biggest change in Lance is his ability to talk. After he said his first words, his speech improved rapidly. Now he's capable of participating in full conversations, but his memory has not yet returned.

This morning, when the two of them return from a walk, Lance heads directly to the bathroom to shower. Doris runs into Fatima in the kitchen and surprises her from behind while she is doing dishes.

"Fatima! I have to confess something, and I need your honest opinion on it. I had a dream last night about Lance. We went on a date and kissed. I know that sounds terrible. Am I an awful person?" Of course, in her dream, a lot more took place, but she's not ready for a full confession. She'll save that for a priest. *Someday.*

"*What?*" Fatima spins around. "Are you sure that's *all* you did in your dream? Just kissing him will change your relationship, and it's complicated enough as it is. What if he starts falling in love with you, and then his memory comes back? What do you think will happen? He won't leave his family for you, and he'll end up hating you. Hell—the whole *country* will end up hating you. Is that what you want? Another problem? You've got to stop thinking like that, Doris."

"I know, I know. Calm down." Doris pauses, unsure if she should say more, but she can't help herself. "And there's more. The other dream is reoccurring. In it, I lose Lance—quite literally.

I wake up in the morning, and he's gone, nowhere to be found. So I'm thinking that if we grow closer, it will cement his trust in me."

"No. You can't forget who he really is," Fatima warns.

"I know you're right; it can't be sexual, but it can still be intimate without sex." Doris realizes how ridiculous she must sound, how desperate. "He remembers nothing about his past, and I want him to connect with me on a deeper level. He's been feeling lost, and so have I. He needs to feel safe here— specifically, safe with *me*. A deeper level of intimacy could make that happen."

Fatima grabs her sister's hands. "What if, and this is a *big* if, he begins to care for you more than he cares for his family or country? Then you will be both a homewrecker and a traitor. You are *not* that person. It's bad enough as it is. He may spend the rest of his life thinking about you, hoping to return to you in some way. You don't want that, do you?"

"No. I know you're right, but I love the sense of security he gives me while I'm lying there next to him—so close to that kind of power." Doris's eyes begin to water. "I wake up every day and look forward to the mornings and afternoons, when we take our walks. I haven't felt this good since Daniel. It's something I've wanted so much, but obviously not like this. I also know very well that he'll remember who he is—and probably sooner rather than later. I'm not dumb. And if he *doesn't* figure out who he is, then what?"

Fatima shifts nervously, then says, "This must stop! The two of you must *stop!*" Her voice vibrates with passion.

Doris is horrified. She can see herself in Fatima's eyes and doesn't like what she sees. Before she can defend herself, Fatima strikes again: "Seriously, Doris. I really want to understand. And honestly, most of it, I can. But *this?* This potential love affair is unconscionable, borderline insane, and absolutely wrong in *every* possible way!"

"I can't stop it!" Doris erupts. *"There,* I said it. Don't you understand that he's mine? Mine to watch over and take care of. At least for now. If he goes, well, *when* he goes, I'll have lost someone I loved. It certainly won't be the first time. But I can walk away with *something:* knowing that I did something right. I know I've made mistakes along the way. Every morning, I wake up and wonder what would've happened if I'd just told the hospital everything when I first found his ID. But I didn't do that for so many reasons. Nothing happened in a clear and logical way. At that point, nothing in New York City was clear and logical. When I got to the courthouse, I realized that it wasn't just an assassination attempt; it was *war.* My mind shifted. I can't explain it, but that realization clouded my every decision. And to be honest, it still does." Doris breaks down, gasping and sobbing into her sister's shoulder.

After a couple of minutes, Doris is able to regain control of her emotions. She releases Fatima from her embrace and looks at her with fear and desperation in her eyes.

"Listen, Doris, I think you have PTSD from what you witnessed on those courthouse steps. Like I've said before, I don't know what I would have done in your circumstances. We live in a different world today than we did before February 4. Neighbors are being pit against one another. Americans are committing acts of terror against their own country." Fatima cups her sister's face in her hands and looks her straight in the eyes. "But now that you have feelings for him, you are in even greater danger than before. I've been doing some digging and have given a lot of thought as to how to contact his family. Now is the time. I think the best thing is for me to contact one of his children. I've come up with a plan, but I won't be ready to share it with you until it's fully fleshed out. But I do have one, and we'll have to put it into action soon."

Doris sits with this for a moment. "That's great, Fatima. At least *one* of us has a plan. And you are right about all of this. I wanted to return him to his family fully functional, but time is running out, and I don't know how much longer his rehabilitation will take." She feels defeated but forces a smile. "It is time to make this happen. How can I help with your plan?"

"There's nothing I need from you now. I just need another day or two to get the details right. I may know someone who knows someone," she says with a smile and a wink. "When I get home from work tonight, we can talk more. This is good, Doris. It's the right thing to do."

Their time together has run out, as Fatima is already late for work. She kisses her sister on the forehead and wishes her luck for her day with Lance. Before she leaves, she warns Doris not to think about her dream until she's had more time to consider the consequences of acting upon her feelings.

Shortly after Fatima leaves, Lance returns from the bedroom, having showered and dressed. He sits down next to Doris at the kitchen table, pulls out a piece of wrinkled paper, and begins sketching what appears to be a house.

"Do you want a better piece of paper?" she asks.

"No, this is fine, thank you," he replies curtly, without looking up at her.

Concerned, Doris quickly responds, "What's up, Elliot? Everything OK?"

"No, not really. I've been thinking we should go somewhere else. Somewhere I can remember, a place I've been before. I think that would help me. I don't remember *this* place, Ribbons. Nothing here looks or smells familiar." He pauses a moment before adding, "I know we're welcome here, and Fatima has been really kind to us, but I just don't have any sense of responsibility here. You do everything for me. There's nothing that you will let *me* do. Do you know what I'm trying to say?"

"No. What are you saying?" She's not ready to leave yet, not without a plan. But at this particular moment, she'd be happy to deliver this man back to his family. She tries to remember what Fatima said about her plan. Something about contacting one of the Dumont kids. Had she said more? She wishes she'd been paying closer attention.

She stands up from the table and walks across the room to turn off a light, stalling for time and hoping he will drop the subject. She knows he's watching her, waiting for her to return before he continues.

"I'm saying I would like to leave. I feel lost here. Look at me. I don't remember anything from my past. Hell, even my name doesn't sound right to me. What's going on here? What are we doing?"

He crumples the piece of paper he was drawing on and throws it against the wall, catching it on the rebound.

This simple mastery of motor movement scares Doris more than it should, and she fights to keep her voice steady. "I know you're lost, but your memory will come back. You've got to be patient."

Lance continues throwing the ball of paper against the wall and catching it, his face turned away. Doris's fear is replaced by irritation.

"Elliot, can you please stop that? I don't want to compete with that frickin' ball of paper!" She turns away in an attempt to hide her anger. She doesn't want him to see her this way. She takes a sip of water from Lance's glass, buying time to regain her composure. She wonders why she's so angry.

Lance stands up from his chair, holding his hands together in front of him, his fingers intertwined. She wonders what he's hiding. He then unclasps his hands and drops his clenched fists to his side. For the first time ever, Doris feels afraid of him.

"What do you want, Elliot? What—"

"Stop it!" Lance screams. "What happened to me? How was I injured? These wounds, all this pain—please tell me. I try not to be scared, but of what, I don't know. I don't even know how to act most of the time. I'm confused when I look in the mirror."

"Elliot, I—"

"Let me finish, please! You're taking such good care of me, and I can see that you care for me, but why? I'm so confused. I'm not sure why I'm here with you. It's like something just isn't right with us, but I don't know what it is. I can't put my finger on it, but I know and can feel in my gut that something is wrong. I'm sorry; I've tried not to ask any questions, but I need to know more. I'm ready." He takes a deep breath before adding, "And there's more: I feel frustrated when I'm next to you. I feel something I can't understand."

Doris gives him a cold smile; her irritation has turned to hurt. His words cut deep into her soul. She sets down the glass of water she's holding and walks over to him. She puts both knees on the chair behind which he's standing and looks deep into his eyes, realizing she's no longer able to protect him the way she was before. Hell, now she can't even predict what's going to happen next. But she also doesn't want to answer all his questions right now. It isn't time for them to have this conversation. Not yet. She needs more time—a couple of days, maybe. This is something she can control; she still holds the power, at least for now.

Before she can say anything, Lance grabs her by the hand and walks her to the front door. Motioning for her to put on her coat and shoes, he opens the door and gestures her outside. Doris follows his lead, but he doesn't say anything as he closes the door and they head down the street.

"Where are we going, Elliot?" she asks as she follows him, wrapping a scarf around her neck.

"We are taking a walk," he replies, turning his head to look at her. "I need to see your smile. It will make me forget that I'm scared of the unknown. I *want* to know who I am, just as you know yourself."

She tenses. She wants to slow Lance down a bit so she can have time to think, time to come up with the perfect answers to his questions. She wishes she had spent more time thinking about what to do once he became functional; all she could do was focus on getting him there. But he isn't a regular patient who can check out of the hospital after recovery. She can't just say goodbye and move on to the next patient.

Suddenly, Lance grabs her arm and stops her, turning her around to face him. His gaze is focused on her eyes. He's practically looking through her as he lifts her chin and smiles. When Doris tries to turn away, he reaches for her collar and lifts it just enough to protect her neck from the cold late-morning wind.

"I feel *something* for you, Ribbons. Maybe you know that, but I just don't know what exactly it is yet." He looks over her head as if thinking to himself and then smiles down at her again. "You know what? Let's make this a date."

Doris opens her mouth to protest, but he grabs her hand and continues toward the crosswalk without another word. As she walks with him, a realization dawns on her, dampening her initial excitement at his desire for a date: *He's only playing the part, reacting to my anger. He's just telling me what I want to hear.* She suddenly feels as if the curtain is going up and he's her leading man. But what part of the play are they in? It feels like the part in which the girl falls in love with the boy. She decides to let down her guard, so she loosens her legs and clears her mind. Doris turns to look at Lance. He doesn't return her gaze, but she knows he has sensed her shift.

This is still *her* play, and she's still the director.

CHAPTER 35

TRUST NO ONE

▷ **Rose – New York Presbyterian Hospital, Day 24**

Rose is still standing by the bedside of the patient—the man who she just realized is *not* her husband. She closes her eyes and says a quick Hail Mary. When she has the strength to look at him again, it just reaffirms the fact that her greatest nightmare has become reality. There is definitely no scar on the right side of his lower back. Had she spent time with him, she would've known sooner. There are some other markers on Lance's body that are unique to him, including a handful of freckles and a tiny birthmark on his inner thigh, but there has been so much on her plate—taking care of her family, managing the media, working with the acting president, and helping make sure the country doesn't fall apart—that she never thought to look for them. At the beginning of this ordeal, she couldn't cope, so she left Lance's care in the hands of her children, the hospital, and government officials. She thought, *Certainly, they are more capable than I am.* But now she knows that wasn't true. Now, everything has changed. Rose can feel her heart rate increase rapidly as rage fills her body.

She opens the hospital room door and runs down the hall to the family's suite. The agents stare at her; then one pulls out a two-way radio and speaks into it: "I think we have a situation."

Rose disappears into the suite and wakes June and Edwina. Then she walks into her sons' rooms and does the same. "Come to the living room now," she says as she leaves each room.

She heads for the living room and, once there, rubs her shoulder along the wall, knocking some of the paintings off-kilter. It is as though she's trying to imitate a horse scraping its rider off its body as it runs alongside a fence. She realizes *she's* the horse—and a damn strong one. She needs to take over and get this rider off her back. She's devastated she didn't pay attention to Edwina's concerns. How did this young girl know? Rose is more than twice Edwina's age, as are all the decision-makers who constantly surround them. Edwina knew on day one, and her mom failed her. She failed them all. But no longer.

Rose thrusts her head into the palms of her hands, repeating over and over, "What a fool! What a fool!" She pulls her head far back, as if trying to dislodge it from her shoulders. Lowering herself to the ground, she raises her knees, grabs her calves, and leans forward, her face against her knees. She cannot lose control. Control is all she has left. She has to stay strong, not only for Lance, wherever he might be, but also—*especially*—for the sanity of their children. *Is it too late?* she wonders.

"Edwina!" she screams. "Edwina! I'm sorry!" She stands back up and slides along the wall again, trying to keep herself from falling.

Edwina, half-asleep, stumbles into the room, then rushes to her mother and tries to hold her up. "What is it, Mom? What's happened?"

Rose's face is red and soaked with tears. "You . . . you were right from the very beginning. You've known all this time!" For a moment, Rose struggles in Edwina's embrace, but eventually relaxes. Edwina slowly releases her mother and stares at her tear-stained face.

When Rose finally speaks, her voice is low and devoid of anger. "*Who* is that man we have been caring for? Why is he here? Where the hell is your father?" she asks before breaking into sobs. "How did they get everything so wrong?" she manages. "They can't even bring in the right president? Did your father just leave us behind? Is he being held somewhere? Is he dead?" Overcome by emotion, Rose grabs Edwina and embraces her tightly.

Edwina's arms close around her, but not in a way Rose would've hoped for. Her daughter is holding back—not that Rose can blame her. The weeks of fraught silence between the two of them ever since that fateful day she slapped her stands between them now, and there's not much of a bridge for either of them to cross.

"Edwina, I'm so sorry. Please forgive me." Then she turns to George, June, and Thomas, who've wandered into the room one by one. "You guys have to help me find your father; I beg you."

"How did you find out, Mom?" Edwina asks.

"The scar. The scar on his lower back. It's not there." The inside of Rose's mouth is raw from biting her tongue and the sides of her mouth, a nervous habit she's had since childhood. Her brain is just mush, thoughts bouncing from one side to the other without any semblance of reason. Maybe Lance is dead, or he's a prisoner in some torture chamber, or perhaps he's being held hostage by their own government. The possibilities feel endless, and at this point, she isn't sure which possible scenario is worse.

"He *must* be alive," Thomas says, bringing a glimmer of hope to his mother's dark thoughts. "I'm sure of it. If he were dead, I think we would feel it in our bones. Trust me on this one, Mom; I know he's out there somewhere. I just wish I knew where and why."

Still sniffling, Rose lets Edwina help her over to a seat at the dining table in the living room. For Lance's sake, they need a plan.

Rose only wishes that in this nightmare of David versus Goliath, her family didn't have to play the role of David. And it seems cruel that they have no idea how many Goliaths are out there. She's convinced that there is more than one enemy at play. It's been exposed that the Brigade has an extensive network, wealthy backers, and connections inside the government. But without facts, these are just theories and speculation.

After a few moments, Edwina breaks the silence. "During my shift a couple of days ago, I also checked to see if Dad's scar was there," she lies, not wanting her family to know that it's been eleven long days since she confirmed her suspicion. This knowledge has been torture.

George steps forward. "And why the hell didn't you tell us?"

Everyone stares at Edwina in disbelief.

"I didn't want to believe it myself. I dunno. I wanted to have a plan in place before I told you guys. And, well . . . no one believed me before," she says defensively.

Rose puts a hand on Edwina's shoulder. "It's OK. I don't blame you. I probably wasn't ready to hear it anyway."

Thomas stands before he speaks. "If Dad is alive, then we have to find him."

Rose is too tired to think clearly. "I don't know where to start, Thomas. None of this makes sense. Director Schultz told me that little factual information about the Brigade has surfaced, and they haven't come forward to demand anything. But it's been so long; surely too much time has passed for that kind of a deal. Wouldn't we have heard something about it by now? Unless someone inside is hiding information from us. That could very well be it. For all we know, Dad could even be buried—a body that was maybe misidentified and went directly to the morgue. There are just too many possibilities on the table right now. I'm sure there are scenarios we can't even imagine." Rose shifts her weight to her other thigh and holds on to the chair with her left arm. "Even if he is alive, is he OK? Has someone hurt him?"

George looks his mother square in the eyes and says, "After all the campaigning he went through, then the attempt on his life, and now being kidnapped? It'd be too much for anybody— even Dad."

"George! Just shut up, man," Thomas says, shooting George a dirty look.

"Guys, let's just think," Rose says. She can't look Edwina in the eyes, as she feels too guilty. Her body is sore and exhausted. There's not a single part of her that feels human. To her relief and gratitude, Edwina begins to massage the tight muscles in her shoulders and neck.

"What do you want us to do, Mom?" Edwina asks. "I know you want us to do *something*. We are here for you."

Rose is hardly listening; Edwina's hands are smooth and strong, working methodically through all the knots and twists Rose has accumulated over the weeks. Her voice sounds like a sweet melody. Rose lets her mind wander to romantic nights under clouds of cool rain, her limbs entwined with Lance's beneath soft covers. She curls herself around the memory and gives way to the comfort of the past. Before she can slip too deep into her reverie, her body jerks at the soft touch of Edwina's lips as her daughter kisses her forehead. "Why have they done this to our family?" Rose asks as she collects the parts of her body that she can still feel and covers her eyes with one hand. "Go find your father."

"Mom, you're not thinking straight. There's nothing we can do," George protests.

"I *said*, go find your father, wherever he may be. Edwina, take your brothers, and start searching." Rose sits up and rubs the sleep from her heavy eyes. "At least I'll know we're doing something. I will manage things here, with June. We can help the three of you from here. I will keep the Secret Service distracted and find out everything I can to assist you."

"But Mom—" Edwina begins.

"Edwina, please." Rose takes her daughter's hand and kisses it, a final peace offering.

Thomas walks over, hugs his mother, and says, "You are right. We need to figure this out. We can't just sit in this hospital, looking after a man that isn't even our father."

Rose's voice is raspy from the lack of sleep and hours spent crying. There's been so much strain on not just her voice, but also her mind and body. She needs her strength now more than ever. Her family's security is at stake, as is the security of the country.

"Guys," George says, "I want to find Dad as much as you do, but isn't this a job for the FBI or the CIA? We're just the First Family. In reality, we have little power without Dad. Those organizations have everything at their disposal: manpower, intelligence, and technology. Let's talk to Director Schultz and get the power of the US intelligence services on this. I'm ready to talk to him; I can take the lead. And what about Director Cummings? Or how about the vice president?"

Rose sits up straight and shakes her head. "You're right, George. They *do* hold the power, and that's just it: they have too much of it. I don't trust the FBI or the CIA, and especially not the lying and incompetent Secret Service. Our government allowed this attack to happen two weeks after your father's inauguration. And on top of that, they brought in a stranger instead of the president of the United States. How the hell does that even happen?!" She stops to collect herself. "Our government let your father down. They let us all down. I have no doubt in my mind that there's someone among us who is responsible for all of this. They've had more than three weeks to make sure that man was your father. Fingerprints, eye scans, and whatever else—I'm *sure* someone has gone through these steps and knows that's not him. And whoever that is, they are responsible for a lot of death. It has to be someone at one of those agencies. We can't trust them. Have I made myself clear? Trust *no one.*"

The room falls silent. No one wants to be the first to talk. Rose looks around at each of their faces and isn't surprised when Edwina is the first to step up.

"I'll go. I can't sit around here waiting while Dad could be out there alone and hurt. We need to get to him before someone else does. And if someone has him, we need to find out who we can trust to get him back. Either way, we need more information." She turns to her mother. "What's your plan, Mom?"

"I don't think the Brigade has him. They would have made a move or bragged about it to the world. If one of the agencies has him, then I don't know. I need to think on that. If they literally just screwed up and brought in the wrong guy, then your dad is somewhere out there."

"But if that's the case, wouldn't he have come forward? If he was at a hospital, he would've told someone who he is," June interjects confidently.

"I agree, but what if he's not conscious?" Rose's mind is spinning, but she feels a new wave of energy. "I have my job cut out: I will handle the government agencies. You guys need to work on all the hospitals in New York that received victims from the attack."

The children look at one another, shooting looks of doubt from one to the other.

Edwina's face hardens. "Guys, all we need is one lead. That's it. Just something to run with. Will it be easy? No. But we must do *something.* I can't sit in this damn hospital one more day, knowing Dad could still be out there somewhere."

Rose takes a deep breath. "Together, we can do this. Edwina, Thomas, and George will go to the hospitals. I will tell the Secret Service agents and everyone else here that the three of you want to visit some victims of the attack—as well as the first responders who served this country so well—by personally attending to them at the hospitals. This is something we should have done to begin with. Too many people suffered and died on that horrible day." She wipes away her tears and continues, "This will give you full access and a reason for visiting every hospital on the list, which we will put together. I will call the chief executive officer of each hospital personally and explain the purpose of your visit. They will grant you full access to doctors, nurses, and patients." She pauses for a few moments before adding, "I will tell James the same thing we are telling everyone else: no one can know the truth. But I hope we are the only ones who know your father is missing. It will buy us time to be first in finding him."

"I will compile a list of the hospital contacts and have it ready by noon tomorrow," June says. She's always been the quiet one, who gets things done without being asked.

"Great," Rose replies, finally allowing a weak smile to find its way to her lips. "I will call FBI Director Johnson and CIA Director Schultz to see if they've found out anything new about the Brigade, and will start doing some digging with people I know and trust. I hope Jennifer Alvarez is one of those people. But for now, we won't tell her the truth either. If I start comparing stories, hopefully I will start to see some gaps and will eventually find out who's lying, even if I have to pit them against one another. On a more somber note, I'll request a full list of every victim who went straight to the morgue, as well as those who died at the hospital. The list will need to include a photograph of each victim. If there are any John Does, June will work with local officials until we identify each one. I want no stone left unturned. This is critical." Rose is aware that the morgues and their unidentified victims have to be part of their search, no matter how awful that thought may be.

"We are on it, Mom. Don't worry," Edwina assures her.

Rose gives Edwina a look that only a proud mother can bestow upon her child. "Then we all agree?" she asks as she walks toward her children, grabbing a small family portrait from the side table along the way. She holds the framed photo to her heart as all her children embrace her in a hug.

Then the room grows quiet as the terrible realization sinks in that Lance is probably dead.

CHAPTER 36

IS THIS JUNE?

▷ **Doris – Santa Fe, New Mexico, Day 25**

The early-morning Santa Fe sun makes the dew droplets on the lawn look like diamonds that fell from the sky overnight. Doris smiles as she enjoys the moment of wonder. "So this is why people live in New Mexico. Diamonds," she says to herself in a whisper so as not to wake Lance.

There's a soft knock at her bedroom door. It's Fatima. "You guys awake?"

Doris opens the door and comes out to greet her, quietly closing the door behind her. "Happy Saturday! Of course I'm up, but he's still sleeping."

"I have an update for you!" Fatima says, bubbling with excitement. "Come have coffee with me."

Doris follows her sister to the kitchen. "Everything OK?"

"Everything is great! I have good news. I finally got the phone number of one of the Dumont twins—June Dumont."

"Wow! That's . . . that's really great." Doris's heart sinks. "How did you manage that?"

"Like I said before, I know someone who knows someone; that's all I can say. Just in case something happens to you, I want to protect them. The fewer people who know, the better."

Doris smiles nervously. "OK, so what's the plan?"

"We are going to call her. Now. I already know what I'm going to say."

Doris looks at her sister. She wants to grab the phone out of her hand, but manages to stop herself from doing so. "I'm sorry—I just don't know if I'm ready. What's going to happen to me? To us?"

"Don't worry. You have to trust me on this. I've thought through some scenarios, and it's going to be OK. I said I will handle it, and I will. You'll see."

Doris nods in agreement, and Fatima dials the number.

"It's ringing," Fatima whispers.

Doris can hear the soft rings. After the fourth, she hears a young woman's voice.

"Hello?" she answers, sounding a little anxious.

"Hello, is this June?" asks Fatima.

"Yes, it is. Who's this?" June replies, her tone suspicious.

Fatima ignores the question, clearly keeping to a script. "I have some information about your father."

"What? What about my father?" June asks. Doris can hear excitement in her voice.

"I want to hear, please," Doris blurts out.

Fatima puts the call on speakerphone, then replies, "I'm sorry to tell you this, but your father is not at Presbyterian Hospital. He was taken to a different hospital on the day of the Courthouse Massacre. He was severely injured, but he's alive and recovering. You don't need to worry."

June gasps. *"Really?* Why do you think this patient is my father?"

Just then, Fatima and Doris hear a scuffle, then some muffled words from June. Suddenly, a man's voice comes over the phone. "This is the CIA. Who the hell is *this?* And how did you get this number?"

"Give me back my phone, James!" June yells in the background.

Without thinking, Fatima panics and hangs up the phone.

"Oh no, that was bad. What did we just do?" Fatima drops the phone and starts pacing.

"I don't know. That didn't sound good. I hope we didn't get her in trouble. Something is wrong there. Lance's daughter, she sounded almost, I dunno . . . relieved when you told her about her father."

Fatima leans against the kitchen counter for support. "Maybe, but she also sounded scared. Why the heck is a man from the CIA grabbing a phone from the president's daughter?"

"Well, the CIA is going to call us back."

"No. No, they won't," Fatima replies confidently. "This is a burner phone, and I also hid my number before I dialed. I told you I would take care of this. What the heck do you think I've been doing for the last week?"

"But that plan didn't work."

"I'm sorry, Doris. It was the best I could do."

"No, I'm sorry that you had to do that and that I've put you in harm's way. This is all so frustrating. Part of me was happy that this all could be ending; the other half of me wasn't ready to lose him. And now I'm just confused and can't see what the next step should be."

"The next step is to get his memory back and create a plan for when his mind finally comes around. What will you do then?" Fatima's tone is almost accusatory.

"I know, I've been thinking about that. I will figure something out. I promise."

"I'm going to run some errands. Try to enjoy your day, honey. Again, I'm so sorry that didn't go as planned," Fatima says as she heads to the door.

Doris lets the weight of her body bury her in the couch. Deep inside, she's relieved it didn't work out. She wants more time, but she also needs a new plan.

CHAPTER 37

GOODBYE, JAMES

▷ **Edwina – New York Presbyterian Hospital, Day 25**

E dwina is sitting in the hospital bedroom she shares with June, but she is out in the living room eating breakfast with the rest of the family. Edwina is still reeling from the conversation with her mother the night before. After ten minutes, she pulls herself together. "Please, God, help me find the strength to find our father. Please." She prays aloud, then joins her siblings in the living room.

"What are you guys eating?" asks Edwina, noticing that the florescent lighting is hurting her eyes this morning.

"Eggs and pancakes," says George. "I'm really getting to like hospital food."

"Good morning, Edwina. I was just on my way to get dressed. You done in there?" asks June.

"I'm done. I'm going to eat; I'm starving," Edwina replies.

Just then, June's phone vibrates, and she steps outside the suite to take the call. Given the lack of privacy, the family members usually take their calls in the hallway or in one of the bedrooms. Everyone continues eating their breakfast, mostly in silence.

Two minutes later, they hear June yelling. Rose is the first to her feet and out the door with the kids right behind her. They nearly fall over themselves on their way out the door and stop in their tracks when they see James and June quarreling.

"What are *you* doing here?" asks Rose in a condescending voice.

"Good morning, Mrs. Dumont. I'm sorry I didn't call first. I needed to get an update from Dr. Kellerman," James replies defensively.

"Mom, James just took my phone from me!" yells June.

"What the hell is going on, James?" Rose demands, her voice now angry.

"I was walking up and heard her say, 'Why do you think this patient is my father?' Someone calling about the president is a matter of national security. The Brigade members are still after him. You can't be taking calls from unknown numbers," James says, turning to June on the last sentence.

Rose walks over to him. Edwina backs away, hoping her mom doesn't slap him. Rose stops just shy of James, then snarls, "Listen, James, you have no idea what that call could've been about. It could've been a relative. You don't know the context; all you heard were some words about June's father, my husband." Rose snatches the phone from him.

"With all due respect, this could be serious. Your lives are constantly in danger until the Brigade members are all found," James says, his tone softer. "I'm on *your* side."

"Really? That's what we thought until we learned you were working for the CIA throughout the entire campaign. You've proved that we can't trust you. Lance was way too easy on you," Rose says evenly.

"I'm sorry. You are right. But can I prove myself to *you?*" James pleads.

"Right now, I just want to be with my family. Goodbye, James." Rose turns back toward the suite with her children close behind her, like a mother duck and her ducklings.

Once inside, Rose is the first to speak. "Tell me exactly what happened on that phone call, June."

June recounts every detail of the short telephone call.

"June, can you please unlock your phone and hand it to me?" asks Thomas. "I want to see the number. We can call them back."

"The number was blocked," June replies.

Rose sits down. "Damn it. The hospital has to be here, in New York City. Let's move forward as planned. Quickly. June, as discussed, please start calling the four hospitals I gave you, and hand the phone to me when you get ahold of the top person in charge. Tell them who you are and that you are calling on my behalf, just as we discussed." She turns to Thomas. "You, Edwina, and George, go get ready; I want you at the first hospital by 1:00 p.m. June will handle any John Does here at Presbyterian." She pauses, then adds, "This is actually good news. It's better than nothing, and let's just remember, at least he's alive and not in the hands of the Brigade. Thank God. We just need to get to him before the wrong people find him."

Edwina sits quietly with her thoughts, wondering, *What woman has our father? And why?*

CHAPTER 38

THE SERVER

▷ **Doris – Santa Fe, New Mexico, Day 25**

Lance and Doris decide to go out for an early dinner. Doris needs some air after the failed attempt at contacting the Dumonts. After walking for around twenty minutes, they reach a small restaurant they have passed several times during their walks over the past week. Doris nods her thanks as Lance holds the dark wooden door open for her, and steps into the charming old-world interior. Red faux-leather booths line the walls, with vintage posters hearkening seemingly happier days. A tall, young female server comes over and leads them to the back of the restaurant, where there are fewer people seated. Lance helps Doris into the small booth by a window, then walks over to the other side and slides to the middle while grabbing a laminated menu.

Since they entered the restaurant, Doris has been thinking about the new man Lance has become over the past few days. Each day, his progress surprises her. She hasn't seen this gentlemanly side of him before. It's like this new person has emerged from thin air—this man of many colors. He takes the liberty of ordering her favorite sandwich for her: turkey on rye with everything on it and extra pickles. He's seen her make it countless times at home. He then pours cream into her cup of coffee, adds one tablespoon of sugar, and stirs it. Again, just like she does at home.

She thinks back to her first feelings for this man sitting beside her. She remembers all the blood on his face and on the ground around him. It looked as if there could be no more blood left in his body. He was lying there patiently, silently asking her to save him. In that moment, she wished the world would open a crack big enough to swallow all the pain and death that surrounded them. Armageddon had reached the steps of the New York State Supreme Court Building. Doris remembers looking up at the sky and making a promise right then and there. In a small voice she said, "God, if you save this man, I will run through the depths of hell for him and bring him back to you safely."

She returns to the moment and watches Lance as a cat would a wounded bird that's about to fly away. She takes in his new-found charm, then realizes it must have been there all along. He certainly had it on the campaign trail. She saw it on TV, where many news commentators called it too smooth, inauthentic. But to Doris, it's pure confidence, and she loves it. It reminds her of Daniel. So much of Lance reminds her of him.

"Why are you watching me like that? I pose no danger, my dear." Lance's voice snaps her out of her thoughts. "The danger would be you and I alone, right?"

Doris is taken aback, afraid, but also excited. She wonders where the hell this came from. "What do you mean, Elliot? Maybe *I'm* the danger. What if I left you to tend to yourself?" She doesn't look at him as she talks, and instead pretends to read the menu, even though he already ordered for her.

Lance looks at her with a half grin that stretches across the uninjured side of his face. His left cheek has lost some of the movement it once had due to the tissue damage.

"So, Ribbons, do you think I've done well? I can take care of myself now." He pauses for the accolade, but it doesn't come. "Have I passed the test? Isn't that what this is all about? Your patient has recovered. Now what's your plan?"

Again, Doris is left suspended in disbelief that this man—her patient, President Lance Dumont—is talking to her in this way. This feisty and flirty man. Is this the *real* him? She doesn't know enough about his real personality, only what she has seen on TV. What is he like in private? She has heard rumors that he was a ladies' man, but there were no women coming out of the woodwork, like with other politicians. His record was clean, which is why many people she knows voted for him. She decides to give it right back to him and see how he reacts.

"I didn't know I was testing you, but I'll tell you something, Elliot. I'll confess that I don't know this side of you. I'm liking our lunch date."

Lance raises an eyebrow as if to call her out on her bluff. "You've been acting as if we are brother and sister—surely, nurse and patient. But here, in this restaurant, we can be something new."

Doris wonders if the earth just flung itself into outer space. Sure, she has wished for words such as these to come out of his mouth, but only in her dreams. She never expected to actually hear them, and she's not certain it's what she really wants. But *damn!* He's good at this dialogue. He can manipulate her, just like her late husband. The two are way too similar, and now she knows she's in dangerous territory. Fatima's advice rings in her head. He's already caught on to her habits and able to predict her next move. Has he been studying her since the day they met? Has he been more mentally aware than she's thought? She isn't sure who is playing whom anymore. She'd thought she was the director of this play, but now she feels more like the actor.

She leans back into her chair as if to get a better view of what's happening. To take it all in. She pulls her long blond hair from behind her back and drapes it over one shoulder. It's a look she knows works well on men.

Lance watches her intently as they sit in silence. She wonders who will make the next move.

The server breaks the tension when she arrives at their table with their food and asks, "Do you need anything else?"

Lance replies, "I think we're good, thank you. We love this place. How long have you worked here?"

"Just a few months. It's my part-time job; I'm also a yoga instructor," boasts the server, her full lips exposing unnaturally white teeth.

With great interest, Doris watches them talk. Certainly, the server is attractive, and Lance, despite his wounds and scars, is still something to look at. Instead of the handsome boy next door he used to be, he now gives off a sexy, rugged vibe. He has an air about him that even the assassination attempt couldn't take away.

After the server leaves, Doris leans in, careful to keep her voice neutral. "What was *that* all about?" She isn't sure if she's teasing and can't understand why her heart feels so easily threatened. For now, he belongs to her, but she knows it won't be for long.

"What? We've seen this server a few times on our walks. We've even said hello to her when we've passed. I was just being polite. Let's enjoy our meals."

He rubs her thigh for a brief second in the silence that follows. She stiffens but chooses not to move. "Your thigh is warm, are you OK? I hope I didn't hurt you in any way by talking to the server. Disappointment seems to turn people cold toward one another." He pauses, looking at her more intently. "I'm sorry. Is it OK that I touched you?"

Doris shifts her torso in the booth with the nervous energy of a teenaged girl at the school prom. She can't tell him the truth: that it felt like streams turning into rivers when his fingers caressed her leg. "Oh, I didn't even notice. Don't worry about it, Elliot."

His eyes register his subtle victory, and his lips once again pull upward into a crooked grin. She glances down, silently berating herself. If only she could've found the right words. Why didn't she simply admit she enjoyed it? She crosses her arms over her chest, trying to settle herself and extinguish the fire his touch lit inside her.

"To be honest, that server kind of irritated me," she admits after a minute. "I don't mean to sound jealous because you were talking to someone else. I just felt like she was interrupting a special moment between us. That's all." She is surprised that her tone sounded angrier than she'd intended. She knows she had no right to say this, because he is *not* hers, not really, but she couldn't help herself.

"Ribbons—"

She doesn't let him finish. "Let's go back home. I don't feel well." Her cheeks are stinging with the thought of him touching her again, but she refuses to let it show. She's the director again, and she's ready for this part of the play to end. She takes two twenties from her purse and places them on the table.

Lance offers her a hand up. As she stands, he puts his lips to her ear. "You know, I've been waiting for you to say something like that, to reveal your true feelings. It makes me feel good. So will you let me start helping you now?"

The scent of his cologne hits her like a hot shower, and she hastily tries to shake it off so she can focus on his words. "What do you mean?"

"Well, you've been taking care of me for as long as I can remember—granted, that may not have been a very long time."

Lance laughs, leading her toward the door of the restaurant. "Now it's my turn."

She looks down and tries to hide her smile, wondering if this is a fever of the heart or of the flesh. She looks back up at him, into his bright-hazel bedroom eyes, and her lips part ever so slightly. *Stop it,* she says to herself as they exit the restaurant.

☺☺

Back at the house, Lance asks Doris, "What flavor of tea do you want?"

"Me? Tea?" She asks, forgetting her lie about not feeling well. Her face flushes.

"Yes, you said back at the restaurant you didn't feel well, so I'm making you tea. What flavor?"

"Oh, yes, chamomile sounds great. It will help me sleep tonight. Extra honey, please." She smiles warmly, anxious to relieve the tension between them. What she really needs is a cold cup of water dumped over her head to cool her down.

Lance asks her to sit on the sofa in the living room. From there, she watches him carry over her cup of tea, which he gently places into her outstretched hands. He then retrieves a kitchen chair and places it directly in front of her.

Just as he's about to speak, she cuts him off. "I'm glad that you want my attention. You could've just sat next to me on the sofa."

Lance stays in the chair and smiles, ignoring her comment.

Ribbon's mind momentarily wanders to a similar moment she shared with Daniel. She shakes her head, and the memory fades away. She doesn't want her mind to be anywhere else right now.

Lance taps her teacup to get her attention. "Let's say I start to feel good enough to make my own money. You know, get a job?"

She shoots him a nervous look. "Why do you want to make your own money, Elliot? We're fine. I pulled enough funds from my 401K to last us several months."

"That's not the point. I would like to buy you something in return for everything you've done." He opens his legs wider, enclosing her legs as he scoots in closer to her.

"What do you mean?" She leans toward him to smell his scent; it always helps calm her when she knows a tough conversation is coming.

"At night, when I can't sleep, I hear this calling to return to some far-off land where there's an ocean. But then the next morning when I wake, I don't see any pictures of myself on the wall or dresser. That's when I think, maybe I don't belong here—in this house or town. I have nothing but the ribbon you wore on your lapel. There's nothing else I remember. It's just me and that ribbon. I need more. Please let me do more."

She tries to speak, but he puts his finger to her lips and leaves it there. Doris doesn't move, nor does she look away. They stare at each other in silence until Lance continues.

"Ribbons, please listen. I want to get a job. I want my own money. Money to do things with you and buy gifts for you. Please."

His voice—sincere and shaky—makes her heart ache. This man could do anything; he already landed the most powerful position in the world, and here he is now, begging for a simple job. She takes a deep breath and holds it. She can hear the wind beginning to howl through the trees outside. Just as she's about to speak, the opening of the garage door floods the house with sound, and she stands up in relief. Just in time. She's not ready for this conversation.

"OK, Elliot, we'll talk about this later; I promise. Fatima is home."

He looks dissatisfied, but he doesn't say anything more as Fatima walks in, laden with bags and envelopes. Doris walks over to assist her, taking the bags and putting away groceries as Fatima grabs some water and sits down at the kitchen table to sort through the mail.

"Dor— Ribbons," Fatima stammers.

"Yes?" Doris turns to look at her sister. She notices the color has drained from her face and she's holding a piece of paper. "Are you OK, Fatima?" Turning to Lance, she says, "Why don't you go ahead and get ready for bed. I'll be there in a few minutes."

"Sure, I'll see you in there. Good night, Fatima," Lance says before heading to their bedroom.

"What's wrong?" Doris asks as she walks over to the table.

Fatima pushes an envelope across the table to Doris. It's small, so the name written across it nearly fills the entire space: *RIBBONS.* Below that is written Fatima's address. Doris's mouth dries up.

"What? This can't be! Someone knows?" With trembling hands, she rips it open, unsure of what bad news it will contain. It feels like lifting an old piece of wood that's been sitting on the ground for years, knowing you'll find spiders beneath it and hoping none are poisonous.

She extracts a single piece of card stock containing a single word carefully printed in capital letters: *RUN.*

CHAPTER 39

SEARCHING FOR JOHN DOE

▷ **Edwina – New York Presbyterian Hospital, Day 25**

George, Edwina, and Thomas huddle around the table to begin the search for their father. Their goal is to interview hospital personnel working on the day of the Courthouse Massacre. Narrowing down the list of hospital contacts and preparing the list of questions for them is a time-consuming task. There are thousands of workers at each of the four hospitals, but June has already shortened the list to just hundreds per hospital—only those individuals who had direct contact with victims of the Courthouse Massacre. They work for the rest of the morning, preparing schedules and strategizing their approach, with the goal of leaving Presbyterian by 12:30 p.m.

"OK, do you think we have everything?" asks Edwina. "Thomas, let's put together four identical binders for each of the four hospitals, containing the names of every person who worked during the twenty-four-hour period following the attack. Maybe leave extra space so we can take notes on each page and highlight anything unusual or helpful." Edwina's heart is pounding. She's relieved to know her father's alive, but she's very much feeling the pressure of time. "We have to be the first to find him, guys."

"Don't you think we know that?" says George sarcastically.

"George, just shut up," Thomas says. "We *will* be the first. Let's just keep our questions focused while sticking to our story: we are visiting to personally thank everyone and learn about their individual stories. I think we should also include shift times and the number of courthouse victims each nurse or doctor engaged with that day."

"The good thing is that everyone's going to want to share their story," Edwina says. "We just have to go off hunches. There's so many people, so much ground to cover—hundreds per hospital. Remember, we especially need to focus on all the John Does, like Mom suggested. That's going to be the place to start in each emergency department, then go from there. What do you guys think?"

Thomas nods. "Great idea. Look for anything out of the ordinary—unidentified victims are the perfect place to start—and remember, we can always circle back to a hospital later. We've got to move fast, so we'll need to split up the interviewees to cover more ground." He pauses, then looks at George. "And don't forget, the press will be watching us and trying to make a story out of our visits, so we can't slip up."

"Mom says she has it all taken care of," George replies. "No press will be allowed inside the hospitals, and we'll enter through the back of each building, with only a same-day notice being given in order to prevent leaks. Mom's back on her game. Once she's on a mission, she's unstoppable."

Edwina sifts through their notes and then straightens up as an idea comes to mind. "Don't you think Dad would have had some sort of papers in his pockets, like notes for his speech? He would, at least, have some kind of identification, right? Presidents carry IDs too, don't they?"

"Hold your horses, young lady," George says, smiling. "I already asked Mom about that this morning. She confirmed that Dad had some sort of ID on him, which is unusual for presidents, but I guess he had asked for one. She couldn't remember why."

"You surprise me, George," Thomas says as he pats his brother on the back.

"OK then," continues Edwina, "so if he did have an ID, then someone who works at the hospital would've had to check him in and verify identification for insurance and to notify his family. They would've found it in his pocket and immediately notified the authorities, right?"

"Maybe, but remember, there was absolute chaos at the courthouse; there's a possibility his ID fell out of his pocket," George says. "But someone *does* know where he is: the woman June spoke to on the phone—not that *that* helps much. Right now, we need to understand how they admit new patients who come through the ER. We need to understand every detail and look for any gaps. That's how we'll find Dad."

Edwina puts her hand on top of her brother's hand. "Thank you, George. I feel better about this already. You know, I feel lucky to have you both as brothers." She high-fives George and Thomas and then looks up at the ceiling, her hands together in the praying position. "Oh God, please help us."

"Come on then," Thomas says, rising from the table. "Let's check out the first hospital."

Rose catches them on their way out the door. "Listen, you three: time is not on our side. I did some digging this morning and found out that every injured survivor of the attack was brought *only* to the top five New York hospitals, this one included. So you don't have to waste your time with the smaller hospitals and urgent care centers. You can do one today, maybe two tomorrow, then one the next day. Be quick and focused with your questions. Good luck, and I love you guys."

The siblings hug and then hurry to their car downstairs, Secret Service in tow.

◎◎

Their first stop is Bellevue Hospital on First Avenue, which happens to be one of the largest hospitals in the entire country by number of beds. Many of the victims were taken here. The hospital's president greets the siblings and brings them to the ER. There, they split up and head off to conduct their own interviews with staff members who worked during the first twenty-four hours of the attack.

Two hours later, during a break, they compare notes on the ER's check-in procedure. They all have the same story: The patient's clothes are removed, placed into a plastic bag, and then attached to or placed below the patient's hospital bed. Nurses go through the patient's wallet for identification and to help with hospital documentation for those who are not able to communicate. Of those who did not have identification on them the day of the attack, some had spouses or friends with them; others could identify themselves. Nothing unusual here.

That afternoon, the three of them witness the chaos from a nearby car crash involving six passengers. The procedure they reviewed two hours ago doesn't appear to be followed. Obtaining identification is not that important at such a critical time, when every second means life or death. The staff first needs to save the patients' lives. The patients' personal belongings are, in fact, bagged—but they are not immediately labeled. Because things are so hectic, some bags are placed on the large counter at the nurses station, to be labeled and documented later, once things have slowed down.

Thomas turns to Edwina. "Are you thinking the same thing I am? If they brought Dad here, only the person who checked him in would know his identity. There's no double-checking. There's so much room for error. A nurse or doctor could write down any name, and no one would be the wiser."

"Of course!" Edwina says excitedly. "A nurse learns a patient's name almost immediately. It seems that if the nurse is too busy, like we just witnessed, he or she might go through the belongings bag later to fill out the paperwork. So anything is possible. The process is a lot less formal than I expected."

Thomas nods slowly. "It seems they only go through a patient's pockets after it's been determined that the patient came in without friends or family and is unable to speak. If the patient can speak, the nurse doesn't even bother going through their clothes to confirm the information provided. Maybe Dad was able to talk and lied about his identity to protect himself. Dad's smart enough to do that, even under duress."

"But if he couldn't talk when he was brought in, someone must have gone through his clothes and found out who he was," George mumbles, biting his nails anxiously. "It would have blown their mind when they saw it was the president of the United States!"

"That's only *if* Dad had his identification on him, and we don't know that for sure," Edwina reminds him. "And why wouldn't someone immediately report that they found the president? All those we've met have been dedicated, hardworking everyday people. They aren't part of militias or intelligence agencies. They wouldn't be motivated to hide Dad's identity, right?"

Thomas jumps in. "Guys, hold on here. Remember that the woman who called June somehow knows that Dad was a patient somewhere other than Presbyterian. She must have seen his ID. Otherwise, how would she know?"

"By *looking* at him—*duh*," snaps George.

Edwina ignores him. "Thomas, you're right. She's aware that a certain patient is the president. But clearly, he's not registered as Lance Dumont. So he has to be listed as a John Doe, just another unidentified patient. We've been told there were many that day. This needs to remain our focus. We can tell personnel that we're trying to help families identify missing parents and siblings. We also need to find out what they do when they have a John Doe. There must be some sort of special procedure for those cases."

"Well, hold on. Let's think about that," George says beginning to pace in a circle. "On the day of the attack, there was so much excitement going on in every hospital. Maybe someone was trying to protect Dad's identity. Things were chaotic, and the news made it clear that some of the attackers had not been caught. Maybe they were worried something would happen to him. Or maybe they just didn't believe it was actually him—like it was some sort of a mistake. I guess that's much more plausible."

"George, stop moving. You're giving me a headache walking in circles like that," Thomas complains. "And even if someone is protecting Dad, they'd still have to give the hospital a name for his records. So maybe the John Doe route isn't the only one we should take."

CHAPTER 40

DON'T LET ME DOWN

▷ **Rockefeller – Langley, Virginia, Day 26**

Rockefeller is trying not to let his frustration get the best of him. He didn't sleep at all last night, as he was busy trying to plan his next step. He decides to skip going into the office this morning. He needs his team to be focused on finding Dumont, so he makes the drive west to the Brigade's headquarters. On the way there, he has time to think about everything that has happened over the last few weeks. Nothing has gone according to plan. He lost a lot of Brigade members during the February 4 attack, but that's what they signed up for. Things got out of control, and he was told Dumont was brought to the hospital instead of being killed.

Thanks to his contacts, Rockefeller has been able to control things at the hospital. He now has people on the inside. His post-attack plan was to make sure Dumont never woke from his induced coma. That was accomplished easily enough by putting the doctor on payroll and threatening him and his family. But then, a few days ago, he learned that the Secret Service brought in the wrong guy on the day of the attack, proving their incompetence yet again. Now he has to find the president.

He parks his car in the driveway of the pale-green house, walks up to the door, looks up at the camera, and nods his head.

The door opens after he inserts his key, and he makes his way inside.

"Everybody ready?" Rockefeller asks, forgoing any pleasantries.

Gruff nods his head as they walk through the next security door. The basement war room feels like home to Rockefeller. It gives him confidence that they can find Dumont.

"I've risked a lot by coming here. But this is important, and we have very little time. I want an update," he barks.

Gruff takes the lead. "Unfortunately, we don't have any good news. In three days, we hit all five hospitals and every New York City morgue. We found nothing."

"What do you mean 'nothing'?" Rockefeller asks, his impatience building.

"Well, most of the patients from February 4 have been discharged. We identified each remaining male, and none was Dumont. We then confirmed that every morgue successfully contacted the family members of each of their original five John Does. We got those names and followed up on each just in case. Everything was legit. No Dumont."

Rockefeller stands and walks to the other side of the room, then turns to his troop. "OK, so now we need to find him. We know he's alive and was discharged. The clear route is to identify every discharged male. How many is that?"

"I dunno . . . probably around two hundred and fifty, tops." Gruff replies.

"Then get on it. I want everyone on this—100 percent focus. Get those names today, and start your work. Be ruthless. Do what you've got to do. Pay who you need to pay, and threaten those who won't cooperate. Don't let me down."

"We're on it. I can put at least six members on this immediately," Gruff promises as he looks around the room. Understanding their commander's orders, the team members nod in agreement.

"Good. Did you take care of the doctor?" Rockefeller hadn't anticipated needing Dr. Kellerman's help for so long, and he certainly can't just get rid of him. At least not right now.

"Yes, sir. We transferred more money to his account. He will make sure Guthrie stays in his coma until you give the orders," Gruff replies proudly.

"Listen, I can't use my connections right now to give you information any faster. But you guys should already have enough access to systems to find out what you need to about those who were discharged."

Gruff nods. "We will be fine. All systems go, sir."

"By the way, any news on the cop? Patient Guthrie's son. Tell me he's just moping around in his small New York apartment, missing his daddy."

"Sir, actually, he's not. He's been busy. We've tapped his phone, placed a tracer on his truck, and my guy has been on him around the clock over the last week."

"What's he been doing? The cop, that is." Rockefeller sits up in his chair, feeling a little less cocky.

"For some reason, he went back to Lenox Hill Hospital a few days ago."

"And? What the hell was he doing there?"

"I don't know. We don't know who he talked to," Gruff answers sheepishly.

"I want eyes on him twenty-four seven. Get someone better on him. I want to know who he meets with and where he goes. Got it?"

"Well, it's too late for that."

"Why's that?"

"Jack Guthrie left the state of New York today," Gruff responds, looking down at the ground.

"Jesus. Where's he going?"

"No clue, sir."

"Don't let your guy lose him, or there will be hell to pay," Rockefeller threatens.

Gruff nods. "Yes, sir."

ꙮ

An hour later, Rockefeller is back at his desk. The drive gave him time to think about his next move. It is only a matter of time until *someone* at Presbyterian Hospital figures out the truth—most likely, the Dumont family. But he's not worried about them. Not right now. The last thing he wants is the Secret Service finding out they screwed up. But he needs to know if *they* know.

He dials the number of a contact to see if anyone has discovered Dumont's not at Presbyterian. She will know.

A woman picks up the phone.

"Hello, Erica. How are you?" Rockefeller asks in as kindly a manner as he can muster.

"I'm good, sir. Thank you for asking," Erica says.

He can almost see her blushing.

"Is the new president in her office?" Rockefeller asks. He can just imagine Jennifer Alvarez sitting behind the desk at the Oval Office, enjoying herself immensely. Having the president put into a coma is one of the easiest ways to get promoted. *Alvarez should be thanking me*, he thinks as he waits for her to take his call.

CHAPTER 41

A CAGED BIRD

▷ **Doris – Santa Fe, New Mexico, Day 26**

Doris hasn't been able to sleep. She's noticed every hour on the digital clock and remembers each: 11:42, 12:17, 1:33 . . . Her mind has been in and out of half dreams, the kind in which you're not sure if you are sleeping and reality blurs with nightmarish thoughts. Finally, she decides to get up. The clock reads 5:49. It is still dark outside, but she needs to wake up Lance now. Time is running out.

RUN. That's all she can think about since she saw that word.

"Elliot, wake up!" She nudges him gently until he stirs and grunts. "I have some good news," she says in a hushed tone, hoping to hide the panic surging inside. "I told Fatima that we're going to leave." She looks for his reaction, but his eyes are still closed. "She said we can stay here as long as we want, but I told her we need to move on and give her back her space."

Lance opens one groggy eye at a time. She nudges him harder, trying to inject some enthusiasm into her voice. "Don't you want to go on an adventure? Away from here, just you and me? We can go to a new place and find you work. Isn't that what you want?"

Finally awake, he asks, "Are you sure, Ribbons?" His words come slowly and a bit suspiciously. "Where will we go? There are no places I remember. My mind is still foggy, and my memory's still shot." A hint of a smile appears on his face as he sits up. "But OK. When do you want to leave?"

"Today, as soon as we can. Let's start packing!"

⊙⊚

Doris lets Lance pack his own things—clothes she bought for him at Lancaster York Gentlemen's Apparel, a local men's store in downtown Santa Fe. She quickly packs her clothes and takes her luggage out to the car in the garage. This time, instead of renting a car for Doris, Fatima is letting them borrow one of her two cars. Doris knows how hard it is for Fatima to let it go, aware there's a chance she'll never see it again. It was the first car Fatima purchased in the new millennium. She bought it when she turned twenty-two and got her first real job as a bank teller. Doris steps back from the faded red car—a 1996 Honda Civic. It was used when her sister bought it, but Doris remembers the good times they had in it and wishes they could go back to that simpler time.

Doris goes back into the house and finds Fatima in the kitchen. "Good morning," Doris says as they share a lingering hug. Leaving Fatima's house is hard. Her sister has done so much for them, risked so much.

"Have you thought about the note?" Fatima asks.

"No, I haven't had much time to think about it." *Except all night,* Doris adds silently.

"Who would have given you such a warning? The postmark wasn't even from New York. It said *Stamford, Connecticut.* Do you know anybody there?"

"No. I think it has to be Angela or Alice. They are the only friends of mine who know you and could've guessed that I'd be coming here. Anyway, I will have plenty of time to think about it in the car." She can hear the dread in her own voice.

"I wonder why they want you to run. Who's coming?" Fatima asks, clearly fearful.

Doris knows she has to be strong for her sister. She grabs Fatima's hands and looks directly into her eyes. "Listen, *you* will be fine. Should anyone come around, you tell them that you haven't seen me. In fact, make it clear that you are worried about me because you haven't heard from me in so long. Tell them the truth: that I haven't been answering my phone." That much was true. She left her cell phone back in her New York City apartment.

"I will be fine; I can handle myself. But I wish you didn't have to go, Doris," Fatima says. "I wish I could've helped more; I especially wish that call with June wasn't a failure. I'm sorry."

Fatima allowed Doris to make the hard decisions about Lance without interfering, and Doris is thankful for that. "The best thing that's come out of this for me is reconnecting with you. It has been such a joy. I should've come here when Daniel passed away. I probably wouldn't be such a mess right now. Hell, maybe I would've made an entirely different decision about Lance if my head was screwed on straight." Doris looks at the floor. "But the past is the past, and I guess that's exactly where it belongs."

"Hey, don't have regrets; there's no need. You've done your best. This will turn out all right. I'll always be here for you if you need anything." Fatima lifts her sister's chin up to look directly into her eyes. "Listen, when this is all over, I'd love for you to come stay with me for as long as you want. Promise me you'll consider that?"

"I promise," Doris replies, wiping tears away while wondering when they will see each other again and under what circumstances. Maybe she will be behind bars. "When Lance comes in here for breakfast, can you give us a moment? For your safety, you can't know where we're going, and Lance and I need to discuss it before we get in the car." Her gut tells her that they should drive to California. She wants to be as far as possible from New York; Washington, DC; and now, New Mexico. But where would they go in California? She doesn't know anyone there. But at least it's somewhere else, someplace safe, for now. And Lance mentioned the ocean.

Fatima nods in agreement just as Lance walks into the room.

"Good morning, ladies," Lance says with a grin.

Doris pulls out the map she purchased in New York City and sits down at the table with Lance. On cue, Fatima stands up and leaves the room so that if anyone comes asking, she can truthfully say she has no idea where her sister is. It's for the best.

Doris spreads out the map on the table. She points out New York, neglecting Washington, DC, and moves his attention across the Midwest and down to New Mexico. Her finger then continues west, ending up at the Pacific Ocean. She needs *him* to want to go to California. It has to be *his* idea.

"What's over here, Ribbons?" Lance's hand runs over the map as though it were smoothing his hair—casual but deliberate. His fingers land on California. "I'd love to see the ocean. I feel like a caged bird that needs fresh air."

The fish took the bait. Time to reel him in. Doris feigns surprise. "The ocean? All the way to California?" She pauses for effect, deciding not to address his caged bird comment. She, too, feels caged, and now it's time for them to fly the coop. "Well then, California it is! We can go to Los Angeles, lie on the beach, maybe even get a suntan! We will leave after breakfast and get a good start on the long drive there."

She flinches when Lance reaches over and takes her hand. Hers is clammy, and she's almost certain he can feel her heart pounding.

"Why am I so afraid when I look into your eyes?" he asks. "I see fear. What are you scared of? Are you sure you're ready to leave your sister?"

Doris smiles, but it feels tense. She leans into his arms, noting his physical strength, and tries to draw courage from his presence. She doesn't want him to know how frightened she is. There is so much they're running from. If he only knew.

⊚⊚

Their luggage is sitting next to the car in Fatima's garage. Doris figures it's best to say their official goodbyes and load the car out of sight from the prying eyes of neighbors.

She thanks her sister again, which turns into many more thanks. While they talk, Lance loads the car with their suitcases and their drinks and snacks. The sisters prolong the moment, neither wanting to be the first to say goodbye. Lance takes the lead, thanking her with a kiss on the cheek and a long, strong hug. He climbs into the car and shuts the door, giving the sisters some last moments alone.

Doris speaks first. "Thank you for everything, sis, really. I'm sorry we have to run—literally! I know this all seems so crazy, I've admitted that, and still think it's all nuts. I know I shouldn't have, but I got up early this morning to watch the news before Lance woke up, as I have almost every day, and major news outlets still believe that people inside our own government colluded with the Brigade. They talk about it like it's a fact. Plus, there are new stories about other extremist groups taking up arms and threatening attacks on the president's allies."

"Why are you telling me all this, Doris? I'm already worried enough."

"I dunno, maybe because I'm trying to rationalize why the heck I'm running across the country with the president of the United States. I need to be sure I'm doing the right thing."

"If doing the right thing means saving him and yourself, then, yes, you are doing the right thing. Think about it, if people on the inside know that President Dumont isn't lying in that bed at Presbyterian Hospital—and I'm sure they must know by now—then it's just a matter of time before they track us both down. To be honest, over the last few weeks, I've been sure a SWAT team will come busting through my doors and windows! People are gonna realize there is no Elliot Greene, and if that hasn't happened already, it's probably going to be soon."

"You are right. Thank you, Fatima. Thanks for everything." Doris doesn't bother with the tears streaming down both sides of her face.

Fatima grabs her hands. "God put this man in your hands. He knew you'd keep him safe. And so far, you have. I'm sorry this all rests on your shoulders. I wish I could do more to help you."

Doris holds on to her sister's hands for as long as she can. "Hey, we've always had each other's backs, and now more than ever." She wants to say so much more, but she just can't find the words right now.

Fatima and Doris hug one last time before Doris gets into the car, closes the door, and backs out of the garage. Doris thinks about their past while hoping they will make it out of this mess alive so they can have a future. In time, hopefully not soon, someone will be coming to Fatima's house, looking for Doris Machado and the president.

CHAPTER 42

TELL ME THE TRUTH

▷ **Edwina – Bellevue Hospital, Day 26**

The next morning, Edwina, Thomas, and George target the next two hospitals on their list, eager to move quickly. In their briefing to their mother last night, they shared what they had learned at Bellevue. Rose told them she had spoken to James and learned that the CIA has been visiting the hospitals in search of injured Brigade members. According to her, James was trying to earn back her trust and was sharing more information now. However, she also warned the kids that the information may be false, noting that she still doesn't completely trust him. In the end, they all agreed that this meant that the CIA would also be looking at the John Does.

The Dumont siblings make it to the first hospital of the day by 7:30 a.m.—Lenox Hill Hospital. The CEO greets them and takes them to the ER to begin their interviews. Once again, the siblings split up and move through the staff, interviewing and updating the notes in their binders as they go along. They finish their rounds of praise and gratitude and then head up to the second floor to meet with Dr. Brian Dansby, the floor's head physician.

"Thank you for allowing us to be here, Doctor," Thomas begins, shaking his hand. "We're thankful for all the work you and your team have done to help the victims of the Courthouse Massacre."

"Thank you for coming to visit us," Dr. Dansby replies.

"Have all your patients been identified?" Thomas continues. "We can help if you're having any issues. We would hate to think any victims from that day are unable to connect with their loved ones. We are here to help."

Dr. Dansby shakes his head. "Fortunately, that won't be necessary. Everyone has been identified, but I understand where you're coming from. In fact, we had a police officer come by not long after the attack, looking for his father. I'm not sure whether or not he found him after he left here. Those were crazy days; we were overwhelmed by the number of people we had to notify that their family members were in our care."

"That must have been a huge endeavor, Doctor," Edwina empathizes. Then, after a moment of thought, she asks, "So was the hospital able to locate family members of *all* the victims?" She says a silent prayer: *Please, God. Please let him say no.*

"Luckily, we were. We now have just a few dozen patients from that day in our care."

Edwina's hope dissipates as quickly as it arose.

"But in one case, it took a week—a patient by the name of Elliot. I can't remember his last name. He never had visitors while in our care, even after a week of being here. It was sad to see him struggle alone. We worked with New York City's program designed for family members to locate victims of the attack. About forty-eight hours after the attack, we submitted Elliot's name after we discovered we were unable to locate any of his family members. In the beginning, the nurses searched his name and made several calls but couldn't find any contacts for him."

Edwina looks at her brothers with hopeful eyes and asks the doctor, "Were you not able to ask this patient for his family's contact information?"

"He had severe injuries and couldn't speak. Plus, he was suffering from amnesia."

"I'm sorry to hear that. So . . . I'm guessing you eventually located a family member or friend of his?" George asks.

"It all turned out OK. Thankfully, he had one of our best nurses looking after him. Doris took care of him like he was family. She took a real liking to him and never left him alone. You know, it happens a lot with nurses and their patients. They can have a special bond, especially after traumatic events, such as the Courthouse Massacre."

"We'd love to meet him and say hello, if possible," Edwina says quickly. "We've met so many victims, and our mother wants us to do anything we can to help them."

"Unfortunately, you can't meet him, as he was released a couple of weeks ago. The nurses said someone, maybe his daughter or son—I can't remember—finally came to take him home. It all happened so quickly. I personally didn't think Elliot was ready to leave; he still had a long road ahead of him to recover his memory, but another doctor signed him out under pressure from Elliot's family member. So strange: I'm gone for a day, and another doctor signs him out. And that doctor left the next day on maternity leave, so I haven't been able to follow up with her. Anyway, I would've kept him here longer, but I can't control *everything*. As I said, it all happened so quickly."

Edwina, George, and Thomas steal a hopeful glance at one another before Thomas exclaims, "That's great news! We'd love to thank his nurse. Is she working today?"

Edwina turns to George, flashing two crossed fingers.

"Again, I'm sorry." Dr. Dansby looks at the floor, noticeably emotional. "She no longer works here. She quit the same day Elliot left. Not surprising, though. She was here for over ten years and went through a great deal during that time. She lost a lot of patients, including her husband a year ago. This is a hard job. Our nurses work every day with patients who get better and leave, but others die. It can get to be too much for them. The nurses said Doris left here in tears." He swallows audibly. "We were close, so she left me a long resignation letter. She was a first responder at the courthouse. In fact, she was the one who found Elliot beneath the courthouse steps. She was experiencing a fair amount of PTSD from that day, but she left before the hospital could set her up with a therapist. I get what she was going through. From what I've seen on the news, the courthouse looked like a war zone that day. I can't imagine being there in person. I don't blame her in the slightest for leaving us, but I wish we could've done more for her. We haven't heard from her since she left. Our calls to her cell phone go to voicemail, and there's been no answer on her landline either. A couple of the nurses have stopped by her apartment, but she's never there. I really hope she's OK."

"I'm so sorry," Edwina says sincerely. Thomas looks solemnly at the ground.

"Thank you for everything, Doctor," says George. "We appreciate it. We would still like to thank the other nurses who were working the day of the attack. Are the nurses who worked with Doris here today? And forgive me if I've forgotten, but did you mention her last name?"

"Machado, Doris Machado," says Dr. Dansby, letting out a small laugh. "She was part of the Three Musketeers, though I suppose with just two left . . . well, that's another story. The other two are Alice and Angela. They were all working the day of the attack and may have been here when Elliot left. Poor ladies—they did everything together. Doris's quitting was especially hard for them."

"Thank you, Doctor," Thomas says.

Dr. Dansby nods and begins to leave, but Edwina calls him back.

"I'm sorry for all the questions, but can you tell me what injuries Elliot suffered? My mom loves stories with happy endings, and I hope this will be one of them."

"Oh, let me see if I can remember." He rubs his temple with his left forefinger. "Yes, I shouldn't be sharing this information, but considering the circumstances . . . the patient had two bullets graze his head—one grazed his left cheek; and the other, the side of his head. He was also quite severely concussed. He had no clue who he was, and he was never able to speak a word. In other words, he had a very severe case of amnesia, probably from the concussion and other complicating factors. He'll need extensive treatment and therapy if there's any hope of his getting even *some* of his memory back. He had one of the most severe cases of amnesia I've seen in a long time. It will be a lot to overcome. Apparently, Doris made sure that the relative who checked him out was planning to get him into therapy right away, but even then, it would take a few months at the very least. Oh, and he had a sprained ankle and bruised ribs. He used a walker during the first few days but was walking pretty well by the time he left. We did the best we could for him in the short time he was in our care." Dr. Dansby straightens his coat. "My best wishes to you and your family, and a speedy recovery to your father. We all hope he'll be back in the White House soon."

Once they are alone, Thomas is the first to speak. "I dunno. The odds here are miniscule. The doctor said a family member picked him up. I think it's a dead end. This is just hospital number two; we have two more to go. We can always come back later if we have no other leads."

"Thomas is right," George says to Edwina.

Not wanting to let this lead go, Edwina speaks up. "Sure, but we did agree to chase *every* lead. So we are going to speak to those two nurses. Maybe this is nothing. But maybe it's Dad."

◎◎

After leaving Lenox Hill, Edwina, George, and Thomas quickly make their way to the next hospital on their list by 2:00 pm. Their destination is NYU Langone Hospital. It isn't as big as the previous two and only took in 138 victims from the Courthouse Massacre. This time, George takes the lead and splits up the list of patients among the three of them. If they're able to get the names quickly and confirm any John Does, then they can send the information to June so she can research each unidentified patient.

After two hours, Edwina stumbles upon a nurse on the third floor who is working at her station. "Hello," says Edwina in her friendliest voice.

The nurse hadn't noticed her and is clearly taken by surprise. "Hello! Can I help you?" Just as she finishes the question, she realizes to whom she's speaking. "I'm sorry . . . I . . ."

Edwina gently jumps in. "You were busy, and I interrupted your work; I apologize. My brothers and I are here at Langone meeting some of the first responders and victims from the Courthouse Massacre."

"T-t hat's very nice of you. I'm sorry about your father; I-I hope he's improving," stammers the nurse awkwardly.

"Thank you for your kind words," Edwina replies softly.

"We saw a lot of victims on this floor. Some had no family members, and some didn't make it. So many sad stories," says the young nurse, her dark bangs almost covering her eyes.

Edwina can tell the woman is nervous. "Were all your patients identified, or did you have any John Does? I think that's what you call them, correct?"

"Correct. In fact, yes, we did. One gentleman."

"Really? Can you tell me about him?"

"I don't know that much. He was in his forties, Caucasian."

As the nurse is speaking, Edwina texts her brothers to come to the third floor.

"What else can you tell me about him?" asks Edwina, a little too eagerly.

"Well, the hospital spent weeks trying to figure out his identity. The NYPD helped, but they never had any luck."

Edwina can barely breathe. She wants more information but can't seem to think straight. She's scared to ask more questions but also can't wait to find out as much as possible. Maybe this is it. After a moment, she can no longer hold back. "What color were his eyes and hair? Was he tall or short? What was his build—stocky or lanky?" At that moment, her brothers arrive, saving Edwina from the embarrassment of asking any more questions about this patient. She realizes she must sound crazy.

Her brothers introduce themselves to the nurse.

Then the nurse turns to Edwina, clearly confused by all her questions but not wanting to disappoint. "OK, so he had brown hair and hazel eyes, and he was around six feet tall. But he was in a coma during his entire stay in the ICU, where I was working."

Edwina's heart skips a beat, and she can feel sweat beading on the back of her neck.

Before she can speak, George asks, "Is he still in the ICU? We'd love to see him and help in any way we can."

"I'm sorry, but he passed away a week ago," the nurse replies somberly.

Edwina begins to cry, her whimpers quickly turning into sobs. Thomas hugs her, holding her so tightly she's not quite sure if he has actually picked her up, because she can't feel the floor beneath her feet. Seconds of silence pass until Edwina finally opens her eyes. She gazes at the hospital rooms that surround them. She wants to run from this place and never see another hospital again in her life, but she simply says, "I want to leave."

"George, will you take Edwina downstairs while I go call Mom and have her look into this particular case?" Thomas asks, and George nods. After thanking the nurse, the three of them head to the elevator.

Ten minutes later, they reconnect in the lobby.

"Guys, this doesn't mean anything," Thomas says as soon as he arrives. "Come on—there are thousands of men in New York City who fit that description. I talked to Mom just now. She said they will take it from here. That's what we agreed on. We need to stay focused; we still have one more hospital to visit tomorrow. Plus, we still need to dig into the story of Doris and Elliot from Lenox Hill." George and Edwina just stare at the floor without saying a word.

It's nearly 7:00 p.m. when the siblings finally leave Langone to head back to their temporary home, New York Presbyterian Hospital. Edwina doesn't speak on the way home, trying not to think of her father lying somewhere in a morgue, unidentified and alone. She barely registers the white lights and antiseptic smell of Presbyterian and doesn't even look at the guarded door they pass. Behind it lies a man she knows isn't her father. Instead, she numbly follows Thomas and George into the makeshift suite to find her mom and June gathered around the dining table. They look up eagerly, and Edwina feels the knot in her chest tighten. A tear runs down her face, but she doesn't brush it away.

"What's wrong? What happened?" Rose immediately asks.

Thomas takes Edwina's hand and begins the download for their mom: "So . . . we think we have a solid lead, but we don't want you to get too excited, Mom. We've only visited three out of the four hospitals on our list. But before we tell you about it, we want to know what you've learned about the deceased John Doe from Langone."

Rose, looking exhausted, forces her lips into a small smile. "June contacted the hospital's morgue, and I sent one of the Secret Service guys over to take a picture of the victim so they can run his image through their database. The short story is, it isn't Dad. Thank God. With the help of Homeland Security, they were able to identify the man, and they're planning to contact his family."

Edwina feels like she can breathe again, relieved that the hunt for their father is *not* over. She was terrified it would come to an end in the morgue.

Thomas, George, and Edwina retell the story of Elliot from the very beginning, starting with their introduction to Dr. Dansby on the second floor of Lenox Hill Hospital. Edwina then recounts Dr. Dansby's description of Elliot's injuries and his condition when he left the hospital. She explains, in conclusion, that two nurses have tried to contact Doris Machado numerous times, but haven't had any luck. Rose nods throughout the story and refrains from asking any questions.

When Edwina finally runs out of information to share, she studies her mother carefully, trying to gauge her reaction. She realizes her mother has aged about five years in the past couple of months, thanks to the toll of the campaign, the assassination attempt, the horrors she witnessed at the courthouse, and the current unknown state and whereabouts of her husband. Her mother's long, black, normally flawless hair is dull and messy. She's no longer wearing makeup, not even lipstick. Edwina's not sure she has ever seen her mother look this way. Her heart goes out to her. Regardless of whether or not their father is ever found, Edwina makes a mental note to spend more time with her mother when this is all over.

Rose sits quietly with this information. Edwina is sure that June knows not to speak until their mother has finished asking any questions she may have.

"Well then," Rose finally says, "the three of you have done an amazing job. Your father would be proud. I know *I* am."

"Hey, look!" George exclaims, turning his phone toward them. "I found an image of Doris on LinkedIn. Check it out!"

The temperature in the room suddenly seems to plummet.

Rose stands and walks to the other side of the table, where George is seated. She grabs George's phone and slams it facedown onto the table.

Shocked, George doesn't move.

"That nurse is very pretty. Your dad has always been attracted to beautiful women. It's his Achilles' heel."

Edwina exchanges a look of bewilderment with her siblings. What exactly is their mother trying to tell them? Is she implying something inappropriate may have occurred between their father and this nurse? She wonders if anything like that has happened before, but she doesn't dare ask. She hopes it's not the case.

"The doctor said that this patient, Elliot, was checked out by a family member," George mumbles, clearly shaken. "Personally, I don't think he's Dad, but we agreed we'd chase every lead, even if it's a stretch."

Edwina wants to say more—to tell her mom not to worry and that this nurse took good care of this patient while at the hospital. That the doctor was impressed that Elliot's health had improved quicker than anyone had thought it would, because Doris tended to him night and day. But Edwina thinks better of it and decides to save this information for a later date. Enough has been shared for the time being.

Rose looks down at her wedding ring, twisting it nervously around her finger. "So the three of you think this nurse could have Dad? Do you think that's who called June?"

"Maybe, but we can't know for sure. It's just a theory," Thomas offers.

"You said a family member checked this Elliot out of the hospital," Rose says as she moves to the sofa and sits down.

June follows and sits beside her.

"Do you know the name of that family member?" Rose asks Thomas. "Let's follow up on that first thing in the morning." She looks at June when she says this, silently assigning her to the task. Rose bites her bottom lip and turns to look at a small framed photograph on the side table. It's a portrait from her wedding day.

Edwina wonders if her mom would rather have her husband in the hands of the terrorists rather than in the arms of another woman, a pretty nurse—but that seems unlikely. What Edwina fears much more than any blond nurse is the government and the Brigade.

She looks at her mother, hoping to redirect this conversation. "Mom, the doctor said that this patient—who most likely is *not* our father—might have his memory back by now," she says, stretching the truth a bit. "The odds are slim, but it is a possibility. I truly believe that if Dad was in his right mind, he would've found a way to safely return to us. This lead just gives us a little hope."

Rose stands and speaks to George, Edwina, and Thomas as if she were leading a team of secret agents. "Here's the plan. Tomorrow, the three of you will cover the fourth hospital on the list and then return to Lenox Hill afterward. In the meantime, we'll find out everything there is to know about the family member who checked out Elliot. I will personally call Lenox Hill tomorrow and get the name and contact information for that person. I'd like to have you guys talk to the two nurses you mentioned—what are their names?"

"Alice and Angela," replies George quickly.

"Well then, call Lenox Hill tomorrow morning and find out when they will be working next. If they really are friends of Doris, it should be easy to get them talking. And if they seem awkward, or if anything seems fishy, then you'll know you may be on the right track. Now go get some rest. I will order breakfast to be delivered at 6:30 a.m."

Rose's expression changes. Edwina notices a vulnerability in her that she's never seen before.

"I love you all now more than ever," Rose adds tenderly. "Thank you for doing all this. I know it's hard, and I'm so proud of each of you." She sits up a bit taller and adds in a more serious tone, "I also know that you might learn things about your father that you'll think I may not want to hear. But I want to know *everything*. Even if you think it will hurt me, tell me the truth."

CHAPTER 43

LET'S TOAST!

▷ **Doris – Los Angeles, California, Day 27**

Doris saw the sunrise in her rearview mirror about three hours ago. Now she can see the downtown Los Angeles skyline as she makes her way west on the 10 freeway. She feels rejuvenated after their six-hour nap at a rest stop just outside of Phoenix. Since then, she's had plenty of time to think about her next step, which is her last card to play. That card is the only person left in her life who could possibly help them.

They arrive at their hotel and park in its underground garage. It is a bright-orange, fifty-four-room boutique hotel located in a quiet part of Los Angeles, not far from the famous Hollywood Bowl. She looked it up on the internet when she was at Fatima's, hiding her search by using Google's incognito mode. It looked like they had availability, but she couldn't make a reservation. Too risky. She just hoped they would still have rooms available upon their arrival. She picked a smaller hotel, knowing that the fewer people they encounter, the less she has to worry about. She puts the car in park and takes a deep breath, hoping she's now a few steps further from danger.

She turns to the passenger seat and looks at Lance.

Before she can stop him, he grabs her face with both hands and gives her a small kiss on the lips. "We're here!" Lance says happily. "Thank you for making this trip with me."

Doris feels momentarily paralyzed. Did he just kiss her? She wonders if he even meant to. Maybe he's just excited to be in a new place. Her thoughts are interrupted when Lance jumps out of the car and yanks their luggage from the back seat.

They carry their bags up the stairs to the lobby, where they find a line of guests waiting to check in. Doris glances at her reflection in the mirror behind the front-desk staff. She changed clothing at the last rest stop and is now wearing a green cotton calf-length dress. Her brown riding boots match her brown leather coat with faux-fur trim. Her blond hair is in a bun. She hopes it's a stronger woman who's looking back at her, not the weaker version of herself she tried to leave back in New Mexico. She wonders who's coming after them and how many people they may be running from. One? A dozen? Or are there hundreds? She shakes the paranoia away, at least for now.

Doris jumps when she feels someone lean in over her shoulder. Then she hears Lance whisper, "Who am I, Ribbons? If I were rich, would I have to buy you? If I were poor, would I have to steal you?" She turns her head just a bit to see him from the corner of her eye.

"What are you talking about?" she asks shyly, feeling his heat on her neck.

"Well, you know I have no money, so stealing would come naturally to me." He says in a voice that's a little too suave.

She turns around and hugs him tightly. She has seen a big change in his personality and his awareness of everything around him. Their stay in New Mexico consisted of a lot of work and stress, but it was a successful endeavor. She was diligent about making sure the TVs and radios in the house were never turned on while Lance was awake. She wasn't ready for him to see his face on the news. But now here they are in Los Angeles, far away from New York and Washington, DC. She wonders if she should make the first move in trying to nudge his memory. *Is this the right place and time?*

They stand close together in the check-in line for another five minutes, waiting for their turn at the front desk. There is only one clerk working. Suddenly, Doris feels a cool, moist breeze rush past her. She remembers they are just fifteen miles from the ocean, and the air here is so different than it is in New York City. She breathes in deeply and closes her eyes.

Lance presses against her from behind and says, "Let's let this music between us play forever. I'm the title of this song, the lead singer, *and* the band." He turns her around until they are facing each other. He looks deep into her eyes and then winks.

She wants to turn away, to pinch herself awake from this dream before a fool is born. He's watching her every move. Realizing this is real, that the shaking inside her is authentic, she bites her lip. Where did this new man come from all of a sudden? Doris smiles. Part of her feels like Daniel reincarnated his soul into Lance's body on that fateful February day.

"Listen," Doris says, "we're going to stay here, in Los Angeles, for just a few days. We can relax, go to the beach, and then continue our adventure."

"How many days?" he asks disappointedly.

"I don't know exactly, but we'll have some fun while we are here. I promise."

"That sounds good. I'm ready for something fun. Anything!"

The front-desk clerk calls them forward. Luckily, the hotel has a room available immediately. Doris has no choice but to provide her real name and driver's license. She's relieved that they let her pay cash for the room and use Fatima's credit card for the deposit.

The clerk gives Doris their room number and two keycards. Then they follow the bellhop to the second floor and take a quick tour of their room. He shows them around, pointing out the thermostat and minibar.

"I love minibars!" Lance announces as if he's just stumbled upon a gold mine.

Doris has no doubt he raided many mini bars on his campaign trail and wonders what thing or person will finally trigger his memory. She might just be ready now.

When the bellhop leaves, Lance follows him out the door.

"Where are you going?" Doris asks, grabbing Lance's arm.

"Whoa, relax! This is a vacation! I will be right back—promise."

Before she can protest, he waves her off and disappears. Seconds turn into minutes, and she begins to panic, possibilities flooding her mind. Maybe his memory came back all of a sudden or someone recognized him. Or maybe he got lost. She never should have let him go. That was a stupid and dangerous decision.

A full half hour later, Lance walks through the door with a big grin. To Doris's surprise and relief, he's carrying a bottle of champagne with a red ribbon tied around its neck.

"What took you so long? I was worried," she says, trying to keep her cool.

"I'm sorry. I had to walk to a liquor store to buy this bottle," he says as he presents his gift to her.

She wants to tell him he can't just leave on his own like that, but she decides against it. The moment is over, and she has learned her lesson. "How did you get the money?"

"I asked Fatima if I could borrow some. I promised her I'd pay her back. I told you I want to start buying you things to begin thanking you," he says as he opens the bottle and pours them into the glasses he brought out from the bathroom.

Doris takes the glass he offers her. "Well then, thank *you*. Let's toast!"

"To what?"

"To adventure."

"OK, to adventure!" The clink of their glasses rings out in the small hotel room.

After they take a sip of their champagne, Lance grabs Doris by the small of her back, pulling her in close, and kisses her neck. She pushes him away and downs her glass of champagne. Lance refills her glass, and just as quickly, she downs this one too. He steps in close to Doris, but before he can grab her, she takes a step backward.

"No!" she exclaims, pushing him away again.

WE MISS DORIS

▷ **Edwina – New York Presbyterian Hospital, Day 27**

After a long, deep sleep in the hospital suite bedrooms, the Dumont family members eat breakfast together at 6:30 a.m. They review the agenda for the day. Earlier this morning, George called Lenox Hill and learned that Angela and Alice are working the day shift. The plan is to visit the fourth and final hospital first, then return to Lenox Hill.

Per protocol, the Secret Service chaperones Thomas, George, and Edwina to hospital number four, the Mount Sinai Hospital on Madison Avenue.

Once there, the three siblings go through the motions, but with less passion than they've had on previous hospital visits. Their minds are on Doris Machado and Elliot, her patient. Edwina hopes their mom will find some information on this woman.

The morning passes slowly with nothing remarkable to note. So far, nothing seems out of the ordinary at Mount Sinai, but they are still careful to write everything down in their binders after each meeting in order to identify any detail that might be a clue. They take time to meet some of the Courthouse Massacre victims who are still hospitalized, asking many questions about each patient's life. They're hoping to get lost in the patients' stories, a welcome reprieve from the hunt for their father.

After a late lunch, the siblings return to Lenox Hill Hospital. A nurse at the first station on the second floor directs them to Alice and Angela, who are just down the hall. Thomas, George, and Edwina find them standing together outside a hub of three hospital rooms situated in a corner of the hallway. All the nurses on the floor have been given a heads-up that President Dumont's children will be returning today to thank those who worked the night shift on the day of the Courthouse Massacre.

Edwina clears her throat as they approach. The sound appears to startle the nurses, and they turn to see who is approaching.

Thomas speaks first. "Hello there! We are sorry to interrupt you. My name is Thomas Dumont, and these are my siblings—Edwina and George. I think the administrator may have mentioned we'd be by today?"

"Oh, yes, of course—hello! I'm Angela, and this is Alice," Angela says with a welcoming smile.

"Our family is devastated by the violence at the courthouse. There were so many innocent people who were injured and killed. We know our dad would want us to thank each of you personally. We understand from Dr. Dansby that the two of you were here to receive and care for many of the victims on that awful day. We are forever grateful for the work you have done. We know it's a tremendous sacrifice. Dr. Dansby said a lot of good things about the two of you."

Edwina watches the two women carefully; it's as if they've prepared for this moment. But they seem genuinely touched by her brother's words.

Alice shakes Thomas's hand. "We are honored to meet the three of you. We have heard about and are touched by your visits to the hospitals. And by the way, we both voted for your dad." The two nurses smile brightly at the Dumont kids.

Thomas flashes a polite smile in return, his voice now just a tad stiff. "We understand from Dr. Dansby you had a patient brought in the day of the attack who unfortunately was not visited by any family members or friends throughout his stay. That must have been so hard for him. I believe his name is Elliot. The doctor said your colleague Doris took good care of him. We are grateful for the extra-special treatment you have given patients, such as Elliot, who've had no one by their side but the fine staff here at Lenox Hill."

"*So* grateful," adds Edwina. "We've been to a handful of hospitals and have heard so many heartbreaking stories like this one—and, unfortunately, so many stories about doctors and nurses who either quit or were forced to take a leave of absence due to the psychological trauma associated with the Courthouse Massacre. Sounds like your friend Doris is yet another unintended victim of the attack on our country."

"I heard you two really miss her," George adds. "We would love to hear the story of Elliot and Doris. Our mom loves when we tell her stories of the victims and their caregivers, people like Doris and the two of you, who've gone above and beyond the call of duty."

Angela nods in agreement. "Doris was a dedicated nurse, like no other I have ever met. This job was all she had. She *lived* for her patients. She spent so many hours here at the hospital; she even volunteered here during her free time. Elliot's recovery was due to her commitment. He was in bad shape when he first came to us. The doctors feared he'd suffered permanent brain damage. His recovery truly was a miracle. We miss Doris, but as you said, that day really did affect everyone here—especially her. She was one of the few of us who was actually on the scene at the courthouse. It had to have been a life-changing experience—and not for the better."

"I'm so sorry," Edwina responds before she starts fishing. "The doctor said Elliot's wife finally found and collected him, and you two checked him out around two weeks ago? That must have been some reunion!" She watches them closely for their response. Dr. Dansby didn't mention anything about a wife or specify which staff member completed the discharge paperwork. She's hoping to catch them in a lie.

"Well, y-yes a family member did come to get him. I don't know if it was his w-wife," Angela stammers, looking at Alice nervously.

"Yes," Alice confirms, though her tone sounds less certain than it did before. "Elliot was never able to talk, so we didn't know anything about his family members. So much effort was put into finding them."

"We'd really love to meet Elliot. Would you happen to have his discharge papers?" Edwina asks casually. "Our mother would like to send personal notes to some of the victims."

"No," Alice and Angela say simultaneously, giving each other a concerned look that does not go unnoticed by the siblings.

Angela quickly adds, "I mean, our files are immediately processed by our discharge department for input into the system. We don't keep the files here after checking patients out. You would need to check with the discharge department. And I think Dr. Dansby was mistaken; we didn't check Elliot out that morning. I'm not sure who did. That information would be in his paperwork."

"I totally understand," Thomas says smoothly. "I'm sure our mother can follow up with the hospital CEO and get that paperwork. What's Elliot's last name again?"

Alice looks down at a folder in her hand, as if she might find the answer to Thomas's question. "Greene. Elliot Greene."

"Are you *sure* you don't know who checked him out?" Edwina asks, sounding more aggressive than she'd intended.

"You know, it was so hectic that day." Angela runs a hand over her hair, not looking at any of them, then adds, "I think it was Doris who took him down to discharge on the first floor. I'm sure they'll know more."

Edwina notices Alice shoot Angela a dirty look. Intrigued, she asks, "So why do you think Doris quit on the same day Elliot left the hospital?"

"Your guess is as good as mine. We miss Doris a lot," Alice says curtly. "Well, thank you both for coming. I've got to get back to my station. Angela, it looks like the patient in 2434 needs you." As if on cue, Angela's handheld computer buzzes.

As the siblings walk to the elevator, Edwina contemplates what was said and what wasn't.

"Stop!" calls a voice from down the hallway.

Edwina looks up and sees Alice running toward them.

CHAPTER 45

THE JOURNEY OF MY LIFE

▷ **Doris – Los Angeles, California, Day 27**

"I'm sorry," says Lance as he steps away from Doris.

"I didn't mean to say no; I just want you to wait here. I'm going to change out of these clothes and into something more comfortable. Don't drink all the champagne," Doris teases as she disappears into the bathroom.

Minutes later, she reappears wearing nothing but a simple black satin slip. Its lace top reveals the sides of her full breasts, while the lace-trimmed side slit exposes the uppermost part of her right thigh. With one outstretched hand, she leans against the wall. The champagne fuels her confidence as she twists her torso back and forth as if trying to rid her body of the stress of the long road trip. In her peripheral vision, she can see Lance watching her. She looks at him with *that* smile on her face. Her blond hair, no longer in a bun, falls freely over her shoulders. She tucks one lock of hair behind her ear, and for a moment, she feels like a movie star.

Lance gently places his glass of champagne on the desk and walks toward her. He doesn't speak; he just looks at her.

Doris is aware of the *new* kind of danger they are in at this moment, but she doesn't care. She's going to lose him soon, so what does it matter? Loss is the one constant in her life. This time, maybe she can enjoy herself, even if only for a moment. After all, she can't really lose something she never had to begin with.

Lance puts his arms around her and holds her firmly by her waist. He then leans forward and kisses her long and hard on the lips. All of the weakness, loneliness, and stress leaves her body in her next few breaths.

He links her hands in his and pushes her against the wall, letting his tongue slip in and out of her mouth. Doris can barely stand, so she closes her eyes. She has not experienced this kind of passion since Daniel, and for a split second, she sees Daniel when she opens her eyes.

Lance removes her slip with one hand without letting go of her other hand, then guides her to the bathroom and turns on the shower.

Doris tries to push him away, but he holds her tightly in his arms. "We can't. We—" She cannot finish her protestation because his mouth hungrily consumes hers.

"I'll be right back," he says.

Returning to the bathroom with the bottle of champagne, Lance steps into the shower with it, then looks over at Doris. He doesn't have to ask her to join him; she steps right in as he turns on the water.

As steam fills the bathroom, they take turns drinking from the bottle of champagne. He gently rubs her in the same way she massaged his injuries so many times. He traces water droplets from her shoulders down her arms and from her neck down to her chest. With each touch, Doris grows more eager to have all of him. She closes her eyes, and her thoughts race, wondering if perhaps this is how she wants to die.

Lance turns off the water, and he and Doris step out of the shower. Gently, he leads her to the bed, where they lie naked on the cool sheets. As Lance massages her thighs, he feels her flesh quiver beneath his fingers. He spreads her legs and climbs on top of her. She lets him inside and moans loudly. Taking hold of one of her breasts, he teases her nipple with his tongue while moving himself deeper inside of her. Doris arches her back in response. She wants him deeper and knows he wants it too. Lance moves his mouth up to her ear and lets out a soft, warm moan as he kisses her earlobe. Her body prickles with goosebumps, and she roughly grabs the back of his neck. They push their bodies together harder until she's not sure where her flesh ends and his begins. They ride each other faster and faster, and Doris grabs his buttocks as he thrusts deeper. She can see him grind his teeth, and she tightens her pelvic muscles to get a better grip on his manhood. His eyes begin to roll back, so she quickens her pace. As he disappears farther into her, they convulse, climaxing together.

Beads of sweat drip from the tip of Lance's nose onto Doris's forehead. He leans in to lick them off, then kisses her softly as they settle into the tangle of sheets beneath them.

Doris wonders where Lance's confidence came from and if this will happen again. Just as the thought passes, Lance slips back into her wetness. He doesn't move, just holds himself inside her until she begins to shake. He drapes a sheet over her and reaches for a pillow, tucking it under her head. The two melt into each other.

Doris can see the lust lingering in his eyes as he asks, "How much can I take from you?"

"Everything. You can take everything," she replies breathlessly, realizing he already has.

He stops for the shortest second before pushing himself deeper inside of her. She wonders how he's still erect, but dismisses the thought just as quickly. *Enjoy the moment,* she silently reminds herself.

He is slow and gentle at first, and Doris feels her nipples stiffen. She grabs the back of his head and pulls him closer, signaling for him to meet her gaze. "Start just above the skin," she commands, her shyness long gone.

Lance leans in and whispers in her ear, "Your skin is like a spool of cotton candy. Just close your eyes, and let me do the work." He navigates her body, starting above the skin, just as she requested. He then licks the beads of sweat from her neck, slowly moving his lips down to her breasts. When he reaches her stomach, she arches her back. He looks up at her and returns the look of excitement in her eyes. He pushes the length of his fingers inside her, and with his other hand, brushes his finger across her lips. As he plants a kiss on her inner thigh, he whispers, "I can walk on water when I'm with you."

Doris gasps as Lance slides forward and enters her again. As he pushes deeper and deeper into her, she arches in a spasm, reaching past his waist to grip his back. Her eyes close as she focuses on Lance's rhythm and rocks back and forth with it. Suddenly, she feels capable of doing anything. Even walking on water, as Lance mentioned, seems possible at the moment. She feels an electricity between their bodies as they again climax together.

Raw with emotion, Doris smiles broadly.

Lance curls his body around hers from behind, cradling her knees with his hands. As she drifts off to sleep in his arms, he whispers tenderly, "Love me if I make you laugh, Ribbons. If I cry, stroke my face with your fingertips. For the journey of my life with you has only just begun."

CHAPTER 46

WAIT; THERE'S MORE

▷ **Edwina – Lenox Hill Hospital, Day 27**

"Wait; there's more," Alice says anxiously. "I don't know why you're interested in this man, but I *have* to tell you something."

Edwina's heart begins to race. *Maybe this is it,* she thinks.

Alice tells the siblings the story of the man who visited the hospital weeks earlier and the threats he made to Alice, Angela, and their families.

"Why didn't you go to the police?" asks George.

"And risk my child's life?" Alice says, clearly shaken by the ordeal. She then looks directly at Edwina and says, "That same man came back when Angela and I were on shift together the day after Elliot left."

"What? He came back? Are you guys OK?" Edwina asks empathetically.

"We are fine—scared, but fine. The first time he showed up, he said he'd be back in a week. And he kept his word. When he returned, we saw him going from room to room again. I don't know if he was looking for Elliot, but he was looking for somebody. I'm risking a lot by telling you this, but I had to tell someone. We were afraid to turn to the police."

"Your secret is safe with us, Alice. We won't jeopardize the safety of you and your family," Edwina says as she puts her hand on Alice's shoulder. "I'm sorry this happened. What did you do when you saw him the second time?"

"We weren't sure he saw us, so we ran in the opposite direction when he went into a room, and then we hid in a janitorial closet for three hours," Alice replies with tears in her eyes.

Edwina hugs her. "Thank you for confiding in us, Alice. We will do our best to figure this out—I promise. Do you and Angela have any idea who he was looking for?"

"We wish we knew. We've been wondering the same thing, but mostly, we're just praying he won't come back. And so far, he hasn't."

The siblings say goodbye to Alice and don't speak again until they reach Presbyterian Hospital.

"Wow. That was not what I expected," Edwina says as they walk down the hallway to their suite. "Clearly, those two have been through a lot. Did you see the way they kept looking at each other? They were nervous."

"Of course they were!" exclaims George. "They were talking to the president's children after having their lives threatened. I'd say they have every reason to be nervous as hell."

"I'm still trying to wrap my head around the whole thing. Who do you think the guy with the hoodie could've been? A Brigade member?" Thomas wonders aloud.

"But what would a Brigade member be doing scouring the hospitals? They still think Dad's here, at Presbyterian," counters Edwina.

"Or maybe they *do* know," says George.

"Well, if they already know about Dad, then our job is going to be a lot harder. For now, I think we need to focus on who checked Elliot out of Lenox Hill Hospital. Alice and Angela said they have no clue who came to pick him up. But I'm sure all the nurses talk, and they must know the truth. But why wouldn't they just tell us? They were so awkward about the whole thing," Edwina says, hoping their mom will know the answer to this question. Her gut is telling her that the nurses are covering for Doris.

Once in the suite, they tell their mother and siblings every detail of their visit to Lenox Hill. Again, Edwina doesn't take her eyes off her mother, watching closely her every reaction.

"Oh my God," Rose says grimly. "This can only be the Brigade. The CIA wouldn't need to threaten, nor would they wear a scrub top over a hoodie. They can hide behind their badges, so it can't be Director Schultz's people. Maybe Schultz told James the truth: that his agents are looking for any Brigade members who're still hospitalized. Then it could be possible that the Brigade is also looking for their members before the CIA gets to them."

"What did you find out about Elliot, Mom?" asks George. "Who checked him out of the hospital?"

"I spoke directly to the CEO, and he was quite helpful. James had sent through a formal request using his CIA credentials to allow the CEO to provide me with the information. A woman by the name of Allison Greene, claiming to be Elliot's daughter, was the one who came to get him. So I asked James to work his contacts and do a search using Allison's driver's license info, which the hospital emailed me." Rose laughs, then says proudly, "I'm going to make James work to earn my trust, even though I may never give it to him. Anyway, turns out there is no Allison Greene with a father named Elliot. What's more telling is that the driver's license that was used during the checkout process was a fake."

For a few moments, the kids are stunned into silence.

"What the hell is going on here?" Thomas says angrily.

Rose has rarely seen him mad. He's usually so level-headed and steady.

"This is it, guys! Elliot is Dad. This is a no-brainer!" George exclaims as if he has just won a game of Clue.

"I'm not quite sure," replies Rose calmly, "but clearly, there is something more to this story. I hope we weren't the last to learn your father's not in this hospital. On one hand, we have the CIA checking every hospital for possible Brigade members, and on the other hand, there's some guy—or guys—going from room to room looking for someone."

"This just means we have to move fast! For now, this Elliot Greene is all we have, and my gut tells me we need to follow this lead!" Edwina exclaims, standing up in the hope of rallying her family members.

June cuts in, excitedly: "We discovered a lot about Doris Machado. Her husband died one year ago. His name was Daniel Bauer, and they never had children. Doris's parents passed away when she was in her twenties, and her only sibling is her sister. Her name is Fatima Machado. She lives in Santa Fe, New Mexico. She never married and also has no children. Mom even got her phone number and address!"

"Yes, and the good news is that this Doris has a simple background," Rose adds. "No criminal record. I had June take some flowers to Doris's apartment to see if she could find out anything."

"I even wore a hat!" June says proudly. "I brought the flowers and sweet-talked the doorman at her apartment building. It's amazing how much people will talk if you're willing to listen long enough. He told me not to bother with the flowers; he hasn't seen Doris in weeks. He has no idea where she went. He said she never takes vacations; all she has done is work since her husband died. I asked where he thinks she may have gone and if he ever saw her with a man. He told me that he's pretty sure the only people Doris has ever had over to her apartment are her sister and a couple of girls from work. And apparently, she hasn't been on a date since her husband passed away. He was a little too forthcoming with his information. I kinda feel sorry for Doris. I'm not totally sure why."

Rose hands a piece of paper to Thomas and says, "You and Edwina are going to Santa Fe, New Mexico."

Edwina is surprised by her mother's response but glad they are on the same page. They need to talk to Doris's sister. She has noticed a change in her mother over the last twenty-four hours; she's back in charge. Edwina smiles at this, happy the mother she loves and admires has returned. They all need their mother's strength right now.

"That is the address of Doris's sister, Fatima," Rose says to Thomas. "I've taken the liberty of telling the Secret Service you'll be going to your grandmother's house in Texas. From there, it's a short drive to Santa Fe. And per protocol, a Secret Service agent will join you on your flight and make sure you get to your grandmother's house safely. Then he will return to New York. It took some arm-twisting, but in the end, I was able to talk Director Cummings into affording you guys a little freedom, sans Secret Service agents." Rose smiles proudly. It's nearly impossible for anyone in the First Family to avoid having Secret Service agents by their side whenever they're in public. Rose explains to her children that she threatened to go public with her displeasure over the agency's mishandling of her husband's first public speech if Cummings didn't grant this request.

Rendered speechless, the kids just stare at their mother.

"What are you guys looking at? Chop-chop! You are on a manhunt and will have the CIA and the Brigade on your heels— or maybe ahead of you. Either we get to your father first, or *they* do. June will get you a burner phone. I love you guys. Be sure to give my momma a hug from me, OK?" Rose's phone rings, and, without batting an eye, she answers it, walking into her bedroom to take the call in private.

Edwina turns to her siblings, hoping they'll say something. She hadn't expected they would get their grandmother involved, but maybe it's a happy twist of fate. She's a bit of a character, but well-meaning and loved by all her grandkids. She has only one rule: they can never call her *grandma;* they have to call her *Honey.*

CHAPTER 47

COME ON, DEBBIE

▷ **Doris – Los Angeles, California, Day 28**

Morning comes too soon. The fog lifts, and time resumes. A wild parrot screeches overhead as sunlight streams in through the part in the curtains.

The rituals of a new day commence. As Doris buckles the straps of her shoes around her slender ankles, she can feel Lance's eyes on her. And though she avoids his gaze, memories of what happened last night bring warm smiles to their faces.

Over their room service breakfast, Doris asks, "How do you feel?"

"I'm so relaxed. I feel so light, as though I could walk on water. What the hell happened last night?"

"*What?*" Doris sputters, her fork suspended midair. "You don't remember what happened last night?"

He gives her a wink that induces her bright smile.

Doris relaxes. Maybe this is the way it should end. They don't need to talk about what happened.

"Ribbons, you said we've got some things to do here, in Los Angeles. What do we need to do? I thought our agenda consisted of lying on the beach," Lance says as he takes a bite of a croissant.

Doris hesitates. The time has come for the truth—or some of it, at least. But she has to start slow. "Elliot, you must know something. We needed to leave Fatima's because people are looking for us. Well, they are looking for *me*. I'm not perfect, Elliot. I've done something bad, albeit with good intentions."

"OK, every person has done at least one bad thing in their life. That's something we all have in common." Lance looks at her inquisitively. "Who is looking for you . . . and why? Is it the police?"

"It's not the police. Well, maybe it *is* the police." She realizes she probably should have said something other than they are running from people. *Damn it,* she thinks. *Too much, too soon.*

"How do we know who to hide from? I don't even know who we should be looking out for."

She takes a big gulp of coffee, as if steeling herself for the truth. She needs to be honest with this part now that she's put it out there. "Well, we should avoid police officers and . . . well, anyone in uniform, really. You know how I always get nervous when we pass by a person in uniform. But overall, let's just try not to talk to strangers unless we have to." She can see the worry on his face.

"So we can't talk to *anybody?*" he asks.

"Not right now, Elliot." She realizes how poorly this conversation is going but can't seem to find the words to fix it. "But please know that you will be fine. Believe me, you will. As time goes by . . . well, what I'm trying to say is that someday in the near future, I'm going to need you to protect me, just as I have protected and cared for you." Doris can see that he isn't quite sure what she's talking about, and she's glad he isn't.

"What did you do wrong? And why are they after you?"

She stalls for time, pretending to fish a speck of something from her glass of orange juice. "It's a long story. I didn't really do anything wrong. It's all just a big mix-up that I need to fix *before* they find me, OK?"

"OK, if you say so," he says as he takes another bite of his croissant.

"It's nothing awful—I promise. Now listen, dear; I need to make some calls in private. Do you mind going for a swim while I do that?" Doris is nervous to let him out of her sight, but she has no choice right now; she needs the room to herself. She hopes that Lance's fresh scars will keep people from approaching him. "Come back in twenty minutes, OK? Do you remember our room number?"

He scoffs at her question. "Yes, of course I know our room number! What do you think of me? I've still got a brain. Jeez. I may not remember the past, but I remember everything we do."

Doris nods, then turns around to go about her task. She's glad he's come around faster than she ever could have imagined. It's a relief knowing that he can think for himself and take pride in his abilities.

After he leaves the room, she calls the front desk. "Hello, can you please help me place a call?"

"Just press the nine key, wait for the dial tone, and then enter the number you're calling," the clerk says, clearly annoyed by the question.

Doris knows better than to place this call from the phone in her room, so she pushes harder: "I'm sorry, but I have tried that, and it's not working." After some time, the clerk gives in and dials the number for her. The phone begins to ring.

"Come on, Debbie; please pick up," Doris begs as she twists her finger nervously around the phone cord.

Debbie Morris was Doris's teacher at Washington State University. She wasn't much older than Doris at the time and led the two-year nursing prerequisites program at the Pullman campus in Washington. She was the type of teacher who was quick to laugh and even quicker to put someone in their place. The two had a rare pupil–teacher relationship and have remained good friends ever since Doris graduated over a decade ago, though it has been eight months since they've spoken. After Daniel's death, Doris kept to herself for a while. At the same time, Debbie went through a divorce.

Debbie is still working at the university, but in what capacity, Doris can't remember. She thinks it may be in administration, as Debbie was tired of teaching. She crosses her fingers, hoping Debbie will answer. She needs to ask for her help in finding a job for both Lance and herself. It is a lot to ask, but Debbie owes her a favor. The job would provide a safe haven for them while also distracting Lance. But most importantly, Debbie may be able to help Doris get in touch with the Dumont family, thanks to her high-level contacts in the state of Washington. She is their only hope.

After the sixth ring, a voice answers, "Hello?"

"Debbie Morris! It's me, Doris," she replies, knowing Debbie is going to want to hear all about her life. There's so much to tell and so much she has to leave out.

"Oh my gosh! How are you? I'm so glad to hear your voice," says Debbie earnestly.

Doris instantly feels a sense of comfort. "I'm good. It's great to hear your voice too."

"Honey, it's not Morris anymore; I finally got rid of that awful name and the memories it carried. Since last month, I've gone by my maiden name. I'm officially Ms. Lewis again, and it feels good."

"Well then, welcome back, Ms. Zelda Deborah *Lewis!*"

"Thank you. It took the university a while to register my name change. Remember how hard it was for me to shed Zelda and have them list my name as Debbie Morris instead of Zelda Morris? I'm sure they still have that name down in their records. It took years to change, and this time was no different. This place hasn't changed. It's still as disorganized and bureaucratic as ever. So what's happening with you?"

"I left New York City," Doris says, deciding to weave in the truth. "I was on the scene the day of the Courthouse Massacre, and I just couldn't handle the hospital anymore. Being at the courthouse put me over the edge." That part is 100 percent true. She is still experiencing flashbacks and night sweats and relying on Xanax to get to sleep every night.

"Doris, why didn't you call me earlier? You poor thing. That must have been awful."

"It was horrific. Aside from Daniel's death, it was the worst day of my life." More truths.

"So now what are you doing?"

"Well, I just spent some time with my sister. You remember Fatima. And . . ." She's uncertain what words will find their way out of her mouth next. "I met someone new." Sure, it's a bit misleading, but that is also true.

"That was fast!" Debbie can't contain her excitement. "I knew you would, honey!"

"Thank you. You've always been on my side." Doris pauses, wanting to move on from the subject and get to the point. "Listen, I'm moving out West. I want to start fresh. So I need a favor: I need a job."

"Hold on! You're coming back here?"

"I'd like to, but only if I can find work."

"We actually do need a lot of help here," Debbie says excitedly, "Things at work have been a mess. Management has cut our budgets, and, of course, there's the usual politics. That hasn't changed; in fact, it's only gotten worse." She pauses, then adds, "God, I miss you, girl!"

Doris sighs deeply. "That's what I've been praying you'd say. And I miss you too. So, listen—I'm coming up there in a few days. I know it's soon. I'm going to bring the guy I met. He's good with administrative work. He's got to come with me, so you'll get two for the price of one! But don't worry; he's a good guy, and you won't be sorry. I met him a few months ago, and he's my first love since Daniel." Doris is surprised by how easy that was to say. *Too* easy.

"I trust you, Doris. Bring your man, and get your beautiful smile up here. I can get you both to work quickly. I now work in administration for the undergraduate program. I'm no longer involved in teaching, thank God; I was done with that years ago! Anyway, let me check around and see what's open. A lot of the old staffers still work here and talk about you. They'll be so happy to see you! It's been a long time, honey."

"This is the best news, Debbie! I would love to see some of the old crew, but I'd especially love to see you."

"And guess what? This must be a sign, because I drive by your old place on the way to work each day and saw a *For Rent* sign just a few days ago! Every time I pass that tiny house, I think of you. The place looks just like it did when you lived there. I'll put down a deposit, if I can, and have it ready for you. Sound OK?"

Doris is about ready to cry with relief. "Thank you so much for everything, Debbie. I promise I'll figure out a way to repay you someday. We will call you on the way to let you know when we will be arriving. Maybe we can meet at the old house? We can start working right away—on Monday, if that's possible."

"All right, that sounds great, Doris! And honestly, this is the *least* I can do for you. When you vouched for me during that work drama ten years ago, you saved my job—well, my *career*. I'm in your debt. And before you ask, no, I haven't met anyone new. I'll give you the full story over a glass of wine when I see you."

Doris takes a deep breath. "I could use a glass of wine . . . or three."

She can hear Debbie typing away and knows her friend is already reaching out to her contacts for them.

"By the way, Doris, what's your guy's name? I'm sending an email now."

"Elliot. Elliot Greene. I promise that neither of us will let you down." Doris feels like she's just been given a new lease on life. "By the way, I lost my phone, so I won't be able to talk to you until then, OK? See you soon!"

Once she hangs up, she checks her watch. It's been over half an hour. She was hoping Lance would be back by now. She heads to the lobby to look for him and finds an unwelcome surprise. He's chatting it up with a police officer in front of the reception desk.

"Good God!" Doris says out loud. "Who else would he be talking to? This man would talk to dogs as well as cats. There's no telling what he would do if he went to the zoo. Dammit!"

There's nothing she can do but approach the two of them and try to extract Lance from the conversation as smoothly as possible. Biting her lip to hide her nervousness, she walks up to them and sees guilt wash over Lance's face.

"Ribbons, this is Officer Washington. We just met here, in the lobby. Officer, this is my girlfriend, Ribbons."

Doris is stunned by Lance's *girlfriend* remark, but she barely has time to enjoy it. "Nice to meet you," she says to the officer, avoiding his gaze. Turning, she gives Lance a stern look and then rubs her nose as if to satisfy an itch.

"We were just talking about the assassination attempt," the officer says casually. It's usually those from faraway places who are dumping their problems on our country, but this time, it came from right under our noses—maybe even from within our government. I was telling your boyfriend that there are rumors on the internet claiming they got the wrong guy, that the man at New York Presbyterian Hospital isn't President Dumont."

CHAPTER 48

SOMEONE ON THE INSIDE

▷ **Rose – New York Presbyterian Hospital, Day 28**

Rose gets up extra early, feeling energized and empowered by her plan. While her kids are looking for Lance, she will spend her time finding out what *really* happened on February 4. She's ready for the truth, no matter how ugly it may be.

She hears her phone buzz and picks it up on the first ring. "Hello, James."

"I'm downstairs. They won't let me up," he says.

She can hear his frustration, and feels the satisfaction that comes with that.

"I will tell them to bring you up now," she says coolly.

"Thank you, Mrs.—"

She hangs up before he can finish.

A few minutes later, she hears a knock at the door and lets James inside.

"Good morning, Mrs. Dumont," James says rather sheepishly.

Rose simply nods, too focused on her goal to be bothered with pleasantries. She sits down and waits for him to speak first. She wants to make this as uncomfortable for him as possible.

"Mrs. Dumont, I hope you found helpful the information I provided you on the Machado sisters," says James.

"Yes, it *was* helpful."

"Please know that I am willing to do anything for you and your husband."

"I hope so, James, because I have a big ask," Rose replies, sitting up a little taller.

"Like I said, anything." He smiles eagerly.

"First, I have a question. What do you think really happened at the courthouse? And don't just spit out media reports or Homeland Security garbage. I want to know what *you* think. No holding back."

James looks even more nervous than he did when he walked through the door. He averts his eyes from her gaze. After stalling for a minute, he looks back at her and replies, "I believe there's more to the story than just the Brigade."

"Go on," she says, not taking her eyes off him.

"My theory is that someone in the Secret Service is involved. Based on my experience at the CIA, I believe there has to be a mole. Someone on the inside had to have helped. They would have provided the Brigade with the details required to allow such a huge attack to happen. Someone on the inside created the gaps in the security perimeter for the Brigade. I've talked to plenty of people on the inside—not just agents from the Secret Service, but also those in the CIA, the FBI, and Homeland Security. Former colleagues of mine. Something larger is at work, but no one knows who is responsible."

"Director Cummings?" Rose asks, feigning surprise.

"I don't know for sure. My gut tells me it's not him, but it has to be someone who reports directly to him. That narrows it down to four individuals, including Cummings."

"Then *that's* my big ask. I want their names, and I want you to do whatever you can to look into all four of them." She pauses. "And let's make Cummings the lead suspect."

"I don't have my CIA clearance anymore. I'll see what I can do, but—"

Rose cuts him off. "No 'buts,' James. I've seen what you can do. I don't care if you have to lie, beg, or steal. Do whatever you need to do. Just move quickly."

"This will take months, at minimum," he says defensively.

"You have a few days. I will talk to Acting President Alvarez. She'll help. Think about what you need, and get back to me. I will help you help me."

"I want this as much as you do."

"We'll see how much you want it, but you've got to work quickly." Suddenly, an idea comes to her. "Why don't you contact Director Schultz on the way out of here and ask for your job back? If you get any pushback, let me know, and I'll talk to Alvarez."

"Are you sure? You really want me to work for him again?" James challenges.

"I don't give a damn. Right now, I'm in a rush. If you bring me some solid information, I will tell you what I know. Quid pro quo. Got it?"

"Do you already have information?"

She takes a little enjoyment in his surprise. "I do. And it's shocking. You *do* want to know what I know. Trust me." She stands up and orders, "Give me an update by the end of the day. Now grab a pen and paper."

"Yes, ma'am," James says as he starts looking through his messenger bag.

"I'm going to give you my phone number."

"But I already—"

"No, you don't have *this* number." She takes the pen and paper and writes down the number of her burner phone.

"You can't have another phone number. If someone finds out, they—"

Again, she cuts him off. "No one will find out, and if they do, *you* will fix it. Listen, James—this is even more serious than you know. I need you to step up to the task. I need urgency from you. If you really love Lance and care about our family, this is the time to prove it. This is literally a matter of life and death."

He looks uncertain, and she can see he's processing her words.

"Life and death—I really mean it. Now go; you have a lot to do today." She leads him out the door and shuts it quickly.

She picks up her regular phone and dials. "Hello, this is Mrs. Dumont calling for Jennifer."

"Yes, ma'am. I will tell Vice President Alvarez—ugh, sorry—the acting president, you are on the line," says the man's voice.

Rose waits only seconds before Jennifer picks up the phone. "Hello, Rose. How are you?"

"Well, thank you. I need a favor."

CHAPTER 49

I LOVE YOU

▷ **Doris – Los Angeles, California, Day 28**

Doris momentarily forgets herself and lifts her head to look at Officer Washington in disbelief. "You don't think that's possible, do you? I mean, the American intelligence agencies could not have screwed up that badly, right? Bringing in the wrong man? Impossible."

"Well, I don't know, ma'am. Anything is possible, and every conspiracy theorist online gets their two seconds of fame. I don't know what to believe anymore. Either way, we'll know more when the acting president speaks to the nation tonight. The military is still on full alert. They believe another extremist group is planning an attack." Officer Washington turns his attention back to Lance.

Just as Doris is about to grab Lance's arm and lead him away, he starts speaking. "Well, you see, there are already counterterrorism policy standards and procedures in place. This type of threat is common, but usually overseas. When the threat is on American soil, that's when things get tricky. But the good news is that Director Schultz has implemented a system to methodically track potential threats such as these. I can't disclose the details, of course. I'm sure that he and Director Cummings are on top of it, Officer. No need to worry. That's *their* job."

Both Doris and the police officer look at Lance in shock, but Officer Washington speaks first, sounding impressed. "How do you know all this, sir?"

Lance turns to Doris with a look that appears to ask the same question.

"Oh, he was a teacher at a military school back East," Doris quickly interjects. "Right, Elliot?"

She turns to Lance and notices he's lost the color in his face. She knows they need to get out of this situation now, before Lance's memory comes back to him right here, in the lobby, in front of this cop.

But Lance chimes in again. "Yes, I was a teacher at the Virginia Military Institute. I taught the cadets political science and international studies. Part of the curriculum focused on national emergencies, domestic-terrorist attacks, and defense strategies." He laughs nervously. "But that's all in the past. Right now, my girlfriend and I are on vacation."

"Look at the time, Elliot!" Doris points to a large clock across the room. "We're running late!" She then turns to the officer. "I'm sorry; we've got to go, but it was such a pleasure meeting you, Officer Washington. I hope you have a nice day."

She grabs Lance's hand and pulls him around the corner, away from the eyes of the officer. Once they're out of sight, she lets out a big sigh and leans against the wall for support. "Thank God that's over!"

"I'm so sorry." Lance's eyes are large and pleading. "I know I'm supposed to avoid anyone in a uniform. I don't know what came over me. And I have *no* clue how I knew all that information. Something in me just clicked, and I wanted to share it. It felt so good *not* to be the dumbest one in the room."

Doris grabs his shoulders. "Elliot, you will always be the *smartest* one in the room—I promise. But for now, just follow our rule about not talking to strangers. And if you *have* to talk to someone, keep the conversation light and talk about the weather or food. Nothing else, all right?"

Lance looks down at the floor and nods. "I am really sorry."

Doris grabs his hands. Realizing he's a bit shaken, she tries to ease his mind. "Hey, on another note, I have some good news. Remember what I said about leaving in a few days? Well, we'll be heading to the lovely state of Washington. My dear friend Debbie works at Washington State University and thinks she can help us. I told her about you, and she promised to look into getting both of us jobs. This is what you wanted, right? To make your own money? It's going to happen, so let's just keep our heads down between now and then."

Lance smiles widely. "This is *exactly* what I wanted. I won't have to be taken care of anymore. I want to see what I'm capable of, especially now. After that conversation with the officer, I feel like I know a lot more than I thought I did." He gives her a kiss, and they head back to the room to take a long nap.

Little does he know how capable he really is, she thinks.

☯☯

After a two-hour nap, Doris and Lance are famished and order room service. They enjoy their dinner in silence. Then Doris takes a long bath to wash away the stress from their conversation with the police officer. She can't stop thinking about what Officer Washington said. Hopefully, the rumors about the president remain just that—rumors. Of course, they *do* have the wrong guy, but Doris is sure that the government is keeping that information from the press. They have to be aware that letting the public know this would create panic. The stock market would crash, and every extremist group would be on the hunt for President Dumont. It would be chaos in the streets. Upon finishing her bath, she lets

Lance know that the bathroom is his. She suggests he enjoy a long hot shower.

Once she hears the water from the shower, she turns on the TV and flips through the channels until she finds coverage of the investigation into the Courthouse Massacre. Instinctively, she looks away from the screen. She hasn't been able to watch footage from the courthouse since that day. She's too afraid of what it might bring about. Would she finally crack? Part of her feels like she already has. She's running with the president. Isn't that proof enough?

Something catches the corner of her eye, and she turns back to the screen. Her stomach tightens. The footage is of an ambulance, but in the background, she sees someone kneeling over a body on the ground. The footage is a bit grainy, but her red overcoat and blond ponytail are unmistakable.

"Oh my God," she says aloud, starting to tremble. The camera didn't capture a front view of either of their faces, thank God, but her profile is visible for a couple of seconds. She wonders if it's enough for anyone to recognize her. She starts to sweat when she realizes that, in today's world of technology, this footage is good enough to be used to identify her. Sure, it would take some work, but that's what the authorities do every day. Maybe it's not only possible to do that; maybe they already have.

Suddenly, she realizes she's no longer alone in the room and turns to see Lance staring at the television. "Look, Ribbons! That's you! You're on TV! I've seen you wearing that red coat. What were you doing there? It looks like a war zone. Who are all those people lying on the ground?"

Her mouth dries up when she sees his look of surprise and horror. A fleeting thought of confessing everything crosses her mind. Maybe this is the moment, but maybe it's not. She turns off the TV and looks at Lance, her voice like steel. "I would be proud to be at that scene, but that wasn't me. And you are right: it *was* a war, an attack against the United States of America and an attempt to kill the president. A lot of people were murdered, and many more were injured."

She stops talking and watches him, waiting to see if any of this has triggered his memory. Her muscles tense in preparation for whatever is necessary—fight, flee, anything. But they haven't prepared her to see him cry. His tears begin to flow, streaming down his face and dripping onto his T-shirt. Her heart melts, and her fear turns to sorrow. This man has been through hell. He hasn't had the time or ability to address the trauma *he* has experienced. Before she knows it, she has crossed the room and is now hugging him as tightly as she can.

"I love you, Elliot. I don't know if you know what that means to me. You are the heart of this little girl inside of me, and you are my boy of green pastures, standing next to me. It's all going to be OK. I promise you: you're going to get better and remember everything."

He wipes away his tears and looks at her like a child who has forgotten to bring his homework to school. "I don't know who I am or where I'm going. Sometimes I fall asleep thinking about the pain of being so lost in this world. But I do know one thing: I'm lucky to have you here by my side."

They finish getting ready for bed and lie down together. Lance is pressed against her side, and all she wants to do is listen to his every shallow breath. The Los Angeles evening is growing cold. It's so quiet she can almost hear him blink. She wonders if he is still awake.

Suddenly he coughs. "Ribbons, you'll always be next to me, won't you? The strings that tie my heart to yours will be there for the rest of my life. You made me strong and shared your food, family, and bed with me. And look at me now!"

"My heart will never leave you, Elliot. That I can promise," she replies.

Understanding his intentions, Doris pulls the covers back, and repositions herself on top of Lance. She gently wraps her fingers around his shaft, then trails her fingers along its length. Astonished by her own boldness, she guides him into her. He grasps at her back and pulls her forward, against his chest. Doris wants to make this last, craving slowness and warmth. Lance takes hold of her hips and pushes himself deeper inside her. After it's over, he curls his body around hers, just as he did last time. He holds her close as he once again whispers gently, "My life with you has just begun."

YOU LOOK LIKE A BALLERINA

▷ **Edwina – San Antonio, Texas, Day 28**

Thomas and Edwina made it to Texas, along with their Secret Service special agents, on a red-eye flight. They were then taken directly to Honey's house on the outskirts of San Antonio. Edwina is proud of her mother for having convinced Director Cummings to allow the two of them to stay at their grandmother's house without Secret Service protection. She'd threatened to go to the media with her suspicion that Cummings's Secret Service agency was ultimately to blame for the Courthouse Massacre. Her mother had been certain that would force his hand, and he would allow an exception to the rule for which there has never before been an exception.

Honey is nearly eighty years old but still strong in mind and body, working for hours in her large yard every day. She has lived in the same house all her life. In fact, she was born in this house, as her mother hadn't trusted doctors or Western medicine. The old Spanish Mission-style house has five bedrooms. While it had been built with only one bathroom, Honey's parents added two more over the years out of necessity. The grandchildren have visited for two weeks every summer since they can remember.

Rose called Honey yesterday to tell her that Thomas and Edwina needed to get out of New York City. Not only did they need a break from the hospital, they also needed to escape the eyes of the media and wanted to visit some of their friends down in Texas and New Mexico. Of course, Honey understood this; she had always wondered why Lance stayed in politics, allowing his family to be constantly scrutinized. Honey was especially surprised when she learned that Edwina and Thomas would be without Secret Service detail. She even offered to loan the kids her old car so they could visit their friends. Of course, that was just a ruse; Edwina and Thomas would not be visiting any friends.

After spending the day with Honey, Thomas and Edwina are able to escape the home of their well-meaning but fussy grandmother. With a renewed sense of urgency, and with Fatima's address in hand, the two embark on their journey to New Mexico. Fatima Machado lives in a suburb of Santa Fe, a ten-and-a-half-hour drive from San Antonio. If they drive through the night, they will arrive as the sun is rising.

֍

Three hours later, they arrive at their first rest stop to use the restroom and stock up on snacks.

"It's awfully flat here, in Texas," Edwina says as she gets back into the car and rolls down her window to take in the fresh country air. Thomas will drive the second shift, and they will continue switching positions until they reach their destination, each getting a chance to sleep.

As the sun rises, they arrive in downtown Santa Fe and find a small motel. They pay cash for a room with twin beds. They're exhausted and are looking forward to a few hours of sleep before heading to Fatima's house.

"You know, I've been thinking," Thomas says as he looks up at the ceiling, "there's a decent chance that Fatima won't be able to tell us anything. Maybe she knows nothing. Even worse, maybe Doris is there, and we learn that this Elliot is really just some random guy. Maybe this is all a complete boondoggle, as they say around here." He looks over at Edwina, and they share a much-needed laugh.

"I have a feeling we're on the right track," Edwina assures him. "All we need is something to connect Dad and Doris."

"I know, I know. I'm just anxious about this, and I want answers. Mom *expects* answers." With that, they both do their best to get some sleep before their big afternoon ahead.

☉☉

Thomas's cell phone alarm rings at noon. Edwina wakes and wonders what this lady—Fatima—is made of. Is she some sort of superwoman or a Santa Fe hippie?

"What if she doesn't open the door? Maybe she left the country?" she wonders aloud. "In either case, we'll have to stake out her house until she appears. We'll have to sleep in the car and take turns watching the house."

"Calm down," Thomas says. "We just have to hope for the best. Now let's get dressed and get going."

"I'll take the bathroom while you change out here," Edwina says.

The siblings get to work changing their appearances. Edwina chops off her honey-colored hair to make her look more like a hipster and less like a typical college student. For added effect, she then uses a temporary color spray to turn the ends purple. Looking in the mirror, she realizes that if she goes through with her plan to become a nun, she will look back on this moment and laugh.

She steps out of the bathroom, takes one look at her brother, and exclaims, "Wow! You look awesome, Thomas! I love it!" Thomas has shaved his full beard, leaving only a 1970s-style moustache, which makes him look like an outsider. He's still handsome, but with the addition of a trucker's cap, jeans, and a flannel shirt, he looks completely different than he used to. They laugh at each other's character choices.

"You know what? I think I prefer this new look! I was tired of looking so boring and conservative," Thomas confesses.

Edwina nods, but her mind is elsewhere. She can't help feeling nervous and afraid. This is the first time since the assassination attempt that she's felt this level of fear. She sits on the edge of her bed and says a few Hail Marys before it's time to leave.

"I'll take a quick look to make sure the coast is clear," she says, cracking the door and peeking outside. "OK . . . clear."

"Jesus, Edwina, it's as if you think the US military is on our trail. You've seen way too many movies. Just act normal. We haven't been alone for a full twenty-four hours, and you're already giving me anxiety! We're going to walk out of here like two normal, up-to-nothing adults."

"OK, OK, but remember, I wanna ask Fatima some questions too. Don't hog all the good ones for yourself!"

The day is overcast and cool. They climb into the car Honey lent them, a silver 2014 Lexus sedan, and make their way to Fatima's house, practicing their questions and arguing over whether or not they will get more truthful answers with sugar rather than salt. Edwina wants to take the aggressive salty approach, while Thomas claims he always has more luck when he uses his sweet charm.

Next thing they know, they are standing at Fatima's front door, ringing the doorbell. A woman in her late thirties, dressed in colorful leisure wear, answers the door. Edwina stares at her for a moment that's long enough to make the woman's smile grow even larger.

"What's the matter? Who did you think was going to answer the door?" The woman reaches out and grabs their hands, pulling them into the house. "Dear, you look like a ballerina! You're so fair-skinned and have such fine, delicate hands. But that *hair*—what happened?"

"Excuse me?" Edwina asks defensively. She shoots a confused look at her brother.

"Well, just in case you're wondering, I'm not Doris; I'm her sister, Fatima."

Bewildered, Edwina studies Fatima's face and, while still holding her hand, moves in closer. Fatima's smile is so bright and wide, but what's completely throwing her off is that it appears genuine. *Damn it! She's using sugar*, Edwina realizes.

"It's a pleasure to meet you both," Fatima says earnestly. "You are President Dumont's kids. I've seen pictures of you." She winks with the confidence of a gentle breeze rippling across a pond on a warm summer day. "You are Edwina, correct? I'm the one who spoke to your sister June on the phone."

"I— how—" Caught off guard, Edwina trips over her words. She looks at Thomas again, but he's simply gaping at Fatima in surprise. "But . . . how did you know we'd come here?"

"Well, first of all, your disguises need some work," Fatima jokes as she gestures for them to sit down on the living room couch. "But that's a good question. My sister and I talked about every possible scenario. We knew that if anyone was going to knock on my door looking for your father, it would probably be his kids. Well, to be honest, we also thought it might be the

FBI—or worse, the Brigade. But here you two are! Thank God it's you," she gushes, making the sign of the cross.

"Well, you're right," Thomas finally says. "This is Edwina, and I'm Thomas." He pauses before adding, "So your sister *does* have our dad. Where the hell are they?"

CHAPTER 51

I'll THINK OF SOMETHING

▷ **Doris – Los Angeles, California, Day 29**

This afternoon, the California sun shines on Doris and Lance as they enjoy a trip to Venice Beach, just as Doris promised. On the way back, they take the crowded 10 freeway toward downtown Los Angeles, the tall buildings reflecting the cloudless blue sky and palm trees that glisten in the sun. Doris remembers a trip she took during college that included a fun weekend in Los Angeles. Part of the purpose of that trip was to get fake driver's licenses for her and her friends in Los Angeles's MacArthur Park. Now, over twenty years later, here she is again, heading to MacArthur Park—this time, with the president of the United States. Life contains many surprises, but this one is for the history books.

They find a parking space near the lake and walk toward South Alvarado Street. Doris hopes she can remember the area. She recalls that back in the day, all you needed to do was walk down the street, and guys would pass by, asking, "ID? Coca? Pot?" They offered everything a college student would need for a crazy weekend. Sure enough, within half a block, a guy walks by and quietly asks if they are looking for an ID, molly, or coke. With marijuana now being legal in California, she guesses much of this guy's business has been taken away. Within the hour, Lance has a new, fairly realistic California driver's license in the name of Elliot Greene. She can see him beaming with pride on the ride back to the hotel. She hopes he feels comfort in formalizing an identity he doesn't even remember. She also hopes the identification will pass the scrutiny of Washington State University's human resources department.

Lance is in a great mood. Doris is glad that things are going his way. Some of his memory has returned, and he seems excited about the possibility of working at the university. Even if he's in just an administrative role, he can still take pride in making his own money. Today's trip to the ocean has given him a sense of happiness Doris hasn't seen in him before.

Once they get back to their room at the hotel, Lance asks, "How about a dip in the pool? I want to swim some laps!"

"Really? So you think you're a swimmer now?"

Despite her words, Doris does not need to be asked twice. She strips off her clothes and steps toward her suitcase to retrieve her swimsuit. At that moment, Lance sneaks up from behind her and dumps a cold glass of water down her naked backside. She screams, turns, and lunges at him, her momentum carrying them to a crash landing on the sofa. Suddenly, there's a loud knock at the door.

"Who is it?" Lance calls out.

"I'm a police officer," comes the loud response.

Doris scrambles out of Lance's embrace as if the sofa were on fire. "What the hell, Elliot?!"

"I'll think of something," Lance says quietly. "Just take a breath." He turns back to the door and calls out, "Wait a minute! Let me get some clothes on!"

"No problem. Go ahead, sir," the officer responds in a much more casual tone of voice.

"Grab a towel, Ribbons," Lance orders. "Then wipe down all the cups and bottles and the toothpaste too—every damn thing we've ever touched. I'll try to hold him off for a bit."

Lance puts on his robe as Doris throws on her own robe and begins wiping things down. She can hear the sound of the door opening as she continues her task. She turns to see Lance standing in front of the familiar-looking officer. She's surprised he isn't in uniform. Panic surges in her chest.

"May I come in?" asks the officer, holding up his identification. He appears young enough to be Lance's son.

Lance manages to keep the officer outside the room long enough for Doris to finish wiping everything down. "My girlfriend is getting dressed. What seems to be the problem?"

"My name is Jack Guthrie, and I'm looking for a woman named Doris Machado. She was a nurse I met at Lenox Hill Hospital in New York City. It was just after the Courthouse Massacre. I was looking for my father, who went missing after the attack. He'd gone to see President Dumont speak and hadn't been seen since. *Now* may I come in?"

Peering out from the bathroom, Doris can see Jack looking over Lance's shoulder, clearly wondering why this guy hasn't stepped away from the door.

Doris wonders how the hell this cop managed to locate her in Los Angeles. If *he* can find her this easily, then anyone can.

"OK, OK! No problem. Come in, if you'd like. You can look around, but there's no Doris here. It's just me and my girlfriend, Ribbons." Lance steps away from the door.

"Well, can I please at least meet your girlfriend?" asks Jack. "Where is she?"

"I'm here," Doris announces as she exits the bathroom.

"Hello, Doris. I'm sorry to surprise you like this," Jack says apologetically.

Perplexed, Lance looks at her. *"Doris?"*

Doris realizes she's never told Lance her real name, but she isn't about to explain right now, not in front of a police officer. She feels a bead of sweat roll down her back. *Think, Doris, think . . .*

CHAPTER 52

A PATHETIC ATTEMPT

▷ **Edwina – Santa Fe, New Mexico, Day 29**

"Right to the point! Of course you want to know where your father is, Thomas." Fatima's smile doesn't fade, but Edwina can see she's nervous. "Well, I'm happy to see the two of you. I'm glad you found me first. The last thing I wanted was a SWAT team breaking down my front door!" Her attempt at a humorous remark falls on deaf ears.

Thomas and Edwina just stare at her, anxiously awaiting a response.

Fatima's expression turns serious. "I know you're desperate to find your father. To be honest, they *were* here, but they left three days ago. Doris hasn't phoned since she left, and she wouldn't tell me where they were going. She wanted to protect me in case the wrong people came looking for them. After leaving Lenox Hill Hospital about three weeks ago, they drove for two days to get here. Doris worked around the clock to rehabilitate your father. When he arrived, he wasn't able to speak. But he left here a new man, speaking and walking. However, his memory still hadn't returned. I don't know if that's changed since then."

Thomas's hands curl into fists as he shouts, "Why the hell didn't she contact the people in charge of his safety once she discovered his identity?"

Incredulous, Edwina can't hold back either. "He's the president of the United States, and she *kidnaps* him? This makes no sense. And you supported this?"

"I know, I know. I asked Doris the same thing; trust me. Her plan sounded like a death wish for the two of them. But Doris didn't ask for this—no more than any of the victims asked for that awful day at the courthouse. But to cut to the chase—the people who oversaw his safety screwed up. We all know that; *you* certainly know that. These same people brought the wrong guy to the hospital. Then they lied to you. Does any of that sound safe to either of you? There's something at play here that none of us know about; that much is clear. The theory of our government's involvement in the attack has been broadcast across every news channel since the beginning. And don't get me started on all the militia groups threatening to finish the job. Who the hell was Doris supposed to turn your father over to?"

"But people just don't—" Thomas begins.

"Stop. Just hear me out. I know you and your family must agree with this theory; otherwise I would've had the Secret Service or CIA at my front door. But instead, *you're* here. Why? Actually, where *is* the Secret Service? I didn't see anyone else in the car when you pulled up."

"It's just us," Edwina confesses. She wants to be mad, but somewhere deep inside, she's relieved to hear her father is alive and somewhat all right. It doesn't sound like he's being held captive, and he's not dead.

Thomas shakes his head. "Well, that is exactly what our mother thinks. It's true; we don't trust the very government that our father leads. Our family gave him to this country, and then the people who were supposed to keep him safe nearly got him killed. Now, they want to finish what they started—the Brigade and whoever it is in our government who is helping them. And, yes, you're right: they probably lied to us from the start."

Edwina's mind is spinning. As she listens to Thomas, she wonders what would have happened if her family had acknowledged her concerns on the day of the attack. Maybe they could've found their father just a few days later at Lenox Hill Hospital.

Fatima says softly, "My sister has done everything possible to keep your father safe. When she became a nurse, she swore to herself that she would dedicate herself to a life of service. Her job was to make sure her patients were safe and looked after. Fate brought your father into her care. Doris has said from the very beginning that she only wants to return your father to you, his family—*not* to the government. That's still her plan: to deliver him to you safely. That's why we called your sister. It was the only number I could get my hands on." Fatima sighs deeply, sounding defeated.

"What a pathetic attempt! Your sister could have tried to contact us the moment she found out who he was. Or maybe the day after, or even the *week* after!" Edwina finds herself becoming increasingly agitated and doesn't really care.

Fatima sounds tired when she replies, "I know. I'm sorry for that. I don't know what to say. What I do know is that her intentions are good. She's not part of some extremist group; she truly wants to return him to you. But you are right, Edwina: she could've done a lot more. I could have as well."

"Damn right, you could have. It seems your sister just wants to keep our dad to herself. What a home-wrecker." Edwina wishes she could inflict physical pain with her words.

"You have every right to be angry, Edwina," Fatima says empathetically.

After almost a minute of silence, Thomas asks, "Do you think they stayed in New Mexico?"

"No." Fatima gets up and returns with an envelope that she hands to Edwina. "Doris received this in the mail the day before they left. This is why they ran."

Edwina opens the letter and reads the only word on the paper: *RUN.* She flips over the envelope to look at the front. "The postmark says *Connecticut.* Do you know who could've done this? And why is the word *Ribbons* written on the envelope?"

"No clue about the postmark. It was probably a friend of Doris's. We assumed that whoever it was probably sent the letter from outside of New York City in order to protect themself. Most likely, it was one of the nurses at the hospital. Doris's life was that job, and she had a few close friends at Lenox Hill. And as for the word *Ribbons,* that's the nickname the other nurses gave Doris because your father was rather fond of the ribbon Doris wears on her lapel. She had it on when she responded to the courthouse after the attack."

"Ribbons. There's a surprise around every corner," Edwina quips.

"As for Doris's coworkers, Alice and Angela, we met them," Thomas adds. "We asked them some questions, and it was clear they were covering up for Doris."

Edwina turns to Thomas. "I'm sure they sent it after their second run-in with the man in the hoodie."

"You know about the man in the hoodie?" Fatima asks, clearly surprised.

Edwina tells Fatima the story of the man's return and how Alice and Angela hid from him.

"Doris mentioned him. It's one of the main reasons why she left the hospital. She didn't want her best friends to be in danger. She also wanted to protect your father. It's likely that man was after *him.*"

"And protect *herself,*" adds Edwina sarcastically.

"Yes, and herself," Fatima admits. "So I'm thankful that you two found me first."

The three of them sit in silence, each thinking about what the next step should be and feeling the pressure of time. The race to find their father has begun, and Edwina and Thomas need a leg up on whomever is behind all of this, whether it be the Brigade or a government agency. Edwina wonders if they are already being watched. Maybe they are leading the wrong people to their father. She doesn't know whom to trust, and picking the wrong door to open could lead to disaster. At the slightest touch, everything could go up in flames.

Edwina has been so caught up in her thoughts, she feels like she's forgotten to breathe for the past ten minutes. She takes a quick breath of air and focuses on the rhythm of inhaling and exhaling until she snaps back to the present moment.

Fatima and Thomas sit next to her, staring at their hands. Edwina feels helpless. They're stuck. They don't know where to go from here. At best, they have a week or two to find their father before someone else finds him first. But they need more information, a tip that will lead them to Doris. Edwina doesn't want to call her mom without having a viable lead and a destination in mind.

"Look, I don't know what else I can say," Fatima says. "I can't tell you what you and your family need to hear. I wish I could. I wish I knew where Doris and your father went. It'd put *my* mind at ease as well."

"What else can you tell us about Doris?" Edwina asks. "She left New York and came here because you are her lifeline. What other lifelines does she have? There must be other people Doris would lean on in a time of need, right? Think hard, please." She has decided to go with the sugar approach for now.

"Well, my sister doesn't have many people in her life. Our parents died years ago. We have no siblings, and neither of us have children. I've never been married, and Doris's husband, Daniel, died a year ago. It was just the two of us until Doris got married after nursing school, and soon afterward, moved to New York City. She loves the nurses she works with, and even spent her free time at the hospital, especially after Daniel died. She and Daniel were great together. She was completely devastated."

Thomas shoots a discouraged look at Edwina. "OK, so it was just you and the nurses in New York in Doris's life? That doesn't give us much. I can't imagine her going back to New York City now that other people may know our dad is missing."

"She didn't have any friends from nursing school?" Edwina presses.

Thomas nods as if Edwina is onto something. "What college did she attend?"

Fatima taps her fingers on her chin. "Washington State University in Pullman. It's a beautiful place, I used to visit all the time. Doris loved it there. I think— no, I'm *sure* she had friends in college, but I don't remember their names. They never come up in conversation anymore. I wish I could remember something. I'm sorry, but that was well over a decade ago."

"Please, Fatima, just think." Edwina leans in, her voice unwavering. She's not going to leave without a destination in mind, even if they have to stay there all night. "We've got to go somewhere from here; we can't just give up. And I know you don't want the wrong people finding your sister before we do, so please keep trying."

Fatima closes her eyes, her brow furrowed in concentration.

Edwina holds her breath as Thomas sits rigidly beside her.

Suddenly, Fatima jumps up off the couch and practically yells, "Debbie! Her name is Debbie!"

Edwina hardly dares to breathe, scared to latch on to something that may give them false hope. She stays seated as Fatima runs the name over and over, tasting it on her lips and nodding to herself until her bright, shining smile has returned.

"Yes, that's it: *Debbie*. I know it is. I'm sure this doesn't sound like much, but it's the only name I can remember. Debbie was one of her teachers. Maybe she's still there!"

"There have got to be hundreds of teachers and administrative personnel at Washington State University," Thomas says. "How are we going to find a Debbie who worked there over ten years ago? And we don't even know if Doris has kept in touch with her. If we chase this, there's a good chance it'll just lead to a dead end. We don't have time for that." He turns to look out the window next to him and pushes back one of its curtains a tiny bit.

"Thomas, close the curtain," Edwina says, and then a flash of white catches her eye. "Wait! Look over there! See that white van? There's no writing on it, and it looks like there's someone sitting inside. I don't remember seeing it when we pulled up."

Thomas looks at the van, and Fatima rushes over, ducking her head in between theirs. Now three heads are crammed into the tiny opening of the curtain.

"Guys, one at a time," Edwina says.

"There's a good chance that your every move has been tracked," Fatima says cautiously. "Trust me when I say I've peeked out this curtain a couple hundred times since Doris arrived. I've turned off the lights and watched for hours. I've stared down every dark van, black SUV, and any car that looks too expensive for this neighborhood. But that doesn't look like one; it's probably just someone's work van. This is a working-class neighborhood, and there are a lot of vans around. And besides, if you're being followed, there's nothing you can do. This journey is dangerous. I accepted that fact when I agreed to let Doris stay here. But to be honest, the more I learn, the more I know she's doing the right thing in keeping your dad safe and out of the hands of the wrong people."

Thomas closes the curtain, and the siblings turn to look at Fatima. "Fatima," Edwina says, "you spent time with my father. Do you think he would turn himself in or try to run on his own?"

"I think the only one who can do anything about this mess right now *is* your father. For now, Doris will hide him well. Your father has put all his trust in her, and she will protect him. Ultimately, he's the one who's going to have to be ready to return to his old life. But, of course, he's going to need his memory back, and until that happens, I think they'll keep running . . . and, of course, looking for a way to get ahold of your family."

Edwina rolls her eyes. "That, I don't believe. But if your sister is going to run, then we will keep running too." Edwina straightens up, a fire building in her chest. "There's only one place to go: north, to Washington."

Thomas gives her an approving look before turning back to Fatima. "Thank you for talking to us and *hopefully* telling us the truth," he says.

Edwina can't help herself. "When we find our dad and Doris, you know we can't protect her, right? Most likely, she will be prosecuted for kidnapping and endangerment—at the very least."

"I know, Edwina. But, as I said before, my sister isn't a bad person. She may have made some poor decisions in the beginning, but knowing what we all know now, it's looking more and more like she did the right thing."

Edwina ignores this. She just wants her father back. She doesn't care about what happens to Doris, even if her intentions are good and in some weird way, she *did* save their father. That's for the courts to decide. She asks Fatima for a pen and paper and scribbles something on it. "Here's the number of our burner phone. Please call if you find out anything—if Doris calls you or if you remember something that can help us, like Debbie's last name."

The three say their goodbyes, and Thomas and Edwina make their way out the door.

Back outside, Edwina looks furtively at the white van parked across the street. The person she saw inside earlier isn't there now. There's a knot in her stomach as she looks back at the house one last time. Secretly, she hopes Fatima will be fine. She knows she'll have enough sense to keep the door locked and lights off should anyone else come knocking. She doesn't want any more death stemming from the Courthouse Massacre. Repeating that thought over and over, Edwina gets into the car and makes the sign of the cross, muttering a few Hail Marys under her breath.

FINGERPRINTS

▷ **Doris – Los Angeles, California, Day 29**

"Jack!" Doris exclaims after finally remembering Officer Guthrie's first name. "What are you doing here, in Los Angeles?" For a second, she wonders if he's the one who sent the letter, but she doesn't dare ask.

"Let me explain, Doris." Jack gestures toward the couch. "Maybe you guys should sit down."

Doris sits, pulling Lance down with her. Lance stiffens at her touch. She can't begin to imagine how confused and upset he must be right now. Jack settles into a chair opposite them. Doris sits up straight, trying to remain composed despite her fear. Maybe this is the moment when everything is revealed. The room feels as if it may become a confession booth, with Jack as the priest, listening intently.

"When I left Lenox Hill, I was pretty upset," Jack begins. "No, I was *destroyed*. After that, I spent weeks searching every hospital, urgent care center, and morgue. I begged my department for resources, and they did help, but no one was able to find my father. After a while, I stopped looking. I had exhausted all avenues. But then I remembered *you*, the nervous nurse from Lenox Hill Hospital, the one who didn't tell me that her patient was a John Doe." He turns to look at Lance. "I thought, *Well, maybe that nurse knows something more. Maybe she can help me, as I have no leads.* So I went back to your hospital and learned you'd quit on the very same day Elliot was checked out of the hospital. Dr. Dansby, Alice, and Angela were all quite helpful in providing me information and answering my questions."

Doris sits in silence, her nerves crawling with unease. She wants to yell at the top of her lungs, "I give up! I have the president of the United States! Just take him!" But instead, she gives Jack a small smile and takes a sip of water. She turns to Lance, but he's staring off into the distance. She wants to keep Jack talking in order to learn what he knows, so she says nothing.

"I'm sorry, Doris," continues Jack. "I know this all sounds crazy, but I've been desperate. I was surprised to find out the two of you had left. The timing of your departures seemed suspicious to me, so with the help of the hospital and the NYPD, I learned there is no Elliot Greene with a daughter named Allison who lives in Seach, Indiana. I also learned the driver's license provided to the hospital was a fake. So then I thought maybe Elliot *could* be my father. I hadn't gotten a good look at him back at the hospital when you and I met. So I had to figure it out myself."

Doris's heart sinks into her stomach, but she finds a way to ask, "Did you tell the hospital or the NYPD what you learned about Elliot?"

"No, I didn't tell anyone. I just want to find my father," Jack replies matter-of-factly.

"So how did you find us?" Doris asks, not quite sure she wants to know the answer.

"It was pretty easy. I found out that your only living family member is your sister, Fatima. Angela and Alice confirmed that the two of you are close. So when I learned you had resigned from the hospital and no one had been able to contact you, I headed for Santa Fe."

"You were watching us when we were in New Mexico?" Doris asks incredulously.

"No, I arrived there yesterday evening and drove all night to get here. According to your sister, I'd just missed you."

"What did Fatima say? Is she OK?" Ribbon stammers, now worried about the safety of her sister.

"She seemed all right. I explained who I am and what I'm trying to do. She was tight-lipped, claiming she had no idea where you'd gone. In fact, she said you were alone. But something about the way she was acting told me she was lying. She was very nervous."

"Can you blame her? A cop from New York City comes knocking on her door, looking for her sister. I'm sure as hell she was nervous."

"There's something else you need to know."

"What is it, Jack? Tell me!" Doris practically yells.

"I thanked your sister for her time, and when I returned to my truck, I was struck over the head."

"Oh my God! Fatima!"

"She's fine. I was attacked, but I was able to fight back, and, uh, it didn't end well for the guy who attacked me." Jack looks down at his hands as if they are to blame. "He's dead."

"Who *was* he?" asks Doris, jumping up from the couch.

"Please sit down, Doris."

Reluctantly, she complies, closing her eyes to calm her nerves.

"He had a Secret Service ID. I killed a special agent."

Doris opens her eyes and sees the shame on his face. "How could've you have known? He tried to kill you!"

Jack doesn't answer her rhetorical question. Doris glances at Lance, who's still staring out the window.

"Immediately after the incident, I went back to talk to Fatima, to warn her. I explained what had happened and told her she needed to get the hell out of there immediately and to tell absolutely no one that I was there. She said she would leave the next day, which is today. That's when she confessed that you were traveling with Elliot. I then took the liberty of stealing a couple of local license plates. I put one on her car and the other on my truck."

Doris covers her forehead with her palms. "I can't believe it. This can't be real. What happened to the dead agent?"

"He's in my truck," Jack replies nonchalantly. "I told your sister she shouldn't return to work or come home until I tell her it's OK to do so. I also told her to leave her phone at home and buy a burner. She has my cell number." Jack pauses before continuing, "Fatima told me you guys have her car and credit card. With that information, it was easy for me to track you to this hotel. And since I'm a cop, the front desk gave me your room number. So here I am."

Lance is still staring out the window as if stunned into silence. Doris hopes the shock of this disturbing news hasn't brought back his memory. *Please, God, not now*, she silently prays.

"OK, Jack, by now, I'm sure you can see that Elliot is *not* your father."

"There's more to the story, Doris. It's the *real* reason I've followed the two of you."

"More? How can there be *more?"* Doris asks in disbelief.

"Just before I left New York City, I got a message from our research department in the NYPD. During their ongoing search for my father, the system detected a fingerprint search and found that the search results matched my father's fingerprints. Our team tried to find out who'd conducted the search, but they had no luck. It turned out to be a classified search performed by some government agency at a higher level than the NYPD. So I was sure *someone* had my father, dead or alive.

"I started calling every contact I had made during my previous visits to the hospitals and morgues, asking if they had conducted any fingerprint searches. Again, I had no luck—that is, until I finally talked to someone at Presbyterian Hospital. She wasn't willing to tell me much because the president is a patient there, and all patient information requests have to go through the Secret Service. But she did mention that there have been agents from multiple intelligence agencies stationed at the hospital since the day of the attack. It sounds like they have control of the whole place." Jack stops for a moment, as if he's still trying to put the pieces together.

"I get it: they are trying to protect the president. But it got me thinking about why an intelligence agency's search might have involved my dad's fingerprints. Is he dead, and they're trying to locate a family member? Or maybe he's a John Doe at Presbyterian Hospital." Jack clears his throat. "I'm sorry, but may I please have a glass of water?"

Doris stands up, pours Jack a glass of water from the tap in the bathroom, and hands it to him. "But this doesn't make sense to me. You should've stayed in New York. If that's where the fingerprint search was conducted, then that's where he is."

"I felt the two of you were my best lead. Before going to the Secret Service or CIA, I had to know for sure Elliot isn't my father. I may be a new cop, but I at least know that every clue is a step closer to solving a case. And after what happened at Fatima's house, I knew *something* had to be up with the two of you."

Instead of focusing on Jack's story, Doris has spent the past couple of minutes thinking about *her* story. How is she going to explain Lance's identity? Every thought that pops into her mind is more absurd than the previous.

"First of all, I'm *so* sorry you still haven't found your father," she says slowly, making sure the sentiment is drenched in empathy. "I'm glad you haven't given up your search for him. I'm also sorry that . . . that I can't tell you much more about Elliot." She pauses, turns to Lance, and grabs his hand. "I don't know who he is either."

Her words do the trick; Lance looks at her for the first time since he sat down.

"What? Is that why you haven't told me anything about my past? I thought you knew, but were waiting for the right moment to tell me, trying to protect me from something awful."

"I've been meaning to tell you this, but the timing has never seemed right," Doris says, wincing at her lie. "I'm really sorry, but you came into the hospital with no identification. The hospital staff tried to determine your identity so they could notify your family, but they had no luck. As time went on, I began to care for you . . . perhaps too much. When Dr. Dansby told me you were going to be transferred to a residential treatment facility, I got scared. I know too many stories about patients who go there and never leave. The system sucks them in. The drugs and dull environment rot their brains, and they stay there forever. I wasn't going to let that happen to you. I-I'm sorry."

As Doris begins to cry, Lance hugs her tightly. "It's OK, Ribbons," he whispers. "You saved my life. I will always owe you for that."

After slowly extracting herself from Lance's embrace, Doris turns to Jack. "Listen, Jack," she begins respectfully, "I know you need to report this, but can I please ask you to wait a couple of weeks before doing so? *Please?* I'm not ready to lose Elliot, and my work with him—his mental therapy—is not yet complete."

She pauses for a few moments before adding, "And now, I have something to tell *you*."

"What's that?" Jack asks eagerly.

"There was a man who came to Lenox Hill Hospital in the middle of the night, not long after the Courthouse Massacre. As he was going from room to room—we think, looking for Elliot—the nurses you spoke to, Angela and Alice, confronted him, and he pulled a knife on them. He knew the name of Alice's son and where he goes to school. He said he'd kill them all if the girls spoke to anyone. That's why we ran."

"Clearly someone is after Elliot. But why?" Jack asks. She can see that he's thinking this through.

"I'm not sure why either, but now I know who: the Secret Service. The man you killed." Jack's news has confirmed Ribbon's suspicions about the government's involvement, but knowing this for certain only makes things worse.

"OK, well, now I have a dead special agent in my truck, and I'm not any closer to finding my father."

"What does your father look like?" Lance asks Jack. "Do you have a picture?"

Doris stares at Lance. She just wants this awful moment to be over and for Jack to leave.

Jack digs into his pocket and pulls out his phone. After tapping the screen a few times, he hands it to Lance, as Doris peers over his shoulder. She sees a man in a suit standing next to Jack, who's wearing his NYPD uniform. It looks like the picture was taken at a recent event.

Jack smiles proudly. "He's forty-seven years old and just over six feet tall, with hazel eyes and light-brown hair. In fact, he looks a lot like you, Elliot. I guess that's why I was so interested in following up on the two of you."

Doris can't believe the resemblance between his father and Lance. She now understands how easy it would have been for the Secret Service to believe that they had the president in their custody. Then it hits her. She picks up her glass of water but is shaking too much to drink it, so she sets it back down. Her mind is racing: *This man's father is at New York Presbyterian! They think he's Lance Dumont. Though maybe not anymore. Now that they've found a fingerprint match, they must know they have the wrong guy. Oh shit!*

"Listen, Jack." She turns to him with a newfound determination in her voice, keeping her hands clasped firmly on her lap to stop them from shaking. "I want to help you. Don't ask how or why I know this, but I feel certain your father is at Presbyterian Hospital. I realize it's Fort Knox over there right now, but that's your best bet. It's your only option. Now that you know Elliot is not your father, you have to go back there and do *whatever* it takes." She can see the confusion and concern on Jack's face. "Jack, I'm sure he's alive. You just have to keep faith."

"How do you know he's at Presbyterian Hospital? What exactly do you know?" Jack pleads.

"Honestly, Jack, I'm not 100 percent sure. And I can't tell you *how* I know, but I feel pretty confident that your father is there. Go back to Presbyterian. *Please.*"

"OK, OK, I will. Thank you. But now I'm neck-deep in this mess, with a dead guy in my truck. You really don't know why a special agent would've been after the two of you?"

Damn it, she thinks. It's the question she was praying he wouldn't ask. "Jack, there are government forces at play here that are far beyond our imagination." She chooses her next words carefully. "I don't know for sure, but I think Elliot may have been involved in the attack in some way, and that's why they're after him. Maybe he works for the government or even the Secret

Service itself. Maybe he knows something he's not supposed to. I don't know. All I'm trying to do is protect him."

"They're after *me?*" Lance asks, clearly overwhelmed by the conversation.

"Elliot, they are after *us*," she replies, taking hold of one of his hands.

Jack nods, then looks at Lance and asks, "How are you recovering, sir?"

Lance hesitates before answering, "I'm tired. I need to rest. It's been quite the day. You understand, don't you?"

"I do." Jack stands, resting his glass on the table. "Thank you both for your honesty and support. Doris, I especially appreciate your advice and kind words. I'll call my captain and see if he can head over to Presbyterian to find out anything else."

"Good luck. And thank you for everything you did for Fatima." Doris bids him farewell with a wave and closes the door behind him. Standing up to look through the peephole, Lance watches him walk toward the stairwell. He then turns to Doris with a confused expression on his face.

"What the hell was that all about?" he demands angrily.

Doris collapses onto the sofa, unable to speak. Her mind is racing. All she can think about is Jack's father lying at New York Presbyterian Hospital, with the world thinking he's President Lance Dumont. But not the *whole* world. Thanks to the fingerprint match, someone knows the truth.

"Ribbons!" Lance snaps.

Doris realizes time is running out. After the improvisation he pulled today, Lance appears to be on the brink of regaining his memory. He's ready for the truth, and she's not.

"Why did you have me wipe down everything in here?" she asks, trying to stall.

"I was sure he'd try to walk away with some fingerprints. Somehow, I knew to do that." Lance's voice is confident, but just as quickly, his tone changes. "What the hell? Why do I know that? Who am I? I'm ready to know, Ribbons. Or should I say, *Doris?* Did I do something awful that landed me in the hospital? You don't have to protect me from the truth any longer. I can handle anything. Or do you really not know who I am? You just kidnapped me, an unknown patient, from the hospital?"

Fidgeting nervously on the couch, Rose looks away. She then says, "You're right; we *do* need to talk. I need to explain everything."

"I want to know who I am and why exactly I was in the hospital," barks Lance, taking a seat next to Doris. "Why has all this happened to me? It feels like we're running from danger."

"Elliot, I know this has been a lot, and I'm tired of all of it. You deserve the truth." She begins to stand up, but Lance grabs her wrist and pulls her back down to the couch.

"How did I get here? How did you choose me from all the patients in that hospital? I'm not blaming anything on you, but you do owe me the truth. Who the hell am I, and why did you take off with me?"

Doris twists her wrist, but his grip is too strong for her. "Elliot." Her voice is calm. "Let go. Please."

"I—" Lance looks down and releases her wrist. "I'm sorry. I just *need* the truth, Ribbons. I know I owe you my life, but it's time for you to tell me everything. Please, Ribbons. *Please."*

His gentle request shatters the last wall of Doris's resolve. She scoots closer to him and looks him straight in the eye.

"Remember the scene you saw on TV last night? The one from the steps of the New York courthouse? All those bodies on the ground?" She notices how intensely focused his eyes are on hers. "Well, you were right: that *was* me on the screen." Doris pauses to let that sink in, but Lance's expression doesn't change. "Televisions around the country are playing that scene on repeat. Like I said, it was an attack on America, and it was an attempt to kill the president of the United States." Again, she pauses. A look of detachment has come over Lance's face. She can see that he still isn't understanding what she's getting at, so she tries again, speaking each word slowly and precisely. "They tried to kill him, but they failed. I was the one on the sidewalk below the stairs—the woman you saw in the red coat. The person lying on the ground was *you*. I was helping *you*. You were shot that day. Twice." Her last sentence catches his attention. She sees something register in him, but he's not quite there yet. She has to be more direct.

"You are not Elliot Greene. And I *do* know your identity. Your name is Lance Dumont, and you are the president of the United States."

CHAPTER 54

AMERICA DESERVES THE TRUTH

C
IA Director Donald Schultz is sitting at his desk, busy with his morning routine. He's been up since 5:00 a.m. and is enjoying his third cup of coffee of the day. He desperately needs this caffeine boost, as he hasn't had a good night's sleep since the Courthouse Massacre.

His office phone rings, and his assistant connects the call, announcing, "Sir, it's James Edwards on line one."

Schultz picks up. "Hello, James. What can I do for you?"

"Good morning, sir. I'm in the area and would like to come by, if possible. Do you have time this morning?"

"Anything for you, James. Stop by in an hour."

"Thank you! See you th—"

Schultz hangs up the phone before James can finish.

☺☺

An hour later, James Edwards, Schultz's old employee and Dumont's right-hand man has made himself comfortable in the oversized chair in front of Schultz's desk.

"So . . . what brings you to your old stomping ground?" asks Schultz, noticing that James appears nervous.

Wiping away a few beads of sweat on his forehead, James replies, "To cut to the chase, I want my old job back."

"But you *have* a job."

"For a man who might never come out of a coma," James says, straightening his tie. "I want to get back to work *now*. I've already made my intentions known to Acting President Alvarez and the First Lady."

Schultz's mood brightens. "Yes, Alvarez called me about you already. I do have to say that I wouldn't want to be on that sinking ship. I've heard things are a mess at the Oval Office. How's Mrs. Dumont holding up?"

"She's as good as she can be under the circumstances. As you are aware, she has been directing anger toward everyone she encounters, so I have been avoiding contact with her as much as possible."

"I don't know what positions are available here, at the CIA," Schultz says, sensing James's immediate disappointment, "but I can hire you on a temporary basis now and find something permanent later. I do have an immediate assignment I can give you. It's very specific."

"Anything, sir. I just want to come back to the CIA," James replies.

"Well, OK. I need your help," Schultz says, trying to get a read on James's true intentions. "You've heard the news: everyone thinks there's some big government conspiracy. That's bullshit. We both know that. The Brigade tried to kill Dumont, and the Secret Service massively screwed up. They are the ones to blame. In fact, if anyone from the US government played a part in this whole mess, it's them—maybe even Cummings himself. And if not him, that weasel that reports to him—Ackman."

"You can't be serious, sir!" exclaims James, sounding genuinely shocked. "I mean, Ackman, maybe. But I don't see Cummings being behind something like that. I'm not sure he's even competent enough to pull it off."

Schultz smiles broadly at James. "Maybe. Maybe not. It was quite the operation. Every intelligence organization in this country has done nothing for the last month and a half except focus on the Brigade and other extremist groups like them. And I get it; they *should*. In fact, here at the CIA, we are doing exactly that. But I want to know how the Secret Service screwed it up so badly. At minimum, I want to know what *they* know and determine what they did wrong. America deserves the truth."

"But what can *I* do?" asks James doubtfully.

"You can do a lot. You are perfectly positioned. Listen, keep your current job. Don't resign. I will also pay you, so you'll get two paychecks. Cummings has practically set up office over at Presbyterian. You can do this assignment by continuing to work as Dumont's guy. You can find out things no one else can. And with full access to the CIA Records Research Tool, CREST, you'll have everything you need."

"I suppose I will. I'm interested," James says a bit sheepishly.

"Oh, and I also need you to watch the First Family. I want to know what they know. Go back to that hospital, and get as close to Rose Dumont as you can. I hear she talks to Cummings and Ackman often, and she's very friendly with our lovely new president, Jennifer Alvarez. Rose will be a great source of information. Get chummy."

"Sir, you want me to spy on the First Family and the Secret Service?"

"You've got it! That's exactly what I need from you. You said you'd do anything, and this is it! Get yourself a damn room in that hospital if you have to. Just move quickly."

"Is this our jurisdiction?"

Schultz shoots him an icy look. *"Everything* is our jurisdiction, James; you, of all people, should know that."

"Yes, sir. I'll be happy to accept the assignment." He clears his throat. "I'm your man."

"Thank you, James. Make me proud."

James shakes Schultz's hand and asks, "Who should I reach out to in order to obtain my log-in credentials and gain access to the database and to CREST?"

"Oh, right. Come back here end of day today, and Sheila will take care of all that. I'll let her know." Schultz, getting back to the work in front of him, doesn't bother with a goodbye.

CHAPTER 55

YOU HAVE A WIFE

▷ **Doris – Los Angeles, California, Day 29**

"Y‌ou were sworn in as president on January 20, about a month and a half ago. You have a wife and four children." Doris stops herself, caught off guard by how matter-of-factly she said, "wife and four children." She turns away from Lance, unable to look him in the eyes.

"I have a *wife?*" Lance's face grows pale. "And *four children?*" He says this as if it's an impossible scenario.

Doris reaches forward and grasps his shoulders to calm him. Lance flinches.

"Listen to me, Elliot. You need to hear the whole story. Please."

After Lance, clearly in shock, stops shaking his head, Doris continues: "On February 4, you traveled to New York City to deliver a speech in front of the courthouse. The city was experiencing some of the worst weather in decades; it was crazy. I remember every news channel questioning your sanity. It was so dangerous; people were slipping on the icy steps of the courthouse. Anyway, during the conclusion of your speech, a devastating attack took place. An attempt on your life resulted in hundreds of individuals being injured or killed. There's never been anything like it on American soil."

She stops to make sure he's listening and understanding. Lance looks at her, his eyes wide and pleading.

"After the attack was over, numerous entities took victims to five different hospitals. They were all a complete disaster. I don't know exactly how this happened, but some government officials mistook someone else for you. They brought him—the wrong guy—to New York Presbyterian Hospital, thinking that they'd rescued the president—um, *you*. Presbyterian's just blocks away from my hospital, Lenox Hill. I really don't know why or how that happened. My guess is that they mistook Jack's father for you. You two look so much alike. You saw his picture."

Lance is no longer looking at her, but she can tell he's paying close attention to her words. She knows she can't stop talking now. "So, as a nurse, I was summoned to the courthouse to help out with the rescue operation. I was wearing a red overcoat—the one you saw on TV—with a red ribbon on the lapel. I found you on the sidewalk at the bottom of the steps, lying in a pool of blood. I was the first person to help you. I brought you to the hospital in an ambulance and haven't left your side since."

Lance's head is in his hands, his entire body trembling beneath her grasp. She looks at him, relieved by her confession but desperate to find the right words to say next.

All of a sudden, Lance's head snaps up. Knocking her hands from his shoulders, he jumps to his feet and sprints to the bathroom. Still seated on the couch, Doris whirls around to face the bathroom and sees water splashing on the counter, on the floor, on Lance. It's as if he's trying to wash himself from her story. She realizes what she's telling him sounds ridiculous, even fabricated, but she can't hide the truth anymore. He deserves to know, no matter the consequences.

When the splashing ends, she stands up and crosses the room, stopping at the open bathroom door. "Elliot, it's all true.

And there's more. A militia group called the Brigade plotted for months to commit this heinous attack. They are American extremists . . . terrorists. They wanted to kill you to prevent you from doing all the things you'd promised to do for this country. Although they didn't succeed in killing you, they did murder almost a hundred Americans. It was a massacre. Hundreds more were seriously injured." A vision of all the lifeless bodies fills her head, haunting her as it has every night since that horrific day. But she's well aware she can't succumb to a panic attack now. She reaches for her cosmetics bag and extracts her pill bottle. She takes a deep breath then swallows a Xanax without water, knowing it will allow her to focus on the task at hand: finishing her story. "It took me a couple of days to realize you were really the president. I had your ID card, but I confirmed your identity by the scar on your lower back."

At this, Lance looks up at her as if he's remembering something. She must continue.

"I was terrified when I learned that many of the Brigade members were still on the loose and that there were likely many more of them who hadn't even been at the scene of the attack. They were making public statements, announcing that they were going to finish the job they started. I didn't know what to do. I figured it wouldn't take long for the intelligence agencies to realize they didn't have Lance Dumont at New York Presbyterian Hospital and they'd soon come looking for you. On top of all that, every news channel kept saying that there was no way an attack of that size could've occurred without help from some entity—or entities—within our government. Each news organization was proposing a different theory of government conspiracy. That's when I began to distrust anyone in a uniform, anyone with a badge, and everyone who works for the government. I didn't— well, I *still* don't know who to trust. All I knew at the time was that a lot of people wanted you dead and I wasn't going to be the one to deliver you to them.

"Then a guy walked into your room one night and threatened Alice's and Angela's lives. Then there was a bomb scare at New York Presbyterian Hospital, where everyone thought you were. Anyhow, I knew I could save you. I couldn't save my Daniel, but I *could* save President Dumont. But time went on, and, well, I-I fell in love with you. And because I loved you, it was up to me to protect you. I wanted to save your life, and yes, I wanted to save myself too. So, yes, I guess I did kidnap you. But my intent was—and still is—to return you to your family."

Lance doesn't move. His hands are gripping the edge of the counter so tightly, his knuckles have turned white. He's breathing heavily, his chest rising and falling rapidly as droplets of water cascade down his face. Doris grabs hold of the bathroom door and puts her face to it, shoving her forehead into the wood, trying to relieve the pressure in her head.

After a moment, Lance attempts to straighten up and dry his face with a hand towel, but his trembling becomes too intense, and he drops it. His eyes are bloodshot.

Avoiding eye contact with Doris, he stares dully at the sink and says in a low, bitter voice, "Why did you let me fall in love with you, knowing damn well who I am? I am the president of the United States, a man with a family, a wife. You *knew* this. How could you do this to me? Now what am I supposed to do, dump the woman who saved my life, and go back to my wife after having cheated on her? What's even worse is that I don't remember anything about being president, my wife, my kids . . . anything at all. I *should* re-member those things, right?" He stares at her with disgust in his eyes. "But most of all, you shouldn't have let me fall for you!"

Doris picks up the hand towel and steps forward to help Lance dry his face.

He shoves her away with an aggressiveness she's never seen in him before. She nearly falls to the ground but catches herself on the bathroom sink. She approaches him again, then holds the towel high over her head and hurls it to the floor. She stomps her foot on the towel repeatedly, as if trying to kill a snake, then screams, "*Look* at that damn towel! Do you see it? Lower your head, and look down at the towel! That's how you looked when I found you. The only difference is that you had blood all over you and two bullet holes in your head!"

"You deceived me!" Lance explodes as he glares at Doris.

She tries to regain her composure by pushing down some of the pain she's feeling, and then lowers her voice. "Elliot. When I saw you lying beneath those steps, you were barely moving. And trust me: I didn't ask for any of this." She makes a grand gesture with her arm, as though motioning to the world around them. "I was comfortable in my life before that day. I wasn't looking for places to hide, and I sure wasn't running from anything. But my life changed at those courthouse steps when I saw all the bodies and blood. The screams and moans haunt me every night." She pauses, just realizing this for the first time: "I changed that day. I guess that's what happened. That's why I can't control how I feel sometimes, and maybe that's why I let myself fall in love with you, Daniel." At that, she sees the expression on Lance's face morph from anger and confusion to hurt. *What the hell did I just say?* She desperately wishes she could take back that last word.

"*Daniel?* That's who I am to you? Just a reincarnation of your deceased husband, so you can redeem yourself by saving me?" A sudden look of realization washes over Lance's face. "You are using me to right the wrong of Daniel's death. But as they say, two wrongs don't make a right. Making a married man fall for you is *very* wrong."

Doris has no reply. She stumbles out of the bathroom and falls onto the bed. She can still see Lance from the corner of her eye. He picks up the hand towel and places it over his head.

Daniel. Of course. It always comes back to *him*, no matter how hard she tries. She closes her eyes and suddenly remembers something from her reoccurring nightmare: the bodies at the courthouse—their faces. They are all Daniel. Hundreds of Daniels lying on and around the steps—some dead, some not. *Oh shit*, she thinks. *What have I done?*

After nearly twenty minutes, Lance walks out of the bathroom. The towel is still over his head, with only his face exposed. "So am I supposed to pretend I remember being the president? I feel like I should at least pretend to know the names of my wife and children, right?" He steps closer to the bed. "But I can't. I can't remember any of it. This does not seem real. I'm not even sure you are telling me the truth. Maybe you are lying to protect yourself."

He steps over to the edge of the bed and, leaning over Doris, grabs her by the shoulders. He then says sternly, "My name is Elliot, not Lance. Maybe *you* have the wrong man."

Doris doesn't want to believe her ears. Without a word, she leans up toward him and wraps her arms around him, hoping he'll feel her empathy. He doesn't give in immediately, but after a few moments, he buries his face in her long blond hair and begins to cry.

A minute later, they break apart, and Lance walks over to sit on the couch. "What will I do now?" he asks miserably. "Let's say I *am* the president of the United States—which certainly sounds like something I should remember, but don't—but if I really *am*, then are you saying the people who didn't manage to kill me at the courthouse are still after me? They want another shot at it, so to speak?"

"Yes, Elliot, I'm afraid so. Very unfortunately, there are people out there who still want to kill you. That man Jack killed, he was after us. He would've killed *us* if we were there. You heard Jack; the man was a Secret Service agent. The one thing I am 100 percent sure of is that there are many people who want you dead, and the only people we can trust are your family members."

He looks at her with empty, emotionless eyes and whispers, "What's worse is that I don't even think I can trust you."

She joins him on the couch. "I'm sorry, Elliot. Can you please just *try* to trust me? It will help save our lives. You can do that, right?" She tilts her head and remains silent until Lance gives her a small nod. Now there's just one thing left for her to say: "Elliot, you should know my name really *is* Doris Machado. I didn't want you to find out the way you did. I'm sorry for that. And you already know that I'm a nurse. You've met my sister, Fatima. She's the only family I have. My parents are dead, as you know. I've been married, but I never had children. I've also never done anything big in my life and have certainly never broken the law . . . until now."

Exhausted, Lance closes his eyes. "I knew your name wasn't Ribbons; I know I gave you that name. But for now, I'd like to continue calling you Ribbons, if that's OK." He doesn't open his eyes to see her response.

Doris doesn't bother wiping away her tears. "Elliot, open your eyes and look at me. You must know that my intentions are good and that everything I've said is true."

"Well, if that's the case, then you've done the right thing for me and the country. For my family, on the other hand, maybe not."

CHAPTER 56

GREENER PASTURES

▷ **Lance – Los Angeles, California, Day 30**

The clear Southern California night brings with it an eerie silence. Doris retires early and alone after telling Lance that the stress of the day's events has left her drained and confused.

It has been an awful day for Lance. Learning he's the leader of the free world, with a wife and children, all in a matter of five minutes, was more than he could handle. It's nearly midnight now, and he can't sleep, especially not in the same bed as Doris. He finds some extra sheets, a blanket, and a pillow in the hallway closet, and makes a bed out of the small couch. It will have to do. Then he goes into the bathroom, digs through Doris's cosmetics bag until he locates the pills she takes to sleep, and swallows two of them.

Hours later, he jolts awake, ready to take charge. He's unsure of what to do with the information he has, but he's sure that he wants to leave Los Angeles. He transports his luggage and clothing into the bathroom and quickly begins to pack.

Doris awakens to see a beam of light streaming into the room through the partially open bathroom door. After a minute of waiting for Lance to emerge from the bathroom, she groggily calls out, "Elliot? What are you doing? It's the middle of the night. Go back to bed."

"It's actually 5:00 in the morning," he calls back, not wanting to stop what he's doing. "I can't sleep any longer. I think we should leave now."

"*Now?* It's still dark outside," Doris protests.

"I've got it handled. I've already packed my stuff. We'll grab a quick breakfast downstairs and get on our way. They open at 6:00." He appears in the doorway, suitcase in hand.

Doris rolls her eyes. "Well, I can see you are ready to go. Any reason for rushing out of here, Lance?"

"Please don't call me Lance." He's irritated and still unsure if everything she said yesterday is true. He wants proof.

"All right, *Elliot*. I'm sorry." Doris sits up in bed. "OK, I will need some coffee, but you're right; let's get the heck outta here!"

"Ribbons, I need proof that I'm really who you say I am." This is all he's been able to think about for the past ten hours.

"Of course!" Doris exclaims. "Let me get the ID I found in your jacket on the day of the attack." She jumps out of bed and rushes over to her suitcase, tossing its contents onto the floor. Finally, she pulls out a rectangular card and hands it to him.

He examines it carefully. A strange feeling comes over him. This guy looks like him—a better-looking, younger version. "I see. That *could* be me. I suppose I've changed a lot, but I'm still not completely convinced. How can that man in the picture possibly be *me?*"

"Well, that's all I've got." Looking defeated, Doris gazes down at the ground. "Wait!" she suddenly exclaims. "Oh my gosh! Proof? There's *tons* of it! It's called the internet!" She returns to the bed, grabs the receiver of the hotel phone on the bedside table, and dials zero. "Hello. I know it's early in the morning, but would you happen to have a computer we can use?"

Hanging up, she smiles at Lance. "There you go; they have a computer! Let's pack and go online just before breakfast, and then we can leave."

Lance feels like she's acting strangely. "What's wrong?" he asks. "You seem different this morning."

Doris silently begins repacking the contents of her suitcase, which are now strewn about the floor. After a minute, she finally replies, "I'm scared, Elliot. I've been scared before, many times, but this is different. Before, I knew what I had to do. I always had someone to take care of, so many patients, and that's something I know how to do. But now . . . now that the government knows it's not you at the hospital, now that a Secret Service agent is dead, all hell will descend upon us. Soon, *everyone* will be looking for you. Some people may want to save you, and others may want to kill you. The problem is, we don't know who's on which side—apart from your family members, of course. But . . . I think I have a plan that puts you in safe hands—those of your wife and children." She doesn't turn around as she shoves the last couple of items into her suitcase and zips it up.

Lance says nothing, but he agrees with her that he needs to get back to his family. However, the idea of returning to a family he can't remember seems strange. He heads to the bathroom and shuts the door; at least the shower is a brief escape from this nightmare. Part of him wishes things hadn't changed. Yesterday, he was happy and excited about their next adventure in Washington.

After Lance finishes shaving, it's Doris's turn to use the bathroom. The two are careful to keep the door closed and remain covered in front of each other. When 6:00 arrives, they head down to the lobby to use the internet before breakfast.

At the small computer terminal, Doris suggests, "Why don't *you* sit down, Elliot. This is about you."

As he takes a seat, he replies, "OK, I'm ready . . . I think."

"Well, type in your name, Lance Dumont, and then click here: *Images.*" She points to a link in the upper left corner of the screen.

Lance follows her instructions, and numerous images appear on the screen. Again, he sees that man who looks like him in the photo on the ID. But the man in all the images is healthier looking than he is, isn't as skinny, and has a face with no scars. As he scrolls through the images, he notices that Lance Dumont is almost always wearing a suit. Lance's hair is longer than his own, and he's definitely a better-looking man overall.

"Well?" Doris asks.

He's not quite sure what she wants him to say. "He doesn't look that much like me."

"You can search for your wife and children: Rose, Thomas, June—"

"No! I can't!" He forcibly pushes his chair away from the monitor, nearly tipping over in the process. He then stands and strides quickly toward the breakfast room.

Doris joins him a moment later and says nothing as she sits down.

"So . . . what's your plan?" Lance asks while chewing his bacon a few minutes later. He wants to trust her but can't help wondering why she didn't tell him the truth before yesterday. She had every opportunity. He waits to ask her more questions. Enough has been said for now, and he can see she's uncomfortable.

Doris finally replies, "The plan is to head to Pullman, just like we discussed. Once there, we will get settled in and have my friend Debbie help us contact your family. She has high-level political contacts in the state, and she'll do anything for me. We will get you to your family after we contact them directly. I will figure out the details when we get there. Give me a week . . . ten days, maximum. I promise, Elliot."

He's still not entirely convinced, but he nods anyway. He doesn't want an argument. For some reason, he's craving alcohol. He wonders if President Dumont likes to drink.

Doris doesn't eat more than a few bites of her breakfast. Suddenly, she pushes aside her plate and leans in. "Elliot, I want you to understand the amount of danger we are in. Once news gets out that President Dumont is missing, you're going to be on the 'most wanted' list."

He doesn't want to talk about this anymore, and she's beginning to really stress him out, so he moves to the seat next to her and hugs her. She turns to look at him as though asking for forgiveness, but now is not the time for that. And he's not even sure if he can *ever* forgive her.

After breakfast, they head straight to their car and load their luggage. Doris slides into the driver's seat. "OK, we're ready. I've mentally worked through the route in my head. We'll take the I-5 North for most of the way. It's a nineteen-hour drive to Pullman plus another seven or eight hours for breaks and naps. Easy." She shoots him a smile that he doesn't return.

Lance settles into the passenger seat, and Doris pulls out of the hotel's underground parking garage. He decides to lighten things up to ease the tension during the drive. "I don't know what's going to happen, Ribbons," he says. "But I do know that you have moved mountains to keep me alive. That much is obvious to me. I will never forget that, and I will always be grateful to you. While we try to figure out how to contact my family, maybe I can take care of *you*, like you've taken care of me. It's my turn. I need to do that for you . . . and for myself. And I agree with your plan: let's get me back safely to my family. I have some time to get myself ready for that. But right now, all I want is for my memory to return."

As Doris glances at him, the love he's felt for her surges back for a moment. Whether it lasts beyond today's sunset is another matter.

She lets out a small laugh. "No matter what happens, we are making history. A history that only an opera could retell."

For the most part, they remain silent throughout the drive—at least until they reach Fresno, where they stop for gas. Doris goes inside to pay with what little cash she has left, leaving Lance to fill the tank and wash the windshield.

"Do you want to know about the state of Washington?" Doris asks after they get back on the road.

Lance nods. He's still thinking about who he is and what that's going to mean for him. He's also still angry with Doris, but knows she is his only way back to his former life.

"Well, Washington is like an enormous green pasture with buildings scattered about," she says. "It rains almost all year round and always smells good. The air is clean, and the city of Seattle is particularly beautiful. I wish we had time to visit it, but we need to drive straight to Pullman, which is a great little college town."

Out of the corner of his eye, Lance sees Doris glance at him, perhaps for a reaction, but he's still somewhere else. He's staring out the window, his eyes feeling glassy and unfocused.

Doris turns on the radio, which swallows up the silence.

Now that he knows the truth, there are certain things he must pull back from for the sake of the family he doesn't remember.

CHAPTER 57

DOUBLE AGENT

▷ Rose, New York Presbyterian Hospital, Day 30

James is running late. He said he'd be here an hour ago, but Rose is still waiting. She wonders if he's been able to accomplish what he promised he would. Time is running out, and she needs help. But is James the man for the job? She guesses she'll soon find out.

There's a knock at the door, and Rose hears James's voice. She rises to open the door, then lets him in.

"Good morning, James. Please have a seat." Rose takes the couch. "Well, you have the floor. What have you got for me?"

"Good morning, ma'am. I have good news," James replies. "I have a new job."

"Congratulations. Well done."

"In short, Schultz wants me to be a double agent. He wants me to keep my job working for President Dumont while also working for the CIA."

"*Again?* That's rich," she says, irritated.

"Mrs. Dumont," James says empathetically, "I haven't stopped blaming myself for what happened to your husband. I love that man. I may have been playing double agent during the campaign, but I never wavered in my loyalty to your family. I would have died for him." Tears start to well up in his eyes.

Rose hands him a tissue and waits for him to compose himself. She's not entirely sure if this is an act. "Thank you for the kind words, James."

"I'm sorry," he says, standing up and wiping away a tear. "I don't know what just happened. I know you want to hear about my meeting with Schultz. As I said, he wants me to keep my position on the Dumont team while spying on the Secret Service and . . . you."

"Good heavens, I didn't see that coming."

"He thinks you have all the inside information. Basically, he wants to blame Director Cummings for everything that happened on February 4. And although he didn't come right out and say it, it seems he'd be happy if I were to discover that Director Cummings was the mole who helped the Brigade."

At this, Rose's chest involuntarily tightens. "Director Cummings. Well, that would be a logical deduction." She's had this thought multiple times before, but now it's not just her own belief. The head of the CIA also thinks Cummings may be responsible.

"He's heard that Cummings spends a lot of time here, at the hospital. Schultz also knows that you are close to Cummings, and of course, Jennifer Alvarez. Schultz wants to know what everyone's talking about."

"Of course he does. That's so him. That old man has been running the CIA for over ten years, and now he wants to run this country. He's ballsy; I'll give him that. Lance never liked him, never trusted him."

"Well, I don't blame President Dumont. Schultz did plant me in his campaign."

"True, but I got a sense it was about more than that. I don't know exactly what though; we never really talked about it."

"So, as I said, Schultz wants me to station myself here, at the hospital, so I can watch Cummings and his people—and, of course, you and your family."

Rose feels triumphant. "OK, James, station yourself here. I will request it immediately."

"Thank you, ma'am."

"But keep in mind, you haven't yet fully regained my trust. Did he give you full access to the CIA Records Research Tool?"

"He did. I received my laptop and password end of day yesterday," James replies proudly.

"Good. If you prove yourself with the next two tasks I have for you, I will let you in on a big secret."

"I am at your service."

"All right, so, first, I need you to locate some people. Their names are Doris and Fatima Machado."

CHAPTER 58

SHE'S PRETTY

▷ **Edwina – San Antonio, Texas, Day 30**

E dwina leans back in the pink plush rollback chair that Honey placed in her room when she was a child, relaxing into its familiar coziness. Her bedroom at her grandmother's never ceases to comfort her, and she needs that comfort now more than ever. She looks to the open door, breathing in the sweet smell of cinnamon and sugar as she listens to the sounds of Honey bustling about in the kitchen. She could use some homemade food right about now, along with her grandmother's wisdom. But that's impossible. Edwina can't risk endangering her with what she knows.

Edwina and Thomas left Santa Fe late yesterday, and didn't arrive at Honey's house until 5:00 this morning. They were exhausted and went straight to bed. Now they need to call their mom.

"Hello?" answers June. There's worry in her tone. "Who is this?"

"It's us, June. How are you? How's Mom?" Edwina asks.

"Mom's been unusually busy. I think she's up to something. She's been waiting for your call. She said she has new information but wanted to wait until you guys called so she can tell us together."

There's a sudden shuffle of noise, and their mom's voice comes over the line. "Thank God you guys are OK! I've been so anxious to hear from you. How did things go in Santa Fe? How's Honey? Were you able to get anything out of Fatima?"

Thomas speaks first: "Honey's doing great. And our hunch was right, Mom. Doris did take Dad from the hospital. She is with him but wasn't at Fatima's. Doris and Dad stayed at her house for around two weeks, so we just missed them. Fatima said she doesn't know where they went. Doris wouldn't tell her, saying that she wanted to keep her sister safe in case the wrong people came looking for Dad—like the government or the Brigade."

Edwina watches her mom's face fall at the news that her husband is with the blonde nurse. She knows this must be painful, but her mom's expression quickly changes into a forced smile.

"Apparently, you and Doris have something in common," quips Thomas.

Edwina realizes that his words might be misinterpreted, so she quickly adds, "What Thomas means is that Doris also believes the Brigade may be working with someone in the government, and that's the reason she didn't deliver Dad to the authorities right away. She didn't know who to trust, and now she will only deliver him to us, his family."

Edwina and Thomas hear George speak up from the background: "I guess we all have some worries about government conspiracies since the Kennedy assassination. If it happened once before, it will happen again. History repeats itself."

Edwina cuts back in so as to keep the conversation on track. "Mom, you'll be happy to learn that Dad was doing well when they left Fatima's house, which was just a few days ago. His health had improved, and he was speaking well." She stalls for a moment. "But he still didn't have his memory back."

"Mom," Thomas says delicately, "I hate to say this, but I think he's safe with Doris. I know it sounds crazy, but Fatima seems like a good person. She's worried that the two of them are on the run, with no one to trust. She was also happy that we were the first to come to her door, looking for Dad. It turns out, Doris and he left Fatima's house after receiving an anonymous letter. She showed it to us. There was just one word written on the piece of paper: *RUN.* And so that's what they did. They weren't totally sure who had sent it, but they assumed it was one of Doris's colleagues at the hospital. You know, the two nurses we told you about."

"And?" Rose asks impatiently. "You said you think you have a lead on where your father might be."

"This is just our best guess: Pullman, Washington. Washington State University is located there, which is where Doris went to college," Edwina says. "It's the only lead we have."

"But why would she take your father there?" Rose asks.

"Fatima said Doris was close to her former teacher, a woman named Debbie, who may still work there. It's all we have to go on right now. We don't even have a last name for Debbie." She pauses. "What do you think, Mom?"

"Good work, you two," Rose replies. "I know all this can't be easy, so please know that I'm proud of you. I think you two are right: Doris will likely seek refuge with someone she knows and trusts, and if this Debbie is the best candidate, then get to Pullman as fast as you can. Oh, and you'll have company. George wants to join the two of you. I will arrange for his travel to Texas tomorrow and call Cummings so he can set up a Secret Service escort to Honey's. He's going there under the same guise as the two of you. Make sure to give the agent the impression you've been busy at Honey's house and haven't left the property. We've done a good job so far at keeping them off our backs, and I don't want to lose their trust."

"Hold on, Mom," Thomas says. "June said you have some information for us."

"Oh, I almost forgot," Rose replies. "I've been using James to gain information. I've also been testing him, and so far, he's proved himself loyal. We may be able to trust him. I told him to get his old job back at the CIA so we can gain access to their database and records tool to help with our search, and Schultz hired him back immediately. I also want to find out if the government knows they have the wrong person here at Presbyterian. I figure they won't tell us, but if James is on the inside, he can find out and help."

"That's great news!" Edwina says enthusiastically.

"Well, kind of," Rose says. "Schultz actually asked James to keep his current job working for your dad and to act as a double agent. He wants James to spy on Cummings and me."

"What the heck?!" Thomas exclaims.

"Schultz wants to place all blame for the Courthouse Massacre on the Secret Service. He thinks Cummings could be the mole, possibly connected to the Brigade."

"OK, well, that's scary since the Secret Service is still guarding Dad," June says.

"That's not Dad, June—*duh*," George says, never passing up an opportunity to be a smartass.

"Right," Rose says, "but I think Schultz might be right. It would explain a lot."

"But why does Schultz want James to spy on *you?*" Edwina asks, concerned about her mom.

"James says it's because I have access to Jennifer and I may be a good source of information for Schultz, which is also suspicious. I don't know who I trust least: Schultz, Cummings, or Ackman. Anyway, I have James looking deeper into Doris and Fatima. I will pass along whatever he finds out. Oh, and keep a low profile in Washington, you hear? I love you guys so much. Please call me after you get settled and when you find out more about this Debbie person. I will also have James research her. I'm sure he can figure out who she is and if she still works there."

Thomas and Edwina agree to stay at Honey's house for a few days before they leave for Washington state so that James can have time to gather more information. They then say goodbye to their family and end the call.

Edwina leans back in her chair, feeling sorry for *both* her parents. Oddly enough, she even feels sorry for Doris, although she's not sure why. She turns to Thomas. "What do you think of Doris? Do you feel sorry for her?"

Thomas smiles wanly. His words come slowly and thoughtfully: "I'm not sure. I do know she has risked everything for Dad, and she's helped him recover. He can now walk and talk, so that's all good, right? She has put herself in great danger for Dad, and I'm grateful *she* has him, and he's not in the hands of a militia group, like the Brigade. But no, I don't think I feel sorry for her. Sometimes I think she's just crazy, and that worries me. I mean, who in their right mind kidnaps a patient from a hospital and drives across the country with them? That's some serious shit. And he just *happens* to be the president, the leader of the free world. But given the other two options of being taken hostage or being killed, I'll choose running with a crazy nurse every time."

Edwina mulls this over, chewing her bottom lip in silence. The question she wants to ask—the one that's been on all of their minds—hangs in the air between them.

"We've all seen pictures of Doris," she says quietly, trying not to let her voice turn bitter. "She's quite pretty. So what do you think could really be going on?"

The room falls silent. Edwina isn't sure if her brother is breathing heavier or if it's her. After a minute, Thomas raises his head, and they look at each other.

"Yes, she's pretty, but Mom is also pretty, and she, not Doris, is the one married to Dad." His voice is firm. "For Mom's sake, let's try not to think anything foolish. Sure, Doris could be infatuated with Dad. I'm sure he's vulnerable right now. If something *is* happening, I don't want to know, and I'm sure Mom doesn't want to know either. So let's leave it at that. We just need Dad back safely, so let's focus on making that happen."

Edwina nods and doesn't say anything more. She knows Thomas is trying to comfort her as much as himself. She can't help but think of what might be going on thousands of miles away.

CHAPTER 59

NOWHERE TO HIDE

▷ **Doris – Pullman, Washington, Day 31**

The twenty-four-hour trip to Pullman, Washington, has gone by quickly. Doris is now in familiar territory, surrounded by fir trees. She rolls down the car's windows to take in the crisp air. The lush landscape and towering trees are a far cry from the skyscrapers of New York City and the rocky terrain of Santa Fe. Pullman looks like it hasn't changed much since she was last here over ten years ago, and she doesn't need a map to remember how to get to her old house. She turns onto the street and recognizes most of the small craftsman houses lining each side. It's like stepping back in time. *If only,* she thinks. Unexpectedly, she feels like she can breathe for the first time since February 4. Soon, she spots the tiny faded-yellow bungalow. It's just 675 square feet, with one bedroom and one bathroom, but it has a generously sized porch in front. That's where the memorable moments took place.

As they pull up to the house, Doris notices Debbie sitting on the porch, wearing jeans and a bright-red shirt. Doris's heart lifts at the sight of her, with her familiar dark-brown curls landing atop her shoulders and warm, genuine smile on her lips.

After stepping out of the car, Doris introduces Debbie and "Elliot" and watches as they shake hands. Debbie, however, hardly glances at Lance; instead, the gaze of her sparkling hazel eyes remains on Doris.

"What's the matter, Debbie?" Doris knows she looks older, but hopes that all the stress of running away with the president hasn't added *that* many years to her face. "You're looking at me like you've never seen me before."

"I'm just taking it all in!" Debbie says brightly. "You are a sight. Lordy! Time has been kind to you."

"Stop it. I look haggard. You're the one who looks amazing! You really haven't changed at all. I can't wait to see how my old place looks! I had some of the best times of my life in this house."

"Well, go on in and get settled," Debbie says with a wink. "Boy, am I glad you're here! I desperately need help at work. Your timing is *perfect*. I even found a job for your handsome new man."

"We'll take anything you've got," Doris says gratefully. "I'm just so happy to be back here, and I'm especially thrilled to see you. You've already done so much by getting me my old house back. I can't believe it was available."

Debbie waves off her thanks. "The Lord works in mysterious ways, my darling. Listen, I know you guys had a long journey, I have dinner plans tonight and a lot to do before that happens, so I'm gonna head out. But I'll see you Monday morning at 9:00!"

"Not before I get a chance to say thank you." Lance steps up, then leans in for a brief hug. "I've heard a lot about you, and I'm grateful for your help."

Doris smiles and lets him unload the suitcases from their car. Taking Debbie's arm, she walks her to *her* car. She's glad her friend is busy all day and this evening, because during the drive to Pullman, they heard on the radio that the acting president will be holding a press conference at 4:00 p.m., and they need to unpack, get in a much needed nap and grab some food before then.

Once Lance has disappeared into the house, Debbie whispers, "What's wrong, Doris?"

"Nothing," Doris says a little too defensively. "We're just wiped out. We've been sitting in the car for twenty-four hours. I'm lucky if I slept four of those hours. I'm exhausted."

"No, I mean, what's wrong between you and Elliot? You guys OK? I'm sensing a strange energy I can't put my finger on. You know you can't get anything past me, girl."

"Everything's fine, Debbie. Trust me. We're just tired. On Monday, you'll see us refreshed and buzzing about."

"O-OK." Debbie smiles, but Doris can tell she's not convinced. "Rest up, and I'll see you then."

Doris waits until Debbie has driven away before she grabs the snacks she bought at the last gas station they passed from the back seat of the car. Entering her old home, she places the bag on the coffee table in front of the couch. She then surveys the mostly furnished space. There's too much brown for her taste, and the flowered curtains seem old and dusty, but she knows beggars can't be choosers. The interior of the house remains charming, with many small touches, such as the nook where an old telephone once sat. For a moment, she wonders why the previous tenants left their furniture behind. *Just be thankful, Doris,* she tells herself.

☯

They wake at 2:00pm and order some food. They eat in silence then take some time to unpack their suitcases and get settled in. Time goes quickly and Doris looks at her watch, surprised at the time.

"Are you ready?" she asks Lance as she sits down next to him on the couch.

He nods, and she takes hold of his hand while using the remote to turn on the TV. The press conference is about to start. She wonders if any of this looks familiar to Lance. Will he recognize Jennifer Alvarez? *Please God, don't let her say the president is missing,* her inner voice tries to convince the outer world.

Media access has been restricted at this and all previous press conferences since the Courthouse Massacre. Back in February, Homeland Security elevated the terrorism threat level to red, as Acting President Alvarez has taken a very conservative approach to security in America.

Jennifer Alvarez appears at the podium without any introduction. Her face looks drawn and weary. "For those of you who are watching, I want to thank you. As you know, we have been on a nonstop hunt for every single Brigade member. Additionally, we have shut down five other similar extremist groups that threaten our security and our democracy. Today, I want to share what I hope will be our largest victory in our fight against domestic terrorism." The acting president adjusts her earpiece and pauses for a long moment. Doris shivers as goose bumps spread across her back. "You are about to witness a live event taking place just outside of Washington, DC, in Reston, Virginia. I have collaborated closely with the FBI on this previously classified initiative, and I want the whole nation to see our commitment and efforts in our fight for this country. The FBI has secured the entire neighborhood and instructed residents to remain inside for their safety." She pauses briefly, listening to her earpiece, then resumes, "We are now switching to live coverage in Reston."

The feed from the press conference switches to live footage of a raid. Armored cars and FBI vehicles have filled the streets and surrounded a small house.

Doris turns up the volume, and the roar of numerous helicopters grows louder.

Alvarez speaks over the footage: "We are panning over to the house so we can get a closer look. I am being informed that the house has been fortified with lead-filled, soundproofed walls. The team on the ground has confirmed that they have located a stockpile of weapons. We can see two enormous satellite dishes on the roof."

Doris stands up on shaky legs and walks closer to the screen, stunned to her core.

The footage cuts back to the acting president, who says, "What you saw on your screen is the headquarters of the Brigade, the extremist militant group of domestic terrorists. The FBI plans to spend the next several days searching the property for any physical and digital evidence that may assist them in taking down the Brigade and capturing its members."

President Alvarez pauses to take a sip of water, then nods a few times, clearly being fed information on her earpiece. She then continues, "Not only have we seized the Brigade's headquarters, we've also taken four members into custody. This is the result of the hard work of the FBI and Homeland Security." She puts her hand up, as if calming a cheering crowd. "But we cannot—and *will not*—rest. This is not the end. We estimate that there are thirty or more members of the Brigade still at large, and we will locate and capture every single one of them!" She slams her hand down on the podium. "These extremists will be destroyed. Make no mistake: there is no room for terrorists in our nation, even those masquerading as patriotic American citizens. Such hypocrisy is unacceptable. These individuals are not patriots; they are enemies of the state. Today's operation serves as a clear message to those who seek to challenge the principles of our democracy. We will not rest until justice is served and those who seek to destroy our way of life are brought to account. Let this serve as a warning to any individual or organization considering such actions: there is nowhere to hide.

We will find you and hold you accountable for each of the lives lost on February 4."

Doris smiles, imagining thousands of Americans cheering aloud in the privacy of their homes. But the acting president isn't finished yet. She's still standing at the podium.

"I want to offer my personal apology for what transpired in our nation. Our intelligence agencies failed not only in protecting us against an attack on our own soil, but also in serving the American people. We have learned that the Brigade spent more than a year planning the horrific events of February 4. This most definitely should have been prevented. As your president, I take full responsibility, and I am committed to bringing those responsible to justice. I will be leading a congressional investigation to uncover any possible government involvement with the Brigade. We will leave no stone unturned in our pursuit of the truth. I ask for your support as we work to uncover the facts and ensure such a tragedy never occurs again. Thank you all, and may God Bless America." The camera follows Alvarez as she steps away from the podium, removing her earpiece and shaking hands with those officials who stood behind her throughout her speech.

Doris silently thanks the heavens that Alvarez didn't say anything about a missing president.

Lance, having been silent throughout the broadcast, finally speaks: "My God, this poor woman has been placed in my position and is taking full responsibility. I feel sorry for her. I can't remember much about her other than a vague familiarity that I can't explain. I still can't piece any of it together. Alvarez must be a good person, and I'm proud of her for making herself accountable to the people of this nation. When I'm better, and when my memory fully returns, I vow to repay her for her service to our country. I also pray that she finds the son of a bitch in the government who assisted the Brigade. I wish I could help somehow."

Doris is stunned by Lance's response. Clearly, his cognitive abilities have significantly improved. While he still can't remember much, his ability to understand and articulate his thoughts on the broadcast indicates that his mind is getting sharper, and for this, she's grateful. She needs President Dumont right now. She opens her mouth to respond, but Lance continues.

"What I can't understand is how little they know. The attack took place over a month ago. She's right: how did a year of planning by a known militia group go unnoticed by all of the intelligence agencies? Something's not right. I can feel it." He turns to look at Doris, as if for support. "And I think you're right as well, Ribbons: we can't trust anyone. The fact that the militia group was able to execute such a coordinated attack suggests that they had governmental accomplices, and Alvarez knows it. That's why she's conducting a congressional investigation. But I have a feeling that she knows more than she's telling us."

Doris relaxes back into the couch and lets out a big sigh. "OK, well, that was a lot to take in. But it's good news they've made significant progress in neutralizing the Brigade. I hope that means there's less to be worried about."

"I hope so too. I can't wait to start work on Monday!" He looks at her like a toddler pleading for more candy. "Can we please just continue leading these pretend lives? I need a little time until my memory returns. Maybe I can assist in developing the plan to contact my family."

"Absolutely! That's a great idea. But the last thing we want to do is put them in danger. We have to do it right. We have to know that everyone around you will be safe when that happens, OK?"

"Yes, yes. That makes sense. I'm so wiped out," Lance confesses.

"I realize that Monday isn't going to be easy for you," Doris says. "You're going to be wondering who's watching you and what they're thinking. We have a lot to hide, so we'll need to be very careful about what we say. But remember, I'm just a smile away from you. I'll make sure of that."

As they get ready for bed, Doris thinks about how they will find a way to contact Lance's family and get him back to them. After she turns him over, she will admit to the authorities that she was the only one behind the kidnapping of the president; there were no other participants. Her lips tighten. The game is not over yet, and she still has a few cards to play.

CHAPTER 60

MISINFORMATION

▷ **Rockefeller – Langley, Virginia, Day 32**

Rockefeller wakes up early. He's feeling pretty good about himself, as yesterday was a productive day. A few days ago, he came to the conclusion that the Brigade's headquarters in Reston may be compromised. Recent missteps by some clumsy Brigade members and complaints to the local police by their neighborhood task force sparked an idea in him. He had one of the lead women on his team make an anonymous phone call to the FBI to tip them off on the Brigade's headquarters. Then, last night, the core team deleted all the computers' hard drives—replacing their contents with a hoard of false information. They planted some true details of their planning of the February 4 attack in order to make the files appear authentic, but the rest was convenient misinformation. Rockefeller had a gut feeling they might be raided, and he didn't want any surprises. He hates surprises.

Today, he's planning to speed up the search for Dumont. It's 7:00 a.m., and he's on his second cup of dark roast coffee, which he takes black. He likes it so dark he can't see the bottom of the cup until the very last sip.

He picks up his phone and calls Gruff, who answers on the fourth ring.

"Hello?" Gruff asks sleepily.

"Why the hell are you still asleep?" Rockefeller demands.

"I'm sorry, sir. I was up until 2:00 this morning. We may have a problem," Gruff replies nervously.

"I'm listening." Rockefeller is tapping his leg like a nervous teenager, his anxiety amplified by all the caffeine in his system.

Gruff clears his throat. "My guy, Diego, followed Jack Guthrie all the way to Santa Fe, New Mexico."

"What the hell? Why did Guthrie go there?"

"He went to visit a woman by the name of Fatima Machado. The strange thing is, we haven't heard from him for three days. Diego watched Guthrie enter the house, then called us to find out who lives there. That's the last we heard from him."

"This is bad, Gruff. I told you we should've replaced Diego. He was too weak for the job. We might be compromised. What ID did you give him? Secret Service or FBI?"

"Secret Service, sir."

"Good. What did you find out about this woman, Fatima?"

"Nothing out of the ordinary. I can't see how they're connected."

"Fly someone out there ASAP. We're running out of time! In the meantime, find out what this woman has been doing—you know, the usual: credit card charges, phone calls, license plate scans. Everything. And get someone to locate Guthrie. His truck will pop up somewhere." He pauses for a moment to swallow his growing anger. "Got any *good* news, Gruff?"

"Yes, I've been putting together the information we have compiled on the males who were checked out of the five hospitals."

"And what did you find out?" Rockefeller hopes there's a lead somewhere in there.

"Well, there were two hundred and twelve males checked out of five hospitals. All the John Does were accounted for in the end. I had six members working tirelessly on this over the past few days."

"Get to the point, Gruff," Rockefeller barks.

"Right. We've performed in-person visual checks on one hundred and eighty-nine of these guys, and we are completing the last twenty today—hopefully, by early afternoon."

"And the missing three?"

"Good math, sir; you are correct. There are three names we haven't been able to identify in the databases we have access to, so we're hoping you might be able to lend assistance."

"Give me the names."

"Brandon Campbell, Sheldon Davis, and Elliot Greene."

"Got it. Now go find this woman—Fatima—and Guthrie!"

"Oh, before you go, sir. Great work on the Reston headquarters and the live coverage by the president herself! Brilliant work."

"All that misinformation will keep the agencies and media busy for the next few days. Gives us some time to find Dumont without them on our backs."

"Damn it!" Rockefeller says as he hangs up. He wonders how so many things can go wrong in such a short period of time. He looks at the piece of paper next to his coffee cup: his list of things to do today. The list is short, but the top entry, printed in boldface and underlined, simply states **_UPDATE DIRECTOR CUMMINGS_**.

CHAPTER 61

STAINED GLASS

▷ **Doris – Pullman, Washington, Day 32**

oris and Lance wake up to an unseasonably warm Sunday morning in Pullman. The warm air envelops them like a comforting blanket.

"I have a surprise for you today," Doris says energetically.

"I love a good surprise!" Lance replies.

"Well then, get dressed; I'm taking you to my favorite place."

As Lance dresses, Doris prepares their picnic lunch, which includes a chilled bottle of chardonnay. She puts the bag with the food, plates, cups, and wine into the car without Lance's noticing. Doris smiles. She wants to share this part of herself with Lance in a location that will cement their time together in her heart—as well as his, she hopes.

As the two head to the car, Lance walks past her to open her door.

"Thank you, kind sir," she jokes with a smile. Then a pang of disappointment hits her. The sexual tension between them, once so thick she could practically taste it, is nearly gone. She's sure it will never disappear entirely, not with all that has transpired between them, but they both know those days are gone forever. He's been somewhat distant since their argument in Los Angeles, and she hopes today will change that.

On the forty-minute drive to their destination, Doris can tell Lance is enjoying it thoroughly; his shoulders are slack with relaxation, and he is humming an upbeat tune. She's grateful that the comfortable rapport between them has been restored. No words have to be spoken to fill the silence, and she wishes he would say something to help mend the hole in her heart. The trees seem greener than normal; the sun, brighter; and the air, fresher, but deep within her, that gaping hole of darkness threatens to consume her. She says nothing of this to Lance as they park, exit the car, and she grabs the bag from the back seat.

"Where to now?" Lance asks.

Doris points to a grassy clearing in the woods up ahead. As Lance follows her there, the gentle breeze flows through her long hair and causes the branches of the trees to sway like waving arms in the afternoon sun. As they approach the clearing, she turns to see Lance looking ahead, toward the edge of a small lake. The water is still and as clear blue as the sky. Doris explains that back in her college days, she would often see a large black swan gliding through the water, like a queen in her castle.

Doris spreads out the blanket and the bag's contents and sits down, her eyes misty with nostalgia and longing, taking in the beauty and earthy scent of the trees surrounding them. But when she looks up at Lance, she can see that he's unsettled.

"What's wrong?" she asks.

"Well, I didn't expect this," Lance confesses.

"Expect what?"

"A picnic. Am I reading this wrong?" The question is laden with tension.

Doris places her hand on the blanket to support herself. She suddenly realizes how Lance is interpreting this outing. A nervous laugh escapes her lips and quickly transforms into a burst of guttural laughter. Lance looks confused and taken aback.

After composing herself, she says, following a sigh, "Oh, Elliot. You have it all wrong. I planned this picnic to end our story on a good note, nothing more than that."

He looks unconvinced, his eyes not meeting hers.

"Look at me, damn it!" she commands, and he does so sheepishly. "You know I love you! But my only true love was Daniel. And because you remind me of him—that is probably why we are here and why I let myself love you." Doris takes a deep breath and pours some chardonnay to fuel her courage. She fiddles with the edge of the blanket as she says, "This is where Daniel and I first met. It's my favorite spot in Pullman, and in all of Washington. We used to come here every weekend and just sit for hours, talking about everything. I—" She stops and looks at Lance, her cheeks flushing. "I'm sorry, I didn't mean to laugh, but this place is about *me*. Not us. Not you. I wanted to share a bit of myself: my history, my Daniel."

She looks away from him and back at the lake. The gravity of her past with Daniel, with whom she shared this very spot dozens of times, weighs on her, making it hard to breathe. At the same time, she can feel that ghost climbing up her throat, trying to claw its way out so it can be seen, heard, and felt. She knows this is what she's been waiting for ever since Daniel's death, but she hasn't had the courage to initiate it. She hasn't had anyone to tell these things to or the ability to process and grieve her husband's death. Maybe this Lance fiasco is a result of that.

"I am sorry. I do want to hear about Daniel," Lance says gently as he reaches across the blanket and presses his hand on her hand. "I really do. Please don't hold anything back, Ribbons. Who knows how many days we have left together, and I want to know everything you are willing to share with me. I mean it."

Doris bites her lip. "This was my place to share with the people I loved the most—not just Daniel, but also my parents and

Fatima, when they visited. There's something magical here that makes everyone speak their truth. I can't tell you how many times I've been to this very spot, probably over a hundred. My fondest memory is being here with Daniel on our one-year wedding anniversary. Back then, he and I would always come here on special occasions." The corners of her lips begin to curve upward, but a hint of sadness holds her smile at bay.

"I'm honored to share this moment with you," Lance whispers. "It's the perfect place. And you're right; there's a unique quality to it that I can't quite identify. It's lovely."

Doris continues softly, "Daniel and I would wake up early in the morning and write in the condensation on our car's windshield. He would write a word, and then I would write another until we'd formed a complete sentence. It became a game. He'd try to come up with a word that worked with the previous one, but I always loved coming up with a word that made it nearly impossible to follow without ruining the sentence. It drove him crazy." A smile lights up her face, despite the melancholy tone of her words. "I'm sorry; I'm babbling. It's just that I miss Daniel, and I see him everywhere I look. Especially today, especially here."

"Don't stop. I want to hear it all. What was he like?"

"He was a dreamer, a poet. He would talk to the stars and carve tiny images on tree trunks. He had a passion for creating his own unique star patterns and held great reverence for all of nature's gifts. He cherished the changing seasons and took delight in their predictable patterns. He believed that timing was everything, and that only nature had the power to keep time. Knowing that helped me to understand why he hated clocks and was generally late to every appointment. She pauses. A sense of guilt rises in her at the thought of her betraying Daniel's memory. It's now more evident than ever that Daniel and Lance are alike, and this realization terrifies her.

"Well then, it sounds like Daniel and I have something else in common: I also hate clocks," Lance says, as if reading her thoughts. "I'm glad you've finally afforded me the opportunity to really *see* you, Ribbons, even as late as it is in this adventure of ours. I'll be gone soon. You'll see and hear me on television, but I won't be able to see or hear you. So tell me more. This is *our* moment. Tell me as if you are writing a love letter with no address. Tell me about your old school friends—anything, Ribbons. I love listening to you talk. Your eyes even change color when you get excited about a topic; they go from sky blue to this amazing shade of gray. Sometimes I count the freckles on your face when you talk." He lifts a finger and traces the air close to her face.

Doris laughs amid her fresh tears, wiping them away with her sleeve. She knows he's waiting for her to say more, but she only looks down at the checkered blanket beneath her.

"Please, Ribbons. Your stories are gifts to me." He offers her a napkin, and she takes it, smiling again.

"Did I ever tell you about my best friend's father's funeral?" she asks. "I may have told you during the drive to New Mexico, but I think you were still on painkillers then." They laugh.

"I probably was, because I don't remember. I would love to hear it. Everything has been about *me* since we met; actually, that's been the case for the last two years, I suppose. Give me something to take back to Washington, DC. Something to cling to when things are awful and I need a moment of escape."

Doris takes another deep breath and stretches her arms above her head. Upon lowering them, she adjusts her position and begins in a low voice. "My best friend's father died of heart failure, and the funeral was held here, in Pullman, on a beautiful but very hot day. Rays of sunlight streamed in through the church windows like the beams of a thousand radiant flashlights. I could see particles of dust dancing in the air. Everyone was dressed in black and moved silently through the space with graceful ease. It all felt surreal. So final. Like this life is it, and nothing will follow.

After the mass and communion, everyone sat in silence, waiting for the priest's words. I recall the awkward quietness in the church. Suddenly, I noticed that the priest was speaking in a whisper, reciting the rosary. Although no one could hear him, I assume everyone realized it, as no one said anything. We all just waited in silence. Even the saints on the stained glass windows appeared to be waiting. I almost burst out laughing because I was so uncomfortable, but I managed to hold it in. And then *it* happened. A baby let out a cry so loud it could've reached the heavens, and it lasted for what felt like hours. But it was the most beautiful cry I had ever heard in my life, and being a nurse, I've heard a lot of crying. It was as if life was being passed from one soul to another. Despite this man's death, I realized at that moment that life goes on." She wipes her face again and looks into Lance's eyes. "And now it feels like I'm in the same spot: mourning one death and breathing life into another."

Lance's face appears blurry through her tear-filled eyes, and she sees that he is crying as well.

"You're right, Ribbons. Both Elliot and Ribbons will soon be gone."

Doris's heart aches at his words; she wants to hear that he will never forget her, that some part of Elliot will never die, and therefore, Ribbons won't either. But she knows she has no right to ask that of him. She only hopes he will hold this moment in his memory forever, as she will.

Two children run past them, giggling. Doris points to the little girl. "Isn't she pretty? I wish I had a child. Perhaps I wouldn't feel so alone."

"I'm sorry I can't help with that, but I wish I could. Children definitely help fill a void in one's life. The rewards are plenty, as are the sacrifices." Lance pauses before asking, "Why didn't you and Daniel have children?"

"Daniel never wanted them. Maybe he had a feeling he wouldn't live long enough to see them grow up. I don't know. But I never pushed the subject, because he was my every pleasure. He was like a gold chain with a beautiful locket, always clinging to me. A brilliant presence. He adored me, and I loved it. I was happy with *us*. I guess part of me didn't want to share all the attention he gave me, and that's probably selfish. Daniel would play the sweetest games with me. Sometimes he'd tickle my feet just to hear me laugh. Oh, and he was fascinated by my waist. He'd sneak up behind me, grab me by my waist, and scare the bejesus out of me. I could never completely figure him out, but I loved his unique ways. He was like no other man I've ever met." *Until recently,* she thinks.

"Well, Daniel had great taste; you *do* have a beautiful waist. I'm sorry he passed away so early in life." Again, Lance reaches over and puts his hand on top of hers. "It seems we are all students of the heart, constantly learning but never feeling like we know enough."

Doris gives him a sad smile as she begins to unpack the food for their lunch. She feels a strange sense of peace wash over her. *I miss you, Daniel,* she says silently.

CHAPTER 62

LONG LIVE DUMONT!

▷ **Doris – Pullman, Washington, Day 33**

Lance and Doris wake up early to prepare for their first day at Washington State University. Lance sets out some fruit and cheese for them to eat. Doris tries to act like nothing is on her mind, but she's not fooling anyone.

"What's going on?" Lance asks. "You seem so anxious. Are you nervous about going back to the campus of your old school? It's going to be great! I'm excited, and I want you to be too!"

"It's not that. I'm excited about today too; really, I am. I can't wait to see Debbie." Doris pauses for a moment before she lets it all out. "OK, you wanna know what's really on my mind? I can't stop thinking about who's going to find us first. Some of those Brigade bastards are still out there, and we can't run from the government for long. It could be a cook or a janitor or even a professor who is an undercover agent or worse, a gunman. I've gotten you this far; I sure don't want something to happen to you now. Going to the university makes me feel so exposed. I dunno—maybe this isn't a good idea. I really just wanted to make you happy and have Debbie help us safely contact your family."

"This *is* a good plan, Ribbons," Lance says. "Let's see how our first day goes. And then tonight, we can discuss how Debbie can get ahold of my family. One thing at a time."

After they finish breakfast, Lance puts on a pair of khakis and a baby-blue button-down shirt, while Doris dons a long-sleeve beige dress she borrowed from her sister. It fits a little snugly, especially around her chest, but it's pretty nevertheless.

They drive to the large campus, park, and walk to the French Administration Building, where Debbie works. Doris stops in front of the red brick building and takes in the view around her, enjoying the memories that come with it. They find Debbie waiting for them in the lobby of the Capital Planning office.

"Welcome to your first day of work!" Debbie exclaims as she hugs both of them in turn. "And listen, I've had some time to think, Doris. There's been a change of plans—well, really a change of *roles* for both of you. I need you to help me with a big project. Wait for it . . . are you ready? It's the university's spring gala!"

Doris tries hard not to grimace. She didn't sign up to help fundraise or plan an event. She'd prefer she and Lance be stationed in the back somewhere, filing paperwork and staying out of sight.

"A g-gala. Wow. How exciting." Doris stammers a bit on the word *gala*. Why can't they just call it a fundraiser? She forces herself to say, "We'd be happy to help with that."

"Doris, you're an awful liar, always were." Debbie grabs her hand and gives it a squeeze. "Listen, I know that's not what you envisioned, but I need more time to find real jobs for the two of you. The gala is this Friday, just four days from today. I've had three people quit over the last two weeks, and I need your help. Please?"

Lance grabs Debbie's free hand. "I love events! I'm more than happy to do anything I can to help. We're just grateful for everything you've done for us."

"Great! Come to my office, and I will get you set up in a temporary space. As I mentioned on the phone, a few years ago

I changed positions. I'm now heading advancement for the undergraduate program. That includes fundraising. I got tired of managing people, especially across both campuses—Pullman and Spokane. It was all too much. Doris, you know my patience is crap. I just couldn't babysit them anymore, with their constant complaining about every little thing. I mean, it's not like we're curing cancer here!" She stops to think for a moment before adding, "Well, I suppose some of them are trying." She gives them a wink and lets out a hearty laugh.

Over coffee, they discuss the gala in detail and the roles Doris and Lance will play. They are tasked with managing the vendors over these final days. They are in charge of pretty much everything, from overseeing catering to ensuring the video presentation is delivered and set up per the technical specifications.

"You know," Debbie says in a low voice, as if anyone else in the lunchroom cares about their conversation, "we have some awesome attendees. Most are corporate bigwigs from Microsoft and Amazon, but we've got some notable political names coming as well. Some of these contacts I made years ago, when they were members of Congress, but since then, they've become big players in our government. In fact, I received a confirmation from the governor's office today, saying she'll be attending, along with one senator and a handful of congressmen. I'm so excited!"

"Wow," Doris says distractedly. She's wondering how all this can play into her plan. These contacts may assist them in getting in touch with Lance's family, but the event itself increases the chance of Lance's being identified due to his increased exposure.

Debbie continues, "My fundraising goal is a bit ambitious, but with the right attendees, I think I can achieve it. The event is going to be held at Ensminger Pavilion. They remodeled it back in 2003, converting it from an old livestock-judging barn into an awesome meeting hall. There are large open floor plans and windows that let in lots of light. It's going to be beautiful."

The rest of the morning is dedicated to introductions. Doris attempts to speed through them to prevent anyone from getting a good look at Lance. She can see his anxiety growing as the hours pass. With every visit to a new department, her stomach churns.

After lunch, they arrive at the security department, where Doris introduces herself and "Elliot."

"IDs, please," says the older security officer, pushing his glasses farther up on his nose so he can better see them. His glasses, round belly, and white beard make him look like Santa Claus.

Doris sets her Starbucks cup on the counter, then hands over their driver's licenses, with hers on top. "We are so excited to be starting work here! How long have *you* been here?" she asks, hoping the question will distract him from the task of reviewing Lance's fake license. It is good, but not good enough to withstand close inspection.

"New York, I see. You've come a long way," the man says, sounding less friendly than Santa Claus.

He looks at Lance's license and holds it up to the light. Doris panics.

"California, huh? Where—"

Doris reaches for her cup and manages to knock it over onto the counter, spilling coffee all over the man's documents on the desk below.

"Oh my gosh!" yells Doris. "Go get some paper towels from the bathroom, Elliot—*quick!*"

By now, the old man has stood up and is using his hands to wipe the coffee off his documents and onto the floor. Without looking at Lance, he says grumpily, "It's just around the corner on your left."

After several minutes of cleaning up the mess, the man has forgotten about the IDs, which Doris had swiftly taken and returned to her purse during the commotion. Doris tries to make some jokes to lighten the mood.

"Thank you for your forms. I think we're done here," says the Santa Claus man.

"Thank *you*. I'm so sorry about the coffee," Doris says in her sweetest voice as they turn to leave.

"It's fine," the man replies. He then says sadly, "You're from New York. Were you living there when the Courthouse Massacre happened?"

Reluctantly, Doris turns back around. "Yes, sir. I was in New York at the time."

"I've seen the footage more times than I should have. It's given me nightmares," the man confesses.

"Yeah, me too," Doris agrees.

"I was a volunteer for the Dumont campaign here, in Pullman. My daughter got me involved."

Lance smiles, and Doris notices a sparkle in his eyes.

Their interest inspires the man to grab his jacket from the chair behind him. He holds up the lapel proudly, "See here—I just got this!"

The pin on his lapel reads *LONG LIVE DUMONT!*

"Dumont wanted to reduce excessive overseas expenditures and increase support for local government—spending money here, locally, in communities like Pullman, improving our schools, police departments, and roads." He shakes his head. "He wanted to make real change. Local change. You know what I mean?"

"Yes, I *do* know what you mean," Lance responds quietly, looking the man square in the eyes. Doris shifts on her feet, their connection making her uncomfortable. She prays the man doesn't see Dumont's eyes staring back at him.

"Well, anyway, I have no doubt that *same* government Dumont was trying to downsize brought him down on that bloody day. I hope he recovers so he can do what he promised."

"Yes, we are all praying for his speedy recovery," Doris says as she grabs Lance's arm and leads him out of the small room and into the dimly lit gray hallway.

She's beginning to realize her decision to come to Washington and get them both jobs at the university was just plain stupid. There are risks everywhere. These thoughts, plus their interaction with Santa Claus, have consumed her by the end of the day. Doris wonders if anyone recognized Lance. Some interactions were awkward, with people staring at Lance for a little too long. She tries to convince herself that this must be because of the scars on his face, but then she remembers what Fatima said the night before they left. Fatima told her the best way to hide Lance might be to keep him in plain sight. And maybe she was right. No one is going to think that the president of the United States is standing right in front of them. The entire world still thinks he's lying in that hospital bed at Presbyterian.

On the drive back to their new home, Lance looks at her and says, "Maybe I should just turn myself in. You heard that man today. I made promises, and people voted for me. Now here I am, hiding from it all."

"Are you kidding me?" Shocked, Doris almost lets go of the wheel. "Turn yourself in, and just *hope* that no one in the government is part of the Brigade? If you're wrong, they could just take you, and you'd be gone forever. That is *not* going to happen, not under *my* watch. I've been thinking about our options, and I just need a couple more days. As I promised, I'm only going to deliver you to your family, no one else." She pats him on his knee. "Don't worry, Elliot. I think I have an idea."

CHAPTER 63

TAKE A DETOUR

▷ **Edwina – San Antonio, Texas, Day 33**

George arrived at Honey's house yesterday. Edwina is grateful she has had a couple of days with her grandmother, but today is the day to leave. After a long breakfast with Honey, the three siblings pack their bags into the Lexus she never uses and say their goodbyes to their grandmother while promising to keep in touch during their adventures. With no overnight stops, the drive from San Antonio to Pullman will take about thirty-one hours. The three of them will take turns driving to avoid having to stop at a hotel along the way. Thomas loves to drive, so he commits to driving the longer legs.

Edwina sprawls out in the back seat and starts preparing for their investigative work at Washington State University. Earlier, she printed out a map of the campus, which she plans to use as a guide for their search. They will have to navigate the entire campus, building by building, until they find the Debbie they are searching for.

George and Thomas share the same taste in music, so they take turns playing deejay. The music sounds like it's getting louder by the minute, and Edwina is too anxious to enjoy the moment. She wants to know if her mother has managed to find out anything. She can't think about anything else.

"Can you guys just turn that off?" Edwina yells, trying to compete with the music.

"Oh, come on; let's have a little happiness," George whines, matching her volume.

"I want to call Mom!" she yells back.

At that, Thomas turns off the music. "Go ahead and give her a call, but I don't know that she'll have any new information yet."

Edwina has already dialed the number and is waiting for their mother to pick up.

"Hello?" Rose answers.

"Hi, Mom; it's me," Edwina says, trying to keep her voice upbeat even though she feels sick to her stomach and wishes she'd had less coffee this morning. She puts the call on speakerphone so her brothers can hear the conversation. "I wanted to see if you found out anything."

"I spoke to James this morning. He doesn't have any information on Debbie, but he does have a list of every teacher Doris had during her time at WSU. However, there was no Debbie or Deborah."

Frustrated, Edwina kicks the back of George's seat.

"Edwina!" George whines again.

"But he did get some information that may help us," Rose continues. "Apparently, Fatima has two cars. One of them, an old Honda Civic, was scanned crossing the California state line seven days ago and was last scanned in Los Angeles just three days ago."

Edwina could kick herself. Why hadn't they asked Fatima for the license plate number of the car Doris is driving? Vehicles can be tracked down nowadays. She read somewhere that people have been trying to fight the new license plate scanners because they consider them to be an invasion of privacy. While Edwina agrees, right now, she's thankful they exist. *We need to be smarter about all these details,* she thinks.

"So where are you now?" Rose asks.

"About six hours from Albuquerque," Thomas hollers.

"Did you hear him, Mom?" Edwina asks.

"Yes, so since you are going to take a detour through Los Angeles on your way to Washington, why don't you guys spend tonight in Albuquerque? Then, in the morning, you can head to Los Angeles. I will handle getting you a hotel in both cities. Call me when you're a couple hours out. I gotta go. Drive safely. I love you guys. Rose hangs up the phone before Edwina can return the sentiment.

George immediately starts complaining about being hungry, so they decide to pull into the next restaurant they see. Forty-five minutes later, they're sitting in a booth at a 24-hour diner just off the freeway.

"There are more Debbies working at Washington State University than one would expect," Edwina says, running her fingers through her hair. "The operator wouldn't give me last names over the phone. She said it's against the university's policy. I mean, I get it, but it's also frustrating."

George has a mouth full of food, but that doesn't stop him from adding his two cents: "What did you think, Edwina? There are, like, thirty thousand students; there's got to be thousands of employees."

"Gee, thanks, Georgie. Your smartass remarks don't help me." Edwina glares at him, and George opens his mouth to show her his chewed food. A snort escapes her, lightening the mood as she turns to Thomas. "Anyway, the operator said they have dozens of Debbies working at the university. It could be worse, I suppose. I just thought this would be easier." After thinking about this for a few moments, she adds, "I guess it's not so bad. Maybe we can split up and knock it out in a day!" She reminds herself that there is power in hope.

George isn't finished with his two cents: "Well, it seems to me that Fatima has to know more. Are you sure you asked her every question you could think of and then some?"

"If you want to ask Fatima more questions, feel free to do so," Thomas says, irritated. "We can leave you here, and you can hitch a ride to Santa Fe. Edwina and I spent hours at her house, asking her questions, but if you feel like we left some stone unturned, please go!"

George rolls his eyes. "Really? Sure, leave me here," he says sarcastically, then stuffs another forkful of pancakes into his already full mouth as Thomas and Edwina look at each other in disbelief. They finish their meals in silence and make a quick stop for gas before getting back on the freeway to spend the night in Albuquerque.

CHAPTER 64

RUN BACK TO YOUR LIFE

▷ **Lance – Pullman, Washington, Day 34**

Lance gingerly opens the bedroom door with his elbow and peers inside. He's surprised to see Doris fully dressed for work and sitting at the small table by the window. He thought he'd surprise her with breakfast in bed—a tray containing bread, cheese, fruit, and orange juice—because she'd had such a rough night. From the couch in the living room, he could hear her mumbling incoherently in her sleep. She smiles at him as he walks in and places the tray on the table in front of her.

"Good morning! What did I do to deserve this?" Doris asks.

"I just thought breakfast in bed would be a nice treat, but I see you are already up," Lance replies as he drags over a velvet armchair from the other side of the room and joins her at the small wooden table.

He sits down and looks out the window to see the sunlight peeking between the mountains and over the treetops. He realizes why Doris loved living in this tiny house. It's so peaceful here, and its size makes it feel almost womblike.

"I slept poorly last night, and from the sounds of it, I could tell you didn't sleep well either. But I've got some good news, Ribbons."

She doesn't say anything, just gazes down at the lovely plate of food he prepared for her.

"Well, my dreams were so real, so vivid." He pauses a moment before blurting out, "They were about Rose."

Doris's head jerks up. Clearly, she's shocked. She doesn't look happy or sad, just completely taken aback. But just as quickly, her expression changes, and she smiles awkwardly.

"Wow! That's good! It's actually *great*, right? We've been waiting for this moment for weeks!"

Lance sees a flash of fear in her eyes, but then she smiles again and pats the back of his hand.

"Yes, this is good," she affirms.

He has been nervous about her reaction to his dream, but he knew he had to tell her about it regardless. He hoped his genuine excitement would make her happy for him.

"It was all so surreal," he says. "I was with Rose and the kids, and we were vacationing in Texas, where my mother-in-law lives. It was summer, and we were barbequing in her backyard . . . Honey!" Lance jumps to his feet, hands on top of his head, eyes wide with delight.

"Honey?" she asks, apparently wondering if he really meant to call her that.

"No, no! I'm sorry—not you! Honey is what my kids call their grandmother. And I-I remember the names of my children. Thomas and Edwina . . . G-George . . . hold on . . . I know, I know . . . and June!" Half laughing, half crying, Lance pulls Doris up by her arms and embraces her, then sends her twirling with a powerful swing of his arm.

"Wow!" Doris exclaims. "You really remember!"

Beads of sweat glisten on Lance's forehead. "Not everything, but I do remember moments in time, like flashes. In fact, I'm not even sure whether I was dreaming last night or my mind was just operating on some other level. I recall eating breakfast with the kids one morning, then being a boy with a butterfly on my shoulder, and then running on the beach with my daughter June. Random experiences just popped in and out of my head all night. My mind is like a racing car without a driver. Even as we are talking, I'm seeing new things. It's hard to control."

"It's OK. Just sit down and relax," Doris suggests, pointing to his chair. "Let's enjoy the breakfast you prepared, and we can talk while we eat."

"My mind is like a Christmas tree, overflowing with colorful and sparkling memories, so much joy in my life. I want to remember more, to see more. I want to hold my children and kiss my Rose." He glances at Doris and sees her expression change. Her smile fades, and tears begin to form in her eyes.

"I'm sorry I've kept you from all that . . . from your family," she says softly.

"No, *I* should apologize. If it weren't for me, you'd be wrapping up a night shift right now, probably chatting and laughing with Alice and Angela, not on the run, risking your life."

Doris sits up straight. She grabs his hand with one hand and lifts his chin with the other. "Look, you are not to apologize to me anymore, not now or any other time. I'm here by choice, and you were brought to me by a singular act of violence. I was meant to find you on the sidewalk beneath those steps; I have no doubt about that. It was divine intervention."

"It *was* an act of God that put me in your hands. If I wasn't here with you right now, I'd probably be dead."

"Maybe. But it doesn't change the fact that I fell in love with you."

"I-I fell in love with you too," Lance confesses as he stands up again and walks over to the window. "But I do need more time. I can't face my family yet. Not like this. My confidence and memory are both just developing, and I need to have a great deal of mental strength to face my wife and children—and most of all, my enemies. Oh, and then there's the entire country to address. But . . . I'm glad in a way, because now I have a reason to stay here with you until I get back to 100 percent. Even with my long-term memory beginning to return, I still need your strength, Ribbons."

Tears now fall freely from her eyes. "I don't know if I can handle it . . . handle *this*." She gestures to the two of them. "Maybe it would be better for me if we can get you back to your family as soon as possible. Then we can both return to our normal lives." Avoiding his gaze, she adds quietly, "And maybe you should call me by my real name, Doris."

The sting of this hits him, and he shakes his head. "Oh no, you aren't doing this to me. I'm not ready for *that* just yet, just like I wasn't ready for you to call me Lance. Let's keep it this way for a few days more, please? I need to ease into all of this; I can't have everything change overnight. I'm not strong enough yet, even with you by my side. Please?" He waits for her to nod, and when she does, he forces a soft chuckle. "Well, anyway, we have some time. It seems this country is running so damn well without me, I don't have to turn myself in for the foreseeable future!"

His joke fails to land, and he can see she's still upset.

Doris stands, apparently angered by his words. "Oh no! You're going back! I didn't risk my life, reputation, and emotions for nothing. The presidency is your destiny. You belong in the White House. Tens of millions of Americans who voted for you want you back, like that Santa-looking security officer. They put their trust and faith in you. You are going back to Washington, DC, back to your wife, family, and job. So don't *ever* say that again. Now eat your breakfast!" She gestures angrily toward the table, and Lance obliges.

He sits down, shoulders hunched. But instead of picking up his fork, he says, "I'm sorry I upset you. I can vaguely remember the feeling of the White House; it was a big, lonely place. It didn't feel like home, but I don't know if it's a place anyone can truly call *home.*" He picks up a small chunk of cheese and looks at it listlessly. He can't hold back his tears. It feels good that he wants to cry until his eyes run dry.

Doris sits down, her tone softer as she says, "It's going to be OK, Elliot. We will *both* be fine."

"I'm thinking that in a few days, we won't be sharing the same table for breakfast." Lance sets down his fork, takes her hand, and kisses it. "We won't be the same—well, I don't know what we *will* be." He pauses, and when he speaks again, he realizes he sounds hesitant, as though he doesn't quite believe what he's saying. "Look, why don't we just toss all of this aside and make a run for it? We could leave the country and start all over again, just the two of us." As the words leave his mouth, the guilt rushes in, accompanied by a faint memory of lying in bed next to Rose. Then just as quickly, the memory fades.

Doris gives him a look filled with compassion. "Elliot, that's sweet, but I know you don't mean it. Besides, we could never do that, and we both know it. It was nice to hear you say it though. Anyway, neither of us really wants that, do we? *All* of your memories will return to you soon. You don't need to run away from your life; you need to run back to it, and I will help you do that, even if it kills me."

A LOT OF MONEY

▷ **Rose – New York Presbyterian Hospital, Day 34**

R ose hears a knock at the door and looks at her watch. He's early.

"Good morning, James," she says upon opening the door. "Come in. I have a fresh pot of coffee." She steps aside. "Any updates?" she asks as he enters the suite.

James pours himself a cup of coffee and then sits down at the table. "Actually, before I give you the information you requested, I have some interesting news for you." He sips his coffee, then looks up at Rose, who is still standing. "The FBI finally decoded the information from the computers they collected from the Brigade's headquarters. There was some incriminating information."

"What? Against whom? Tell me!" Rose is so excited, she can't contain herself.

"You might want to sit down for this one."

"Just tell me!"

"Cummings."

Rose's heart sinks as she walks to the couch and drops into its comfort.

After taking a moment to regain her composure, she asks James about the information they found on Cummings and what will happen next. She tells him to make sure Schultz doesn't find out about this, as she doesn't want to give him the pleasure of being right. She plans to ask a favor of her friend Jennifer Alvarez.

Changing the subject, Rose asks, "So tell me what you've learned about the Machado sisters' whereabouts?"

"Well, I'm waiting on a couple of reports, but I expect to receive one of them, regarding Fatima's car, by the end of today. I'm hoping the Civic's plates will be detected in another scan. On the Debbie front, I'm afraid I don't have any news, but I'm still digging. I hope that the information I furnished regarding Doris and Fatima Machado was of assistance to you."

"Very much so," Rose lies, there was nothing really new in his report. Apparently, there's not much to dig up on these women. Until now, they've lived rather ordinary lives. After a few moments of silence, Rose says, "There's something you should know, James."

"Yes, ma'am?" James asks.

"I'm glad you're sitting down." She pauses for effect, then says calmly, "The president is missing."

"Excuse me, Mrs. Dumont?" James furrows his brow, clearly confused.

She realizes her claim sounds outlandish. "The man down the hall is not Lance. I don't know who he is, but he's not my husband. I've done a body check, and it's not him. *Trust me on this.* It seems that the Secret Service screwed up and brought in the wrong man. We also know that Lance was taken to Lenox Hill Hospital after the attack and then was checked out a few weeks ago under a false identity: Elliot Greene. We now know that he is in California with his nurse, Doris Machado."

After Rose has finished filling in the details for James and answering his questions, she sits back, hoping she has a trustworthy partner in him. She doesn't have a lot of other candidates for the job.

After a long silence, he asks, "What if we work together, Mrs. Dumont?"

Rose smiles and reaches across the table to put her hand atop James's hand. "First of all, from now on, please call me Rose when we're alone."

"Yes, ma'am—I mean, Rose."

"So . . . I also have to come clean with you about something else. Edwina, Thomas, and George are not at my mother's house in Texas. At the moment, they're in Los Angeles, since that is where Fatima's license plate was last scanned." Rose details the kids' trips to Fatima's house. She then shares with James what they learned about Doris's motivation for running with Lance, including the man in the hoodie and the threats he made to Alice and Angela. She goes on to explain that the kids were initially heading to Doris's alma mater in Washington, looking for her old teacher/friend Debbie, but are now heading to Los Angeles to look for any possible leads on Lance's whereabouts.

James leans back in his chair, looking stunned. "Well, all I can say is that I'm shocked all this has happened under my watch, and while I'm somewhat hurt and annoyed, I'm also quite impressed." He smiles. "At least now I can assist you, and hopefully, by the end of the day, we will know everything there is to know about this Debbie. What else can I do?"

"Same thing as before: get me information when I need it and help me figure out who we can trust and who was really behind the Courthouse Massacre. But first, let's build a small team of allies who will help us attack our enemies. I do think we can trust FBI Director Anita Johnson and definitely Jennifer."

"Oh my God! Have you told Ms. Alvarez that the president is missing?"

"No. I'm not ready—not until we've fully fleshed out our plan. For now, this stays between us. I need to do this *my* way, James."

"Understood, Rose."

⚉⚉

After James leaves, Rose decides to have a conversation with Cummings. She can't tell him what she knows, but she wants to tell him off before his arrest, which should be imminent. She hopes he's in his temporary office down the hall. Now she finally knows why he stationed himself here part time. She should've trusted her gut from the beginning and acted then, but it's too late now.

Three Secret Service agents greet her as she leaves her suite. "I'll be down the hall," she says without looking at them.

Rose arrives at Cummings's door and pulls her phone from her purse before entering so she can access the notes she has prepared for this conversation. She's planning to accuse him of being involved in this mess but will stop just shy of accusing him of being part of the Brigade. The congressional hearing will handle that. She wants to provoke him for the satisfaction of a verbal attack and to observe his reaction. She has nothing left to lose.

Just as she's about to knock, she hears a voice coming from inside the room. It's muffled, but she realizes she can hear better if she puts her ear against the door.

An agent gives her a sideways glance and starts to walk over, but she puts her hand up and he stops. Rose can make out Dr. Kellerman's voice. She presses harder against the door, and she can just barely make out his words: "Yes, sir. I understand. Guthrie is still in his induced coma." Then silence. She wonders if Cummings is in there, and she just can't hear him.

"Yes, the Dumont children have continued their twenty-four-hour coverage, but they still seem clueless," the doctor says. She can tell by his tone of voice that he's nervous. She checks the door handle and finds it unlocked. Opening the door, she is surprised to see Dr. Kellerman alone in the room, holding a phone to his ear. He looks even more surprised than she does.

"Who the hell is that on the phone?" she demands as he ends the call and puts the phone in his pocket.

Rose can hear the footsteps of the agents approaching, and before she knows it, they are at the door, staring at the two of them.

One says, "Excuse me, Doctor. What are you doing in the director's office?"

"I-I just had to make a phone call," says Dr. Kellerman weakly.

"Excuse us, please," Rose barks as she motions for the agents to leave. As soon as they do, she slams the door behind them. "I will ask you again, Doctor. Who were you talking to? And how the hell do you know that isn't my husband in the room next door?"

Rose hears a scuffle in the hallway. She turns to see James burst through the door, which he closes behind him. "Is everything OK, ma'am? I left my cell phone in your suite, and your special agents said you were in here."

"No, James, it's not. It seems that Dr. Kellerman has been lying to us. He knows that isn't Lance in the room next door, and he has been keeping that poor man in an induced coma," Rose says. The anger in her feels like it's burning a hole through her chest.

"What the hell?" James growls, pulling out his CIA-issued SIG Sauer P226. Rose had forgotten that he'd be walking around with a concealed weapon now that he's working for the CIA again.

"Sit down, and tell us everything. From the beginning," Rose commands.

"I'm sorry. I'm so sorry," Dr. Kellerman says softly, his voice trembling. "Please don't kill me."

"Just talk, and I won't," says James in an even voice as he walks closer to the doctor, keeping the gun pointed at him. Rose is impressed.

"That was a man by the name of Gruff on the phone. I don't even know his last name. Gruff is his code name. It all started a few days after I started looking after the president. I was approached by this man outside of my apartment building. I don't know how he knew where I live. He threatened me and my family. He gave me instructions to keep the president in an induced coma until I was to be given instructions to, well, end the coma and terminate his life. If I didn't do what he said or if I reported it to the authorities, he would kill my family. I believed him. I still do." The doctor is sweating through his well-tailored light-blue button-down.

Rose and James look at each other, silently acknowledging the fact that their worst fears are being confirmed.

After a few seconds, Rose asks, "Who is that man lying in the bed next door?"

"I'm not totally sure. Gruff calls him Guthrie. If Gruff knows I'm telling you all this, he *will* kill my family."

Rose ignores this and asks, "How long have you known he's not the president?" She's not quite sure she wants to hear the answer.

"I pulled the patient's fingerprints about three weeks ago. Gruff gave me an adapted pulse oximeter with which to do so— you know, the thing a nurse puts on your finger to test your oxygen level and heart rate." They nod, and he continues, "A couple of days later, Gruff told me the patient wasn't the president. He also put a lot of money in my bank account." He pauses. "A *lot* of money. And again, he threatened to kill my family if I didn't continue cooperating and keeping my mouth shut. He and his men watch my wife and kids while I'm at work. Sometimes he calls me and tells me what my kids are doing in the schoolyard. Please, please don't get my family killed. I'll do whatever you say. Just protect me, *please.*"

CHAPTER 66

JUST HEAR ME OUT

> ▷ **Doris – Pullman, Washington, Day 34**

After an eventful morning, Doris and Lance made their way to Washington State University and are now in a meeting with Debbie regarding the gala. First on the agenda are the table assignments. Doris listens listlessly as Debbie runs through them: the hospital board, chairman, and president will be at the head table, and the big donors and politicians will be seated nearby. Next, Debbie plows into the details on the guest speakers' presentations, allowing them to cement the timeline of the event.

Doris tries to stay focused, but all she can think about is the new man sitting next to her. President Lance Dumont has recovered his memory, but he didn't run. He didn't call the authorities and report her. She isn't sure what she'd expected, but it wasn't *this.* It feels something like how things were before his memory returned, before she told him everything. So much has changed, yet nothing has. Except that she feels like she doesn't know Lance Dumont.

"Doris, you with us?" Debbie prods.

Doris nods her head and smiles.

"Let's move on to the AV presentation," Debbie suggests. "I thought it would be nice if we show some slides of the progress made with the money raised at last year's gala. We can also give a quick overview of the university's financials for complete transparency, as this is the first year we are under budget, so it's definitely something we can brag about. Doris, you will need to work with the CFO on the budget information, and make it simple so people don't lose interest. It can't be more than a page with a few numbers. I will get the other information and have someone from our communications department make it look great. You should work with them as well.

"I couldn't get any entertainment that was a good fit for the event, so please make sure the AV company sends us a list of what music will be played. Maybe they can add some additional lighting, and project images on the walls, showing the undergraduate program at WSU. Elliot, why don't you meet with our historian right after this meeting and work with her on pulling images?

"OK, well, I think that covers it for today! We have only three days to go. Does this all seem doable? I realize it's a tight timeline."

When Doris doesn't respond, Lance answers for her: "I think these are great ideas. Nothing to add from my point of view. It's too bad about the entertainment, but it sounds like the night's agenda is pretty full as it is. If you can email us those contacts, we'll meet with them this afternoon." He stands and walks over to Debbie. "Thanks again for letting us be here, Debbie. We know how important this gala is to you, and we won't let you down. We have plenty of time. We can do this."

Of course he can, Doris thinks. *The president of the United States can certainly handle putting together some historical images.*

"Thank you both for coming at the right time. You're absolute lifesavers! So, over the next couple of days, you will need to spend time at Ensminger Pavilion, and you'll do the final walk-throughs with all the vendors on Thursday. That will take a full day, so you'll need to call the vendors today so that it's on their calendars."

◎◎

When he arrives home with Doris at the end of the day, Lance makes them sandwiches, and they get settled on the couch in front of the television.

Just as Doris takes a bite of her sandwich, Lance turns to her and says, "I remembered something new today when Debbie was talking about projecting pictures from the university's history on the walls. As part of my inauguration protocol, I worked with Homeland Security to help establish a secret code. It's a code that was created for a situation exactly like this—verifying the identity of the president when it's in question. I don't think they ever could have predicted this exact scenario, but it was intended for use in the event of a hostage situation."

"What?" Doris sits up, nerves tingling. "I'm not following. I hope you don't think that you're a hostage. You're free to go anytime, *Lance*."

"No, no, no! Of course I don't think I'm a hostage. But it gave me an idea. Just hear me out, please."

Doris can tell he's excited.

"We've been trying to figure out how we can return me back to my family safely, right?"

She nods, hoping he will get to the point quickly.

"Well, at the gala, we can use this code I created!"

"*What?* In front of two hundred people? That's not how I pictured it happening." Although she's not really sure how she *did* picture it happening. Maybe placing a call from Debbie's office directly to his wife or one of his kids. But definitely not in front of the entire country. There will be quite a few reporters at the gala. She gasps for air, realizing that she has forgotten to breathe.

"We can use the gala as an opportunity for me to decipher the code publicly. We can display it using the presentation equipment we are managing. Debbie said the governor, a senator, and some congressmen will be present. It's the perfect place to do it!" He meets her gaze. "This might be our best chance."

Doris puts down her sandwich and turns her face away. She just needs a moment to collect herself. It feels like everything is happening too quickly. The gala is in just three days. But she doesn't have a better idea right now and doesn't want to ruin Lance's moment, so she asks, "What else do you remember about this code?"

"I had to create the code and go through the program for hours. It took an entire day. It's a brand-new security measure, and I'm the first president who has been given the opportunity to create such a code. The best part about this idea is that there'll be reporters at the event. Even though it's local media, there will be live coverage. It's perfect! Debbie has already been working with the biggest local channel. So now all we need to figure out is how to get the elements I need to decipher the code."

"And how do we get your family here? Wait, you don't remember the code?" She is already seeing the hurdles in this plan.

"That's not how it works. It's a dynamic code that I decipher, not a memorized password. They feed me numbers, symbols, images, and words to help me with the code. I'm sure I can do it! We just need to figure out who we can trust to administer the code. Few people know about it—just a handful, really. I wish there was a way to reach Rose without going through any federal agency. She would be able to figure this out. Oh, that's another recurring memory: my life with Rose."

At the mention of his wife, Doris's mind shifts. She wonders if she's already lost him. She was hoping for just a few more days with Elliot, not Lance Dumont. She looks at the man sitting next to her and tries to imagine him without his beard and shaved head. She remembers thinking how handsome the president looked during the inauguration. If something really is going to happen during the gala, then she's going to have to get Elliot looking like Lance Dumont. This is starting to feel like an impossible task.

Lance breaks her train of thought. "My only wish is to get home safely, without any drama, and especially without risking the lives of my family members." He pauses for a moment, apparently deep in thought. "I do want to go back to my job and family, Ribbons. I don't want to rush this, but this code thing seems like our best chance for a safe exchange. I know this is faster than we've planned."

She can tell he's tip-toeing his way through this conversation. She doesn't know what to say, so she keeps quiet.

He stretches his long arms over his head and sways them back and forth until he finally collapses onto the couch. She watches him, her heart torn. He's clearly ready to go back. But she's not sure she can handle everything that needs to be done to make that happen while simultaneously dealing with another loss. Wondering if she has a choice, she realizes she has no more say in the matter than Lance did when they left the hospital. With that thought, she turns to him and forces a smile.

"I know you're right, Elliot. I . . . I can't pretend I'm thrilled by how suddenly all of this is happening, but it *is* our best shot at getting you back where you belong. Let's come up with a safe way to contact Rose, and we'll figure this out. I'm with you all the way. For now, can we sleep on this and decide first thing in the morning?" Another thought creeps into her head. This one, she can't hold in, so she asks, "What will Rose's first reaction be when she comes face-to-face with me?"

Lance lets out a nervous laugh. "She'll be jealous. I'm sure she won't be happy to find out that I've been alone with a pretty woman for so long. Rose is beautiful and soft spoken in public, but she's quite tough. The best scenario would be to have her in attendance at the gala, along with all four of my children. Think we can do that?"

Doris wonders if this plan is a pipe dream, but she doesn't want to burst his bubble by saying so. Instead, she says, "We'll see what we can do. I've seen Rose many times on television. She is very beautiful. Your whole family is beautiful."

"Thank you, Ribbons. But even if we do manage to pull this off, I'm pretty sure I'll have a full-blown panic attack in front of the entire world," Lance confesses. "Then what happens if I can't decipher the code? There will be all those people in the room and millions more watching from their homes." He cups his face with his hands as he takes deep breaths.

She leans toward him and pries his hands away from his face. "You'll be great on Friday night."

"Maybe, but it's not just me I'm worried about." Lance looks at her. "I'm worried about who's going to protect you after Friday. I promise I'll do everything in my power to make sure you aren't charged with any wrongdoing. I thought about this a lot last night. It'll be my first presidential pardon."

She gives him a small smile. Pardoning his kidnapper could carry a political cost that he may not be willing to bear upon his return to the White House. "I know you'll do everything you can for me, and I know *you* will be fine. You don't have to worry about me. I didn't have much going for me in New York anyway—just my job and a few friends. I'm sure my apartment is gone. I haven't even been paying rent on it. They probably sold all my possessions. I walked away from everything. I'm not really sure what I was thinking. Who knows—maybe I'll move to New Mexico. Fatima said I should stay with her when this is all over."

"Well, you know, I've got a brother who has been single for a long time. We look a lot alike, though he's not quite as good-looking as me. His name is Joe." His joke makes her laugh softly. "I'd be jealous, but it'd be great to know you are safe, happy, and still in my life."

Doris looks him up and down. "Who said you're good-looking?"

They laugh as he moves closer and puts his arm around her. "Call it a hunch." He pauses, then, in a more serious tone, says, "Never second-guess yourself, Ribbons. You did the right thing. Your intentions were good from the beginning—and your actions, brave. You've given me another chance in life, and your sacrifice for this country will be repaid. I will make it all right. I promise." He stands up and spreads his arms.

Doris also stands, and walks into his embrace, wrapping her arms around his waist and pressing her face against his chest. After a few moments, she raises her head, wipes the tears from her cheeks, and extracts herself from his arms.

"Elliot, you know I love you like a kid loves candy, but all of this laughing and crying has made me tired. Let's turn in for the evening."

He smiles down at her. "I've been thinking about how we can contact Rose."

"What's your plan?"

"My chief of staff, James Edwards, was my right-hand man. I'm sure Debbie can get ahold of him pretty easily with a call or two to one of her contacts. I think we can trust him."

"I don't know if that's a good idea. I made a promise to myself that I'd return you to your family, no one else."

"And I agree, Ribbons. James will make that happen. I think it's the safest option."

"No, not James. I would rather Debbie call Rose."

"Excuse me?"

"I just thought of something. Remember when I told you Fatima and I called your daughter June?"

"Yes, I remember."

"Well, the guy who took the phone from June said he was with the CIA. And then later, we heard her call him by his name: James."

CHAPTER 67

PITCHING PENNIES

▷ **Edwina – Albuquerque, New Mexico, Day 34**

The siblings arise Albuquerque at 6:00 a.m., eat breakfast, and get on the road to Los Angeles. With a few stops along the way, they make the drive in about fourteen hours, reaching Los Angeles at 8:00 in the evening. Their mother booked them a hotel so they can stick around until they learn more about their dad's location.

It's a cold Los Angeles evening. Edwina shivers, unprepared for the cool weather after their stay in Texas. Thomas and George straggle in after her, weighed down by their luggage. The three check into their room, which contains two double beds and a sofa bed. A coin toss results in George settling for the sofa bed.

After dropping off the suitcases, George leaves to grab some food to go from a Jack in the Box down the street. Twenty minutes later, he returns with three bags of food.

Edwina is looking out the window at the dark California sky and wonders how this nightmare will end.

"What's the matter, Edwina? Did I order too much food? I paid for it with my own money, if that's what you're worried about," George says as he unloads the bags.

Edwina extends her index finger and gently traces a line down the surface of the window. "I just miss Dad. With a single glance, he always knew just what I was feeling. He made us laugh when we were sad or hurt. Remember when he'd do all those counting games using our fingers and toes? I feel like the strings of his heart tied us all together. And now, I feel like we're broken without him. I'm sorry," she says, her voice faltering. "I know I'm speaking as if we'll never see him again, but I . . ." Her voice trails off as tears stream down her face.

Thomas rises, handing her a napkin and wrapping his arms around her. "We've got to believe we will see him again," he whispers. "It's not as though he's in Guantanamo Bay or being held underground by the Brigade. He's with a nurse who is probably trying to help him. And whatever our suspicions are about Doris Machado's true intentions, I don't think he's in any real danger." He pauses for a moment before adding, "Unless we don't find him first. Now let's get some sleep."

Thomas and George call it a night shortly after finishing their food, but Edwina is too tired and anxious to fall asleep. She double-checks the hotel door to make sure it's fully locked, then walks over to the window and peers out onto the street. A homeless man smokes as he walks slowly down the dark, empty sidewalk. There are no suspicious-looking pedestrians and no vans, but she feels anxious all the same. She sinks down into the large gray armchair by the window.

After some time, Edwina closes her eyes, hoping sleep will come. Instead, she thinks of her father, back when they used to pitch pennies on the sidewalk while their mother shopped inside her favorite boutique. It was a game her dad loved to play with each child until they were too old to be interested. Edwina remembers one lonely afternoon when her mother was sick, and her father discovered her alone in her bedroom. Her father sat down on the bed and said, "Hey, Edwina. You know, one day when I'm no longer on this earth, say something to me. Just talk to me as if

I were next to you in the room, like I am now. Can you promise me that? Because I *will* be next to you. You won't be able to see me, but I will be there." Edwina promised him she would.

Finally, early on this cold Los Angeles night she drifts off to sleep, contemplating what she would say to her father if he were here now.

CHAPTER 68

EYES AND EARS ON THE GROUND

▷ **Rockefeller – Langley, Virginia, Day 34**

R ockefeller can't stand the confinement of his office. He misses his days in the field—not just being in his twenties, but also experiencing firsthand the thrill of the chase. Now he does everything from his command center; he literally phones it in. Sure, it's nice to have all the power, but still. And besides, this chase is different. Locating the president has proved more difficult than he expected.

He leaves his office and begins pacing the dark hallways of the fifth floor. The thick walls provide him with a sense of comfort, at least. His special phone vibrates in his jacket pocket. He takes two deep breaths before he answers.

"I have information on those names," Rockefeller says before Gruff can say anything. He continues down the gray hall until he reaches the door to the stairwell, which he opens.

"I have a couple of updates for you too, sir," Gruff says. "One is rather urgent."

Rockefeller doesn't like Gruff's tone. All he's had recently is bad news. "OK, you first." He can practically hear Gruff sweating.

"Well, sir, Dr. Kellerman is missing. He didn't report to the hospital yesterday, and his house is empty. He and his family are gone."

"What the hell? Are you guys getting dumber by the day?" Rockefeller kicks the bottom step of the staircase leading to the sixth floor, relishing the sensation of pain. "I thought the doctor was on twenty-four-hour watch?"

"No, he wasn't. We didn't think it was necessary. I—"

"I don't want you to think anymore, Gruff. Just do what I say from now on. That's *it*. If you aren't sure, damn it, *ask me!* Kellerman must've told someone, or he just got cold feet. Either way, he's going to be trouble. I hope it isn't already too late. Use that woman to find him. What's her name?"

"Tracker," says Gruff with a bit more confidence.

"Tell her that this is an elimination assignment. I don't care what it looks like at this point. This will give the media another distraction. We need to find Dumont. We can't let Kellerman start talking, or *everyone* is going to be looking for the damn president!"

"Yes, sir. Tracker can handle it—no worries. She's a sure thing."

Rockefeller wants to believe Gruff, but things are slipping out of control. "She'd better do this right. Make sure she finds out if Kellerman's told anyone anything. Bring him to me if necessary, or torture him. Whatever takes."

"She will love to hear that," Gruff replies.

"OK, so I have information on the three names you gave me from the discharge list. It was very easy to get information on two of them. I will be sending over their home addresses after this call. But my search expert couldn't find anything on the third guy. She said nothing comes up in any of the databases we have access to."

"Which name is it?" asks Gruff.

"Elliot Greene. My search expert came up with a number of matching names in the Tri-State Area, but none matched both Greene's description and age. On top of that, there was no Elliot Greene with a daughter by the name of Allison."

"Strange. What do you want me to do?"

"Go to the hospital where he was checked out, and ask around until you have answers. Find out who his nurse was, who signed his release documents, and who personally checked him out. You know the drill: eyes and ears on the ground, Gruff. Do it today. At which hospital was Greene treated?"

"Lenox Hill, same one the cop was at the other day," Gruff says eagerly, like a schoolboy who knows he has the right answer.

"Damn it! This can't be a coincidence. Get on it!" Rockefeller kicks the step again, the pain relieving his tension. He then asks, "Hey, what are my other updates?"

"The last twenty males on our list were all visually checked out. Nothing came of them."

"OK, and what about our guy Diego in New Mexico. Hear from him yet? Is he still missing?"

"Still can't get ahold of him, sir. But I did send one of our best out there—Holmes. He went to that woman's house—Fatima Machado. She wasn't home. He went to her work, and she hasn't been there for a few days. He watched her house overnight, but she never returned. No car in the driveway or garage."

"Damn it, damn it, damn it!" *Can't anyone do anything right?* Rockefeller thinks. He needs answers, not more questions and dead ends. "Listen, Gruff, there's something here: First, Jack Guthrie going to New Mexico, then this Greene patient from Lenox Hill, then Diego disappearing, and now this Machado woman going missing."

"Sir, after Holmes gave me the update, I had our team do some research. Turns out, she has two cars. One car hasn't turned up on any ALPR scans since Diego was there. And the other car, well, the last place its license plate was scanned was Sacramento."

"*Califrickenfornia?*" Rockefeller can barely contain himself now.

"That's correct."

"So get Holmes to Sacramento!" Rockefeller bellows.

"Already did that. Holmes is in the air as we speak. He should be landing within the hour."

"Good. Have the team keep checking the ALPR scans. And where's Jack Guthrie?"

"He's been off the grid since Fatima Machado's house, sir. His truck seems to have just disappeared. I've got a guy on it."

"I need some good news *and soon.* The next time we talk, you'd better tell me someone's been located or eliminated." Rockefeller doesn't wait for a response. He ends the call and kicks the step one last time.

CHAPTER 69

MADAM PRESIDENT

▷ **Rose – New York Presbyterian Hospital, Day 35**

Rose is up early this morning. She's got a busy day ahead of her. Days ago, she decided to pull June off ICU duty, feeling no need to keep up the charade. There's no point in having them waste their time maintaining a twenty-four-hour watch over a stranger.

Rose is excited to get any information she can on Debbie. The kids are in Los Angeles, waiting to hear from her before they head up to Washington. Just as she finishes applying her Chanel Rouge Allure lipstick, there's a knock at the door of the suite.

As she makes her way through the main room, she wonders how much longer she has to be held hostage in this hospital, but right now, she has bigger fish to fry, as they say.

"Come in, James," she says upon opening the door.

"Good morning, Rose," he replies and takes a seat on the couch.

"Any news about Doris's old teacher from WSU?"

"I'm sorry it's taken so long, but it appears that there was no instructor with the first name of Debbie who taught nursing when Doris attended school there."

Rose frowns. "That's impossible. Edwina said—"

"I know, I know. But we pulled each instructor's name from her transcript, and there was no Debbie or Deborah."

"So then, what now?" Rose asks, deflated.

"Well, I have some good news: Fatima's car crossed the Washington state border four days ago. They may well have been heading to Pullman. The data obtained from the license plate scans is delayed by a few days, so by today's end, we should know if Doris is in Pullman."

"That's great news! I will tell the kids to head up there right away."

As Rose texts Edwina, Thomas, and George, James continues his briefing: "The other piece of good news is that three of Doris's instructors still work at the university." He hands her a piece of paper. "Here are their details. One of these teachers will know something about Doris or Debbie."

Rose reads the list aloud: "Zelda Morris, Alexandra Moore, and Lisa Irving. OK!"

"So give the kids this list, and send them to Pullman. For now, it's all we have to go on."

"At least it's something, James."

"Are you ready for our outing?" James asks enthusiastically.

"Are you kidding? I'm so excited, I could barely sleep! But I'm a bit sad to be going back to the White House without Lance."

☺☺

They land on Air Force One after a forty-five-minute flight to Washington, DC. Jennifer Alvarez was kind enough to send the 747, mostly because Rose wouldn't agree to the trip otherwise. She wanted to set the tone, not just for the meeting with Jennifer and Cummings, but also for the press. The nation needs to know that the First Family is still around, because things are going to change very soon.

When Rose and James arrive at the White House, Jennifer meets with them immediately. They will meet with Director Cummings afterward. Rose takes a seat next to Jennifer on one of the large beige sofas in the oval office. James sits down on the sofa opposite them.

"Good morning, Madam President," James says.

"I just can't seem to get used to that title," Jennifer confesses.

"You've earned it, Jennifer. Especially after that raid. Brilliant!" Rose says, placing her hand on her friend's leg. "Lance would've been so impressed."

"Thank you," Jennifer says. "Speaking of, how's he doing?"

"Pretty well. He's in the state of Washington with a blond nurse," Rose says soberly, testing the waters.

Rose can tell Jennifer isn't sure if she should laugh or not. After a moment, she smiles confusedly and asks, "What exactly does that mean, Rose?"

"I'm sorry; I know I shouldn't joke about something so serious. I need to tell you something." Rose takes a deep breath, hoping the oxygen will give her the strength she needs to tell this story again. "The president is missing."

Rose spends the next twenty-five minutes of the meeting catching Jennifer up on everything that has happened since the day Rose looked for the scar on Lance's back. She is relieved to see that her friend appears genuinely surprised by the news. At this point, Rose wouldn't be shocked if Jennifer already knew. She agrees to let Homeland Security assist her in her search for Doris and Debbie, but she asks Jennifer not to tell Director Noakes that the president is missing.

After the pair wrap up their conversation, they ask for Director Cummings to be brought in to join their meeting. Each of them has her own questions for him. Both the FBI and Homeland Security prepared the acting president for this moment. No matter how this meeting goes, the outcome will be the same, but this is Jennifer's favor to Rose: a face-to-face confrontation.

"Have a seat, Director," Jennifer says as Cummings enters the room.

After they've exchanged pleasantries, Cummings asks, "So, to what do I owe this pleasure?"

"As you are aware," Jennifer begins, "I've just launched a congressional hearing on the Courthouse Massacre."

"Yes, Madam President. I'm well aware. It seems that my agency is the focus of this hearing, but I have nothing to hide. We did our best with the information and time we had. Originally, I suggested to—"

Rose cuts him off. "Don't even say it. You could've stopped Lance from going to New York City that day! A warning wasn't sufficient. If you truly weren't prepared, you should've told him the event couldn't take place!"

"Cummings," James interjects, "we have evidence of your involvement in the February 4 Courthouse Massacre. It's over."

Rose watches Cummings closely, hoping for a reaction that may offer enlightenment regarding his culpability. She deeply hopes that this sixty-year-old man had nothing to do with the Courthouse Massacre, but the evidence appears to prove otherwise.

Cummings jumps to his feet. "How dare you accuse me of such a thing, Edwards! Did Schultz put you up to this?" The director turns to Jennifer. "Madam President, if there is any evidence that points to me, it has been falsified. I had absolutely nothing to do with the attack. Sure, mistakes were made, but I was not involved! Surely you don't believe the CIA!"

Jennifer puts up her hand to silence him. "It's not the CIA that has the evidence; it's the FBI, and I believe them," she says, slapping her hand on a stack of classified documents on the coffee table. The sharp sound serves as an exclamation point to their allegations.

Cummings shakes his head so aggressively, so desperately, that Rose fills a bit sorry for him. "No, no, *no!* This can't be happening! Whatever is in those files is wrong. Have you even looked into the head of the Uniformed Division, David Ackman? He'd be the first person to set me up! If it's not him, then bring in Donald Schultz. He's the one with the skeletons in his closet, and he knows where the bodies are buried."

"Director," Jennifer begins, her voice steady but with a hint of anger, "the raid on the Brigade's headquarters in Reston produced information that will be nearly impossible for you to disprove. You will never see the light of day!" Her face flushes as she stands up, yelling now: "What you did on February 4 is pure evil, and I hope you rot in hell!"

Rose has never seen her like this.

Cummings stands and walks to the door of the Oval Office. Before he exits, he turns around and says solemnly, "On the day of the attack, I observed Schultz standing amid that terrible mass of bodies on the ground. He was bent over a young man who appeared to be one of the attackers. I could see he was talking to the man. A minute later, I saw the man's body convulse and then suddenly stop. I know how a body reacts when it's hit by a bullet. Schultz shot that man right then and there. After he walked away, I approached the man to visually assess his wounds. I refrained from verbalizing my thoughts to Schultz; however, I believe my observation provides insight into his character. I have come to the conclusion that he lacks credibility and trustworthiness. Goodbye, Madam President."

As soon as Cummings opens the door, five FBI agents take him into custody.

CHAPTER 70

ROADBLOCKS

▷ **Edwina – Pullman, Washington, Day 36**

"**G**ood morning, sunshine!" George yells, yanking open the curtains.

Edwina opens her eyes and isn't quite sure where she is. Yesterday was long, as they drove for nearly nineteen hours straight, only stopping for gas, bathroom breaks, and convenience store snacks. They'd left Los Angeles at 5:00 in the morning after learning from their mother that Fatima's car was seen crossing the Washington state border several days earlier. It wasn't until well after midnight that they checked into their hotel room. This time, James had utilized his new covert resources at the CIA to book the room undetected, with neither the reservation nor the funds used for payment able to be traced by the agency.

This is the siblings' first morning in Pullman, and they are greeted by fog and heavy rain. During their drive yesterday, they reviewed their plans to ensure a productive start today.

Once awake and caffeinated, Edwina begins to take charge: "Remember, guys, there are many Debbies at the university. As agreed, we will make sure we meet each of them. We must be focused. The Debbie we learned about from Fatima was a professor in the undergraduate program for nursing over ten years ago. James said he couldn't find any Debbie who worked for the university back then, but he did give us a list of three of Doris's professors who still work at WSU. Let's start with these names and see if they remember Doris or Debbie." As she hands the handwritten lists to her brothers, she adds, "I've split up the list. One name for each of us."

George rolls his eyes, and Thomas elbows him hard.

"I think you're right; we should split up," Thomas says. "If we stick together, people will quickly figure out who we are. But if we split up, it's less obvious, *and* we can cover a lot more ground." Thomas turns around and looks at Edwina. "And we've got to do something about George."

"Guys, I'm standing right here. What did I do this time? I'm not staying here at the hotel, if that's what you're trying to say."

"Relax. You're going with us. We need all the help we can get—even *your* help. But you look too much like yourself: George Dumont. Edwina's going to help you fix that. I think you'd look great as a stoner type—you know, a little groggy and grungy, like you just got out of bed. Wait, you already look like that!"

Edwina laughs and says, "While I think that would be a great look for George, it's not going to get the job done. We've got to look presentable so faculty members will let their guard down and help us out. Let's give you a nerdy look, George. We can stop by a drugstore and grab some glasses on the way. Then, when we get to the university, you can buy a cap and sweatshirt with the university logo. That should be good enough for you to pass without anyone thinking twice about it. No one is expecting to see a Dumont on campus when his dad is lying in a hospital bed across the country."

They finish their breakfast while watching the news on television.

Suddenly, George turns up the volume. "Guys," he says, "look at this!

They all freeze when they see the following headline appear in a graphic near the bottom of the screen: *DUMONT'S DOCTOR FOUND DEAD.*

"Oh my God!" Edwina exclaims as she blesses herself. She can hear the reporter, who's talking rapidly, but none of his words are making sense; her head can't seem to process them. After a minute, she says, "Please say this murder didn't take place *at* the hospital." All she can think about is the safety of their mother and sister.

"No," replies Thomas, "it seems it happened somewhere in Ohio. His body was found behind a hotel off the highway. He and his family were hiding in a hotel room there after they left New York City."

☙❧

The siblings spend the rest of the morning talking to their mother about the murder and trying to refocus on the task at hand: finding Debbie. The three of them look at a map of the university and break it up into three sections: Edwina will take the administration office; Thomas, the human resources office; and George, the university education programs office. They also split up the three names they were given: Alexandra Moore, Lisa Irving, and Zelda Morris.

With their maps in hand, they get in Honey's car and make their way to the Pullman campus. It is now late morning, and nearly every unassigned space in the parking garage has been taken. They figure that the more people, the better; they will be less conspicuous. They agree to meet back at the car in two hours.

Edwina makes her way to the administration office inside the four-story French Administration Building located in the middle of the campus. The building also houses the student services department. When she arrives, she finds no one at the reception desk, so she locates a chair and makes herself comfortable. Thirty minutes later, a lanky guy around her age appears behind the front desk.

She stands and walks over to him. "Good morning," she begins. "I'm here to see Zelda Morris. She asked me to drop by today. Said she'd be in the office all day. Is she in?" She crosses her fingers behind her back, hoping the receptionist will at least steer her in the right direction since she isn't sure exactly where Ms. Morris's office is located.

The guy appears half asleep even though it's almost noon. He pushes his long black hair away from his face and behind his triple-pierced right ear. "Ms. Morris? She isn't here right now; not sure why she told you she'd be in the office all day," he says without looking up from his phone. "We have our yearly gala this Friday, so she's at the venue, here on campus. She'll be back just after lunch, so why don't you give me your name and number, and I can call you when she's back. Or you can just stop—"

In her excitement, Edwina cuts him off: "Thank you!" She certainly isn't going to give him her name and number. "I, uh, I'm actually starving and need to get some lunch, so I'll just pop by later. Thank you again." She then leaves to meet her brothers.

Edwina arrives early to the meeting place by their cars, so she waits for them. Finally, an hour later, the guys show up and share what they've learned so far.

"Were you guys able to find Lisa Irving or Alexandra Moore?" Edwina asks.

"No," answers George, "Alexandra is off today. She'll be back tomorrow."

"Same for me: Lisa Irving is at some conference, returning in two days," Thomas says with a tinge of discouragement. "How about you, Edwina? Any luck?"

"Maybe," she replies. "Zelda Morris is actually here on campus, but she won't be back from an off-site event until after lunch. So I've gotta head back there in a bit."

Disappointment hangs over them like a dark cloud ready to burst. Thomas and George agree to go get some food, then go to the nursing department to see if they can find out anything there. Edwina is too anxious to eat; she just wants to head back to the administration office.

☯☯

Edwina is standing in front of the lanky guy's desk, smiling broadly.

"Excuse me?" she asks in her sweetest voice, which is practically painful for her to employ.

The guy's still looking at his phone. When he finally looks up at her, Edwina realizes he's kind of cute, and her smile presents itself more naturally than before.

"Hi," he says softly and without a look of recognition. "How can I help you?"

"Hi. I was here before lunch. You said that Zelda Morris was off-site but was expected to return after lunch, so here I am! My name is . . ." She pauses, momentarily unable to recall her fake name. The cute boy has caught her off guard. "Sara," she manages.

"I'm Gabe," says the guy, pushing his hair back behind his unpierced left ear, "and it's *Debbie* Morris. She hasn't gone by Zelda in years. In fact, she now also uses her maiden name: Lewis. I did tell her someone came by looking for her, but she said she wasn't expecting anyone today. She's in her office now. Do you want me to call her?"

Edwina's heart feels like it may have stopped. She braces herself against the counter, hoping the guy doesn't notice. Debbie. Could this be *the* Debbie? After she recovers, she replies, "Yes, please do! Tell her Sara is here. I'm a friend of a friend. In fact, just tell her I'm a friend of Doris Machado's." She wasn't planning on using Doris's name just yet, but the excitement of learning that this woman is actually named Debbie has her off script.

After a couple of minutes, Debbie greets Edwina in the reception area. After leading Edwina to her office, she asks, "So how do you know Doris?"

A bit stunned, Edwina searches for the right reply. Finally, she answers, "Doris Machado? Oh, she's a good friend of my father's." Now Edwina is going *completely* off script. "His name is Elliot." Her stomach is doing somersaults. She wonders if this woman can see the sweat she can feel beading on her forehead. She certainly doesn't want to bring attention to it, so she avoids wiping it off and just keeps smiling.

Debbie opens her mouth, but she remains silent, and her once-friendly face becomes unexpressive, as if she is trying to conceal her reaction. In fact, she looks nervous now, just like Edwina feels.

"Excuse me, Sara, I didn't catch your last name."

Edwina wants to run. She yields to the demands of her forehead, and wipes away the sweat before it has a chance to run down her face. This is going horribly. "Harris, ma'am. Sara Harris."

"So your father's last name is Harris too?" Debbie asks, her tone now suspicious. Her knowing expression resembles that of a teacher who has just caught a student in a lie.

Edwina doesn't have time to think, and she realizes with horror she can't remember Elliot's last name. She knows it's not Harris, but it's too late now. She's been caught off guard. "Yes, of course, Elliot Harris." *Damn it*, she thinks.

Debbie stares at Edwina as if she is looking for further explanation. Finally, she says, "I'm sorry Sara, but I was mistaken. I don't know a Doris Machado. Again, I'm sorry." She stands up and shows Edwina out to the reception area without another word.

CHAPTER 71

A PLAN IN PLACE

The gala is this Friday night, just two days from today. Doris and Lance have been out of the office all morning, meeting with vendors for final walk-throughs to confirm floral arrangements and ensure the correct audiovisual equipment will be delivered in proper working condition. Debbie is a stickler for detail, and they want to please her, so they are checking everything in person, including deliveries to campus. Lance wants to spend more time with the audiovisual equipment vendor, so Doris leaves him at the venue and goes back to the house to make them some lunch.

She is surprised when she looks out of her kitchen window to see Debbie's bright-blue Toyota Camry pull into the driveway. Doris walks outside to greet her, worried something might be wrong, even though she feels on top of everything they've been working on for the gala. Debbie embraces her, but it's not her typical bear hug; it's light and brief, and Doris knows something is bothering her.

"Hey, girl! Why do I have the pleasure of a surprise visit?" She can't hide her suspicious tone.

Debbie looks over Doris's shoulder. "Is Elliot here? I called the venue, and they said you went home for lunch."

"He's still checking out the audiovisual equipment. Why? What's wrong?"

"Let's go inside."

A bit concerned, Doris leads her into the house, and they sit down at the kitchen table.

"I had a very strange visit from a young woman this afternoon," Debbie says uneasily. "She mentioned you and Elliot."

Doris can feel the blood drain from her face as she asks, "What? Who?"

"It was some girl in her early twenties. She said she knows you and that she is Elliot's daughter. Said her name was Sara Harris. When I heard the last name, I asked if that was her father's last name as well. She said yes. I thought it was strange that you show up in town, and a few days later, a girl who says she knows you comes into my office, asking about an Elliot Harris. She appeared very nervous, all sweaty and fidgety. It seemed too much of a coincidence, so I wanted to ask you about it. I have to be honest with you, Doris: my gut is telling me something is wrong here. What are you keeping from me? I know there's a story; there always is. And you *know* I always find out the truth. It's my talent." She smiles proudly.

"Oh no," Doris murmurs as worry clouds her face. "You are going to need a drink after I tell you this. And yes, you are right: there *is* a story. It's why I'm here, actually." Doris stands up to retrieve a bottle of chardonnay from the fridge and pours two full glasses before returning to the table.

"You know I love a good story, girl," Debbie says conspiratorially.

"I know you do. But this one is hard to believe."

"Just tell me!"

"OK . . ." Doris takes a deep breath. "Elliot's real name is Lance Dumont."

Confused, Debbie asks, "So he changed his name to Elliot Greene to avoid having the same name as the president? That's a little extreme. Is he running from something? And what does that have to do with the girl I met?"

"You don't understand. Elliot Greene *is* Lance Dumont, the president of the United States." Doris enunciates each word with deliberate slowness, as if addressing someone of advanced age with hearing difficulties.

Debbie's face grows white as she registers Doris's words. Suddenly, Lance enters through the front door, whistling a jaunty tune to himself.

"How did you get here?" Doris asks him accusatorially.

"Huh? The florist gave me a ride." He squeezes Doris on the shoulder, then looks at Debbie. "You will be pleased to hear that the audiovisual company is going to throw in another HD projector and some extra Bose speakers at no additional charge. Awesome, right?" When she doesn't respond, he furrows his brow. "What are you two talking about?"

Doris winces as a piercing screech fills the air—the sound of Debbie shoving her chair back and rising to her feet. Lance instinctively steps back, but before he can react, Debbie is already in front of him, gripping his face firmly with both hands and turning his head from side to side. She scrutinizes him intently, her eyes wide and unblinking. "It *is* you." She lets go and steps back, wrapping her arms around her waist as if to protect herself. "I can see it now. But . . . but *how?* I'm sorry, but this makes *no* sense."

Doris doesn't know where to begin, but to her surprise, Lance takes over.

"Debbie, why don't you sit down. This is a long story," he says gently.

Over the next thirty minutes, the two of them proceed to tell Debbie everything, beginning with the moment Doris found

Lance on the sidewalk beneath the courthouse steps. They cover their time at the hospital, hoodie guy's visits and threats, their stay at Fatima's house, and the warning note that led them to go to Los Angeles. They complete their tale by recounting their run-in with Officer Jack Guthrie and his story about the Secret Service agent who tried to kill him and whose body is probably still riding around with a mad cop whose dad was mistaken for the president and is lying in a hospital bed at New York Presbyterian Hospital. As she tells the story, Doris feels an overwhelming sense of gratitude. She watches Lance in amazement as he tells parts of the story from his perspective. He takes it upon himself to defend Doris's actions, eloquently explaining why she made the decision to abduct him rather than turn him in to the authorities. Doris suppresses her urge to cry, but she feels like she's been given a reprieve from the guilt that's shrouded her every moment since they left Lenox Hill. *Thank you, Lord*, she says to herself.

She turns to Debbie and can see the toll their truth has already taken on her dear friend. Doris moves to the chair next to her and scoots it close enough so that she can put her arm around her confidant. "I'm sorry, Debbie. I'm sorry we dragged you into this mess. I didn't know where else to turn. We were desperate, and I needed your strength, your help."

"When were you going to tell me this?" asks Debbie, her voice devoid of emotion.

Exhausted, Doris rubs her eyes. "I wanted to find the right time. And I wanted to have a plan in place."

"And do you have a plan now?" Debbie asks, finishing her glass of wine.

"Actually, we do, but we need *your* help." Doris smiles at her friend apologetically.

"I don't know how *I* can help," Debbie says, clearly uncomfortable. "Really, I'm a nobody, and my bigwig connections are all indirect, made through alumni."

Doris retrieves another bottle of wine from the fridge, grabs a glass for Lance, and fills up all three glasses. She gestures for Lance to take her seat next to Debbie, figuring that Debbie's apprehensions will subside if the request comes directly from the president himself. On cue, he sits down and places his hand on top of Debbie's.

"I think our plan can also benefit you and the university. It involves the gala," he says calmly.

Doris smiles to herself. President Dumont is speaking, and he's a pro at pitching ideas.

Lance continues, "As we mentioned, our goal is to safely return me to my family, without risking another assassination attempt. After what happened with Officer Guthrie at Fatima's house, we know the Secret Service is close to finding us, so we have to act quickly. The gala is just days away, and it presents the perfect opportunity."

"How so, Elliot?" Debbie's tone is different now, less fearful. "I'm sorry . . . Lance . . . or Mr. President . . ."

"Lance will do just fine. So, our idea is that I will decipher a secret presidential code that will reveal my identity to the country."

"Excuse me? A *code?* What kind of James Bond stuff is this?" Debbie asks with interest.

"Nothing quite that fancy, but close." He smiles, then continues, "They will project a series of numbers, images, symbols, and letters on the screens at the event. My job is to use that information to decipher the code, and in doing so, I will be able to prove I really am President Lance Dumont. The code will come from Homeland Security. We're still trying to figure that part out. I will decipher the code in front of the guests at the gala, and with it being live on TV, it'll help ensure my safety. It's a long story, but this code was created for situations just like this one, when the government needs to properly identify a sitting president who's been taken hostage. Er—which isn't necessarily accurate in this case," he adds with an apologetic glance at Doris.

Doris nods. "If we can get the First Family to the event, it will be even better. Here's what's in this for you, Debbie: we can promise the media that a major announcement will be made, and provide them with the specific time in advance so that they can prepare to interrupt national programming to deliver a 'breaking news' alert." She turns to Lance and adds, "Maybe your family members can remain in their vehicles, and enter just minutes before you come onstage to decipher the code! That way, they'll be safe, and we'll keep our cards close to our chest."

Doris feels proud of herself as Lance smiles at her. The plan is good. She glances at Debbie to see her reaction, only to find her staring, face frozen, at the table in front of her. She's not moving, and only the slight rise and fall of her chest indicates she's breathing. Doris can practically see the gears turning in Debbie's mind. She stands up, walks over to Debbie, squats down, and takes her scared friend's hand in her own, whispering her name, "Debbie? Debbie?" Debbie's head slowly turns toward her.

"I know this is all so much to take in, and I'm sorry for springing it on you like this. But we need you, Debbie. We really need you. Our *country* needs you."

"I don't know . . ." Debbie says timidly.

Doris squeezes her hand tightly. "I know you're scared. Trust me, I am too. I have been for a long time. But this is the only way we can think of—the safest way—to get Lance back to his family. Nothing can go wrong with the governor, the senator, and some congressmen there." She is aware that she is trying to persuade herself more than she is trying to convince Debbie, but the words sound reassuring as they leave her lips.

Debbie lowers her eyes and slowly nods her head. "This is crazy."

"Please, Debbie," Doris implores. *"Please."*

Time feels suspended as they await Debbie's reply. Lance stands motionlessly behind Doris. After several long moments of tension, Doris finally succeeds in making eye contact with her old friend, and a single unspoken word passes silently between them.

CHAPTER 72

MIRACLES

▷ **Rose – New York Presbyterian Hospital, Day 36**

Rose woke up later than usual this morning and is now enjoying a cup of coffee. She wishes she could just leave this damn hospital and return to her home in Columbus, Ohio. But she can't. She's not sure when that day will finally come. She pushes it out of her mind and picks up the *New York Times.* She is scanning the day's headlines when there's a knock at the door. She's sure it's James.

"Door's open, James!" she yells.

He enters and joins her at the table, where they briefly discuss the day's top news stories. Then her cell phone rings. She looks at her watch; it's nearly 9:00 a.m. She sees that it's her assistant, Valerie. Lately, Valerie's main job has consisted of keeping everyone away from Rose.

"Good morning, Valerie," Rose answers.

"Good morning, Mrs. Dumont," Valerie replies. "Ma'am, I know I'm supposed to keep all calls at bay, but this one's kind of unusual."

"Why is that?" Rose asks, absentmindedly flipping through the newspaper.

"The call is from an employee at Washington State University. She said if I tell you the password, you'll take her call. Her name is Debbie, and the password is—"

Rose tosses the newspaper aside and puts the call on speakerphone so that James can hear.

"Valerie, I don't need the password. Please put the call through," Rose says in the calmest voice she can muster.

"Hello?" she hears a woman's voice say.

"This is Rose Dumont," Rose says matter-of-factly, trying to keep her cool. *Don't scare this woman off,* she tells herself, not wanting another hang-up, like the one June experienced.

There is a moment of silence on the line until the voice finally says, "Hello, Mrs. Dumont. This is Debbie Lewis."

James taps Rose on the shoulder and hits the mute button. "Tell her to call your burner!"

"Hello, Debbie. This is not a secure line." Rose gives her the number of her burner phone and asks her to call it right away. She then hangs up and grabs her burner, which rings almost immediately.

Before Rose can finish her hello, Debbie says, "I'm a friend of Doris Machado, the nurse who looked after your husband at Lenox Hill Hospital after the attack."

"I know who you are," Rose says coolly, "and I know about Doris and Lance—that he's alive and not here at Presbyterian with me." She pauses before adding, "Is he OK?" *Breathe, Rose, breathe,* she says to herself, closing her eyes as she waits for the answer.

"Yes, he's fine. His memory has just returned. He wants me to let you know that he's OK and has a plan for his safe return."

"I want the same thing. Now, can we talk about making immediate arrangements to safely bring him home to his family?" Rose tries her best not to sound either threatening or desperate.

What she really wants to ask is why Lance himself didn't call her, but that's a conversation to be had with her husband, not this stranger.

"There is going to be a gala on the Washington State University campus this Friday, where the president would like to decipher the Dumont Code he created for Homeland Security."

"What code?" Rose asks, a little irritated that this woman knows something about her husband that she herself doesn't know. She looks at James. He nods.

"I don't know the details, but a code was created to help authorities confirm the identity of a missing president." There's a long, uncomfortable silence on the line.

"Go on," Rose orders sternly, reminding herself to breathe.

"Well, there will be around two hundred and fifty guests in attendance, including our governor, a senator, a few congressmen, and many top executives from large corporations. The president wants to be delivered safely to you and your children. He's not sure who to trust, and said that you would know how to make this happen."

Rose's mind is running at full speed. She can see that the same is true for James.

"Tell her we'll figure it out, and we'll bring the code," James whispers in Rose's ear.

"Debbie? I will figure it out. I *do* know who we can trust. And I will bring the code. What time is the event?"

"This Friday at 7:00 p.m., Ensminger Pavilion."

Rose looks at the time on her phone and realizes the event is less than seventy-two hours away. She can hear some rustling of papers over the line. "Are you there?" she asks Debbie.

"Yes, ma'am. I'm sorry. I'm just doing my part, as I found out that Elliot is the president only a few hours ago."

"You are doing the right thing, Debbie. We will figure this out together."

"Elli—er—Lance, said you would say that. He knew you would figure it out. He said he's seen you pull a lot of rabbits out of your hat over the course of your marriage. I think he even used the word *miracles*." Debbie laughs nervously.

Despite wanting to respond with a smart-ass comment about her marriage to Lance, who is currently running around with some blond nurse, Rose refrains from doing so and instead replies, "Well, I don't know if anyone could call them miracles. Lance has a habit of asking for the impossible, but I will figure this out for him . . . and for the country. Please tell Lance that James can be trusted and will manage the logistics from here on out. And tell him Homeland Security, the CIA, and the FBI can be trusted as well."

"I'll do that," Debbie replies. "The president would like the code to be projected on the screens at exactly 8:00 p.m. He wants you and the children to be there, of course, but he says you'll need to wait in the car until shortly before the code is projected."

Rose is torn between anger toward Lance and relief that he's alive and well. She asks Debbie to pass on a message to her husband: "Please tell him that I love him and I'm grateful he's alive." And with that, she ends the call.

CHAPTER 73

SOMETHING'S UP

▷ **Rockefeller – Langley, Virginia, Day 36**

Today marks the three-month anniversary of the day Rockefeller quit smoking.

"Good to see you, old friend," he says as he pulls out a crisp, clean cigarette from his pack of Marlboro Reds. He smells it and can already feel the respite it will provide. Life has been hell. He still can't find the president. He lights the cigarette and basks in the warmth of the flame on his face. "God, I've missed you." He inhales as if he were taking the last breath of his life.

Over the last twenty-four hours, he has learned that Doris Machado was Elliot Greene's nurse at Lenox Hill Hospital. Her sister is Fatima Machado, the woman who is now missing after having been visited by Jack Guthrie, who is also missing. The only good development is that it appears certain that Elliot Greene is Lance Dumont. There's no other explanation for the series of coincidences.

As soon as he finishes his cigarette, he lights another.

There's a knock at his office door.

"Sir?" his assistant asks as she opens the door.

"Yes, Susan?" he replies, smiling.

"You quit smoking, sir. And you can't be smoking in the building. People are going to freak out."

"So let them freak out. I don't care. If anyone complains, tell them to come see me. I dare them."

"Yes, sir," Susan says, quietly closing the door.

Just then, his special phone rings. He extracts it from the breast pocket of his blazer. "Talk to me, Gruff. I see Tracker took care of our doctor. Good job."

"Thank you; she did. She said it took her some time to get information out of him. Short story is that you were right: the doctor talked."

"Dammit! Who did he tell?"

"The First Lady and James Edwards."

"Ugh. Who else?" Rockefeller asks.

"Just those two."

Rockefeller lights his third cigarette by using the burning tip of his second. After a moment, he says, "Strange I haven't heard anything about this. I know the First Lady is still at the hospital. Doesn't make any sense."

"They must be keeping it quiet."

"I doubt it. She probably told Alvarez during her trip to the White House." He takes a deep drag and can almost feel the reaction of the neurons in his brain. Smoking has always helped him think better, sharper. "But what doesn't make sense is that Alvarez isn't doing anything. There's been no rumblings within the agencies. This kind of thing would find a way of getting out; it always does. It's impossible to keep something this big quiet. Something's up, Gruff." He pulls out another Marlboro and smells it. "Tell me where the hell Doris Machado and Lance Dumont are."

"Fatima's Honda Civic was last seen crossing the Washington state border five days ago."

"Five days ago?! Damn, those scanners are slow!"

"It takes two to three days for the government to get those reports, sir, and *we* get them even later."

"I know, I know. Where's your guy—Holmes? And any news on the cop or Fatima's other car?"

"Neither license plate has shown up anywhere. But Holmes is already back at the Sacramento airport. He's boarding a plane to Seattle in ten minutes."

"Good. I will call my contacts." Rockefeller smiles as he hangs up the phone. *You're not in the clear, Dumont,* he thinks as he inhales.

CHAPTER 74

RIBBONS HAS LEFT THE BUILDING

▷ **Doris – Pullman, Washington, Day 37**

t's the day before the gala. Doris wakes up feeling exhausted. Her dreams felt so real that she wonders if she was actually awake the entire night. Her mind was busy entertaining the various outcomes that may await her: being handcuffed and escorted to prison, having a confrontation with the First Family, experiencing a rush of adrenaline that sees her scaling the buildings of Washington State University in a bid to escape the authorities. Now her nerves are buzzing. Sitting on the edge of the bed, she promises herself that she will stick to the plan and play it safe. In just over thirty-six hours, this will be over.

By the time they finished with Debbie, yesterday afternoon had turned into night. There had been a lot of discussion about the risks associated with their plan. The most important risk to mitigate is security. They know they are up against a lot. Attempts on Lance's life have been made since February 4: the man with the hoodie at Lenox Hill, the bomb scare at Presbyterian, and the Secret Service agent at Fatima's house. They stayed up until midnight last night working out every detail for tomorrow night's event. It will be a night that America will never forget. Doris feels proud to be part of something bigger than herself.

When she enters the kitchen, she's not surprised to see Lance already there. She smiles at him, takes a seat, and says, "Good morning; hope you slept well! How are you feeling about tomorrow?"

She misses sharing a bed with Lance, but she was aware that had to end when she told him about his identity. Since that conversation, they have been respectful of each other's space and on their best behavior, even though her mind sometimes wanders back to memories of their nights in Los Angeles. She shakes this out of her mind and takes a seat at the table.

"I'm feeling OK. Not nervous," he replies as he pours them some coffee and sits down. "I'm just sad about the kids. It's hard to know they are here, in Pullman, and I can't see or hug them. I hate it. Tomorrow has to work perfectly, for everyone's sake."

"I understand. In about thirty-six hours, you'll be reunited with your family. We're almost to the finish line." Doris isn't sure what he wants to hear. All she can think about is what's going to happen, and it scares the hell out of her. His future is predictable, whereas hers might end up being behind bars.

She tries to keep the conversation light. "So tell me about your children, Lance."

"Lance?"

"Yes, I think it's time. Elliot and Ribbons need to go. Their jobs are pretty much done at this point. Don't you think?" She can't look at him. Part of her wants him to keep being her Elliot.

"You're right, Doris." He says this in a tone that's both mocking and sad. "Though I prefer Ribbons; it's a great name."

"Ribbons has left the building!" She forces a smile and raises her coffee cup, and he reciprocates.

"Cheers!" they say in unison.

"So, about your children, tell me anything." Doris genuinely wants to know more about them, especially since she might meet them tomorrow.

"Well, the best place to start is with my favorite, Edwina," he says proudly.

"Favorites aren't allowed," she teases.

He nods. "True, but everyone has a favorite; we just aren't supposed to talk about it. My other three kids know, but they don't seem to mind—thank God. Edwina is our moral compass. She's steady, smart, and quick on the draw—so to speak. She's strong, yet emotional and connected at all the right times. We click. She has street smarts and can read people accurately and quickly. I wish I had her talents. Odd thing is, she wants to be a nun."

"A *nun?*" Doris is sincerely surprised and impressed. "She sounds like quite a force."

"That, she is," Lance confirms though Doris can see that his mind is far from here. She's already losing him.

All of a sudden, the stove timer rings, and Lance stands and grabs their plates. "Well, hi-ho, hi-ho, it's off to work we go!"

☺☺

After dressing themselves, they get in the car and head to Ensminger Pavilion to do another run-through with the vendors, review additional security plans, and ensure the audiovisual equipment is functioning properly.

Lance leads the way into the building and through the lobby, in the direction of the double doors leading to a full view of the auditorium. Inside, the vendor crews are moving various objects into place. As they wait for their contacts to arrive, Doris notices Lance's body tensing. His shoulders straighten and push back, and he lifts his head, staring directly at the far corner of the room in front of him. Following his gaze, she notices a man clad in a janitor's gray uniform, pushing some plastic wrapping and other debris with a broom. As the janitor continues to sweep, Lance keeps staring at him.

Doris lightly touches his forearm. "What's the matter, Lance?"

"I know this is strange, but that janitor looks familiar." His gaze doesn't shift. "Maybe James put someone he trusts here to make sure everything is secure for tomorrow night's event, or maybe Homeland Security knows the plan now, and *they* have people here."

Before Doris can respond, Lance marches over to the janitor. She hurries after him, catching his initial words.

"Can I help you?" he asks the janitor.

"I don't think so, unless you wanna grab a broom," the janitor replies sarcastically.

"Maybe you should keep your eyes on your work, then," Lance says with a snark.

"Chill, man. I was just kidding." The janitor shakes his head and leaves in the direction of the lobby.

Lance turns to Doris, visibly shaken.

"Lance, did you really recognize him?"

"I don't know." He shakes his head, shoulders slumped. "Maybe I'm being paranoid. When I ran for office, I knew I would have to get used to the fact that many people around me aren't what they appear to be. I don't think I told you this, but not long after I was elected, I learned that James had been working for the CIA. He'd been a plant from the beginning. I forgave him, as I knew he had just been doing his job and that he really *was* a friend to my family members and me. We were close."

"I'm sure that when you're the president, it feels like you can't trust anyone, and many people are not what they seem. I get it.

I'm sorry; that must have shocked you when you found out about James."

"It's fine. You know, I actually want to thank *you*." He chuckles.

"Thank *me*? What for?"

"For giving me a bit of my old life back—a time when I didn't have to worry about who I can trust and who might be looking to do me harm. Simpler times—doing things like sitting on the porch, taking a long walk, eating at a restaurant, and having a picnic." Lance smiles widely.

"Well, you're welcome, Mr. President." She turns away so he doesn't notice she's blushing.

He straightens up and says, "Now let's get back to business. To ensure the event looks impeccable for the television cameras, I've ordered flowers that will extend in a continuous line from one end of the head table to the other, with a slight dip in the middle to help frame the speaker's podium."

Hearing this makes her anxious. She hopes the cameras won't notice her. While Lance heads over to inspect the podium, she staggers to a lone chair. Legs wobbling, she sits down and leans forward, lowering her head into her hands. She feels like crying, but no tears come to her eyes. Tomorrow night, she will leave Ribbons here at Ensminger Pavilion and go home as Doris Machado. This terrifying thought dries up the saliva in her throat and threatens to choke her.

Does this man really have the power to make her untouchable? Is it even possible to kidnap the president of the United States of America without any repercussions? She snorts softly. It's a pipe dream at best. Even worse, the media will be all over her as the president's crazy kidnapper who fell in love with him. She'll have to go into hiding if she doesn't wind up in prison first. But she *did* fall in love with him. And technically, she *did* kidnap him. Even if it was for all the right reasons, she doesn't know if America will understand. She pictures her image on a TV screen: a miserable figure lurking in the background of a perfect photo of Lance and Rose. The same image is emblazoned across every newspaper. She's sure that's what she'll be made out to be: a homewrecker, a criminal, a stalker, a psycho. *Maybe* she *is* all those things. Her body goes limp, her head growing heavier in her hands, but for some reason, she has the urge to laugh at the insanity of it all—so she does.

"What's so funny?" Lance's voice causes her to lift her head. He's striding toward her with a confused smile. "I haven't seen you laugh in a long time."

"I was imagining my picture in every newspaper across the country. What do you think the headline will read?"

"I'm not sure, but I've already thought about *my* headline. If I'm unable to decipher the code, it'll read *CRAZED MAN THOUGHT HE WAS THE PRESIDENT.*" Lance laughs and Doris joins in.

"Thank you for making us both laugh," she manages.

He grabs her by the hand, and they exit through the rear of the auditorium. As they walk, they are greeted by the fresh, clean scent of rain that has just passed. He guides her to the edge of the lawn, where the rose bushes hide them from view, and asks her to sit on the bench. As she gets settled, he picks a rose and kneels down in front of her. He then places the rose in her shirt pocket.

"If it weren't for you, Doris, I'd be dead—or even worse, brain dead. You walked across broken glass for me. You gave me time to heal, and prepared me for the main event. And maybe the best part of what happened is that you saved the little boy in me. I will take more time to romance my wife and play card games with my kids." He looks down and then adds, "You know, I think your headline should read *RIBBONS SAVES THE PRESIDENT.*"

Doris fights back tears, replacing them with a chuckle. She then gestures for Lance to sit next to her. "How do you think Rose is going to handle this?"

"Aside from tomorrow's event, that's all I've been thinking about. Will she accept me with open arms? I don't know. At the gala, she will have to perform for the sake of the cameras and the country. She always does the right thing, no matter what. But will she really take me back into her heart?" He stares off into the distance. "I hope so. All I can do is pray right now and focus on deciphering the code. I'm powerless over the outcome with Rose. The rest of the crap, I can deal with."

She gently nudges him. "You know something? When I removed your clothing at the hospital, your socks didn't match. And when I learned your identity, it confused me. Could the president of the United States leave the White House wearing socks that don't match? What's *that* about? Didn't you have people for that?"

It feels like they are surrounded by the energy and excitement of spring's arrival. A soft wind blows rose petals onto their laps. Lance picks one up off his leg and holds it in front of them.

"First of all, don't ever tell anyone about my mismatched socks. No one! Even if you go on to write some tell-all book about your experience." He gives her a boyish wink. "You see, when I get up in the morning, the first thing I do is put on my socks."

"I've noticed. Why is that?"

"I love getting up early, as you know, so I always keep socks beneath my side of the bed. That way, I can find my socks without turning on the light. I don't want to wake Rose. I love watching her sleep, and it's sort of a tradition; my dad did the same thing for my mom. It's a love language in our family. Making sure Rose is able to sleep in is one of my ways of showing her love. And Lord knows, I don't want to upset a sleeping woman! That's sort of taboo. And that's why my socks don't match sometimes. It's hard to see in the dark, you know." He laughs, realizing he hasn't even told *Rose* why his socks sometimes don't match. He promises himself that he will tell her as soon as he gets home. If he makes it home.

Doris smiles. "OK, that's enough of that. Let's figure out some details about tomorrow night."

"About that, I have a request." Lance turns to face her. "I want you to wear your red ribbon. It'll give me the comfort and confidence I'll need. I will always be indebted to you." Doris opens her mouth to reply, but he holds up his hand. "I've written an order for your safe return to New York. I will give it to James tomorrow. It ensures you'll get your old job back, and most importantly, it will wipe the slate clean for you. There will be no prosecution nor investigation pertaining to our recent experiences. And all information related to this matter will be sealed and remain confidential until both Rose and I are long dead. I promise, you will be safe, Rose." He puts his hand over his heart for emphasis.

Doris takes his hand from his heart and holds it tightly in hers. "Thank you for that, Lance. I trust you completely." She smiles warmly at him, grateful for his concern for her safety. "And about tomorrow night, there's a back room in the building. Debbie will have armed guards stationed there. She told them that it's where we're keeping some of the jewelry for the silent auction. That's where you will be stationed from the time we arrive until you walk up to the podium at exactly 8:00. The television crews are to be let in ten minutes earlier to begin filming. Their cameras will have been set up prior to the start of the event. They are expecting speeches from the university's president and the governor. They know there's a surprise in store—something big—but that's it. I can't wait to see the look on people's faces when they realize what's happening. We'll be making history!"

"Yes, we will." He squeezes her hand tightly. "I'd like James to come to the back room and walk with me to the podium. Please ask Debbie to bring him to me at 7:30. I need to talk to him before we walk out. I hope he and Rose haven't encountered any hitches in their side of the plan. It was a lot for me to ask of Rose, especially given all that has happened." He lets go of her hand and looks at the wet ground. "I don't know how we are going to pull this off. I can't imagine Rose and the kids making it to Pullman without the media's notice. But that's what James does; he makes the impossible possible. He's just going to have to break about twenty laws to make this happen. Guess I'm going to have to pardon him too." He sighs. "Well, I think our job here is done. Let's go home."

"Yes, Mr. President, let's go home." Doris laughs, and Lance shoots her a surprised look. "I'm kind of kidding," she says, "but you'd better get ready for the changes to your name and title. As for me, I'm going to miss being called Ribbons." She pauses. "But not as much as I'm going to miss you."

CHAPTER 75

THE PRESIDENT IS MISSING

Rose is busy packing for her upcoming trip to Washington when she hears a knock at the door. She's expecting James so they can finalize the details for the gala, but he's early.

"Hello?" she asks from behind the door.

"It's James, Rose."

She opens the door and ushers him into the suite. "I didn't expect you for at least another hour. I was packing. June is doing the same. Is everything OK? Are we still set for our 11:00 flight to Washington tomorrow morning?"

"Everything is still on schedule, but there's something you need to see right now." James's face tells her what she needs to know: there's a problem. "I don't exactly know what it is. My contact at NBC News called to tip me off. They are doing a special report on the president. Turn on the TV."

Rose grabs the remote and switches on the television, worried about what she may see. *God, please don't let it be a photo of Lance with that woman,* she thinks.

455

"This is Jennifer Kim. Welcome to a special NBC News break. The president of the United States is missing." The headline below the anchorwoman mirrors the announcement in bold capital letters.

"James, what the—? How do they know?"

"I have no clue. But I have a feeling we are going to find out soon."

"We have reached out to the White House for information on his whereabouts. The patient who is in a coma at New York Presbyterian Hospital is actually a man by the name of Vince Guthrie, a forty-seven-year-old New York native. The president's doctor, Dennis Kellerman, who was found dead behind his hotel just days ago, left a note at his office. Before he fled New York City with his family, he directed his staff to give the note to NBC News if he were to go missing or be murdered."

"This can't be happening. Why didn't you stop this, James?"

"I couldn't. My source wouldn't tell me what the report was about."

Jennifer Kim continues speaking, her face remaining solemn. Rose can imagine the woman's inner excitement at being given the privilege to break such a huge story. "In the note, Kellerman said he was contacted a week after the president was admitted to New York Presbyterian Hospital. Kellerman was coerced to keep the president in an induced coma until given further instruction. The man who gave him the orders claimed he was with the Secret Service. We don't know how high up the chain of command this goes. We have reached out to the White House for details, but as of yet, have not received any response. Kellerman claimed in the note that the Secret Service agent threatened to kill his family if he did not obey the instructions. He said the same man threatened his wife in their home in Central Park South after she took their kids to school one day. Apparently, their every move was under surveillance."

"Oh my God, that poor woman," Rose murmurs as she turns off the TV. "I can't watch this anymore. What are we going to do? The media is going to be everywhere. We can't make it to Washington now that the world is watching."

"Mrs. Dumont, we *can* do this," James says, taking her hand. "Alvarez and Noakes will make it happen." He pauses before adding, "*I* will make it happen."

CHAPTER 76

TWENTY-FOUR HOURS

D oris and Lance arrive home a bit early this evening, after a long, emotional day at the venue. The day's weather has been full of surprises. The morning was clear and sunny; then the rain came for an hour and departed just as quickly. This evening's sunset is looking to be spectacular. The colors in the sky seem too beautiful to be real. Doris and Lance sit on the porch to enjoy the scenery.

"This is a beautiful view," Lance says. "You must miss living here. It's a far cry from New York City. Have you thought about staying in Pullman after this is all over?"

"It *is* very pretty. I forgot about the view from the porch," Doris replies. "Daniel and I spent a lot of time sitting out here when we first started dating. It's a shame you and I haven't had time since we arrived to fully enjoy it. I feel like we've been too preoccupied with fear, the gala, and contacting your family. But to answer your question, no. I think I will go live in Santa Fe with Fatima. I'm going to need the warmth of that beautiful New Mexico sun after all this." She stands up and walks inside.

Lance follows her into the house and says, "You know what, Doris? You never told me what I was like before we got to Fatima's house."

She pretends as though she didn't hear his question. She doesn't want to end a good day on a bad note. Changing the subject, she asks him to turn on the TV so they can wind down a bit before bed. She is hoping to catch the evening news.

The first thing they see is the headline *PRESIDENT MISSING, SERCRET SERVICE RESPONSIBLE.*

Neither Doris nor Lance is able to move for what feels like ten minutes. They are stunned into silence by the pandemonium they see on television—scenes outside the White House filled with media trucks and a large crowd. Many people are holding signs, including one that reads *WHERE'S OUR PRESIDENT?* and others that say things such as *DOWN WITH GOVERNMENT* and *TRUST NO ONE.* It's mayhem.

Lance is the first to speak. "All hell is breaking loose. The Secret Service is who tried to have me killed? It was a Secret Service agent who tried to kill Officer Guthrie. No wonder Rose told Debbie only the FBI, the CIA, and Homeland Security would be helping us. Was Director Cummings behind the Brigade and the attack? That's hard to imagine. He is such a gentleman. I really liked him."

Doris can feel Lance's body shaking next to hers. Not knowing what to say, Doris simply puts her arm around his shoulders.

"Things couldn't be worse. I've got to get back there, Doris. The country is going to collapse, and I don't know if it can wait twenty-four hours." He stands up and begins to pace the room.

Doris turns off the television and says, "You know something? You are going to decipher that code for the entire world to see. And yes, it can wait twenty-four hours. Listen, I love you now more than ever, as any good friend would. This will all come to an end tomorrow, and everything is going to be OK. The Courthouse Massacre changed everything in this country. You will be leading a very different America when you return to power. In the meantime, you are going to be strong—not just for the country, but also for your wife and children."

He kisses her hand and replies, "You are right, twenty-four hours is a short period of time, and we need to do this right. But please know that I will never forget us. These memories will always be close to me. They will be my safety net. Just like the stars that come out at night after the rain stops, you will always be there."

Blushing, Doris says, "If you are nervous tomorrow when you are waiting in the back room before heading to the podium, use your index finger to draw pictures on the wall of anything that brings you happiness. Daniel would do that when he couldn't sleep or right before a big presentation, and it worked every time; I promise." She knows her ability to help Lance is quickly coming to an end. After tomorrow, he will be out of her life forever.

"Where were you when I was single?" Lance laughs and gives her a wink. "I *will* miss you, my good friend, my nurse, my saving grace."

CHAPTER 77

BORROWED TIME

▷ **Doris – Pullman, Washington, Day 38**

The morning of the gala arrives quickly. The first sounds of the day announce themselves: the creaking of the bedroom door, followed by a patter of approaching footsteps. The air is thick with the warm, nutty aroma of freshly brewed coffee, laced with sweet notes of cream and sugar. Smooth fingers trail the length of Doris's arm, tapping lightly on her skin.

"I brought you some coffee, Doris," a kind voice says. "You're going to need it today!"

Struggling to blink away her sleepiness, Doris sits up, expecting to see Daniel. Instead, Lance comes into focus, singing a sweet and silly song, the kind you make up as you go along. She can't help but smile before taking a sip of the coffee he hands her.

Lance smiles back at her and says confidently, "Today's the day!"

He leads her toward the kitchen, hooking his arm into hers as they walk down the hallway. Doris tries to concentrate on the floor, but her skin is sizzling beneath his touch, not just due to her romantic memories of their time together, but also as a result of her relief and sadness. Lance is strong, both mentally and physically, so her job is done. The thought of that frightens her more than anything else. *Now what?* she wonders.

461

"Look, I've made you waffles for breakfast," Lance says, pulling out a chair for her. "It doesn't do justice as a thank-you for all you have done for me, but it's a start."

"Waffles? Well, I won't eat them unless there are strawberries in the batter!"

"I didn't forget, not on a day like today. My mind feels sharp, and I'm ready for tonight. If I had forgotten the strawberries, I'd have a slim chance of deciphering the code." Lance winks as he serves the waffles. He then takes a seat directly across from Doris at the small kitchen table, where they eat in silence for a few minutes.

Lance speaks first. "Tell me what happened when you first brought me to your sister's house. How bad was I? I don't remember, and I feel like I should know. I'm sure Rose and the kids will ask me about it."

Doris agrees. He and his family should know. "Well, when you were at the hospital, the doctor wasn't sure you would make it, physically *or* mentally. There was so much bleeding in your brain. You could have had a massive stroke and died." She takes a deep breath before continuing. "We were at the hospital for just eight days, and it was rough—feeding tubes for the first five days, dozens of scans, tests, and long nights. But your condition improved a little bit each day. By the time we left the hospital, you were doing all right physically, though your brain was far from recovered. You still had no memory and weren't able to speak. When I realized we were in danger, I made the decision to take you to Fatima's house. Five days after we arrived there, you began to speak."

Lance shakes his head in disbelief. "How did you repair my brain? I don't remember any therapy or medication. It just felt like all of a sudden I woke up from some dark place, and there we were at Fatima's house."

"To be honest, I hadn't ever been responsible for providing therapy to an amnesia patient. I'm embarrassed to say, I went online and consulted with Dr. Google."

Lance doesn't try to hide his surprise. "Wow! OK, so what did Dr. Google tell you to do?"

"I stumbled upon an article from a European neurology institute that I found intriguing. The therapy is based upon the principle of creating a precipitating activity that can help trigger a patient's memory. It is called stimulation therapy. The types of triggers mentioned were pain, anger, sex, and cold-water immersion."

Lance's eyes widen, but Doris doesn't let him interrupt.

"Hey, I didn't make this up! I was desperate. I then found a case study from Brazil that talked about using the element of surprise as an emotional trigger. So, to cut to the chase, I decided to try a combination of surprise and anger. The method I came up with involved letting you fall asleep in a dark room. There had to be no light at all—pure darkness. I'd wait until you were in the REM cycle of sleep, and then I'd pass a feather across your face, slowly at first, but then I would do it more aggressively until you'd wake up. After a few days of this, you began to come back. You were more present. Thank God! I was emotionally and physically wiped out and not sure how long I could continue administering the therapy. There was a lot of crying in the beginning, but I would hum or sing a song to calm you. In the end, I have no clue if it was actually time that healed you or the therapy. But now none of that matters. Here we are, and you're back to normal." She can see that he's fully engrossed in her story. He was right: he needed to know the details.

He leans across the table and takes her hand. "Thank you. For everything."

"I don't know if I deserve thanks, Lance. Frankly, my experience at Fatima's was complicated. I began to develop feelings for you. Here I was, the caregiver again, just like I was for Daniel—with a man who looks and acts so much like he did. I was confused and exhausted. On top of that, I was barely sleeping because of my reoccurring nightmares about the scene at the courthouse. Maybe that's why I latched onto you so strongly in Santa Fe. I dunno. I'd previously failed someone I cared about, and I wasn't going to let it happen again."

"You didn't let Daniel down. Cancer let him down," Lance says solemnly. He takes her hand and kisses her forehead. "You, Doris, *you* saved me. You gave me freedom at a time when I had just lost it as a result of becoming president. You gave me unforgettable moments of laughter and levity. And more important than all that, you gave me my life back. I'm a better man because of you. I have no regrets, and you shouldn't either."

"I don't know what to say." Doris feels like a great weight has been lifted from her shoulders.

"You don't need to say anything. But you do need to heal and find enough self-compassion to forgive yourself. You are a *hero,* Ms. Doris Machado!"

"Hardly! But thank you," Doris says with a laugh. "I didn't expect any of this. I certainly didn't expect *us.* But it happened, and I promise to have no regrets. Ultimately, I just wanted you to recover, and I tried to create moments of happiness and laughter along the way. And there were many. Now it's time to say good-bye. We are finally done running. There are no more lies to tell, and there is no need to hide anymore. I am so lucky to have spent this borrowed time by your side."

CHAPTER 78

THE INNER POCKET

▷ **Director Schultz – CIA's Gulfstream V Turbojet, Day 38**

Somewhere above the Midwest, Director Schultz is seated comfortably, enjoying his favorite lunch: a classic Reuben sandwich. He and his assistant are reviewing plans for the additional security needed at tonight's gala at Washington State University. Acting President Alvarez called him after NBC broke the news about the president's disappearance. She first thanked him for his help in her investigation of Cummings. She then said she needed some of his team members to provide backup for Homeland Security, who would replace the Secret Service in guarding the First Family during an upcoming event at the university. Schultz replied that he found it strange that the family would be attending an event when their father is missing, but Alvarez assured him it was for good reason.

Acting President Alvarez stated that his agents would collaborate with Homeland Security to provide a comprehensive range of security measures at the university during the event. It had been announced the previous night that Homeland Security would be taking over the normal role of the Uniformed Division of the Secret Service. Following the announcement by NBC of President Dumont's disappearance, the public outcry over the Secret Service's involvement in the "Presbyterian Scandal" prompted Acting President Alvarez to relieve the Uniformed Division of their duties until the congressional committee completes their investigation into the Courthouse Massacre and the president's disappearance.

When Schultz received the call from Alvarez, he immediately sent over the best of the best within his team. And even though all she'd asked him to do was send a small team, he felt it was necessary to fly across the country to see for himself what is really going on with the First Family. Then, when he learned that Homeland Security and the FBI would be going, he knew something was up: a full-fledged search for the president. How can they be looking for the president of the United States and *not* request the presence of the director of the CIA? He wasn't going to be excluded, so he ordered the jet.

Schultz takes another bite of his sandwich, then dumps the rest in the trash. What he really craves is a cigarette. Suddenly, he feels his cell phone vibrating in the breast pocket of his blazer. It's his special phone, so he excuses his assistant, waits for her to step into the lavatory, and then takes the call.

"Gruff?" he answers.

"Hello, Rockefeller."

"You on location?"

"Yes, sir. The beautiful state of Washington. Spent most of the night in the air. Wasn't easy to get here with all the connections. Damn commercial airlines. Are you sure this is how you wanna do this? Just you and me?"

"We can't trust anyone else to get the job done, can we Gruff? That's been painfully obvious over the last few weeks."

"I'm ready to take one for the team, no matter the risk."

"That's why you're my right-hand man, Gruff. Tonight is your night to go down in history."

CHAPTER 79

GOODBYE, RIBBONS

▷ **Doris – Pullman, Washington, Day 38**

L ance asks Doris if he can drive to the gala. He explained to Doris that it will be the last time—at least for the next three and a half years—that he will be able to drive a car himself. He remembers the shock of being told that presidents aren't allowed to drive, unless they're on private property. Back then, he was completely convinced that it was safe for a president to drive, but that, like so many other things, wasn't true. There are many dangers that constantly surround a sitting president. *Now* he understands.

It's just before 6:00 p.m., and Doris has her red ribbon pinned to her dress, just as Lance requested. As they walk out the door, Lance says, "Thank you for wearing the ribbon."

"Of course, but please don't tell anyone the story. I want it to be *our* story." She smiles at him for what could be the last time. They both know that the ribbon represents so much more than words can describe.

In the garage, before they get into the car, Lance stops Doris and grabs her hand. He kisses it while looking into her eyes. "Thank you for everything, *Ribbons*."

He holds the passenger door open, and she climbs inside Fatima's old Honda Civic. He then walks around to the other side and sits down in the driver's seat. They remain silent throughout the drive to Washington State University.

The first thing Doris notices upon arriving on campus is the number of security personnel, many more than they requested. She looks at Lance. "And so it begins. It looks like they're ready for you. I figured Debbie would be on top of it, especially with James's and Rose's help."

They drive to Debbie's workplace, the French Administration Building, which is connected to the Lighty Student Services Building. The parking spot they agreed on is located at the front of the building, just sixty yards from Ensminger Pavilion. Lance parks the car, and they make their way up the sidewalk, at the end of which, they enter the grand lobby of the French Administration Building. As planned, they find Debbie waiting for them. She waves to the security personnel and gives them a thumbs-up.

"Well, look at the two of you!"

Debbie embraces both of them, but Doris can tell she's not quite herself. Her hug is too hasty; her smile, too wide. She's nervous.

"You both clean up so well! I've already met with James and reviewed the details. He has what's needed for the code and will begin displaying it at 8:00. He'll meet you in the back room at 7:30 to discuss the process, just as you requested, Mr. President. He also mentioned that there is a protocol that must be followed after you decipher the code."

"*If* I decipher the code." Lance nudges Debbie and smiles. "I may need a drink or two to loosen up my nerves."

Debbie's tone remains serious. "I have no doubt that this event will go exactly as planned, Mr. President. I'm going to go back to the gala now. My assistant, Mariam, will be here at 7:15 to bring you to the venue. There's a tunnel connecting this building to Ensminger Pavilion. It provides direct access to the back room. As promised, there will be armed security personnel just outside the room. James has arranged that with Homeland Security."

When Doris attended school here, she learned that there are over seven miles of steam tunnels under Washington State University. They were built during the 1930s, when the university relied on coal. The tunnels have a width of five feet and a height of six feet, which makes it easy for people to navigate them if necessary. Today, they are used for communication infrastructure, heating, and electricity.

"Well, look at you, Debbie," Lance says admirably. "Maybe there's a place for you on my staff. You're just full of surprises."

Debbie leans in for another hug. "Good luck, Mr. President. It has been a pleasure to serve you. Doris, I'll see you at our staff table just before 8:00."

Doris watches her scurry away. Lance turns to her, reaching forward to adjust her crooked ribbon. She breathes him in, longing to hold his hand and never let go.

"Are you ready to be the president of the United States?" Doris asks softly.

Lance looks her up and down. "You look so beautiful, Doris. It's as if you're standing on a water lily, with the moon and a million stars in the sky shining down on you for the world to see." Suddenly, he grabs her by the shoulders and looks deep into her eyes. "Tell me, did we ever make love? I mean, the real thing. Did we?"

"Why do you ask?" Doris tries to shrug off the awkward chill running up her spine, flooding her brain with the memory of his touch. "What do *you* remember?"

"*Everything*," Lance answers, and then turns his head to the side and looks toward Ensminger Pavilion, where the gala is getting underway.

"Goodbye, Mr. President." She brushes away the tear before it can fall from her eye.

"Goodbye, Ribbons."

They hold each other in a tender embrace, aware this is the last time they'll do so. With a reluctance to part, they remain wrapped in each other's arms, cherishing the moment. Doris considers kissing him goodbye but decides against it. Her heart is already broken enough. She holds him a little tighter and draws a deep breath, wanting to take in all of him before they part.

Debbie's young assistant, Mariam, arrives at that moment, and they let go of each other. With her six-foot stature, long black hair, and full figure, Mariam exudes an aura of authority. She leads Doris and Lance through the tunnel to the back room, where Lance will wait for James. Doris pauses, hesitant to leave Lance's side, but Mariam assures her all will be fine. Doris turns away, looking back one last time to see Lance's gaze fixed on her. Smiling softly, she taps the ribbon on her chest and then slips out, fighting back tears. Now all she wants is a drink to settle her nerves.

She makes it to Ensminger Pavilion quickly, but before she's even halfway through the Ensminger lobby, she hears someone call her name. She hopes it's one of the vendors she has been working with over the last week.

"Doris Machado?" the voice calls out louder this time.

Doris doesn't recognize the voice, but when she turns around, she does recognize the face. It's Edwina Dumont, Lance's favorite child. Doris straightens her spine as Edwina approaches her, leaning forward like a mongoose poised to strike.

CHAPTER 80

YOUR FATHER'S FAVORITE CHILD

▷ **Edwina – Pullman, Washington, Day 38**

E dwina has been waiting for this moment since the day she learned that the woman in front of her had run away with her father. This is why she ignored her parents' request that she remain in the SUV until minutes before her father's stage appearance. Her mom couldn't stop her from leaving, so she sent Edwina's brothers along to make sure she'd be safe.

Doris Machado looks nervous, as she should, and Edwina can see that she is forcing a smile. After a few moments of silence between them, Edwina hears Doris's voice for the first time.

"Hello, Edwina," says the nurse. "I've been looking forward to meeting you. I've heard so much about you."

Two figures appear on either side of Edwina, flanking her: George and Thomas. Her backup.

"Do you love him?" Edwina spits, her voice on the edge of uncontrollable fury. "My father, did you sleep with him?" Her body shakes with anger, her hands clenched into fists.

Before Doris can respond, Thomas steps forward. His face, while no less pained than Edwina's, bears the hint of an apology. Edwina wants to smack him but focuses on Doris instead.

Doris puts up her hand to stop Thomas. "I admire your audacity, Edwina. I completely understand. You love your father in the same way all little girls in this world love their daddies. You shouldn't be any different just because your father happens to be the president of the United States."

"And *you*—" Edwina snarls.

"I'm sorry, Edwina," Doris interrupts calmly, her head held high. "I'm sorry that the Brigade tried to kill your father. I'm sorry the Secret Service let the assassination attempt take place and that their leader was involved with the Brigade. I'm sorry my two best friends and their families' lives were threatened. I'm sorry your dad was shot twice and lost his memory. I'm sorry for all of it, truly."

Edwina doesn't care about this woman's apologies. "That's not what I asked. Answer the question."

"OK, yes, over time, I did develop feelings for your father. I fell in love with him."

"I knew it!" Edwina exclaims, surprised that Doris admitted it. The confession deflates her a bit.

"Edwina, I know you are your father's favorite child." She looks at Thomas and George. "I'm sorry, guys." Refocusing on Edwina, she says, "But now, Edwina, I understand *why*: it's because the two of you are so much alike. You're both strong-willed people who have made a commitment to serve others: he as the president, and you as a nun."

"I hope you aren't saying that because you expect me to forgive you. I'm not looking to be a priest," Edwina says sarcastically.

"I mentioned it because I realize now that the three of us share a life of devotion. Before this, I had a quiet life. I hadn't dated anyone since my husband, Daniel, died a year ago. Heck, *I* was practically a nun. My life was fully devoted to my patients, which was, unfortunately, to my own detriment. I'm not quite sure I was even aware of it until I started having feelings for your father, who, coincidentally, looks and acts so much like my Daniel. I finally connected with someone again. But my point is that I was too devoted. I neglected my own needs, mental health, and family because I was solely focused on my patients. But I now realize it's possible to prioritize both my patients and my personal life."

"But you knew who he was, that he had a family," Edwina says. She thinks about the sacrifices and loss her father has experienced in his quest for a life of service and wonders if being a nun will also mean putting others first. And at what cost to her own life?

"Listen, I know everyone tends to look at life's choices as black and white or good and evil. But you and I know it's not that simple. Everything takes place in the middle—the gray area. That's the truth of life. It's why we have religious and political leaders to help us through the murky parts. This is where we all operate on a daily basis, but when we *judge,* we conveniently place people into neat, distinct categories, like black and white. Having said that, I think that both history and God will judge me favorably. I did what was right at the moment, and your father is safe."

Edwina opens her mouth, but no words come out. She realizes that this woman is not a villain, but instead, just another imperfect human. She also knows there's truth to what Doris said, but she's certainly not ready to forgive her.

The group is suddenly interrupted by a Homeland Security agent who exchanges a word with Thomas before escorting the three siblings to their table. Edwina and George look back over their shoulders, but Doris is already gone.

CHAPTER 81

THE SPIDER AND THE FLY

▷ **Doris – Pullman, Washington, Day 38**

"Doris!" Debbie says as she snakes her way through the crowd. "Hey! How are you holding up?"

In response, Doris snatches Debbie's glass, drinks the rest of her wine, sits down, and pours herself another very full glass. She's beyond glad to see Debbie; she needs a friendly face right now to stop her nerves from fraying completely.

"I don't think I can do this. Can I just leave and pretend none of this ever happened?"

"It's too late. As they say, you made your bed, and now you have to lie in it. But don't worry; you're fine. You *will be* fine. I still can't believe all this. How the hell did it even happen?" Debbie puts her arm around Doris's shoulders, and they share a nervous laugh.

Doris notices four men heading in their direction, all dressed in black with earpieces. Homeland Security. She checks her watch. It isn't time yet. The four men stop a few feet from their table and then part to make way for an older man in similar attire.

"Doris Machado?" he asks curtly.

Doris nods.

"I'm with Homeland Security. Deputy Lee. Please come with me."

Doris blanches and tosses back the last of her wine before standing up on trembling legs. *This is what you get,* she reminds herself. What did she think would happen once they found out what she did? No matter how many times Lance promised that nothing would happen to her, it was always improbable that she would walk away from all this without repercussions.

"Wait!" Debbie springs to her feet. "I'm coming with her."

Deputy Lee turns to her. "I'm sorry, ma'am, but you'll need to stay here. Ms. Machado must come alone."

"But—"

Doris squeezes her hand briefly. "I'll be OK, Debbie. Just wait here, please."

Leaving Debbie to protest helplessly behind them, Doris follows the short, thick-framed deputy, flanked by four more agents. She tries to keep her back straight and head up, but the curious stares and whispers from the crowd threaten to shatter her defenses. She can't help but tremble and sweat. Her gaze falls to the floor. This is the moment she has feared most. She knows what's about to happen: they'll apprehend her, ask questions, cuff her, and take her away. Permanently. She swallows back the lump in her throat, hastily recalling her lawyer's phone number, which she has repeated over and over to herself in preparation for this moment.

The doors of Ensminger Pavilion open, and she feels a touch of relief as the evening air cools her skin. This may be her last moment to enjoy fresh air for a long time. The agents walk her over to a large black SUV with tinted windows, where another Homeland Security agent is waiting for her. The female agent opens the door and orders Doris inside. She's surprised she is not

475

yet in cuffs. It's all so civilized. As she climbs inside the SUV, her heart nearly jumps out of her body.

"Hello, Doris," says Rose Dumont, looking like a spider who just caught a fly.

"M-Mrs. Dumont! Ma'am—I m-mean First Lady . . ." Doris sputters. She didn't prepare herself for *this* moment, being alone with Lance's wife. She simply prayed that nothing like this would ever happen.

Rose looks at her head-on, her face stoic. "I didn't plan on our meeting. In fact, I didn't expect any of this. My first inclination was to have you immediately taken into custody, and let Homeland Security deal with you."

Doris can see the satisfaction on her face.

"How is he?" Rose asks.

Doris is speechless. She wants to open the door and run for her life. She'd rather be interrogated by the FBI than have a face-to-face conversation with the First Lady, the woman whose husband she's been hiding out with for the past month, the wife of the man she fell in love with.

"Elliot is doing well," she manages to choke out. "He's strong and smart and ready to return to his obligations. He's—"

"Ah, yes," Rose interrupts, her tone turning even colder. Doris shrinks in her seat. "Elliot Greene, wasn't it? How, if I may ask, did you have the nerve to give my husband—the president of the United States—a new name and identity, and then run away with him?"

There is so much to say, but shouldn't Lance be the one to explain it to his wife? His way and in his words—they agreed that's how it would happen, but now she's been forced into this unexpected confrontation. She needs to tread carefully, yet she doesn't know which way to turn. How can she ever explain this to Rose without sounding insane? She knows everything she's done looks like it was premeditated, but it wasn't. Every moment since the attack seemed to snowball into the next moment, forcing her to navigate one threat after another. No part of their story was planned in advance, but every version sounds crazy. *She* sounds crazy.

"It doesn't m-mean anything. *Elliot,* that is," she explains hastily. "It's just a name that came out of nowhere to protect his identity. I-I panicked when I found out he was the—all I knew was that I couldn't share his real name."

Rose's eyes blaze. "To protect his identity or to protect yourself? You changed my husband's name so you could play your little game and act the savior. I expected you to be honest. But perhaps you aren't being honest with *yourself.* You kidnapped my husband. Don't fool yourself, Doris; you were protecting *you.*"

Doris bows her head. "You're right; I *was* protecting myself. I can only imagine what you're thinking."

"For your sake, I hope you can't. You wouldn't be here," Rose says dryly.

"I-I'm sorry. You're right; I don't know what you're feeling, and I can't imagine what you've been through. I'm sorry for all of it. I'm especially sorry for hurting you and your family."

CHAPTER 82

STAY ON THE GROUND

Lance checks his cuff links and looks at himself in the mirror. He's clearly not the man he used to be just over a month ago.

James arrived ten minutes ago, and they have been catching up.

"James, did you ever suspect Cummings was behind all this?" Lance asks his confidant.

"Cummings was the most likely culprit since he was in charge of your protection. But to be honest, I *was* a little surprised. He doesn't seem like an extremist. I'm sure he was not happy with your campaign platform that threatened to diminish his agency's power and resources, but to try and have you assassinated? And to cause so much collateral damage? That's hard for me to wrap my head around. But I guess that's just Washington, DC. You never know who you can trust."

"Yeah, I actually liked Cummings. I was surprised as well. He's the one who tried to convince me not to go to New York. We actually fought over it."

"I dunno. Maybe it was because he wasn't yet ready for the attack or had something else in mind."

Suddenly, they hear a commotion outside—an argument followed by a loud bang on the door, as if someone is trying to break it down.

James draws his gun and aims it at the door. "Down to the ground, sir," he commands Lance in a low voice. "Now!"

Lance hears the sound of a muffled gunshot, followed by two more in quick succession. "What the hell is happening, James?!"

"Just stay on the ground," James orders. "Let's get you out of here—back through the tunnel."

Just as Lance begins to stand, he hears a voice from outside the door: "Mr. President, you all right? It's Homeland Security."

"We aren't opening the door!" James yells back. "Not until I've confirmed the area's secure."

"Mr. President!" a male voice shouts. "Elliot!"

Lance's eyes widen. "What the hell?" he says under his breath.

"It's Jack Guthrie, NYPD. I met you and Doris at the hotel in Los Angeles!"

"Dear God. It's the son of the man who they thought was me. I know him. Let him in, James."

"I can't, sir. Protocol."

"I don't care. Open the damn door *now!*" Lance's patience is all but gone. He's the president, this is his night, and he's going to take control.

James begrudgingly opens the door. In walks Jack Guthrie with two Homeland Security agents at his side.

"Jack! What the hell are you doing here?" Lance asks.

"He just shot someone who killed one of our agents, Mr. President," says one of the agents.

"Gruff," Jack answers breathlessly.

"What?" Lance is lost, but he wants answers. He needs to focus on deciphering the code in ten minutes, but now *this* is happening.

"That's who I killed; his name was Gruff. He was one of the top guys in the Brigade. His real name was Gerald Jones. He reported to a man named Rockefeller, the mastermind of the Brigade. I've been following Jones for the past week," Jacks says, his voice now calm.

"Cummings's guy?" James asks.

"Actually, no. His boss *isn't* Director Cummings; it is CIA Director Donald Schultz, otherwise known as Rockefeller." Jack says matter-of-factly. "Mr. President, if you recall the story I told you in Los Angeles, the man who tried to kill me in Santa Fe had a Secret Service ID."

"I remember, Jack," Lance says, but his mind is reeling from what he's just learned about Schultz being the mole—the man in charge of the Brigade. He's having a hard time focusing.

"I told you I had killed the agent, but I hadn't. I've been holding him hostage, and after a lot of threats—and maybe a little torture—I learned that he worked for the Brigade. The Secret Service ID was intended to implicate Director Cummings as the leader of the Brigade. He was to be the scapegoat for the Courthouse Massacre. This guy, Diego, worked for Gruff and told me where I could find him. And I did. I followed him and saw him meet with Schultz twice. Then I followed Gruff all the way here, to Pullman. He landed this morning and met with Schultz again here, in Washington. I've been on his tail all day. When I saw him quickly approaching this building, I knew something was up. Then, when I saw him pull a weapon, I shot him."

"Sir, if I may," interjects James, "this story sounds a bit . . . outlandish?"

"May I take out my phone?" Jack asks one of the agents. "I have proof."

"Let him get his phone," Lance demands.

They watch as Jack navigates his phone. He then holds it up, the screen facing Lance and James. Lance watches the scene play out. There's a man tied to a chair in a dark room. His face is bruised and bloody; his eyes, nearly swollen shut. There's another man in the room. He's masked, but from the sound of his voice, Lance knows it's Jack. The man in the chair confesses that he works for Gruff, who in turn works for Rockefeller, the man who gave the orders to kill Jack Guthrie. He divulges details about the day of the attack and the Brigade's search for President Dumont at the hospitals and morgues, with orders to terminate the president's life once he was found.

Lance turns to James and asks, "Is Schultz here tonight?"

"I'm afraid so, sir," James replies somberly.

"I haven't deciphered the code yet, James, but you know what to do: apprehend your boss, Schultz, *now!*" bellows the president of the United States.

CHAPTER 83

STAY AWAY

R ose shakes her head, thinking about Doris's apology. How dare this woman say she's sorry! Did she assume Rose would somehow forgive her? She dismisses the thought for now and asks the question she really wants an answer to: "Why would you run with the president of the United States? I've had extensive background searches conducted on you. You have no criminal background, no connections. You lived a simple life up to that point. Why would you do this? I have my own theories, but I need an answer from you."

"I've asked myself the same question a thousand times. Things were chaotic during those days in New York City. I was on the scene at the New York State Supreme Court Building on the day of the massacre and was the first one to find Lance there on the sidewalk beneath the courthouse steps, bloodied and broken. The scene that surrounded us was horrific—the sounds of people dying, others crying out for help or screaming in pain. It haunts me in my sleep . . . every night, every time I close my eyes."

Rose remembers the very same scene, but from the inside of the SUV, which, thankfully, softened the cries that Doris heard. She nods. The visuals and sounds often visit her in her sleep as well. But she chooses not to respond to Doris; she's not going to give her the respect of a shared traumatic experience.

With tears now streaming down her face, Doris continues, "It took me a few days to realize that the man I was caring for was President Lance Dumont. At around the same time, a man visited Elliot's room in the middle of the night." Rose considers correcting her mistake of calling him Lance instead of Elliot, but ultimately decides against it. "I wasn't there, but my coworkers Alice and Angela were, and they confronted him. Turns out, he had a knife. He knew things about their families and threatened their lives if they told anyone about his visit, and he said he would be back. Then the bomb at Presbyterian was found, and on top of all that, the media was reporting that the Brigade was threatening to finish what they'd started. And of course, there were the conspiracy theories about government involvement, which, as you know, turned out to be true. That's why I ran. I was scared for my life and the lives of Angela, Alice, and their families. And of course, I was afraid for Elliot's life as well. I didn't know what else to do. All I knew is that the scary hospital visitor would be back to finish the job. So we ran."

Rose looks at the woman sitting on the seat next to her. Just as her kids said a couple of weeks ago, she's pretty. Despite her uncertainty about wanting an answer, her gut compels her to ask the next question: "Do you love him?"

"I did love him. *Elliot*, not Lance," Doris confesses. "But Elliot no longer exists. Just like my deceased husband. And with both men, there is love left over. But I'm not in love with Lance Dumont."

Doris asks Rose for some water. Rose hands her a bottle and a tissue. She watches as the nurse wipes her tears and drinks the water. While she feels no pity for the woman, she does feel an unexpected combination of relief, jealousy, and—surprisingly—empathy. She wonders if she would have done the same if she was in Doris's shoes, especially now, in hindsight, given what she knows about the involvement of Cummings and the Secret Service. Of course, she can't share these thoughts with Doris. She's not going to give her that. Rose wants to speak, but she also wants to hear more from Doris. Lance will be taking the stage in the dinner hall very soon.

"I'm sorry, Mrs. Dumont. I never intended to hurt you and your family."

When Rose finally speaks again, her voice lacks its accusatory edge, but a certain firmness remains. "To be honest, I don't know what would have happened to Lance had you immediately reported his whereabouts to the local authorities. Maybe the Secret Service would've killed him; maybe not. I really don't know. You took a gamble, and it paid off. I'm not good at thank-yous, but I *am* grateful that he made a full recovery under your care. And knowing Lance, I'm sure he will reward you for your service to the country, and maybe you deserve that. But I also deserve something from you. I'm asking, or rather, *telling* you to stay away from my husband and our family for the rest of your life. We have been through so much and would like to move on. I, for one, would like to start fresh with my husband. That's all I ask of you. This is over, Doris."

"Yes, of course I'll stay away. You must also know that I will take this entire experience to the grave. I made that promise to your husband as well. No one else will ever learn what happened, at least not from me. I want to go back to my simple life."

Rose feels this is a fair deal, but she does have one last piece of advice for Doris. "You had to have known that there was going to be no fairytale ending for you." She watches Doris straighten up, trying to appear unaffected by her words. She then adds, "In the future, remember that while love can be idealistic and romantic, it's not sustainable if it's based on false pretenses."

Doris nods, wiping away her tears.

"Thank you for delivering him back to us in good health." Rose pauses, then adds, "Oh, and I hope his socks match." And for the first time, she cracks a small smile, which Doris returns.

At that moment, there's a knock at the window, which signals their time together is over. Lance is going to try to decipher the code. Rose quickly exits the SUV and doesn't look back.

CHAPTER 84

GIVE ME YOUR GUN

▷ **Lance – Pullman, Washington, Day 38**

Lance looks in the mirror again and straightens his scarlet tie. He must play the part tonight, decipher the code, and get back to his old life. He checks his watch, it's two minutes before 8:00. He asked James to delay the deciphering of the code by ten minutes. James tried to dissuade him, but Lance insisted, and James acquiesced.

"Where are they?" Lance asks impatiently.

"Sir, I'm sure Director Noakes will be here soon," James reassures him. "Give him another minute or two."

As if on cue, there's a knock at the door. James makes his way across the small room and asks, "Who is it?"

"Keith Noakes. I've got him with me," Noakes replies, his voice measured.

James opens the door and ushers in the two men.

"I heard you need to talk to us, Mr. President. Is everything OK, sir?" Director Donald Schultz inquires, his voice as cool as the air outside.

Lance readies himself. "Why did you do it, Schultz? What did I do that caused such hatred in you?"

Schultz steps back defensively and stammers, "What the hell are you talking about, Dumont?"

"And you claim to be such a patriot. A proud American. You disgust me!" Lance shouts. "You are an evil man, and you can't hide behind our flag after committing such a heinous crime!" He yanks off his suit jacket and hurls it onto the chair next to him.

"I honestly have no idea what the hell you are talking about!" Schultz shouts in return. "Can someone please fill me in?! If I'm being accused of something, then I have the right to know!"

"You '*have the right*'? How about all of the people you murdered on February 4? They had the right to live!"

"I don't know what you're implying. Do I need to call my lawyer?" Schultz asks sarcastically, his mouth twisted into a contemptuous smirk.

"Give me your gun, Noakes," Lance says coolly.

"I can't do that, sir. He's not worth it!" Noakes pleads.

Something cool touches the back of Lance's right hand. He looks down to see a SIG Sauer P226.

"Thank you, James," Lance says, grabbing the pistol without taking his eyes off of Schultz.

"Have you lost your mind, Dumont? I already thought you were crazy; now everyone's going to see that their president's gone mad," Schultz says with a chuckle.

"Don't do it!" Noakes yells.

But it's too late, pistol in hand, Lance leans back and swings as hard as he possibly can. He hears the sound of bones breaking. Blood oozes from Schultz's nose and mouth, his hands instinctively clutching his face.

"You deserve the scar you'll have from that!" Lance spits. "You should've died that day, but you couldn't even manage that. You ran like a coward. You're the one who's responsible for all that violence and death!"

Lance switches the pistol to his other hand and lands a blow to the other side of Schultz's head, forcing him off balance. He falls to the ground.

"One was for all the Americans you murdered. The other one was because the first one felt so good," Lance says evenly. And it *did* feel good. He's never been violent, never even been in a fight. The adrenaline fuels him as a smile sneaks its way across his face.

Noakes and James say nothing. They only look at each other, unable to look the president in the eye. Lance can see their fear, the uncertainty of what's going to happen next.

"That's what happens when you cling to hatred, maintain the status quo, and prioritize self-preservation over doing what's right, Schultz. I will see to it that you rot in a cell. And I will make sure you are *not* secluded from the other murderers in prison, so you will get what you deserve. You'll be lucky if you're still alive after a week," Lance snarls. Then, as if transformed, he turns and reaches for his suit jacket, slowly pulling it on one arm at a time. As he catches his reflection in the mirror, he realizes he doesn't remember ever feeling this good.

He turns to Noakes and commands, "Get him the hell outta here! I have a code to decipher."

CHAPTER 85

COMPLETE TRANSFORMATION

▷ **Doris – Pullman, Washington, Day 38**

Doris reenters Ensminger Pavilion and joins Debbie back at their table in the dinner hall. As she takes her seat, she notices that staff members are closing the room's multiple doors. Debbie looks relieved to see her, but Doris can hardly muster a smile in return; she's too drained and emotionally broken. All around her, gala attendees are gabbing happily, enjoying their dinners. She wishes she were one of them, just a regular guest.

Doris picks at the food on the plate in front of her and gulps down another glass of wine, determined to evade Debbie's pointed glances and raised eyebrows. But just as she's starting to get comfortable, the alcohol dulling her emotions, a wave of murmurs and gasps ripples through the room. People are standing up and pointing toward the left side of the stage.

Doris stands, assuming Lance is approaching the podium. As she surveys the scene, she spots armed agents at every entrance and imagines a flock of them encircling the building from a wide perimeter. The thought is reassuring but devastating. Just two hours ago, Lance was as free as a bird—no locked doors, no security detail, no bulletproof SUVs, and no agents guarding his every move. Now, he once again belongs to America. *He always has,* she has to remind herself. *He never belonged to me.*

Now everyone in the room is standing, pointing, and chattering. Two Homeland Security agents walk across the stage, followed by another man: the president of the United States of America. The audience gasps. Doris can feel the heat from the bright lights of the nearby news cameras. But what she notices most is the complete transformation of the man she parted ways with just under an hour ago. Over the past forty-five minutes, James and his team must have worked hard to make Lance look like his old self again. Scars still run deep across the side of his face, but she can barely see them from where she's sitting. His beard is gone, and he looks so much younger. His skin is glowing, thanks to the talent of the makeup artists. The cheap suit she bought him has been replaced by a perfectly tailored dark-blue suit, a deep-red tie, and gold cuff links, making him look much more regal. The expensive suit hides Lance's slim build. He never managed to gain back all the weight he'd lost following the attack. He often joked about wanting to go back to his "fightin' weight." Despite that, it looks like nothing ever happened to him. Doris looks down at the table, her heart pounding. His transformation has shaken her, made her feel so small and irrelevant. Before she can give this any more thought, the room darkens and all the monitors light up—just as they planned.

The screens are all over the place, visible from every seat within the four walls of the dinner hall. As soon as the lights go down, images begin to appear on the screens. At first, there are numbers, followed by letters and symbols, then complete words. Doris cranes her neck, whispering them to herself as they appear: "Shelter . . . Home . . . Street . . . Butterfly . . . Eye . . . Ribbon." She freezes. It can't be. But she ignores that thought.

She imagined this moment. What she didn't imagine was the audience's reaction, their shock at seeing the president of the United States standing on the stage in front of them. The entire country has been consumed by the Courthouse Massacre, the hunt for the Brigade members, the news of Secret Service involvement, and the announcement that the president is missing. And now this.

CHAPTER 86

MAY GOD BLESS AMERICA

▷ **Lance – Pullman, Washington, Day 38**

The moment has arrived for Lance to decipher the code that he helped create, the "Dumont Code." For the last few days, he has been pushing himself to remember the time, just two months ago, he spent developing the code in that somber room inside the Homeland Security building in Washington, DC. Without Doris's knowledge, he spent the last two nights making notes and testing his memory of the code while she slept. If he had been honest with her, he would have told her that he was doubtful he could decipher the code. But now, that has changed. Having another near-death experience just moments ago ignited a confidence he'd been worried he had lost. Although he's not proud of it, he's also feeling the high from pistol-whipping Director Schultz. The man is a demon. But no punishment can serve as justice for all the lives that were lost and the hundreds of people who were injured.

The lights from Lance's position behind the podium are blinding, their heat increasing his senses. He closes his eyes for a moment of reprieve and takes a deep breath. *You've got this,* he says to himself. He opens his eyes and looks again at the series of numbers, letters, symbols, words, and images from his life. The final image is of a red ribbon. There it is again: the word, then the image. He stops and grabs on to the podium for support. He looks at the image again, squinting his eyes to make sure that's really what it is—a red ribbon. Of course he was attracted to Doris's red ribbon! When he was an infant, his mother would always wear her hair in a high ponytail tied with a red ribbon. The ribbon would often dangle over her shoulder, and he would play with it. The coincidence scares and comforts him all at once.

He snaps himself back into the moment as his memory is being triggered. The code he created is based on unique memories from his life: scrambled letters from Greek words he remembers from his fraternity days. A symbol of a rose from ancient times of the Round Table of King Arthur as a nod to his Rose. Numbers representing dates significant to him, like the exact year and day he became homeless and the day when Rose told him she was pregnant with their firstborn, Thomas. Lance employs simple personal word associations with the displayed words and applies transposition and substitution methods to convert all symbols, images, and numbers into letters. He then converts them into a Route Cipher using a large ten-by-ten grid.

Eleven minutes have passed, and his grid is nearly complete. The crowd is so silent that Lance feels as if they can hear his heart beating. He knows that there are more than fifty variations of his dynamic code, each one of them correct. What is unique about this code is that he must *decipher* what is provided, not *encipher* it. He just has to get this right.

After another five minutes, he straightens his spine and puts down his pen. His voice is strong as he recites the code slowly and clearly: "K-T-P H-U-V-B-N I-O-N-G-C-I-T Y-U-M-T

I-V P-E-W-R-B-N M-U-I-P." As if to punctuate the deciphered sentence, a drop of his sweat falls from his face onto the paper.

The audience remains silent, unsure of what to do next. Everyone simply stares at him, waiting for something to happen. Lance holds his breath as he turns to Homeland Security Director Noakes. He sees the flash of a blue light on the director's electronic tablet. Noakes looks at the screen and then back up at Lance with a single nod. Lance's shoulders shake with relief as he feels James's arms slide around him. He doesn't try to stop the tears. He doesn't care how he looks; he has correctly deciphered the code. His nightmare journey is over, as sweet as it was at times. He looks up at Rose and then at Doris, her red ribbon shining like a beacon in the night. Without the two of them, he would be nothing.

Rose and his children join Lance on the stage. After embracing each of them, he smiles and speaks into the microphone: "I know none of you expected to see the missing president suddenly show up out of nowhere and then decipher a code to verify his identity. The Courthouse Massacre was an attack on our country by American citizens. It's crazy to think that our neighbors, friends, and even leaders were the ones who inflicted this upon us. We lost too many lives on that horrific day, and I was one of the lucky few to have been spared by the angels." Lance looks directly at Doris, then turns to look at Rose. "But I am especially blessed to have my wife and kids by my side tonight. Without the hard work of the First Lady, my children, James Edwards, Jennifer Alvarez, Jack Guthrie, Anita Johnson, and Keith Noakes, I wouldn't be standing up here today, and the terrorists who led the attack wouldn't be behind bars."

The audience members can't control themselves. Thunderous applause is accompanied by shouts from the crowd: "God Bless the First Lady!" and "Dumont Lives!"

Lance motions with his hands to quiet the crowd. "Tonight, we embark on a new journey. We stand united, as one shoulder leans on another and another, and together we will carry enough water for everyone in the country to drink. Not just for the lucky few. We will see flowers grow where blood was once spilled on the steps of the courthouse, a park that can be enjoyed by all. Individual liberties must be protected and celebrated, especially at a time when we are weakened by fear. We will not lead the world with new wars; instead, we will melt guns and helmets to make toys for children who have nothing. Together, we will silence the weapons of death so our children will never have to hear them. United, we will shelter the homeless and heal the sick. Although I am no longer sick or homeless, I have had firsthand experience with both of these hardships in my lifetime." The audience members exchange surprised glances, and whispers begin to circulate.

Lance signals for silence again. "People need our help because a hand that is closed is no hand at all. The sick and homeless are victims of our medical and financial systems. As a country, we will not only open our hearts to these victims, but also, and perhaps more importantly, open our wallets to get our fellow Americans the help they need. Local help. Strong schools, safe streets, and local jobs make a country great, not the strength of our bloated national agencies. Tonight, I stand in front of you and vow to make these changes to make this country stronger than ever. Let's have hope. God has given us another day, another chance, and love will win another war! Thank you! And may God bless America!"

The audience members spring to their feet, erupting in joyous applause, hoots, and whistles that continue for a full six minutes and thirty-six seconds. This speech will be regarded by many as the defining moment of the decade. Tonight, a fragile America can rest assured that a brighter tomorrow awaits her.

Lance looks at James, who is now standing by his side, and says, "I'm sure glad I met you. I think everyone wishes for someone like you to be a part of their life. You're the big brother I never had, James. Thank you for everything you've done for our family." Lance turns to him and gives him a big hug, and the applause grows even louder.

Lance walks over to his Rose. He reaches out to her, and she grasps his hands. They gaze into each other's eyes, tears welling up and streaming down their cheeks to their necks. They embrace tighter than they ever have before, as if trying to make sure they don't slip away from each other again.

Lance whispers in her ear, "I forgot how beautiful you are. When I saw you from the podium, it was like a theater curtain had risen, and there you were, the star of my dreams. There were times I wanted to call you. I wanted to hear the sound of your voice, but I just couldn't. I somehow lost *my* voice in all this. Now I have it back, and I hope you'll get used to hearing it again. I'm sorry, Rose. I'm so sorry for everything." He closes his eyes, wanting everyone to be gone when he opens them so that the two of them can be alone. He wonders, just for a moment, what he would do without Rose in his life.

After a short silence, he says, "If I had to do it all over again, run for office and take the oath with you by my side for the world to see, I would. And for the support you gave me, I will always love you as if you are the very rain that nourishes the earth. You remember how much the two of us used to enjoy standing in the rain, letting the droplets land on our heads? We would wipe each other's faces with our wet hands and laugh, waiting to see which one of us would run inside the house first. Let's keep doing that, OK?"

Rose laughs and nods in agreement.

He doesn't want to let her go. He hopes that tonight he can make love to the best friend he has ever had.

Lance sees his children nearby. They are standing together, waiting for their parents to come to them, their faces wet with tears. Lance closes his eyes and imagines himself holding the hands of their small children that are yet to be. He's grateful to be alive and hopes he will live long enough to meet his grandchildren. But for now, he makes a silent vow to himself to never withhold the words *I love you* from his children, and to deliver them generously to his wife.

CHAPTER 87

I WILL MISS YOU

▷ **Doris – Pullman, Washington, Day 38**

Doris promised herself she would wait until Lance's speech is over before leaving the building, and she keeps that promise. She is so proud of him—of his recovery and especially of his speech, which she knows was partially unscripted. She watches him as he stands onstage, holding Rose. Even from this distance, she can see the intensity of their embrace. She wishes the hugs they shared were as deep, but they weren't. Theirs were sweet and sincere, but they were very different than what she is witnessing now. She shakes off the jealousy and remembers Rose's words: *no fairytale ending.* As she gazes at Lance and Rose, her dark side silently wishes for any signs of tension between them, knowing that challenging conversations lay ahead. But she doesn't see that at all. She sees raw emotion and love, just like what she shared with Daniel, so she turns away.

This is her cue. This Cinderella needs to run away from here before everyone sees her for who she is: just a simple nurse from New York City, nothing more. Despite all the joy that surrounds her, she feels only sadness. Regardless, she lifts her chin to face the crowd and readies herself to walk away with whatever pride she has left. She is confident that she did the right thing, even if it was partly for the wrong reasons. Her eyes gather moisture, and she finds it hard to swallow. She looks back at her Elliot one last time and says in a whisper, "I'll miss you. Oh, how I will miss you."

Debbie appears by her side and offers to walk her out. Doris smiles softly, and together they walk arm in arm. There are so many people in the aisles, it's as if they're walking in slow motion. She looks up and is comforted by a familiar golden dust swirling in the bright lights. She watches the particles float magically through the air as she moves through the crowd. This is *her* moment—like the baby in the church. She wonders if this has all been a dream from which she's about to awaken. But then a woman bumps into her, and music begins to play. *Not a dream.*

As they approach the security guards at the door, Doris stops. She can't help herself—one last glance, one last hope. She turns and stands high on her tippy-toes—and then it happens. As if by magic, the crowd parts just enough for her to catch a glimpse of her Elliot, not Lance. Just as she is about to turn back around, she catches his eye, and his lips form the words *Goodbye, Ribbons.*

Once Doris and Debbie have shown their identification and received clearance to leave the building, they make their way to Doris's car.

"Why don't I drive you home? You can get your car tomorrow," Debbie suggests.

Doris shakes her head. "No, thank you, my beautiful friend. You've done so much for me and for Lance. I love you, but I need to be on my own tonight. I haven't had time to be alone with my thoughts for a very, very long time."

"I understand, and I love you too," Debbie says, enveloping Doris in of one of her comforting bear hugs.

Doris climbs into Fatima's old Honda Civic, takes a deep breath, and begins to sob. She cries so hard that her body shakes and convulses. She can't stop herself and doesn't try. After nearly ten minutes, she begins to feel the relief offered by her tears. She reaches into her purse to retrieve a tissue. There, she finds a red ribbon with a beautiful blue stone in its center. Beneath it is an envelope with *Ribbons* written on the front. She knows the handwriting. She wants to open the envelope, but instead, her fingers seem to take over, digging through her purse until they finally extract the tissue. She wipes her tears, not looking at the envelope. She raises her hands and places them on the steering wheel.

"Don't do it, Doris," she says aloud, hoping the sound of her own voice will convince her. She needs all the strength she has left to make it home safely. She pushes away her purse until it falls onto the floor in front of the passenger seat, just out of reach. Then she holds her head up, looks straight ahead into the dark night, starts the car, and heads home.

As soon as she steps through the front door, Doris kicks off her shoes and pulls her dress over her head. She wants to shed the weight from the night. She has never been to an event like that, and is sure she will never attend another for the rest of her life. Just thinking about everything that happened overwhelms her. She wants to sleep and wake up far away from here. The letter will be best left in her purse, next to her dress and shoes on the floor. Sleep will be her refuge from the day's painful events.

Doris makes her way to the bedroom, lies on the bed, and closes her tired eyes. She will never forget this night, but at this moment, that's all she wants to do. Her heart can't take any more of it. Thankfully, her body takes over, affording her mind a welcome break as she falls into a deep sleep.

☺◉

As Doris heads to the sunlit kitchen to make some coffee, she passes a calendar on the wall that reminds her that so much time has passed. What will she do now? A nearby church bell rings, reminding her of her wedding day. She misses Daniel and the life they once had.

She can't believe she slept so long and double-checks the time on her phone. *Now what?* She wonders. She wants to feel relief, a sense of a new beginning, but she can't. She remembers the letter in her purse and walks to the front door to retrieve her purse, shoes, and dress. On the way to her bedroom, she promises herself she won't open the letter. Not yet. She knows it may provide a short reprieve from the loneliness she's feeling, but the comedown won't be worth it. She knows she can't read the letter alone—or maybe even ever. She laughs at herself. Of course she will read his letter.

The sound of the coffee maker brings back memories of her brief time here with Lance, and her years with Daniel. Doris takes two mugs from the upper cabinet without realizing she only needs one. As she begins pouring the coffee, she recognizes her mistake and returns the extra mug to its place in the cabinet. She takes a sip of coffee and feels it warm her empty stomach. She drinks more, hoping it will fill the emptiness she's feeling inside. Taking a seat on the couch, she wonders if the last five weeks will be the apex of her life.

Doris is startled by the sound of the doorbell. She places her hand on her heart to calm it as she walks to the front door. She tightens her robe and checks her reflection in the mirror by the door, feeling her chest constrict with anxiety. Maybe Lance couldn't convince Homeland Security to leave her alone, and now they're here to take her away. Perhaps they are here on Rose's orders . . . or even Edwina's. Doris doubts she was able to sway either of them with her words.

"Who is it?" she calls out, hoping she can just send them away without having to open the door.

"It's me!" answers a familiar voice.

Doris can't believe her ears. Rushing forward, she undoes the latch and flings open the door. There, standing on her doorstep, is the one person she has missed desperately over the past two weeks, a warm, kind face that reminds her of her younger, happier days. For a moment, both women stand frozen, just savoring the moment. Then Fatima stretches out her arms, and Doris falls into them, sobbing into her sister's shoulder. She buries herself deeper in her sister's embrace, rocking from side to side in silence, save for her muffled sobs. Fatima's familiar scent of vanilla laced with lavender provides comfort like nothing else can.

Fatima rubs her hand soothingly along Doris's back, tracing shapes and circles with her fingers, just like they used to do when they were kids. Their connection hasn't been broken by time or distance. Neither of them speaks. There is nothing to say at the moment—no judgment, no regrets. Here is Fatima, saving her yet again. Doris thinks about the times they saved each other as kids, taking blame for the other in front of their parents and helping with each other's homework in subjects where one of them exceled more than the other.

After Doris's tears subside, she straightens up and grabs Fatima's suitcase. "Come on in. I'll get you some coffee." She smiles to herself, looking forward to using the other mug after all. "You can change into your pajamas. We're not going anywhere today! We can watch movies, order in comfort food, and share a couple bottles of wine."

Fatima's laugh is like music to her ears. Doris hurries to the kitchen as her sister gets changed and situated on the couch. She brings over the two coffee mugs and hands one to Fatima before settling on the couch, placing a pillow on her lap, and tucking her legs beneath her. Fatima takes a sip of coffee and then turns to Doris, searching her face. Doris knows what she's looking for: cracks that reveal she's falling apart.

"I'm OK, Fatima." Doris shrugs, unable to keep the sadness from her voice. "It's not all bad. There were no surprises. It wasn't a fairytale ending, but it was a happy time in my life."

"Then why do you look so sad?" Fatima presses.

"Last night, I found an envelope in my purse."

"And what did the letter say?"

"Well, that's just it. I haven't opened it yet."

"What are you waiting for? Let's open it now!"

Doris retrieves the envelope from her purse in the bedroom and returns to her sister on the couch. She untucks the flap and extracts a single sheet of paper.

"It looks like a poem," Doris says.

"Read it! I can't wait any longer!" Fatima's excitement fuels Doris's own.

"OK, OK," Doris says, clearing her throat. She holds the top and bottom of the paper with both hands, one at the top and one at the bottom, as though reading a royal proclamation. She begins:

> *I didn't know who you were or where you were from.*
> *I will miss you.*
> *I didn't meet you when I was supposed to, and I had to leave.*
> *I will miss you.*
>
> *I didn't know where you lived, but I passed you by a thousand times.*
> *I will miss you.*
> *I saw tears gather on your cheeks, and soon they gathered on your lips.*
> *For that, I will miss you even more.*
>
> *I wanted to reach out to touch you,*
> *but you just looked at me.*
> *Then, I couldn't see you.*

I almost lost my nerve
and posture
and all my lines.
I will miss us.

I wanted to see the color of your eyes for myself,
But by then, it was dark, and I couldn't see you.
I didn't hear you say goodbye or the door close be-
hind you.
So I waited.

I didn't know you from behind,
and I wanted to follow you.
But I lost you.
I wanted to talk to you.
But I couldn't find you.
I will miss us, and I will miss you.

"That's beautiful, Doris," Fatima says as she brushes away a tear. "What else does it say?"

Doris looks at the paper again. It's just the poem, no signature. She flips it over and discovers four lines: the name of a bank, a username, a password, and a short note.

She reads the note out loud: "Thank you for everything. Now go enjoy your life. Finally, you have no one to take care of but yourself. The best is yet to come to you, Ribbons. With love, Elliot."

Doris gives her sister a sad smile, places the letter on her lap, and stares out the window, wondering, *What if?*